MAKING GHOSTS DANCE

GREGORY E. BUFORD

Foreword

While this is a work of fiction, the situations described herein are inspired by actual events and circumstances.

This book is dedicated to my mother, Doris.

PRINCIPAL CHARACTERS

Pech Borin - Leader, Eastern Sector (Khmer Rouge)

Quynh – Vietnamese-Cambodian child

George Granger – Director of Investigations, International Rescue Mission

Chris Kelly – Vice-Consul, US Embassy, Cambodia

Arthur Behal – Owner, Spanky's

General Hem Bora – Commander, 911 Parachute Regiment

General Thul Chorn (Ret.) – Prime Minister, Kingdom of Cambodia

David Finto – Regional Security Officer, US Embassy, Cambodia

Lisa Kelly – Second Secretary, US Embassy, Cambodia

Mai – Daughter of Chris and Lisa Kelly

Yun Naren – Former Second Deputy Chief, National Police Anti-Trafficking Unit

General Sochua Nika (Ret.) – Head, National Police Anti-Trafficking Unit

General Chet Pannha – Deputy Chief, National Police

General Chea Prak – Commander, Brigade 70 (PM's bodyguard unit)

Chea Phyrom – Son of Chea Prak, Nephew of Prime Minister Thul Chorn

Mao Vannak – Chief thug and right-hand man of Chea Phyrom

Sambo Rithy – President, Sambo Rithy Party

General Nhim Saray – Minister of Interior and National Police Chief

Paris Jefferson – Deputy Chief of Mission, US Embassy, Cambodia

General Phann Phalla – Commander-in-Chief, Royal Cambodian Armed Forces

Leonard Perry – Regional Sales Manager, Henderson Chemical

Richard Schroeder – Ambassador, US Embassy, Cambodia

PROLOGUE

Phnom Penh, September, 2002

A convoy of black Toyota Land Cruisers raced along the center stripe of Monivong Boulevard, hazards blinking. Blue-and-red official license plates meant no one would question its speed or motive. Chea Phyrom's bodyguard sat stoically in the passenger seat—the boss always liked to drive when he'd been drinking—as they made their way to the Heart of Darkness, but the group had fallen off course following Phyrom's drunken lead.

"Sir, you need to turn left."

Phyrom yanked the wheel violently, steering the SUV down an unpaved side street, forcing oncoming cars and *moto*s to veer off course. The alley was full of people: men playing cards, a naked baby sleeping on a *krama*, children amusing themselves with improvised toys. Phyrom slammed on the brakes, and his vehicle skated across gravel. A woman cooking at the base of a wall squinted into the oncoming headlights. *Crash!*

By the time Phyrom realized what he'd done, his buddies in the trailing vehicles had already made a hasty retreat. He'd have to catch up with them later. An old man tore his clothes. Children wailed in horror but shied away from the mutilated body. Dust motes swirled in the halogen glow of the remaining headlight.

"Sir! Sir! We need to go now."

Phyrom plunged the car into Reverse while street people pounded on the windows, mad for revenge. It was now or never; in the throes of mob violence, all Cambodians were equal. He floored it and rammed into a line of vehicles now blocking his escape to the rear. A brick fragment hit the windshield, cracking it sensationally.

Phyrom's friend Chandaran, who had been more or less passed out in the backseat, began to wake. "What the hell——?"

The rear window of the Land Cruiser shattered inward, spraying glass on all three men. A teenager scrambled through. The bodyguard turned and placed a bullet in the chest of the intruder with his K-59. Chandaran began to pummel his savior in the head and neck.

"You idiot! You could've shot me! You stupid idiot!"

Phyrom stabbed the car into Drive but couldn't clear the wall in front. Once more in Reverse would do it. The reflection of a flame flickered on broken glass. A man was dousing the hood with fuel from a portable stove. Someone waved a torch.

"Stop them," Phyrom ordered. "Stop them!"

The bodyguard fired two shots out the window. Both men fell.

Phyrom punched the accelerator and scraped free of the wall, scattering the crowd and driving over bodies. He drove a short distance and stomped on the brakes. Time to teach a lesson. He got out and strode to the back of the car. The crowd advanced. He reached through the shattered window. Thirty meters. He opened a gun case. Twenty. He waited. Closer. He pulled out an old RDP. The mob hesitated.

"Come get me! Come on!"

Phyrom wiped the blood from his face, aimed from his hip, and emptied the magazine. Several people slumped to the ground, and the rest ran. He watched them flee, still squeezing the trigger.

Five minutes later the shattered SUV skidded to a halt on Pasteur Street. The two friends swaggered into the Heart of Darkness, followed by their bodyguard, his K-59 tucked in the small of his back. Bouncers checking lesser patrons for weapons moved hastily aside.

Phyrom slapped a "beer girl" on the ass. "Hurry! I'm sobering up."

CHAPTER 1

Fourteen years later. Quinn

The moment Quynh woke in the morning, even before she opened her eyes, she noticed the terrifying absence of her grandmother's sounds: the thump of utensils, the clearing of her throat, the words of her songs. The mouthwatering smell of *baa baa saa* did not fill the air, the hut did not shiver with early morning ritual, and incense did not burn in front of the old photos. Her grandmother lay still on the straw mat where she'd slept beside her.

"Grandma, wake up. Get up!"

She dropped her head on her grandmother's cold breast and cried for a long time. She smelled her grandfather's cigarette.

"Stop your crying! She's—" The old man's mean words were broken off by a fit of coughing.

Quynh snatched her grandmother's prized comb and ran out of the hut toward the river.

"Come back here!" he screamed after her, but she knew he was no longer able to run.

On most days, her grandfather sat outside the hut with other old men playing cards for money. Sometimes, if he won, he would go away and come home in the late afternoon, falling down and singing and ready to fight. On those days she would go see Chinh, and that's where she was running now, her vision blurred by morning mucus and tears.

Chinh wasn't at the river. Her favorite uncle lived there with his pigs on a small houseboat he'd built himself using scraps of houses washed away by the

1

monsoon. Chinh treated her kindly and let her stay on his boat when she had no chores. Sometimes he wanted her to touch him between the legs, and then he gave her a little money, which she was careful to hide from Grandfather. Chinh told her that if she talked about it with anyone else, she couldn't ever come see him again. That was the last thing she wanted, and so she kept her mouth shut. Sometimes, he touched her too. She didn't talk about that either.

While she waited on the riverbank for Chinh, Quynh used two hundred riel he had given her and bought some tamarind candy from the Khmers who ran the small dry-goods store tethered next to his boat.

"Why are you crying?" the Khmer woman asked her. The village kids sometimes made fun of her because she had a gimp leg and walked funny.

"Leave me alone."

"Okay, what do I care, you brat!"

The woman disappeared into the depths of her floating store-home.

There were not many Khmers, or Cambodians, in the village. Another family of them ferried people across the river on a flat boat big enough for a bullock cart. Grandfather didn't like them. He said her village had not always been in Cambodia but had once been part of Vietnam, a rich and powerful place full of beautiful people. He said the Khmers hated the Vietnamese and had done horrible things to them in the past.

"Thieves! All of them," he'd said.

Chinh sometimes had a Khmer girlfriend.

Quynh sat on her haunches on the bank. She scratched the scabs on her thighs until they bled again. She peed into the silt, generating a tiny puff of dust, and watched the yellow stream disappear like magic. Her grandmother was never coming back. Just like her mother never came back. She threw her candy into the water, and the hungry river gobbled it up; she no longer had a taste for it. She jumped onto Chinh's boat and waited, but when he came home he had a girlfriend with him.

"You can't stay here," he said, so she climbed up the bank and went home.

Quynh's aunt and uncle arrived with their grown son, Minh, and brought food and clothes of white. They shaved Grandfather's head. Uncle Due bought a coffin, and temple monks came in the evening to chant. They asked for twenty thousand riel for the cremation, but the family didn't have it, so Grandmother had to wait four days until they lit the fire to cremate a rich man.

"Who will take care of me now?" Grandfather asked.

It was agreed he would leave their village and move in with his daughter and her family. Uncle Due said nothing, but he spent a lot of time walking in circles.

Grandfather pointed at Quynh. "What about the girl?"

Uncle Due stopped pacing. "We have twelve children. Ten of them are girls. We cannot take any more."

Quynh waited until the men began playing cards to sneak inside the hut.

"Please, Di. Let me come with you. I can work. I can carry water."

Her aunt looked away.

Quynh laid her head across her aunt's lap. "Please, I won't eat a lot of food. I won't bother Uncle Due." In spite of her best efforts, she was blubbering.

"Hush. You are not coming."

"Then what's going to happen to me?"

Quynh spent the rest of the day in a hammock under the hut, listening to the men laugh about their stupid game as if her grandmother wasn't dead. If she couldn't go live with her aunt's family, she would stay in her village with her grandmother's spirit. Then she would be okay. She would live there and take care of herself if it meant she could stay. She would also have Chinh and her friends, and so she wouldn't be all alone. This was something. She didn't want to be all alone, especially at night.

Quynh woke early to find the adults standing around her.

"Wake up," Uncle Due said. "We're going on the river."

Quynh slid from the hammock and looked around at the lined faces of her relatives. There was something they weren't telling her, and it wasn't good. Uncle Due frightened her.

"I don't want to go, Uncle."

Grandfather coughed. "You'll do as you're told."

"They'll bring you home tonight," Auntie promised.

Quynh knew when adults were lying. She licked her lips and made a run for it.

Grandfather grabbed at her but was too slow. His sharp fingernails scratched her arm. Uncle Due caught her by the hair and soon had her over his shoulders, sliding down the riverbank toward Chinh's boat.

"Help! Help!"

Grandfather, Auntie, Chinh, neighbors—everyone she'd ever known—stood there and did nothing, as if they'd never seen her before.

"Grandmother! Grandmother!"

Uncle Due dropped her hard onto the deck. Quynh scrambled to her feet and ran. Her uncle grunted and kicked her feet out from under her, landing her flat on her back and unable to breathe. Stars came out in the daytime. The light turned to darkness and to light again. She wouldn't try to run away anymore.

As they drifted from the shore, Uncle Due and Chinh crouched, smoking, at the rear of the boat while Quynh squatted near the pigs, clutching Grandmother's comb and numbly watching the river turn over on itself. Cousin Minh rode with them but never opened his mouth to talk to her.

⋏

Chinh didn't point the boat toward land again until the sun set in orange-red behind them.

"That's it," he announced, pointing to a village clustered along the shore.

He steered into a shallow inlet ringed by thatched huts, slicing through a dense carpet of plastic bottles and dead fish. A blue pipe spat out a foul-smelling brown liquid that gurgled into the water and disappeared in bubbles. Quynh used a twig to poke at an upside-down fish's white belly as the boat ran aground among a dozen or so long canoes that looked just like the ones the fishermen used in her village. The canoes were tethered by ropes staked up the bank, and their rudders and nets lay idle in their bows, meaning the day's fishing had ended. Strangers stared from the high perches of their stilt houses but made no sign of greeting.

"Hurry up," Chinh said impatiently, slipping into the opaque water. "We're here."

Quynh climbed down into an adjacent canoe and walked across it to land, preferring to keep her feet dry. "But Auntie said we'd go home tonight."

Chinh smiled at her. "Don't worry," he said, but she didn't trust him.

Quynh followed the men up the sandy bank while Minh stayed behind to mind the boat. At the crest of the slope she could see a village somewhat larger than her own with a pagoda at its center. Chinh and Uncle Due conferred and then headed across a weedy lot toward some brick buildings they said was the main part of town. When they reached this crossroads, Uncle Due asked directions in Khmer of a group of men loitering on a corner. Quynh couldn't understand what they said, but she didn't like the way the men looked past her uncle at her. The men of the village summoned a boy and gave him some orders. He took off running, beckoning the three travelers to follow.

"Come on, Quynh," Chinh said, grinning. "See if you can run as fast as he can."

Quynh ignored him, preferring to stare at her feet as they followed their guide through the narrow, twisting labyrinth of the village. At one point a group of shirtless boys giggled at them from below as they walked a plank over a ditch choked with water hyacinth. One of the boys laughed at the rest, taunting his friends from the back of a water buffalo.

After Uncle Due stopped a few more times to ask directions, they caught up with their guide in front of a home that was not up on stilts like the rest. A crowd of children had gathered to witness the excitement. From the doorway of the house a fat Khmer woman sized up Quynh the way people did pigs in the market.

"Come here," she said, and all eyes turned to Quynh.

Chinh gave her a nudge. "Go."

Quynh didn't budge. She knew they were tricking her, but she didn't get the joke. The woman slipped on her sandals and walked over. She dug in Quynh's hair, inspected her hands. She pinched Quynh's face and grimaced at her teeth. She put her hands in Quynh's pants and touched her, but not in the same way Chinh had. She brought her face close and sniffed.

"How old is she?"

The two men looked at each other and laughed.

"Well, fifty is the most I can give you for her."

Uncle Due slapped his head. "But I heard people get three hundred dollars for virgins."

"That girl can't be more than six! She can't cover my expenses just doing blow jobs."

"She's very healthy. Doctors came to her village."

"She looks like she's never eaten. I'll give you sixty and that's all."

Quynh tugged on Chinh's shirt. "What are you talking about, *Bac* Chinh?" He ignored her. She pulled harder. "Tell me. Tell me."

Uncle Due accepted a fistful of green money Quynh had never seen before. He gave some of it to Chinh, who folded it and put it in his pants, grinning broadly. None of this made any sense to Quynh. What were they doing? Why was the Khmer giving them money?

"Come on. Let's go," Uncle Due said.

The Khmer woman clutched Quynh's forearm. They were going to leave her!

"No!" Quynh cried. "Don't leave me! I want to go with you. I know how to make rice."

Chinh squatted beside her. "This is your mother now. She will—"

"No, Bac Chinh! No!"

"—take care of you. She's going to send you—"

"No!" She grabbed for him. He backed away. "Don't leave me!"

"—to school with rich boys and girls and feed you well."

"Please, Uncle! No, Uncle! Don't leave me!" She scratched at the hand on her arm.

The Khmer woman gripped Quynh's chin and made her look. "Everybody calls me Mama."

"No! No!"

Arms around each other, the men strode away.

"Wait! Chinh! Wait!"

Quynh tried to bite Mama's hand, and the woman slapped her hard across the face. Her eyes watered, her cheek burned, her ears rang, but she wouldn't give up. When Chinh was too long gone, Mama released her at once, sending her falling into the slime.

"You owe me sixty dollars now," Mama growled. "You're not going anywhere."

CHAPTER 2

Chris Kelly adjusted his cap and sunglasses and stepped onto the pockmarked street in front of the Golden Lion Hotel. He felt unsure of himself as a group of eager men surrounded him, pleading for a fare.

"Moto? You want moto, sir? Sir! Moto!"

Cambodians called this the cool season, but Kelly was sweating his ass off.

One *moto-dop* held up a finger. "Where you go, sir? You want to party? You want girl? I take you best place."

"I want to go to Svay Pak," Kelly said quietly.

The man's eyes narrowed. "Svay Pak, ah? Okay. No problem."

"How much?"

"Take thirty minute. You pay as you like. No problem."

Kelly climbed on the back of the man's motorcycle, and soon they were cruising along Sisowath Quay, dodging wheeled carts of tropical fruits, noodles, ice cream, soft drinks, sugarcane juice, and precarious pyramids of baguettes with their vendors' cries of *"pain! pain!"* On Kelly's left the new king's framed likeness smiled benevolently from its perch high above the entrance to the Royal Palace. On his right a buckled promenade of rosy-brown laterite bordered the riverfront for more than a mile, beyond which the muddy waters of the Tonle Sap joined the blue waters of the great Mekong. Small shacks littered the opposite bank, their roofs of corrugated tin weighted down with old tires.

They continued past the sports bars and tourist restaurants—Spanish, French, Thai. Wary pairs of young women in sandals and halter tops, sunburned middle-aged men with fanny packs, and seasoned expatriates enjoying a smirk at the tourists all shared sidewalk tables facing the river, all nursing their designer coffees like diverse devotees of a lackadaisical cult. They passed the red-light district, which, at two o'clock in the afternoon, was still sleeping off the previous night's binges. A sign in front of a backpacker hostel read "Sex Tourists Not Welcome." They crossed the river on National Route 8 between heavily fortified garment factories.

"Svay Pak here," the moto-dop called after some time.

Crude development of some sort or another had been constant along the length of the highway since Phnom Penh, and there was nothing to distinguish this particular patch of road, nothing to signify its unique importance. The moto-dop wagged his left hand in the air and left the pavement between a shack selling canisters of cooking gas and a more substantial shop-house advertising dentistry services. The dentist lay sleeping in a hammock, his calloused feet greeting passersby. The moto-dop drove ten more minutes off the main road between fallow paddies and stopped at the intersection of two dirt streets that was the heart of Svay Pak.

When the dust cleared, Kelly noticed the stench first: charred meat, animal waste, fish drying in the sun. A number of men loitering in an empty storefront looked not at all surprised to see a sunburned tourist turn up in their shit-hole village a dozen miles from the middle of nowhere. Below a string of tattered pennants celebrating some long-gone festival a bare-bottomed toddler sucked on a sponge picked from a stagnant puddle. Plastic bags littered a vacant lot where a neglected spirit house sat slightly askew atop its post. An adolescent playing pool in a bar on the corner dropped his cue and came running.

"Sir, you looking girl, sir? We have many, many girl." The boy stretched his arms wide to demonstrate "many, many."

Kelly nodded.

"No problem. Come with me, sir."

Flanked by a happy cohort of village urchins, the boy led Kelly down ever-narrower paths between ramshackle huts of bamboo and rice straw thatch. Women toiled and socialized at outdoor kitchens. Men in floppy hats tended livestock pens. Kelly's guide finally poked his head in the door of a wooden house a cut above its neighbors. A smiling matronly figure wearing pink pajamas welcomed them with her palms together in front of her, and Kelly entered without bothering to remove his filthy shoes. The house was plain but well built—the floor made of wood, not dirt—and on a sofa squirmed a selection of skinny girls ranging from six to maybe sixteen years old. A man lay stretched out on the floor in a dark corner, a cap over his face.

"My name Mama." The woman jabbed her thumb at her chest. "You looking for girl?"

Kelly pointed at a tiny thing in a blue dress, about the same age as his own daughter. "I want the little one." She was exactly what he was looking for.

"This girl," Mama said, pinching the girl's cheeks, "she do very good yum-yum for you."

"Me like yum-yum very much. I do for you," the girl said flatly.

Mama beamed. "You like?"

"I like a lot. How much?"

"Five dollar for yum-yum. For boom-boom you need bigger girl. This one too small."

"Okay. Then I'll take that one too," Kelly said of a girl who might have been thirteen. That hadn't been part of the plan. "Where do we do this?"

"Come."

Mama slipped on a pair of plastic sandals and led Kelly around the corner to a two-story cinder-block guesthouse and upstairs to a room furnished with only a double bed and a ceiling fan. She left him alone. Presently a man entered with the two girls grotesquely overdone with makeup. Kelly sat on the bed and beckoned the girls to his side.

He glared at the pimp. "Get the hell out."

"I wait outside two hour." The man closed the door behind him.

"Good idea, dumbass."

A whistle blew somewhere outside, followed by furious footsteps. Kelly wrapped his arms around the girls, lay back on the bed, closed his eyes, and the door flew off its hinges, showering them with splinters.

Policemen wearing balaclavas poured into the room dragging the hapless pimp with them. A pair of them tackled Kelly on the bed.

"Get the hell off me!"

Before Kelly knew what happened, they had flipped him and cuffed him behind his back. He watched another policeman knock the pimp to the floor and begin pounding him in the face with his bare fists.

"Hey," Kelly cried, "that's police brutality!"

The girls flailed their legs as two men grabbed them up roughly and hastened out the door. A well-dressed woman ran close on their heels speaking soothingly in Vietnamese.

The police dragged the suspects to their feet and marched them down the steps to the street. Mama was there, ranting and shaking her fists. A policeman grabbed Kelly by the hair and forced him into the backseat of a decrepit police car.

Kelly kicked at the door. "That hurt, you son of a bitch!" A policeman in the front seat gave him a puzzled look.

The police shoved the pimp, dejected and bloody, into a similar car a few feet away. The girls were nowhere in sight. Spraying a great cloud of dust behind them, the cars raced through the tiny village toward the highway, leaving Svay Pak to carry on much as before.

When the entourage crossed the river and reached the great roundabout at the foot of the Japanese bridge near the French embassy, the car carrying Kelly stopped on the hectic roadside. An officer undid the cuffs, and Kelly stepped into traffic. The police sped away, leaving him to massage his wrists amid the normal Cambodian chaos. Kelly quickly flagged down a moto-dop.

"Where you go, boss?"

"Boeung Salang."

⋏

Chris Kelly trudged up three flights to Land & Sea and breathed a sigh of relief to find George Granger waiting for him as planned.

George got up with a wince, his thighs pushing the table across the tile floor like it wasn't there. "Congratulations!" He crushed Chris's hand in his and then pulled him in for a chest bump. "You look like you could use a beer."

"Jesus, George. I think you broke my hand." He wasn't entirely joking, and he wasn't really in the mood to celebrate.

"Oh, sorry about that. Man, that Hawaiian tourist getup really suits you."

Chris looked down at his shirt. "Yeah, well, just trying to look the part, you know."

"Hey, why the long face? You alright?"

"Yeah, yeah, I'm fine," Chris said, massaging his eyes. "It's just...it's just the whole thing was really...disturbing."

"Yeah, I'm sure it was. But you know what? You got not one but two girls today. And on your first go-round."

Chris nodded agreement, but he was thinking about the four he left behind.

"Now, come on," George said. "Sit down, and let's pop a top to a job well done."

They sat down, and George poured a single glass of Angkor, letting foam overflow onto the table. Chenda, the rooftop restaurant's young owner, dropped in one cube of ice with a lithe hand.

Chris raised his glass. "Cheers," he said without conviction. Ice in beer. That's one thing he'd never get used to. "I see you're going to make me drink alone again."

George grinned. "Well, not if you just give it up altogether."

Chris drained his glass in one breath and banged it on the table with a foamy smile. "Please don't make me kick your ass. Please."

"Wouldn't dream of it," George said, holding up two massive hands in supplication. "Drink on."

Chris poured himself the rest of the bottle while his teetotaler friend laughed. Bad beer had never tasted so good.

"Did you know they kicked the door in? Scared the hell out of the girls—and me too."

George sighed. "I'll bring it up with Sochua."

"A lot of good that'll do." The Cambodian police weren't exactly known for their finesse. "Where are the girls?"

"They should be turned over to us within an hour or two, and we'll take them out to Shelter 4."

"I'd like to come out and see them when I can."

"Yeah, I'll let you know. Probably be a couple of weeks before we get 'em settled. Listen, I got to go back to the station."

"Am I going to see you at Jack's this week?"

"You bet. Hey, excellent work today."

Chris let Chenda bring him a second round while he watched George limp down the stairs, cursing his bad knee. Although they might seem an unlikely pair—he, an admittedly clean-cut junior diplomat, and George, a former cop who looked more like a professional cage wrestler—their cause united them, and he had a genuine affection for the amiable giant.

"You want eat?" Chenda asked.

It was tempting. Chenda was a brilliant cook. She was also one of the first girls International Rescue Mission had successfully freed in Cambodia and had, at the age of seventeen, turned a two-hundred-dollar loan into a successful restaurant and guesthouse and employed a number of IRM's charges over the years.

"No. I'd better go home."

"Ooh, you such good husband," Chenda remarked with no hint of sarcasm. "You wife so lucky."

"Whatever."

Chenda chuckled and turned away. The heat had abated somewhat. Chris gazed east across the city: rush hour at peak; Lang Ka temple; the kids' carnival on Koh Pich; the Mekong. He could finally breathe. And when he did, he found himself choking back the pent-up emotion of the day.

Chenda handed him a paper napkin. "Hey, hey, you okay?"

"God, they were *so* young. They were just...they were just...little girls. One of them was about the same age...the same age as my—"

"Okay, okay," Chenda said soothingly. "Everything be alright."

Chris shook his head. "I don't know, Chenda. I don't know if everything's going to be alright."

CHAPTER 3

Christopher Kelly, vice-consul, American embassy, Phnom Penh, Kingdom of Cambodia, adjusted his tie and smiled at an anxious man through the bulletproof and blast-proof glass of Window #2. The man placed his palms together in front of his face, a greeting Chris returned before switching on his microphone. Paying his first-tour-of-duty dues issuing visas wasn't exactly the glamorous lifestyle he'd had in mind when he'd joined the Department of State, but at least it was never boring. His wife, Lisa, now on her third diplomatic assignment, had utterly detested her window duty in New Delhi—a famously punishing first tour—but Chris had to admit he found the visa mill tolerable, if not interesting, at times.

Lisa and their six-year-old adopted daughter, Mai, had eased into a comfortable routine in Cambodia. Lisa loved her work in Political—even if she did work too much—and Mai had adjusted easily to first grade at the local French school. Phnom Penh wasn't the worst place in the world for him to do a first tour—his best friend in A-100 got sent to Port Moresby—but, at the same time, it wasn't exactly Paris. The State Department considered Cambodia an "extreme hardship" post, and millions of its citizens could still recount atrocities of the Khmer Rouge era. But that's not what kept Chris awake at night.

The importance of international sex tourism to the local economy could be seen after dark in virtually every bar and restaurant in Phnom Penh, and for a particularly perverse niche of that trade, Cambodia represented ground zero. The Kelly family's welcome to the country had been a prominent sign just opposite Potchentong Airport that read "Have sex with children in this country, go to jail in yours. This notice paid for by the United States of America." Entire villages specialized in providing children—often sold into slavery by their own parents—to fulfill the twisted fantasies of a multinational flood of visitors that arrived unabated. When Chris met George Granger at an unofficial embassy happy hour, "it was love at first sight"—Lisa liked to say—because George introduced him to International Rescue Mission.

IRM, a small nongovernmental organization based in New Zealand, had been in Cambodia since the 1990s, offering material and moral support to victims of human trafficking and pressuring the government to bring perpetrators to justice. After conducting a routine criminal background check, George had invited Chris to become involved. Energized by volunteer work for IRM and with his wife and daughter happy, Chris could live with the drudgery of manning visa Window #2, which, he joked, stood for "no more than two minutes per customer."

Ready, set, go. "Good morning," he said to the visa applicant in Khmer. "Please put your right index finger on the red light."

Chris demonstrated from his side of the glass the manner in which the man needed to orient his finger over the device for him to be able to capture the needed biometric data.

"Thank you. Now your left."

The man did as he was told and then crammed a ream of stained and mutilated documents through the slot under the window. Behind Chris someone opened the door to the office, and warm air gushed through the window slot, carrying the pungent body odor that permeated the visa applicants' waiting room.

"Jesus," Christine Short, a fellow junior diplomat, exclaimed from the window next to Chris's. "Close the door!"

Chris put his finger under his nose and removed the man's application for a tourist visa from the pile of papers and looked it over.

"Who will you visit in the United States?"

"Grandmother."

The man pressed against the window a picture of a perturbed elderly woman slouched in a chair. Having now nearly exhausted his knowledge of the Khmer language, Chris continued through the interpreter, Triv Sophal, standing ready at his side.

"How old is your grandmother?"

The man looked at his hands for help before blurting out "Eighty-eight."

Chris sighed; he'd been secretly rooting for this guy. "Then according to your application, your grandmother is only twenty years older than you. How do you explain that? Do you have any assets in Cambodia? A house? A business?"

The man shook his head.

This was not going to end well. "Where do you work, sir?"

The applicant pressed to the glass a picture of a much-younger self standing proudly next to a bicycle rickshaw.

"You drive a *cyclo*?"

The man nodded.

They'd come to the part Chris hated. "Sir, I'm sorry, but I'm not convinced you are being entirely truthful, and I'm not convinced you will return to Cambodia before your visa expires. I cannot issue you a visa, but you are welcome to apply again in the future. Have a good day."

The man turned and slunk away.

Chris switched off his mike. "Poor guy. I should have told him he's just wasting his time."

"You say something?" It was Short from Window #3.

"No, just talking to myself."

"We understand this job lends itself to heavy drinking, but talking to yourself we cannot abide."

Chris laughed; the grind in Consular engendered a certain dark camaraderie among the junior officers "doing time" there. Short, in particular, made no secret of her disdain for the work; she'd put Phnom Penh on her bid list only because Cambodia would issue a two-year visa to her same-sex partner, something not every country would do. Chris switched on his mike. "Number thirty-nine, please. Number thirty-nine."

A stocky man with close-cropped hair wearing jeans and a red polo confidently approached the window.

"Good afternoon. Your application, please?"

The man responded in slightly accented English. "How's it goin'?" He shoved the requested document and his passport through the window slot. "You need anything else?"

"That will be all for now."

Intrigued by the man's speech and demeanor, Chris studied the applicant for a moment. He could have been a bouncer in a hostess bar or a bodyguard, yet the rings on his fingers and what might have been a legitimate silver Rolex on one thick wrist implied he was neither. He had a distinctly gangster-like aura about him that was more than the sum of its parts. Clearly impatient with the proceedings, the man looked repeatedly and ostentatiously at his watch.

"Could you take off your sunglasses, please?"

The applicant stood stock-still before jerking off his glasses with a snort.

"For what purpose would you like to visit the US?"

"Fundraising. I'm going to America to raise money for my charity."

The man's record appeared on the screen at Chris's side. The information did not surprise him.

"Sir, I am not able to issue you a visa. You violated the terms of your last visa, which makes you permanently ineligible for another one."

"What are you talking about?"

"Sir, you stayed in the US for three years after your last visa expired."

"You can't refuse me! Do you know who I am?"

"Sir, I don't know who you are, but I can refuse your visa. This interview is over. Please leave the room."

The man pressed his index finger against the glass. "You're gonna be sorry, you stupid motherf—"

"Sok, please remove this man from the building."

Sok, the local guard on duty in the waiting area, gingerly placed his hand on the man's shoulder. The thug made an obscene gesture and took off with Sok on his heels.

Chris closed his window shade and got up to stretch. This sort of thing happened occasionally, and it was best to take a short break.

"Man, what did you say to that jerk?"

Jim Johnson, head of the consular section and himself an unmitigated ass, stood behind Chris with a concerned look.

"'No.' I said, 'no.'"

"Yep. That would do it."

"It was clear-cut. He overstayed his visa after he flunked out of some community college in LA."

"Well, keep up the good work."

Johnson had his issues, but at least he never second-guessed his officers' decisions. He looked over Chris's shoulder at the computer screen, his eyebrows raised in interest.

"Do you know who he was?"

Chris shrugged. "Haven't the slightest idea. Who?"

"His name sounds really familiar. Just another typical MRE, I guess."

"MRE?"

"Morally Repugnant Elite."

"Ah." Chris raised his shade. "Number forty-three, please."

CHAPTER 4

"**Well, thank goodness** the rest of the Texas contingent is here. Come on in, and I'll fire up the karaoke machine."

Wearing a "Jack's Bar" T-shirt, Jack Durrant, another first-tour diplomat at the embassy, ushered Lisa and Chris Kelly into his party with a flourish. Chris liked Durrant and appreciated his dry wit on the visa line. Durrant had turned the unfinished third floor of his embassy-provided housing into perhaps the best bar in Phnom Penh, complete with pool tables, darts, disco ball, overstuffed chairs, and a twenty-foot-long L-shaped bar, in front of which sat a by-invitation-only crowd of diplomats, expatriates, and well-to-do Cambodians drinking all the most fashionable cocktails. Though drinking at Durrant's was entirely free of charge, he did accept donations in kind, and nowhere in the country could be found a more impressive selection of hard-to-find and top-notch spirits.

Durrant often surprised his guests with great feasts of Southern-fried chicken or magnificent rib eyes, which were able to thumb a ride from the commissary of the American embassy in Thailand once a month or so on a US military flight. On a Thursday night, a good third of the American staff of the embassy could be found at Durrant's—the locally hired staff did not often socialize with the Americans outside of work—not to mention the Germans, Australians, and even a few Japanese. The French were invited but did not come.

Lisa wagged her head. "I swear to God, Jack, if I have to tell you one more time that I'm not from Texas—"

"She's just jealous," Chris teased. "Don't listen to a word she says."

Durrant laughed. "Hey, your buddy George is over there at the bar drinking ginger ale and flirting with my girls."

"I didn't know you owned them," Lisa said, hands on hips.

"And they sure don't look like girls to me," Chris added, earning him a punch on the arm from his wife. "What? I'm just saying they're adults." He shrugged.

George Granger turned to them and grinned. "I'm not flirting with anybody. Molly gave me that ultimatum years ago."

One of George's interns at International Rescue Mission, a young law student, sat next to him drinking tequila shots under the indulgent gaze of Durrant's beautiful bartenders—former prostitutes who now made a better and cleaner living working for tips at Jack's.

George wrapped a tattooed arm around Chris's neck. "Let me ask you something, man. Does it bother you that your wife earns more than you?"

"Damn, George, what is this—1925? When are you going to crawl out of your cave and learn to walk upright?"

"Naw, I'm serious." His goofy smile suggested to Chris anything but seriousness.

"Does it bother me? Are you kidding? I insist upon it."

Lisa, holding the rank of second secretary, was indeed several years Chris's senior within the State Department, having passed the entrance exam on the first try instead of on the third, like he did, a fact she would never let him forget but that, to her great chagrin, caused him little concern. On the contrary, not having passed the exam the first time had given Chris the unplanned opportunity to spend a great deal of time with Mai during the first several years of her new life with them, something he didn't regret and, in retrospect, couldn't imagine having passed up.

Lisa kissed him on the cheek. "Trust me, George. I'm not after him for his money."

Nagashima, the very drunk intern, slurred, "Chris, can I get one of your cards?" and hiccupped loudly.

"He won't get a card," Lisa explained to a general audience. "The embassy won't pay for business cards, so he won't get any, as a matter of principle."

Chris retreated behind the bar to help fill drink orders. Everything Lisa had said was true. "Cheap bastards. The embassy won't even get business cards for the ambassador. What kind of employer won't pay for business cards?"

"So when people ask for Chris's card, I have to give them one of mine—which I pay for out of my own pocket—and let him write his information on the back." As Lisa said this, she handed Chris one of her cards for this purpose.

Chris snatched the card and wrote his number on the back. "Cheap. That's what they are." He handed the card to Nagashima. "Here you go, Intern." He called all the State Department interns "intern" and figured he may as well extend the courtesy to IRM's intern as well. "George, ask me how many days the US government gives its employees for maternity leave."

Lisa rolled her eyes. "Oh, Lord, not that again."

"They're so damn cheap—"

"Hey, Chris," interrupted Jim Johnson, the consular section chief, red-faced and loud from drink. "Congratulations, dude."

Johnson held up his hand for a high five, and Chris gave it a lazy tap. "Did I do something worthy of congratulations?"

"You know that jerk at your window this morning?"

Chris groaned. There were only two kinds of Foreign Service officers in the Consular section: those who liked to swap visa window stories after work and those who did not. Johnson fit famously into the former category. Either way, visa adjudications were not the sort of thing to be discussed in public.

"Jim, uh, do you think this is the right—"

"I had Sophal look him up, and guess what—he's the prime minister's nephew."

"Interesting." Chris excused himself to go to the bathroom just to get Johnson to shut his face.

Durrant followed him into the hall. "Dude," he whispered, "can you believe this shit? The head of the frickin' consular section bragging about turning down visas like this at a party? What a dumbass."

"Yeah, no kidding."

"Idiot." Durrant shook his head in disgust and turned back toward the party.

Chris grabbed his elbow. "Hey, you don't think this could come back to haunt us, do you?" Durrant was in his fourth year at a visa window, and he knew the way things worked.

"What? Jim running his mouth off? Yeah, he could get his ass in big trouble."

"No. I mean turning down the prime minister's nephew for a visa."

"Naw, I wouldn't worry about it. If the prime minister was going to give him a referral, he already would've done it. He must be like the black sheep of the family or something."

"Yeah, I guess." Still, Chris couldn't get his mind off it.

Lisa touched Chris's hand while he was driving. "Hello?"

"Oh, sorry. What?" They were leaving Durrant's later than usual since Mai was spending the night with a friend, and the wide thoroughfares of central Phnom Penh were deserted. Chris tapped the horn as they passed the American ambassador's residence; the guards waved.

"I said, 'what are you thinking about?'" She sounded a little tipsy.

"I was just thinking about what Jim said. I knew there was something about that guy. He was such a thug." He entered the roundabout at Independence Monument and took the first exit onto Suramarit Boulevard. A late-night noodle vendor served a line of moto-dops from his cart on the corner.

"What are you talking about?" She was definitely tipsy.

"Thul's nephew. The guy I turned down for a visa."

She made a face. "Oh, that."

"He looked like such a thug. Jim said he's the prime minister's nephew."

"Yup, that would explain it."

Chris laughed at his wife's undiplomatic remark. The septuagenarian prime minister of Cambodia, General Thul Chorn, was a first-rate gangster, and Lisa's work had made her something of an expert on him. Thul had enriched himself, his family, and his supporters at the expense of the Cambodian people, foreign donors, and his country's natural resources and environment. He skimmed money off the top of much-needed foreign assistance; he pocketed the proceeds from the sale of publicly owned lands to foreign logging concerns; and he had a finger in every major pie in the country. Thul burdened his impoverished nation with more government ministers than any country in the world, often redundant offices that he passed out like so much candy to reward friends and relatives and which came with official salaries of as little as a couple of hundred dollars a month but included all the power needed to get filthy rich. So rich, in fact, that it had become standard practice for those who would hold ministerial positions to make a sizeable donation to the Swiss bank account of the PM's "charitable foundation," though, Lisa had assured Chris, the practice was officially denied at all levels.

"No more!" Lisa cried, sticking her fingers in her ears. "Don't talk to me about that man."

Chris wound his way to their home in the wealthy residential district of Boeung Keng Kang. Even in BKK most of the streets remained unpaved and without lights, but the presence of the mansions of many high-ranking Cambodian government officials ensured the neighborhood had electricity most of the time. American diplomats got to live in homes that, in the words of the embassy's general services officer, "reflected the power and prestige of the American government. Meaning, the Kellies lived in a mansion—by local standards—as well.

Chris pulled up to the gate in the high wall surrounding their compound, and a moment later Bunroeun, the night guard, swung the thick doors inward to let him drive in.

"Well," Chris said, parking the Land Rover under the carport, "his nephew won't be getting a visa."

"No more visa talk either." She leaned toward him in the dark. "Have I ever told you how good-looking you are? Kiss me."

"I think Bunroeun is watch—"

She cut him off with a passionate kiss.

"Goodness, woman," he said when she let him come up for air, "I need to get you inside, don't I?"

"Uh-huh," she said, struggling in the dark to find the door latch. "You know, I don't feel so good."

Chris helped Lisa upstairs and into bed, and by the time he brushed his teeth, she was snoring loudly.

CHAPTER 5

The following Thursday Lisa Kelly stumbled ungracefully through her back door. "Man, I'm starving." She was happy they'd be skipping Durrant's happy hour tonight because she was wiped out.

Mai attacked her with hugs and kisses. "Mommy! Mommy!"

Chris and Mai had already sat down to supper, preparing to eat without her—not such a rare occurrence of late. Lisa was making a name for herself at work, and, as she had had to point out to her husband on more than one occasion, working late came with the territory.

"Look, I'm thrilled you're on the fast track," he'd tell her—and she believed him—"but we're looking for a wife and mother, as well as a secretary of state."

She wasn't particularly surprised to see that George Granger, Chris's new best friend, was at their dinner table too. "Hey, George." She hugged his neck before he could get up. "Why don't you bring Molly with you next time?"

Mai yanked on her sleeve. "Mommy, why are you working late *again*? Why?"

Thankfully, Chris came to her rescue. "She's got to work extra hard, or else they may send us to Ouagadougou."

"What? Guaca-poo-poo?"

"Ouagadougou."

"Waga-hoo-hoo?"

Chris shook his head gravely. "Trust me. You do not want to go there."

Lisa sat and served herself some green beans. "God, I could eat my arm off."

"No, Mommy. Don't eat your arm off, silly."

"No lunch again today?" Chris asked.

"Well, not exactly. Ambassador Schroeder had lunch at the Japanese embassy, and I got to take notes. They've brought their own chef from Japan, you know. The food looked fabulous."

"You didn't get anything?"

"Not a single bite."

"Poor, poor, baby," Mai teased.

Lisa thumped her gently on the head and turned back to Chris. "So tonight's the night y'all are going to Spanky's, right? But I thought they weren't on the pedophile circuit."

"They're not, really. But George wants me to meet the owner. A guy named Arthur. Wine?"

Lisa offered her glass, pleased Chris would be out with George tonight; not only was he a retired cop, he was also a former Texas Tech linebacker who could pick up her muscular six-foot-two husband and twirl him around in the air like a child if he felt so inclined. Phnom Penh was a dangerous place, and Chris's volunteer work took him into the worst parts of the city.

"Are you going, like, undercover or something? Are you going to wear false beards and moustaches?" she asked.

"Nope," Chris said. "We're going as ourselves this time."

"Perfect. I'll be so proud."

Lisa wholeheartedly approved of Chris's involvement with International Rescue Mission; the cause was, of course, just, and, having renewed purpose, he didn't complain as much about slinging visas all day. Yet, she knew his efforts to rescue children from prostitution necessarily took him places no wife would ever want her husband to go, and she wasn't above the occasional sarcastic comment.

"Spanky's? Someone's going to spank you, Daddy?" Mai looked at her father with chocolate eyes, her fork poised over a loaded baked potato, her all-time favorite.

Lisa laughed. "Someone'd better not. That's all I've got to say." She immediately regretted saying it; for obvious reasons Chris didn't like light to be made of his work with IRM. This was another conversation they'd had a number of times.

Chris sighed. "Honey, we've talked about it before. You know I don't want to go to these places. Please don't make jokes about it."

She took his hand. "Sorry. I was just teasing."

"It's just not very funny."

"Okay. You're right. It's not funny."

During this exchange George had tactfully engaged Mai in a discussion of world geography of which Chris and Lisa caught the tail end.

"Okay, mister. I'm telling you there is no such thing as a country called Hungry."

"And I'm telling you, madam, there is a country called Hungary."

"Nope. That is ridiculous! That would just be too funny."

Moaning, George dropped his shaggy head in his hands. "Okay, okay. Maybe you're right. But I know for sure there is a country called Turkey."

"Turkey? Ha! Gobble, gobble, gobble. There is no country named Turkey. That's the silliest thing I have ever heard."

George threw his hands in the air. "Okay, I give up! You win. Gobble, gobble, gobble."

⊼

"Girls?"

"Girl, sir?"

"You want girl all night?"

"You want get high, big brother? I got good *yama*."

Chris ignored the pimps and pushers and took the stairs two at a time to the beat of eighties hip-hop music wafting from the bar above. Two municipal policemen slept on the landing below a sign reading "This is Drug-Free Business." At the top of the stairs a smiling beauty flanked by two muscular brutes invited Chris forward into the neon glow of Spanky's. He raised his arms and laughed as one of the bouncers frisked him lightly before the other passed a handheld metal detector over his body to the tune of Funky Cold Medina. Cleared, he ran a gauntlet of emaciated Asian women in high heels, fishnet stockings, miniskirts, and leather.

"You want girl?"

"Mmm, me hungry," purred another, licking her bright-red lips.

Chris suppressed the urge to laugh and waved them away. "You know, actually, I'm gay."

George sat alone at a table facing the door, looking twice as big as anybody in the place.

"Am I'm late?" Chris asked him.

"Nope. Just walked in."

At the long bar dominating the room sat no less than three people Chris knew well. Two of them were employees of the American embassy, and one of them was the number three at the Russian embassy. He knew for a fact that the two Americans' wives were out of town—one of them on medical evacuation to Singapore and the other gone to Vietnam on a six-week temporary assignment. Sergei's wife was probably in town but couldn't care less if he went to Spanky's or not. One of the Americans, the Centers for Disease Control chief, offered Chris a nod but did not come over, deeply engaged as he was in conversation with a fawning young lady. No doubt he'd be bragging about his conquest at the next poker party as if she weren't in it for the money.

The clientele were mostly middle-aged Western men in pairs or alone talking with prostitutes half their age. Chris supposed that Arthur liked his "girls" to keep their dates buying drinks for a while before they snuck away with them to one of many purpose-built hotels within a short stumbling distance. It was still early, and perhaps three dozen women lined the walls looking hopelessly bored, waiting for customers.

"George!" A more modestly dressed woman bounced across the room and wrapped her arms around George like Daddy's favorite girl. "George! Why you not come see me more? I mad at you."

She affected an exaggerated pout and then hugged him again. Someone began massaging Chris's neck and shoulders.

Whoever it was had skills. "Man, that feels good," he drawled. "But... uh...no thanks."

He received a playful slap on the shoulder.

"Who this one, George?" George's waitress friend asked.

"Oh, this is my friend Chris. Take good care of him for me. Chris, this is Srey Mao."

Chris offered his hand, and Srey Mao acted like she didn't know what to do with it, leaving it hanging in the air. "You looking for girl tonight, Mr. Chris?"

"No thanks, but it's nice of you to ask."

"You sure? Good woman can be good for you."

"Yeah, I'm sure. I already have a good woman."

Srey Mao, all smiles, gave a quick flick of her head, and Chris's masseuse slapped him again, this time harder.

"Bye," she sang, dragging her nails through his hair as she moved away. "See you later."

"Srey Mao's good at keeping the dogs at bay for us," George noted with a smile, his eyebrows bouncing. "Maybe wrong choice of words there. She keeps the ladies in check, anyway. Don't feel bad—they'll find plenty of other takers."

Srey Mao climbed onto the third stool. "What you want drink, Mr. Chris? Maybe Angkor Stout?"

"I didn't realize Angkor made a stout. Sure, why not?"

"Just ginger ale for me," George said, "and whatever you want for yourself."

"Whatever you say, boss." Srey Mao beckoned a waitress and whispered the order to her.

"Thanks," George muttered. "Hey, can you go see if Arthur's awake?" He stretched his leg out in front of him, grimacing.

"I go see."

Srey Mao disappeared through a doorway hung with beads.

"Hey, George," Chris said.

"Whut?"

"How'd you mess up your knee? Football?"

"Don't like to talk about it."

"Oh, okay." Chris had previously encountered George's odd reticence to talk about himself. In fact, he knew very little about his friend's life before he'd come to Cambodia several years ago "to save the world." "The Lord brought us here" was all he'd say and then change the subject. And he never touched alcohol. "We don't have to talk about it."

"Good."

The waitress brought their drinks.

"Well," George said after a minute, "it wasn't no big deal. This petty criminal named Tommy Cantalupo shot me by accident. I took early retirement. That's all."

Sray Mao walked back into the room followed by a lanky giant with salt-and-pepper hair to his waist.

"George," the man boomed, turning every head in the bar. "Your money's no good here. Srey Mao! Another round for my friends. What are you drinking? Are you hungry? Well, you can eat some nachos. Srey Mao! Nachos!"

George clasped his friend's hand. "Arthur, I'd like you to meet my good friend Chris."

Arthur grabbed Chris's hand in both of his and shook it wildly. "Well, any friend of George's is a friend of mine! Hey! Are you hungry? You want some nachos?"

"You just ordered us some. Thanks."

Arthur threw his hands up. "Srey Mao, where are those damn nachos?"

Srey Mao dropped off her stool and sauntered toward the kitchen.

"Hey, Arthur, listen," said George. "Chris's a new volunteer. I want you to take care of him."

Arthur pumped Chris's hand again. "No shit? Well, anything you need, you let me know. Seriously. By the way, George, was that your little adventure over in Svay Pak?"

"Yep. In fact, that was Chris's first job."

"For real?" Arthur slapped Chris on the back. "Well, good job, Chris-boy."

"What did you hear?" George asked. "Anything we need to be concerned about?"

Arthur shook his head. "Nothin' serious. Just the usual noise."

"Good."

"Well, listen, guys, I gotta roll. Nice meetin' ya, Craig. You good people, man. Keep up the good work."

With that Arthur floated to the next table. "Hey, man. How the hell are ya? Somebody get these guys some nachos. On me!"

George waited until Arthur was out of earshot. "Arthur's quite a character, but don't underestimate him. He's helped us a lot. Although, it's best to come see him early if you need him sober."

"I can see that."

"In a former life he actually studied classic French cuisine at the Cordon Bleu in Paris. I've seen the certificate."

"Hmm. I wouldn't have guessed."

"He's also an admitted ketamine addict. It keeps him more or less a happy drunk."

"And he's on our side?"

"Yep. Supposed to be. He doesn't let any underage girls work here, and he's been giving us valuable information for years. He's knows everything that goes on in this town, and he's got the right connections or he wouldn't have been able to stay in business as long as he has. *And* he's got the best Tex-Mex this side of the Mekong."

"That's not saying a whole lot."

"Nope. But it's true anyway."

Srey Mao arrived with a plate of loaded nachos, sat down between them, and quietly sipped from her glass. Chris took a bite. Not bad, actually.

George took in the room. "Well, whattya think?"

"I have to admit, these aren't bad."

"No, man. The place, not the food."

"Oh." Chris looked at the men he knew from work, wondering how they reconciled this in their minds. Their children played with his at the embassy Christmas party. They went to the same parties. They worked together.

"What?"

"Oh, I was just thinking about those guys over there from the American embassy. I wonder how they go home to their families." Chris wasn't naïve enough to think this sort of thing didn't take place back home, but there was a clear "when in Rome" mentality among Cambodia's foreign community that thrust the practice front and center. "They seem to think that since they're in Cambodia, anything goes."

"Hell, on a good night you'll find half a dozen guys from the embassy here."

Chris showered to rid himself of the dust and sweat of the day and the stale smoke of the bar. He checked on Mai and in the light from the hallway watched her sleep for a minute. She lay on her side, tightly hugging a talking teddy bear given to her by Lisa's father. On her nightstand was a framed favorite photo of Lisa on a rusty playground slide with baby Mai, chubby and grinning on her lap, reaching out to Chris, the photographer. He had been dead set against that trip, protesting that Mai hadn't even settled into her new home with them on the American embassy compound in New Delhi.

Lisa won out, gently arguing that he had a tendency to be overprotective, an accusation he unapologetically admitted was true. They'd flown to Cochin on India's Malabar Coast, where they rented a converted rice barge with a crew of three and overnighted on the spectacular Kerala backwaters. When they'd seen all there was in Cochin, they hired a car and driver to take them to the remote hill station of Munnar, where, during the Raj, British bureaucrats and Christian missionaries had escaped the oppressive heat of the lowlands. With Mai strapped to Chris's back, they toured the tea plantations and hiked among giant eucalyptus and cascading waterfalls. The trip had gone off without a hitch, and Lisa had rubbed that in his face a bit, teasing him for worrying.

Chris kissed Mai on the forehead and closed her door, thinking that just because that trip hadn't ended in disaster didn't mean it had been a good idea.

When at last he crawled into bed, Lisa snuggled into the crook of his arm—she never could sleep without him—and he felt safe at last.

"How much is it," she whispered, "for sex at Spanky's?"

This was the last thing he wanted to talk about. "I'd like to forget about it."

"I'm just curious."

"Three to five dollars for oral sex, ten for intercourse. For twenty bucks you can have breakfast together in the morning."

"Are you're kidding?"

"No, and Spanky's is expensive; it's for foreigners. George told me the places where the Cambodians go cost two thousand riel."

She shuddered. "God, that's cheap. What's Spanky's like?"

"Well, you see stuff like it on TV, but it's hard to believe it really exists until you see it with your own eyes. But it's tame compared to a lot of places—foreign couples go in there to eat."

"Gross." She sounded like she'd just eaten canned asparagus. "Nice place for a date."

"And the women there are at the top of their profession."

"What do you mean?"

"I mean they're the survivors—freelancers. The probably got sold as children by someone they knew, like the two girls I got in Svay Pak. They eventually worked off the price paid for them and finally got old enough and savvy enough to break out of it somehow. Then they realized they could freelance and make more money than they could ever possibly hope to earn in any other profession. They're social outcasts; they can't read or write, and they know no one's going to marry them. That's when they ended up at places like Spanky's and Martini's, and who can blame them?

"Arthur claims he doesn't let any minors work there, and from what I saw, I think that's probably true. Honey, can we please change the subject? I just really don't want to think about Spanky's for even one more minute. It's bad enough to go there in the first place. I don't want to have to relive it at home."

"Okay. I'm sorry. You had another nightmare last night. Same one?"

"Yeah."

Lisa stroked his cheek. "I want you to know I'm proud of you—for what you do. You've rescued two girls. That's amazing."

"Actually, one," he said. "George told me a woman came to the IRM shelter claiming that the older girl was sixteen and that she was her mother. They knew it was bullshit, but there was nothing they could do. They had to let her go."

They lay awake for some time without speaking, Lisa up close next to him while he tried to clear his mind of where he had been and what he had seen that night.

She yawned and kissed him gently. "Do you want to make love?"

He sighed. Last thing on his mind now. "Not anymore. I told you I didn't want to talk about Spanky's."

"Sorry."

She likely could have changed his mind with little effort—and he kind of thought she might—but, instead, she began to softly snore. Chris didn't move a muscle; she used to sleep in his arms like this when they were newlyweds, but not so much these days. Long before the Foreign Service, they had honeymooned at the Oriental in Bangkok, courtesy of his in-laws, the Millers, dining on Som Tam, crab curry, and classical Thai dance before sneaking away from the overbearing luxury to the public water taxis on the Chao Phraya. They'd made love in a forest clearing in a public park in Ayutthaya at Lisa's insistence.

"You're out of your mind," he'd said. "We'll wind up in jail."

"I don't care. I want you now on the ground."

Altogether, it was rushed and uncomfortable, but they had a good laugh about it afterward.

They got shanghaied by a tuk-tuk driver who dragged them to a gem shop to get a commission. On Koh Phi Phi they rented a scooter and rode without helmets and shoes and made love once or twice a night to the sound of geckos—*erk, erk*—climbing the walls of their beachfront bungalow. They lay naked in bed until noon, Lisa in the crook of his arm, her head on his chest, he with his thigh between her legs to her pubis, intertwined from head to toe like they were now.

He kissed the part in Lisa's hair; he knew exactly where it was. A lot had changed since those carefree days—career, life, and the big one: parenthood. Of course, things had been different since Mai. He recalled something his grandmother had once told him and now understood the truth in it: until you have young'uns, you're newlyweds. Things *were* different, but in a good way. For him, Mai completed the picture begun with Lisa, and he felt utterly conscious in that moment that he was fortunate beyond his wildest expectations.

As he drifted to sleep on a wave of contentedness, however, his childhood voice reminded him that his grandmother had made that remark to excuse his father's psychological abuse of him and his mother, and he found himself wide awake again and brooding.

CHAPTER 6

Quynh did not like the place they called the "shelter." She knew it was far from Mama's because it took a long time to get there in a car. There were already a lot of girls living in the shelter, but she didn't know why; men didn't come there looking for girls.

"We took you away from Mama so you wouldn't have to do yum-yum anymore," the shelter ladies told her.

"I want to leave!" Quynh hadn't forgotten Mama's warning that if she ever ran away, Mama would find her and kill her. "When can I go back?" she asked, but no one ever gave her a straight answer. Sometimes at night she was so afraid, she would cry.

At first, Quynh spoke to no one, and the other girls in the shelter teased her for her silence, calling her *yuon*—a word the Khmers used when they wanted to be nasty to the Vietnamese. Worst of all, she had to go to school. The oldest girl in her class told everyone Quynh had the "aid" disease, and so no one would play with her.

The big girl pointed at her. "She's a *sray kouc*," she said, a "broken girl," which is what people called girls who did yum-yum and boom-boom for money.

Quynh didn't even say anything. That's how she felt—broken—and she would always be broken, and she wished she did have the aid disease, because she just didn't care what happened anymore.

After she had been living at the shelter for several days, the *barang* man who had come to Mama's looking for yum-yum came with a pretty Vietnamese lady.

"He wants to talk with you, Quynh," the Vietnamese lady said.

Talk to her? This was very surprising. Quynh stayed inside the shelter's house and didn't go out in the yard to meet him. She was safe there because no men were allowed inside the shelter house. They had told her this.

"He did not really want yum-yum," the lady told her. "He was just pretending so he could bring you here."

This didn't make any sense at all, and Quynh hated him for lying to her. How could she pay her debt to Mama now? Mama was nice to her and a good cook, and she told Quynh she could stay with her and Papa forever.

The Vietnamese lady led Quynh into the yard and made her sit next to the liar-man, who put his hand on her head—on her head, no less!—and mussed her hair.

"Liar!"

She kicked him in the shin and ran to the other side of the yard. She thought she would get in big trouble, but nobody said a word.

A

International Rescue Mission had never believed child sex was on offer at The Black Pussy, a well-established expatriate hangout with—to quote George— "a decent reputation, as far as whorehouses go." However, the name had come up during a routine look at the numerous pedophilia websites, chat rooms, and blogs. Chris's mission—his first of this type—was simple: flirt with the hostesses, profess to get turned on only by little girls, listen and gather information.

Lisa gave him a long kiss at the door. "Be careful. I'll wait up for you."

"You don't have to. I know you're tired."

"I know, but I'm going to anyway."

Bunroeun, the night guard, opened the gate, and Chris left his bubble of safety for the seedy nightlife of Phnom Penh.

"Moto! Moto!" he shouted into the darkness. Somewhere in the distance a small engine roared to life.

The short ride to Phnom Penh's sprawling red-light district took a little longer than it might have because the moto-dop took a circuitous route through the Tonle Bassac district. Only when he reached the river at Rainbow Bridge did the moto-dop turn north toward their destination. With the newly developed Koh Pich—Diamond Island—on their right, the brand-new Sofitel and the Aeon Mall construction on their left, and the ultra-luxurious NagaWorld Casino a beacon in front of them, it seemed Phnom Penh was looking more like Bangkok and Ho Chi Minh City every day. Still, it had a long way to go, and Chris was glad of that.

He didn't mind the moto-dop's leisurely approach; he'd negotiated a fixed price for the fare, and, anyway, he wasn't in a hurry to get to his destination. Reconnoitering The Black Pussy would surely be easier—and safer—than last month's trip to Svay Pak, but it still wasn't the kind of thing he'd ever want to do. At last, the moto-dop dropped him in the middle of the action, and the onslaught began.

"Hey, mister! What you want?"

"Blow job? You want blow job?"

A tout dropped open a laminated accordion of lewd photos. "You take look, sir."

The riverfront was nearing full swing.

A middle-aged man grabbed his arm. "Sir, you want full-body massage, sir?"

"Sorry, pal, you're not my type."

Chris laughed at his own joke and headed toward the neon outline of a giant black cat poised to pounce from a rooftop. Here there were no streetlights, but a full moon and the red bulbs of rent-by-the-hour hotels provided eerie but adequate illumination. At "blue chair" cafes, Cambodians ate and laughed heartily, the ground beneath them littered with a day's worth of spent napkins and discarded bones that skeletal dogs nipped at from the perimeter. A pair of men—Europeans, he guessed, by their clothes—bargained with two women in an open doorway and then followed them upstairs, congratulating each other as if their success was not a foregone conclusion. Japanese tourists filed off an immaculate bus and ran to the safety of an upscale Thai restaurant, chased by a group of children with outstretched hands. Chris enjoyed the scenes in the lighted rooms and store-fronts from the darkness of the street: three generations crowded around a TV, a man poring over accounts, children in pajamas playing with a puppy, strangers locked in embrace.

In front of The Black Pussy, one moto-dop stood apart from the others, enjoying his smoke. Chris briefly caught his gaze. He took a deep breath to steel himself for the night's work; if he did this a thousand times, he'd never get used to it.

The man flicked his cigarette onto the ground. "Moto?"

Chris pushed the door and walked into powerful rays of blue light. A pair of women in thongs and high heels played pool by the door, while on a nearby sofa a compatriot straddled a man's lap, whispering in his ear.

"Hey, Joe," purred one of the women playing pool, eyeing Chris as if consumed by desire. She leaned far across the table to take a shot and present him with an unmitigated view of her backside. In some other universe he might've found her tactics comical.

"Sorry. My name's not Joe."

He made his way to the bar.

"Hello! Welcome to the Pussy," half a dozen beauties chimed.

"Angkor Stout, please."

"No. No have. You drink Black Panther?"

Chris nodded and climbed on a stool. The bartender set a beer and an empty glass before him, and another young lady draped herself over his back and poured. Chris picked up the can.

"You know you can sell these for twenty bucks each on eBay. Empty."

"What you talk about?" The woman gave Chris's ear a little kiss.

He flinched. Okay, so this was a different ball game! Here, with adult women, his authentic participation in this bullshit was at least conceivable. No woman but Lisa had touched him like that in more than a decade, and he felt on the verge of losing his nerve.

Another customer at the bar, a large man with a ponytail and "Lucy" tattooed on his bicep, came to his rescue by butting into the conversation.

"No shit?" The man pushed away the woman kissing his neck. He was Australian, or maybe a Kiwi.

"No shit," Chris affirmed, sighing with relief. "Apparently, quite a few people like to collect beer cans from out-of-the-way places. You can get fifty dollars for a can of Black Death, but I forget where that's from."

The woman on Chris's shoulder spun him on his stool to face her. "My name Tammy. You buy me drink?"

"Tammy? Sure, but how 'bout you get the next round?"

"You funny boy. Me got no money. I work for you."

She stepped between Chris's splayed legs and clasped her hands behind his neck. This move recalled for Chris the time Janie Pillow had cornered him in the church basement in middle school, offering sex in exchange for beating up some boy who'd wronged her. His heart was pounding now just as it had then.

"Sorry, just a minute." He reached into his pocket and pulled out a digital recorder that looked like a mobile phone. He'd almost forgot. "Uh, text message from my wife."

He pushed a button and placed the device on the bar.

"Now where were we?"

"Here," she breathed wetly in his ear.

The hair stood on the back of his neck. "I wonder if you can help me out," he blurted.

"Tammy" ran one gaily manicured nail in a line from his Adam's apple down his chest, pausing at each button.

"Mmm. I do anything for you."

"I'm looking for a girl."

"You think I boy?"

With a giggle she tossed her long black hair. Chris had always loved long hair. Her finger reached his jeans and tried to slide in the top. He arrested her hand a little too quickly. George had told him in his training about one volunteer who'd gotten in a little too deep too quickly on an assignment and didn't surface for two days. It had ended his marriage. But this wasn't a problem for Chris. Whether anyone but Lisa would believe him or not, these women were a complete turnoff. He found the situation sad and pathetic, and the ridiculous outfits, makeup, and behavior had exactly the opposite of their intended effect and brought to mind a similar horrible experience in Tokyo during Lisa's second tour.

Mai had attended *hoikuen*—nursery school—a mere stone's throw from Japan's Imperial Palace while Chris made good money teaching English to businessmen and bored housewives. He'd gotten invited to the bachelor's party of a student and was the only *gaijin* in the group. After barhopping for hours, they wound up at a run-down theater where a troupe of half-naked women entertained a crowd of businessmen with lewd dances and crude jokes. For the finale, the women lay down on thin futons with their legs spread wide to the audience. The men lined up for their favorites and took turns as their friends shouted words of encouragement. Utterly disgusted, Chris had, literally, run out the door. That's what he wanted to do now, but he kept his cool.

"Why you shy? I thought you looking for girl."

"I am. How about you and something younger?"

"How old you think me?"

"You're fine. I'll take the two of you."

"How old you like?"

"Very young."

"We no have little girl here. You want take me and Susan? She only seventeen."

"Sounds good. If you can stay up all night." He nearly laughed out loud at how stupid that sounded.

"Ooh, baby. We go all night for you."

Again, he had to stifle laughter. "Is Susan the youngest girl here? I really want a young girl."

"You not get virgin here." She made disapproving clicks and punched him playfully on the arm. "What wrong with you?"

"You know what? I gotta go. I'll come back later for you and Susan."

Tammy grabbed her drink and disappeared behind a curtain of beads. A much older woman immediately presented the bill.

Chris pointed at a charge. "What's this?"

"You drink—three dollar. Girlfriend drink—seven dollar."

He paid and headed for the door.

"Hey!" It was the Australian. "What's your problem?"

Chris turned around. "Excuse me?"

"You one of those perverts that likes little girls, huh?"

Even if the man hadn't been built like a tank, Chris still would've left in a hurry. It was not only common sense but also part of his training to never engage. The risk of a confrontation in lawless Phnom Penh was never acceptable.

As Chris threw open the bar door, a shove from behind hard enough to give him a mild case of whiplash flung him headlong into the crowd of moto-dops at the curb.

For his safety, local men from International Rescue Mission followed Chris on every assignment, but he had never met them and didn't know who they were. It was one of these men, he presumed, that now dragged him to his feet and pulled him running across the street.

"Vite! Vite," the man exhorted as his moto choked to life. Chris climbed on, and they took off.

His neck aching, Chris looked back at the blue silhouette of the Australian and fought the urge to make a rude gesture, realizing, to his chagrin, they were on the same side.

⽊

In a dingy hotel room Chris Kelly stared, slack-jawed, at a brown girl in a white dress that billowed in the parched air. The silent child didn't tremble with fear or appear lost in a distant place; she closed the door and fastened the bolt.

Stop! Kelly backed across the room and collided with a shabby mattress. He sat down, and it creaked beneath his weight. She took his hand.

"I think we can get started now," he muttered.

That was the signal, but he heard nothing. No one came.

She placed a tiny hand on his shoulder, and he fell back on the mattress, his legs dangling over the edge of the bed.

"Please stop! No!"

Chris bolted upright in the darkness. "Stop!"

"What's wrong?"

"I don't know. What happened?"

"You were screaming," Lisa said groggily. "What is it?"

"I don't know. I guess I was thinking about…" Chris reached for his mobile and shone its light around the room. There was only Lisa and some laundry on the floor.

She turned over. "Go back to sleep."

He spooned her tightly. At first light he gave up on sleep and crept into the living room. He sat on the couch and tiredly waited for the day to start.

Chapter 7

LAX. Two-hour flight delay.

With the zeal of an unrepentant addict, Leonard Perry sat down to an expressly forbidden plate of baby back ribs and a beer and mentally exhorted his wife to kiss his ass. Perry, regional sales manager for a company selling chemical and other additives for concrete—"most people have no idea what concrete can do"—loved his new job. And his promotion—more importantly than furthering his career—meant he could spend a great deal of time on the road away from said wife, as well as fulfill a lifelong dark ambition. This, his inaugural trip, would take him to India, Vietnam, Thailand, and Indonesia, with a brief stop in Japan on the way home, and would last almost three weeks, including a weekend getaway to Cambodia he planned to make under the radar from Bangkok. This personal jaunt had been on his mind for days; even in church he'd gotten a hard-on just thinking about it. When they'd stood for the Doxology, he'd dropped something on the floor between the pews in order not to embarrass himself.

His boss and predecessor, Tom Apikian, who knew well how to have a good time on the road, had, with an impish grin, told Perry he expected a "full activity report" upon his return. Yet despite Apikian's gusto, Perry knew he wouldn't be able to give his friend a true account of his extra-vocational activities in Southeast Asia, and he'd be in the peculiar position of having to fabricate tales of his ceaseless rutting in Bangkok's notorious Patpong brothels in order to hide his much more vile exploits with children in Cambodia. No big deal; he'd learned how to keep a secret.

⟁

This was not the first time George Granger, IRM's director of investigations, had been to the Apsara 2 Hotel. On a normal day burly security guards welcomed trucked-in groups of Japanese, Taiwanese, and Koreans on "golf and sex" holidays, wealthy locals who came to visit "girls" they maintained for exclusive use, and Western pedophiles who traveled alone and took pains to keep things on the down-low. And although the Apsara 2 happily catered to the erotic fancies of all its patrons, it specialized in the lucrative sale of virginity and all that implied—a snug vagina, innocence, freedom from disease, and, as some idiots believed, the ability to cure them of HIV/AIDS—and that's where its real bread and butter lay.

This wasn't a normal day. The security guards had hightailed it, and Granger sat with an International Rescue Mission team in a van in the parking lot, twiddling his thumbs and waiting for the "all clear." A tip from Arthur at Spanky's had led Granger to target the Apsara 2. His investigators quickly found obvious evidence of human trafficking, underage prostitution, and virginity selling. He then handed over a legal complaint to Sochua Nika, head of Cambodia's antitrafficking police, who had conducted her own investigation. In an impressive demonstration of Sochua's influence and her unit's professionalism, not only did management of the hotel not get tipped off during the investigation but Sochua also got sign-off for a raid of the hotel—the largest ever for both IRM and her fledgling unit—from her boss, chief crook and head of the National Police, General Nhim Saray. At least for now, Sochua was kicking butt and taking names. Granger figured she'd better watch her back.

Nguyen Man, an IRM counselor, grabbed Granger's arm.

"Look."

Armed men wearing balaclavas emerged from the building herding several handcuffed prisoners to a waiting van. Some of the hooded policemen got in with the suspects while the rest climbed into the back of a pickup, and the two vehicles sped away.

With the departure of Sochua's elite anti-trafficking troops, a municipal policeman gave a knock on the IRM van, and the team piled out. Dozens of women and girls—many of them crying, some of them madder than a hornet in a Coke can, most of them quiet—were being ushered from the hotel toward two waiting buses. IRM Assistant Legal Director Song Mongtray walked alongside the file of women and girls, speaking to them in Khmer.

"You are not being charged with any crime. You have not broken the law. We do not work for the government. We are not with the police. We are here to make sure your rights are protected. We will be with you when you talk to the police, and then you will be released. We will help you find a place to sleep tonight."

Nguyen Man followed, repeating these words in Vietnamese.

Granger watched the sad procession, knowing these ladies had every reason to be afraid. It hadn't been but a few years ago, before Sochua's arrival on the scene, that women and girls would be released from jail beaten and raped or even sold to another brothel by the police themselves. Or they'd simply be released onto the street after questioning, and competing brothel owners would be waiting outside police headquarters with free transportation and promises of shelter. Since Sochua arrived, things had gotten much better, and the police routinely asked for IRM's assistance, particularly where children were involved, whether IRM had participated in the investigation of a particular brothel or not.

The IRM team divided up and got on the buses. On Granger's bus a number of the women produced cell phones and began ranting at high volume. Nguyen walked the aisle speaking to the women and girls, trying to gain their trust. Granger loved his work; it gave him a sense of purpose he'd never found anywhere else. Hard to believe it'd be nine years in September.

One of the women reached out and pinched him hard on the arm.

"Ow! That really hurt."

"My boyfriend come hurt you, mister. You have big trouble."

He responded in Khmer. After all this time his Khmer still sucked, but it was good enough to surprise people. "Sit down, little sister. In two hours you can go anywhere you want."

The woman stared out the window, nostrils flaring.

⋏

While suspects were being led out of the Apsara 2 Hotel, Deputy Chief of Mission Paris Jefferson was eating lunch in the cafeteria of the US embassy—fish *amok*, her favorite. She had fallen in love with Cambodia as a junior officer—and become fluent in Khmer—and could now reasonably be considered the State Department's leading expert on the country's complicated political landscape.

"Paris! There you are."

Jefferson turned to see USAID Senior Democracy and Governance Officer Allison Rosenburg hurrying her way. Rosenburg was clearly upset. She navigated across the crowded dining room and took a seat opposite.

"Pang Sokkruen died this morning in prison," she blurted.

Jefferson dropped her head in her hands. Pang had been one of her oldest and dearest friends in the local human rights movement, and now she was indirectly responsible for his death. She pushed her lunch away. She'd need to inform the ambassador; he'd want to issue a statement. Anyway, she'd lost her appetite.

Almost exactly a year before, Pang had come to her residence late in the evening to ask for help. He and seven other activists knew they were about to be arrested on trumped-up charges, and he came to Jefferson asking they be granted asylum in the US, like longtime opposition leader Sambo Rithy, who'd fled the country in 2013. Pang had expected a sympathetic ear in Jefferson. After all, it'd been she who'd driven Sambo to the airport in her official car so he could avoid arrest. But she didn't offer Pang the same courtesy. Harboring Sambo was now widely regarded as a mistake. The Cambodian government had not backed down, and Sambo now lived in comfortable exile in LA, where he showed little interest in returning to resuscitate an almost nonexistent opposition movement.

Jefferson and Pang had known each other since her first assignment in Cambodia from 1995 to 1997, and she'd spoken frankly with him that night in her home.

"How has Sambo's leaving helped the country? Stay and fight for your rights!"

"Not when there is no chance it will bring success."

Convinced the Cambodian regime wouldn't risk improving US-Cambodia relations—and not insignificant bilateral aid—by imprisoning the activists, Jefferson pushed. "Sokkruen, sooner or later somebody has to be willing to stand up and get arrested."

"Paris, I'm not young. I cannot stand going to prison. Please."

In the end, Pang stiffened his spine and returned home. When the police came for him at three a.m. the next morning, Pang Sokkruen went to jail with dignity and said to a reporter, "Sooner or later, we Cambodians have to be willing to make sacrifices for what we believe in. Now is that time."

US-Cambodia relations suffered, the Chinese cynically filled the Cambodians' budget gap, and the eight activists remained in jail awaiting trial on charges of criminally defaming the prime minister. And now there were only seven.

"I wonder," Jefferson said, "if we can get an autopsy."

Rosenburg laughed through her nose. "The government cremated his body immediately, citing—and I quote—'safety concerns.' They told his family only after the fact."

Jefferson massaged her eyes. It was times like these that tested her hope for peaceful change in Cambodia. "I guess that makes it a little difficult to do an autopsy, doesn't it?"

⅄

Chea Phyrom liked pizza. He'd developed a taste for it while a student—he had technically been enrolled, anyway—in Los Angeles in 2001. He liked it so much, in fact, that he'd paid an expatriate Sicilian who ran Phnom Penh's only Italian restaurant to manage the construction of a brick pizza oven on his new palatial estate in the Grand Phnom Penh International City development. The Italian hadn't wanted to do it, but Phyrom could be very persuasive.

He was poolside with half a dozen friends—some were friends and some just hangers-on—and just about to sink his teeth into the oven's inaugural *margherita*, when he was interrupted by his effeminate assistant, Kong.

"This better be fucking important," he growled at Kong to the mirth of his guests.

"It's Mao Vannak, sir." He was holding Phyrom's mobile.

"Give it to me." Mao didn't call unless it *was* fucking important. He took the phone. "What is it?"

"The Apsara 2 Hotel has been raided by the police," Mao said.

Phyrom stood. "I'll be back in a minute," he said to his guests. The girl brought for him by his friend Lim held on to his hand.

"Don't go," she drawled coquettishly.

Phyrom snatched his hand away; he wasn't in the mood for games—especially not with these cheap whores. He walked across the yard toward the house. The police had raided his favorite hotel. Somebody was going to pay.

He put the phone to his ear. "Explain," he demanded.

"General Sochua's unit," Mao said. "They raided the hotel this morning and took all the girls away with the help of a foreign NGO."

Phyrom shouted with rage. "Sochua! How dare she fuck with me! Where are the girls now?"

"They were taken to the NGO's shelter in Ang Keo."

"Bitch!"

"How do you want me to handle it?"

"I want them back! And I don't care how you *fucking* handle it! I want them all back at the hotel by this time tomorrow!"

"Yes sir."

"And I want you to find out who these foreigners are. I want to know everything about them."

"Yes sir."

Phyrom hung up. He could go back to his pizza. Mao would handle it. Mao did what the fuck he was told.

CHAPTER 8

There was no school today, so Quynh played on the shelter roof. She liked to dance there between the billowing rows of drying clothes and sheets. She was also there to get away from the chaos below; a whole bunch of new women and girls had been brought into the shelter yesterday, and things were crazy. From her vantage point she could spy on the women and girls below as they played or went about their business of cooking, cleaning, arguing, and gossiping. She felt so tall! She could look over the wall surrounding the shelter yard—the girls weren't allowed out unless it was to go to school—and see many things: water buffalo grazing in the field across the way, the men laying bricks for the walls of what would be a grand house, the customers at the fizzy drink stand on the corner. In the schoolyard several dozen boys chased a ball of paper and cello tape around the red-dirt expanse. She felt free on the roof—and safe. She wasn't sure how long she'd been in the shelter, but the moon had come and gone at least twice. It seemed that if Mama were going to come after her she would've done it by now. Still, she had nightmares.

A moto was coming down the road, and this piqued her interest. It wasn't a moto-dop but a policeman. The policeman who always waited in front of the shelter stood and squinted.

"He's there to keep bad people out of the shelter," they'd told Quynh when she asked about him.

"Like Mama," she asked, hoping this was true. But the adults had just looked at each other and not answered.

When his fellow officer stopped in front of the shelter, the regular police-man nodded and hopped on behind, toting his big gun. The two continued further down the track and stopped to pick up a third policeman who'd been sleeping in the shade of the drink stand, a similar weapon on his lap. The driver then headed back the way he'd come, leaving only silence and dust in their wake. Quynh watched them until they were out of sight. Who was going to protect her now?

Quynh lost interest in the view and went back to hiding among the clotheslines. After a bit, a distant, strange grinding caught her attention, and she ran back to the edge of the roof. She was excited to see a line of fancy vehicles rumbling down the road. In the middle of the pack were two big buses lurching back and forth like boats on the ups and downs of the road. Sun reflected brightly off the vehicles' shiny parts. Three teenagers on a bicycle overtook the convoy. Across the street, the old woman mind-ing her grandchildren looked up from her cooking to admire the unusual procession. The parade finally rolled to a halt in front of the unguarded gate of the shelter.

Big men wearing gray clothes emerged from the cars. A few of them had small guns on their belts, some of them carried long sticks, but most of them had nothing in their hands. The men gathered at the gate of the compound, and the only one among them dressed in black pounded his club on the gate. Quynh couldn't see the man's face because he was too close to the gate. The yard man with no teeth slid open his tiny window and peered out.

"Open it now," the man in black said.

The yard man turned around and looked at the women arrayed be-hind him. Everyone had stopped their doings. Even the birds were silent. Something was wrong. With shaky hands the yard man undid the chain and lifted the bar. The gray men rushed in, knocking him over.

The men wanted the women and girls to get on the buses. Most of them just did what they were told, but Quynh could tell they didn't want to go. A few of the women ran; the men grabbed them by the arms and hurt them. The cleaners and the cook sat on their haunches and did nothing—the gray men weren't interested in them—but the yard man seemed to try to help the men. The cleaners gave him dirty looks. Then the yard man looked up at the roof. He pointed.

Quynh scrambled away from the low wall. She had to hide! She didn't know where they were going, but she knew she didn't want to go with these men. She ran the length of the roof; there was nowhere to go! Then she saw the tank that held water. She squeezed under among the whitewashed pipes and dead geckos and kept quiet. Her breath blew a cicada shell. She waited. Maybe they had forgotten about her. Maybe they hadn't seen her. Just when she thought she'd come out, she heard the slap of sandals. She watched in terror the gnarled feet of the gardener as he walked among the clotheslines, ripping down the drying things and getting closer. Her hiding place didn't work; he walked straight to her like he'd known everything.

"Come out of there!" he said.

Before she even had time to answer he'd grabbed her foot and was dragging her out.

"No! Stop!" she cried.

He pinched her arm above the elbow and marched her down the stairs. It hurt but not bad enough to make her cry. In the yard, one of the housekeepers spoke to her in a soothing voice.

"It's okay, Quynh," she said. "Just get on the bus."

Quynh did as she was told and took a seat next to one of the older girls. The girl was crying and rubbing her head. There was a commotion outside the bus, and everyone got up to look. Quynh couldn't see over the heads, so she put her head out the window. Far down the lane a blue van approached, trailing a great cloud of dust, passing the line of vehicles. The van slid to a stop at the front gate of the shelter. A red-faced barang lady jumped out, marched up to the man in black, and stuck her finger in his face.

"What the hell do you think you're doing? Get those women off those buses!"

Quynh gasped. This was the first time she'd ever seen a barang speak Khmer. And it was the first time she'd *ever* seen a woman speak to a man like that. She was mesmerized. The whole busload was.

The man in black twisted the braid of the woman's hair around his fist and forced her to her knees in one swift motion. He jerked back her head and growled through a clenched mouthful of rotten teeth. "You'd better be careful. We have enough money and power to make ghosts dance."

He released the woman with a shove that sent her sprawling onto the ground.

"Bastards!" she yelled. "We're not afraid of you! Bastards!"

The men got on the buses and in the cars, and the convoy began to move. The foreign woman stumbled alongside for a while, shouting and slamming her fist on the side of the bus. Quynh could almost reach out and touch her. The woman finally stopped and watched them go. She looked very unhappy. Quynh waved to her and smiled, but the woman did not wave back. She was kind of pretty.

⚓

George Granger got a call from a slightly hysterical IRM secretary telling him that Shelter 4 was under attack and that Jane Hightower, director of IRM Cambodia, had raced off to save it. By the time he got there, the show was over. It took a while; he'd bought the land on the shabby southwestern edge of greater Phnom Penh where real estate was cheapest. This was back when it was just him and Jane in the office. Jane had named it Shelter 4 not because IRM had three other shelters in Cambodia—Shelter 4 was the only one—but because it was off National Route 4 just past the airport. He found her sitting on a cinder block in the center of the yard with her head in her hands. The gates were wide open to the world.

Granger pulled his jeep into the yard and climbed out. "Jane! Are you alright?"

She nodded without looking up. He looked around. The normally lively compound was a ghost town. Even the chickens had run off. "Well, can you tell me what happened?"

Jane shook her head. Granger limped over and put a hand on her shoulder. "Darn, Jane. You could've gotten yourself killed."

She shrugged him off. "Shut up."

"What happened to the police?"

Jane shot him a nasty look. "Who knows? They just vanished into thin air!" She got up and rounded on him. "I called everybody! Nobody at the Ministry of Interior knows anything. Nobody in Anti-Trafficking knows anything. Nobody at the Ang Keo police station knows anything. None of them knows a goddamn thing."

Granger kept his mouth shut. He'd known Jane for a long time, and he certainly knew when to let her rant.

"They took them all, George! They walked the fuck in here and took them!" She kicked over her cinder-block chair. "And they all had military license plates."

At that moment Samean, the gardener, walked around the edge of the house. He began to sweep the yard with his straw broom as if nothing had happened. Jane ran at him with a crazy yell. Granger reached out to grab her, but she was too fast. Samean dropped his broom and froze like a startled jackrabbit. Bad move; Jane was a black belt in everything. She nailed him in the mouth, and they both doubled over, Jane clutching her hand and Samean, his bloody mouth.

"Get out!" she shrieked in Khmer. "Get out!"

Samean took off as if the Devil herself was after him.

Chapter 9

"**Bye, sweet pea.** I love you."

Chris Kelly patted his daughter on the head as he dropped her off at school after lunch. Motos, tuk-tuks, cyclos, and chauffeured cars dispensing juvenile passengers crowded Okhna Hing Penn Street, honking and waving each other out of the way. Vendors weaved in and out hawking Petit Ecoliers and chewing gum to the schoolchildren. Ecole Française Louis Pasteur, arguably the best school in Cambodia, closed every day for a two-hour lunch break—a fact that drove Anglophone parents simply nuts and led Francophone parents to wax nostalgic for the France of their parents' youth. Luckily for the Kellies, the school was next door to the American embassy. When they didn't arrange a lunchtime playdate for Mai, the family—often just Chris and Mai—ate lunch together in the embassy cafeteria. Afterward, Mai could play on the embassy playground until it was time to go back to class. She had started *Cours Préparatoire*—first grade—in September with hardly a word of French, and by Christmas she was practically a native speaker. On a good day Chris could get Mai across the street and into school before he sweated through his shirt.

"I love you too, Daddy. Daddy, when I get home, will you play Sea of Darkness with me?"

Chris's mobile phone rang in his pocket.

"What's Sea of Darkness, sweetheart?" It was Hassan Hosseini, a junior officer in the political section. "What's up, Hassan? Hey, can you hang on just a minute?"

"That's when we get on the bed, and you try to push me off the bed into the Sea of Darkness. The floor is the sea, you see. Hey, that's funny—'sea, you see.' Do you think that's funny, Daddy? Daddy?"

"Uh, yeah. That's funny, sweetheart. You run off into school now so you can play soccer before the bell rings. Wait! Give me some sugar first."

Mai gave him a hug. "Bye, Daddy. You're my hero!"

As always, Chris waited until she got through the school gate.

"Sorry, Hassan."

"Can I have some sugar too?"

"In your dreams. What's up?"

"There's a meeting in the Chandler Room in ten minutes. The DCM wants you there."

"Me? Why?"

"I don't have time. Just come to the meeting."

"I'm just across the street and on my way."

Chris threaded his way through the lunchtime traffic wondering what Paris Jefferson, the deputy chief of mission, could possibly want with him, a first-tour junior officer who was not even in Political. He'd had no occasion to work directly with Paris but knew her well because she'd been the family's embassy social sponsor upon their arrival in Cambodia. At a welcome party she held in their honor, Mai had put her arm next to Paris's and said, "Look at our arms. You could be my 'bobological' mother," the concept of a "biological" mother having been a recent topic of discussion in the Kelly household. Paris, who was African American and not Indian like Mai, didn't bat an eye and replied, "Well, I certainly hope I might have a daughter like you someday."

Mai beamed. "Why don't we pretend we're sisters?" she said, cementing their relationship. From that moment on the pair had greeted each other with "hey, big sis," and "hey, little sis" everywhere they met.

Chris took the embassy stairs, figuring Paris's summons had to have something to do with the consular section. A few months before he'd arrived, three local employees had taken advantage of a junior officer's inexperience and a glitch in the system to swipe a few American visas and offer them to the highest bidder. Had something like that happened again? He arrived to find the conference room already full and the atmosphere sober. George Granger sat against the far wall whispering heatedly to Jane Hightower of IRM and a man Chris didn't know. Paul Richter, the embassy political chief, was there as well. This definitely wasn't going to be about the consular section.

"George? What on earth are you doing here?"

Paris closed the door. "Chris, go ahead and take a seat. We've got a lot to cover. Ladies and gentlemen, not all of us know one another. Over here is Lane Connelly, in charge of Legal at International Rescue Mission, and George Granger, their director of investigations. Going around the table we have Jane Hightower, director of IRM Cambodia; Hassan Hosseini, a political officer here at the embassy; Ouk Daravan, from Children's Rescue Center; Laura Forbes, State Department intern; David Finto, regional security officer; and Chris Kelly, a junior officer in the consular section, who has also been doing some volunteer work for IRM. Last, but not least, is Paul Richter, head of the political section. I don't know where AID are, but we're going to start without them. Jane, why don't you tell us all what happened?"

Chris had met Jane Hightower when she personally interviewed him for his volunteer role at IRM, and even then her reputation had preceded her. Lisa privately called her Jane Goodall. To Chris, the nickname was apt not because she resembled Goodall—she did—but because her zeal for IRM's mission brought to mind the single-minded purpose of the famous chimpanzee whisperer. A twenty-year veteran of Cambodia, Hightower had come to town in "the bad, old days" as a staffer with the UN Transitional Authority in Cambodia. At that time she'd witnessed firsthand the way UN troops distorted the local economy by selling their matériel and rations—"You should've seen the number of hand grenades on sale at the Russian Market in those days," she'd told him—and drove thousands of desperate women and children into prostitution at a time when a dollar could mean the difference between life and death. George told him few foreigners knew Khmer as well as Hightower, who spoke a rough street version of the language she'd learned from prostitutes. She'd decided to stay on in Cambodia when she married a local and had only returned to her native England once since setting foot in Southeast Asia—she'd purportedly found her old home stifling.

Hightower fixed her eyes on the table in front of her and began, her voice trembling with rage.

"This morning at ten o'clock, a convoy of vehicles bearing military license plates arrived at our shelter in Ang Keo. About two dozen armed men entered the compound and kidnapped forty-eight women and forty-nine girls, eleven of whom had been living at our home for some time and the balance of whom were there as a result of the raid on the Apsara 2 Hotel yesterday. The victims were loaded onto two buses and simply driven away while our staff watched.

"Despite the fact that Phnom Penh Chief of Police Sok Aun himself knew we were housing the women and girls and agreed to provide the home with adequate police protection, several witnesses to the event said there were no police officers present at the time of the raid. The night before and earlier this morning there had been armed policemen guarding the compound."

Chris was stunned. If thugs could just waltz into an IRM shelter and make off with a hundred people in broad daylight, then what was the point in trying? He listened to Hightower with growing disgust.

"We have already made several calls to Chief Aun, but our calls have not been returned. We have reported the kidnapping to the Ang Keo district branch office of the Phnom Penh Police Department, and the officers have assured us the event never happened. As for IRM, our investigative and undercover operations are indefinitely suspended while we concentrate on figuring out where these women and girls are and ensuring their personal safety."

A mobile phone rang. Regional Security Officer David Finto looked at his phone and raised an eyebrow.

"Sorry. I have to take this." He left, and the room grew quiet for a moment.

Chris noticed a bandage on Hightower's right hand. "What happened to your hand, Jane?"

George dragged a finger across his throat. "Not now," he mouthed.

"I cut my knuckles on the gardener's teeth," Hightower said testily.

Lane Connelly elaborated. "Apparently, the security guard-slash-gardener at Shelter 4 did everything he could to help the bad guys get all the shelter residents on the bus." Lane was the guy George had been whispering to when Chris showed up. He looked like he might be twenty years old, if that. "She lifted the poor guy completely off the ground."

Chris felt sick. Shelter 4. That's where she was, the little Vietnamese-Cambodian girl—the one he had rescued. She would have been at Shelter 4.

Finto returned. "You're not going to believe this. The embassy is being picketed by protesting prostitutes."

Every head turned automatically to the window even though it was impossible to see the front of the building from the room.

Paul Richter sniggered. "Wow, try saying that fast five times." Lisa, who reported directly to Richter, had told Chris of her boss's habit of saying odd things at odd times, not an altogether desirable quality in a senior diplomat. "What are they protesting?"

"They're carrying signs in English protesting IRM's raid on the Apsara 2 Hotel. They say American funding of IRM is interfering with their ability to make a living."

The room erupted in exclamations of consternation and disbelief. Hightower, sitting next to Chris, mumbled a slew of curse words.

Paris cleared her throat. "Interesting. Now, let me tell y'all about the man who may be responsible for what happened this morning." She passed a large photo to her left. "His name is Chea Phyrom. He's the classic story of a spoiled son of a rich and well-connected Cambodian. His father, Chea Prak, is not only one of the prime minister's oldest buddies and head of his personal bodyguard, he's also his brother-in-law, making Phyrom the PM's nephew."

Chris took the offered picture of Chea Phyrom from Jane Hightower. The prime minister's nephew...

"As a young man he'd gotten into trouble many times," Paris continued, "but he was completely untouchable as far as the police were concerned. That was until about ten years ago, when he gunned down a bunch of people in front of dozens of witnesses. It seems he was drunk and ran over a woman and a baby, then shot up a crowd of people after they tried to catch him."

Chris carefully studied the photo. It was of a young unsmiling adult wearing a white button-down and tie. It could've been a school picture. The subject didn't look familiar. Chris passed the photo to Laura, the intern, on his left.

Paris connected her laptop to the overhead projector. "The prime minister came out and made a big show of saying that nobody is above the law in Cambodia, etc., etc., and they actually put Phyrom on trial. Well, thanks to the testimony of his bodyguard, Phyrom was cleared of the charges of shooting all the poor folks—that was pinned on a friend of Phyrom's named Lor Chandaran—but Phyrom was found guilty of manslaughter in the car accident and sentenced to a couple of years in prison. The bodyguard was found guilty of shooting somebody too, and all three of them got sent to jail, and nobody could believe the good luck. Laura, could you get the lights?

"Well, guess what? It *was* too good to be true. While Phyrom was supposed to be languishing in prison—now, this is the good part—he was actually photographed by a Cambodian-American volunteer for Human Rights Watch who happened to be on vacation in China, where Phyrom had been put up in style, probably by his uncle. When NGOs protested to the Cambodian government about this, the prime minister claimed that Phyrom had been acquitted on appeal in a secret trial and spirited out of the country for his own safety."

The lights went dim, and Paris began a digital slide show: a man walking in Tiananmen Square, its iconic Mao portrait as backdrop, a dark shadow— probably a finger—in the upper right corner.

"So when it came out that Phyrom had been living as free as a bird in China, the bodyguard, who was still in prison, decided to change his testimony to match Lor Chandaran's, which blamed Phyrom for everything, and—surprise, surprise—the bodyguard wound up 'shot while trying to escape.' And not only was the bodyguard shot while trying to escape, a letter in his handwriting was supposedly found in his cell in which he took the blame for everything. I swear to you, I am not making this up.

"Human rights groups cried 'foul,' the Cambodian government ignored them, and Phyrom returned to Cambodia to make his fortune in the international sex industry with a particular emphasis on little girls. Some people say he got in good with Chinese organized crime, who funded his triumphant return to Cambodia since his father didn't want to do it. And there you have it: this is the man Jane believes is behind what happened this morning."

"How do you know it was him?" Richter asked, directing his question at Hightower.

"Phyrom's chief bulldog is a bloke named Mao Vannak, and he was leading the operation. I personally witnessed this. He threatened me. And besides, I spoke to Sochua Nika—she's the head of the National Police's Anti-Trafficking Unit, for anyone here who doesn't know—about an hour ago. She wasn't at liberty to divulge her sources, but she implied she has people on the inside of Phyrom's organization."

George nodded. "Chea Phyrom. Yep, that would make sense. Anyway, if Sochua says it, I believe it."

Paris went to the next picture: a man wearing shades getting into the back of a black SUV. It could've been anyone. A woman was holding his hand and looking over her shoulder. She was quite beautiful.

"Who's the woman?" Chris asked. "His wife?"

Paris shook her head. "No. I believe that's his sister, isn't it, Jane?"

"Yeah, that's her. Before the attack, of course."

"So about a year or so ago," Paris explained, "Phyrom's sister was the victim of an acid attack."

"Oh my God!" Laura exclaimed.

"Apparently, she barely survived. The alleged attacker was a disgruntled cop."

"A cop," Chris mumbled. People gunned down, the raid on Shelter 4, an acid attack. What next?

"I don't think they ever caught him."

Paris pressed a key on the computer, and another photo appeared. A thirty-something thug was aiming a handgun directly at the camera at close range.

Chris gasped. "That's him." All eyes turned to him. "I know this guy. Did you say he's the PM's nephew?"

Paris nodded. "I can't imagine you would've had any dealings with the likes of him."

"If he's who I think he is, I turned him down for a visa several months back."

"Well," Paris said with a wry smile, "I'm glad to see the system worked. Laura, turn on the lights. We need to talk strategy."

⚊

"Hey, man. Working hard or hardly working?"

Chris jumped. "Huh?" The answer was 'hardly working'; he hadn't been able to focus on anything since today's unusual meeting. George had been able to confirm that the little Vietnamese-Cambodian girl—her name was Quynh—had been among those taken. Chris's boss, Jim Johnson, was studying him with a stupid grin on his face. "Oh, sorry, it's just this Apsara 2 Hotel thing."

"Yeah, what's up with that, huh?" Johnson looked over at Christine Short at her desk next to Chris's and lowered his voice to a whisper. "Sick bastards, screwing kids, man. We ought to just cut their dicks off, if you ask me. What are you working on?"

The visa windows had closed at two, and Chris had been sitting at his desk in the consular section working on a large stack of immigrant visa applications—without making much headway. "Does the name Chea Phyrom mean anything to you?"

"No. Why?"

"The name came up in a meeting we had after lunch about the raid on International Rescue Mission's shelter. He's mixed up in it. And if it's who I think it is, he was one of our unsatisfied customers."

"Let's stick his name in the computer and see what we got." Johnson pulled Chris's keyboard to him and tapped some keys. "Well, look at that. He's the prime minister's nephew that you turned down for a visa a while back."

"Yeah, that's what I thought." Chris recalled the man's threat: *You're gonna be sorry.* "Small world, isn't it?"

"Yep. These top-echelon fuckers are all related to one another."

"Hey, people are trying to work in here, you know," Christine Short said without looking up from her work. "Just saying."

"Yeah, right?" Jack Durrant of Jack's Bar fame said from his identical desk behind them.

Johnson moved his tongue around in his cheek for a moment and then tapped Chris's shoulder. "Hey, come into my office for a second. I need to talk to you about something."

Chris sighed and followed Johnson into his office. "What?" He hoped it wasn't about his mother-in-law again.

Johnson closed the door. "I just want to talk to you about a little something you might be interested in."

"It's not Amway, is it?"

"No, but that's pretty funny. Check it out: there's a group of about six of us here at the embassy—now, this is totally secret—who go out once a week or so and get some girls and kinda get our groove on, if you know what I mean." Johnson pumped his fists rhythmically while thrusting his hips and grunting. "Strict code of secrecy and all that. What happens in Vegas, stays in Vegas—know what I mean? Some of us thought you might want to join us tonight for a little 'guys' night out.'"

"Really? No, I think I'll just get my groove on at home."

"It's okay, man. We know a little place off the beaten path where no foreigners ever go. We practically own the place."

"I guess I'll have to live vicariously, Jim. But thanks for asking."

"Dude, listen—"

Enough. "Jim. Just leave me alone about it."

"Okay, okay. No prob, dude. If you ever change your mind, just let me know."

"I'm not going to change my mind," he said and left Johnson standing there.

Walking back to his desk, he thought about Johnson's wife, Alma, one of Lisa's best friends, and his twin daughters, who were in the ninth grade at International School of Phnom Penh. One of the girls played softball; the other was into horses. Chris looked at the clock and gave up on getting any work done for the rest of the day. When he left work half an hour later, the daily afternoon rain had come and gone, and there were no protesting prostitutes in sight.

CHAPTER 10

General Thul Chorn, prime minister of the Kingdom of Cambodia, stood behind his desk in his official residence scowling at his brother-in-law, Brigadier General Chea Prak, commander of Brigade 70, the prime minister's personal bodyguard.

"Why has Phyrom behaved so stupidly?" Thul thundered.

Minister of Interior and National Police Chief Nhim Saray watched with amusement as Chea squirmed, waiting for the PM to answer his own question. If there was one man in Cambodia who could compete with Nhim for Thul's loyalty and affection, it was Chea, and this was just the most important reason the two men loathed each other with such alarming intensity.

"I know," the prime minister cried. "The answer is Sochua. She is the one to blame for this!"

"General Sochua?" Chea said. "Sir, Phyrom has caused you nothing but trouble. Why do you continue to protect him?"

"He is your son," the prime minister hissed. "And my nephew! None of this would have happened if Sochua hadn't raided Phyrom's hotel! She created this problem!"

"But, sir, Sochua had authorization for the raid of the Apsara 2 at the highest level. Without that, Sochua would have done nothing."

"Yes," the prime minister roared across his desk at Nhim. "How could you have let Sochua raid that hotel?"

Chea Prak's pivot was no surprise to Nhim—the man at the "highest level" to whom Chea had just tactically referred. Nhim expected no less and would have done the same to his former friend. They'd played this dangerous game so long and with such vigor, it seemed to Nhim absurd that they had initially fallen out over a girl, of all things.

"Sir," Nhim replied calmly, "if I had known the Apsara 2 was one of your nephew's hotels, I would never have permitted the raid."

The brouhaha created by Chea Phyrom's latest outrage was of little importance to Nhim as long as it didn't reflect badly on him. In the immediate term that meant countering Chea Prak's attempt to redirect the PM's ire.

"Well, *she* knew! Sochua's gone too far this time!"

Nhim relished the PM's outrage at his own anti-trafficking chief. One year ago, Thul had forced him to name retired Army General Sochua Nika to head his new anti-trafficking unit. Nhim, disdainful of politics and politicians and with no political power base of his own, watched in awe and disgust as Sochua deftly used her high-profile position to catapult herself to semi-stardom and garner wide international support. She even wrote a goddamn book—in French, no less—prompting some fool writing in *Le Monde* to dub her "the Conscience of Cambodia."

Nhim feigned astonishment. "Sir, Sochua has been unfailingly loyal. Surely you can't be thinking of sacking her?"

"And why not?" the prime minister spat.

Of course, Nhim knew firing Sochua risked her public martyrdom, but he also believed his boss underestimated the degree of dissatisfaction among the general populace and the power that someone as charismatic and politically astute as Sochua could derive from it. Thul's pride wouldn't let him consider the woman could ever present a credible threat to the succession of his son, but Sochua was ambitious, and she was no fool. Better to get rid of her now rather than later.

"Sochua is the Americans' darling. You know they'll throw a fit if you fire her."

Nhim's challenge had the desired effect. As so many people were saying these days, the PM did seem to be becoming daft in his old age.

"They think we can't even clean our asses without their permission," Thul screamed. "This is my country, and I can do what I want here!"

Nhim nodded. "Of course, sir." Mission accomplished.

⚔

Chea Phyrom paced despondently in his private office in a building that bore his name on Norodom Boulevard, his father, Chea Prak, berating him over the phone.

"Your uncle is not happy," the old man growled. "The US is already talking about cutting aid because of your little stunt."

Phyrom hated his father. "Yes, I know." He hated the way he spoke to him as if he were a slow servant.

"All he would have to do is put you in prison, and everybody would be happy. Do you understand? All our problems would go away."

"I understand."

"Your uncle won't do that, but you're making things difficult for him. You're an embarrassment."

Phyrom said nothing. He'd heard that too many times to count.

"It was a stupid mistake. You should've have just let them have the girls. You shouldn't put the PM in this position."

"Sochua should never have raided—"

"Shut up! Don't. Say. Another. Word. Until this goes away, keep all the girls out of sight. Lock them up if you have to." With that, Chea Prak ended the call.

Phyrom barely resisted the urge to throw his phone at the window. Instead, he attacked his punching bag, a useful device installed last year after he cracked his second-story window with a glass paperweight. In twenty-five years their relationship had not changed, and he hated himself for it as much as he hated his father.

⚔

Director of IRM Cambodia, Jane Hightower, entered a packed conference room at the Sunway Hotel and took a seat behind a microphone. She was followed closely by her legal director, Lane Connelly. Connelly's eyes were bloodshot, his expression grave. Jane supposed she looked like shit too; none of them had been getting any sleep. She chugged water from a bottle, cleared her throat, and read hoarsely from a prepared statement to the diplomats, government officials, and journalists from the Associated Press and regional news outlets assembled before her.

"The whereabouts of ninety-seven women and girls who are believed to be victims of trafficking remains a mystery two days after a morning raid on our shelter, during which they were forcibly removed by men in vehicles bearing government number plates. We appeal to the government of Cambodia to take immediate action to locate the abductees and prosecute those responsible for their abduction."

Hightower paused and looked at Connelly for a moment, who only stared back at her, puzzled. Connelly and George Granger had insisted on the press conference—to call international attention to the incident—but they didn't understand that the thugs running the country simply didn't give a damn about international pressure or anything else but lining their pockets.

"Jane?" Connelly whispered in her ear. "What are you doing?"

Hightower shook her head. "Screw this." Reporters began to whisper. She crumpled the paper in her hand and tossed it aside. "Well, that's all I have to say. I guess we'll take questions now."

Connelly sighed, and numerous hands shot up. Hightower pointed at Lance Cockerell from AP.

"Ms. Hightower, let me read from a statement issued by the US embassy this morning. Quote: 'We are particularly concerned about accusations of police complicity in the raid of the IRM shelter.' Were those accusations referred to made by your organization, and do you believe there was police complicity in the raid on your shelter?"

"I don't know where those accusations came from, but I'll make some now. Certainly there was police complicity in the raid—if not by commission then certainly by omission. Absolutely no doubt." She nodded at Larry What's-His-Name from *The Cambodia Times*. "Larry, go ahead."

"Why are IRM offices closed?"

"We're closed because our staff are afraid to come to work. Our office was broken into and ransacked last night, and confidential documents were removed. We've asked repeatedly for police protection, but our requests have been ignored."

"Ms. Hightower, have you been threatened?" someone shouted from the back of the room.

"Yes. Rith, your turn."

"Municipal Police Chief Sok Aun said yesterday evening that he was unaware of the raid on the IRM shelter, that he had as of yet received no report of the raid, and that his office had received no request from IRM for police protection. How do you—"

"Then he's lying. And we have repeatedly asked his office for protection."

Connelly covered the microphone. "Jane, how is that helpful?"

Hak Da from *Rakusmei Kampuchea* raised his hand and just started talking. "How do you respond to allegations made yesterday by a group of sex workers protesting outside the US embassy that your organization illegally incarcerated them after their removal from the Apsara 2 Hotel?"

Hightower imagined wrapping her fingers around Hak's skinny neck. She and Hak both knew he would never write anything critical of the government. "First of all, those women outside the US embassy yesterday were not the same ones taken from our shelter. I have been shown the security tape from the embassy; they were not the same people. Those women were either paid or coerced into conducting that demonstration. Second, we incarcerated no one."

"At least one woman," Hak continued, "has claimed she was injured during your raid on the Apsara 2 Hotel. Did you treat anyone for injuries?"

"We didn't conduct the raid. The Anti-Trafficking Police under the direction of Sochua Nika with the authorization of National Police Chief Nhim Saray carried out the raid after conducting their own investigation and determining underage prostitution was going on there. No one reported any injuries to us, although many of the victims reported abuse they suffered while working at the hotel." Hightower pointed at a man in the front row—the new guy for the *Bangkok Post*. She couldn't remember his name even though he'd tried to buy her a drink in the bar at the Le Royal.

The man stood. "John Lim, *Bangkok Post*. How did the girls end up at your shelter?"

"The *women* and girls were taken in for questioning to the Ministry of Interior. After statements were taken from all of them, they were referred to our shelter by the Ministry of Social Affairs. At that point they were free to leave or go with us."

"How many of them chose to go with you?"

"All of them." Hightower wanted to call on Cockerell again, but the guy from the *Bangkok Post* kept on.

"A complaint filed this morning at Phnom Penh Municipal Court states that you incorrectly identified these people as prostitutes and held them against their will. Do you deny that claim?"

"It's ridiculous. If the adults want to leave, we give them as many condoms as they can carry and then take them home."

"So you do hold children against their will?"

Connelly put a cautioning hand on Jane's arm. She pushed him away. She wasn't going to be humiliated by this rookie trying to make a name for himself at her expense. "Any country in the world will hold children until their welfare is ensured. The only problem is that the government is not doing it here. It shouldn't be us taking care of these girls, but in the absence of any government body to do it, we have to do it. The media obviously don't understand this, and they harp on confinement. We have a Memorandum of Understanding with the Cambodian government that gives us legal authority to hold the girls until we deem their situation safe."

"Does the government conduct any oversight of this process?"

"Nope. The government conducts no oversight."

"Leaving the potential for abuse wide open—"

"I won't have a philosophical argument about all these things. People who have not worked with trafficking victims don't understand what we are up against. The system is definitely not perfect, but without NGOs like us, there is no system at all. Take the standards of a rich industrialized nation and try to apply them here in Cambodia at the grass roots level, and you'll see how hard it is." Hightower pointed to a man she was pretty sure worked for the Cambodian Interior Ministry. She was catching her stride. "Go ahead."

"The Ministry of Interior issued a statement this morning disputing your claim that the women were abducted. The ministry said the women escaped from your shelter with the help of passersby. Is the ministry making this up?"

Of course, they're making it up, asshole. "We are not in the business of running a jail! That's the stupidest thing I've ever heard!"

Connelly pointed to his watch. Hightower said, "Okay, we'll take two more questions."

A man in the rear of the room stood, still reading the lines of a text message on his mobile phone.

"Ms. Hightower, I've just received word from a credible source at the Ministry of Interior that Anti-Trafficking Chief Sochua Nika has just been fired. Would you care to comment?"

Bastards! Hightower wanted to scream out loud; Sochua was the only one in the whole bloody government worth a damn. "Yes, I'll comment. What do you expect? We're living in a bloody mafia state!"

Connelly again covered the microphone—no doubt to council her against defaming the government—but she was done.

"You'll have to excuse me," she said and stormed out the room.

Pete Kennedy, a contractor with Oxfam by day and a volunteer undercover operative for International Rescue Mission by night, hadn't read the paper in several days or yet returned a call from a junior diplomat at the British embassy, and so he didn't pay any attention to the black SUV parked on the busy corner when he rolled up on his moto. He honked his horn and waited for the night guard to open the gate of his modest compound. As usual, the bar across the street was full of tourists slaking their thirst after a visit to Tuol Sleng in the next block, and a long line of moto-dops waited to spirit them back to their hotels. And, as usual, Kennedy figured he might walk over in a bit himself. Without much to do at night—he wouldn't go home to London to see the wife and kids for two months—admittedly, he'd been drinking a little too much of late. Looking at his watch, he confirmed it was past five o'clock; the guard should already be on duty.

Cursing the man for being late to work a second day in a row, Kennedy parked his moto in front of his rented bungalow and removed the padlock. He pushed open the metal doors, rolled his scooter under the carport, and chained it to a metal post. He turned to close the gate behind him and found four large men standing in his driveway. They all wore gray.

Kennedy didn't wait for an introduction. He broke and ran around the side of the house, but there was nowhere to go; the compound wall was high and topped with rusty spikes designed to keep intruders out. They cornered him before he could lock himself in the unused servants' quarters.

Kennedy threw up hands. "Hey…guys. Can we talk about this?"

The men began to beat him with their fists, and he rolled up into a ball. What was the point in resisting? When he woke up in the hospital, the nurse told him his night guard found him unresponsive when he showed up for work two hours late.

CHAPTER 11

Retired General Sochua Nika found the current situation extremely irritating. If the prime minister had let Chea Prak's idiot son rot in jail like he should have done back in 2002, or if he had simply told Chea to rein him in, none of this would have happened. Nobody but the prime minister would give two grains of rice for Chea Phyrom—his own father would love to see him behind bars or worse. General Nhim Saray, head of the National Police and Sochua's boss, hated the younger Chea almost as much as the elder, and Sochua herself couldn't stand the little shit. Nevertheless, the PM again and again came to the rescue of his nephew out of some irrational and illogical notion of clan loyalty that clearly ran counter to his own political and personal interests.

Sochua lay on her bed fully dressed, furious, a prisoner in her own home. She'd tried to leave her house this morning, only to have a petulant young colonel of the National Police inform her that she was to remain at her residence until further notice. Her raid on Chea Phyrom's hotel had been provocative, yes, but not on a scale unprecedented in the regular tit-for-tat battles that took place among the handful of power elite, and there had always existed an implicit understanding that, once in a while, Phyrom needed to be taken down a notch or two for his own good and for the good of the PM as long as it didn't hurt too much. But this time, Phyrom overreacted and drew the ire of the international community at a time when the prime minister was doing everything he could to prove to the world that the rule of law reigned supreme in Cambodia. And who got the blame for it? Why, she did, of course.

Predictably, the PM would now feel the need to thumb his nose at the foreign purse-holders just to prove to himself and the world that he's no man's lapdog. Obsessed with standing up to those who provided his operating budget and mindful that she, more than anyone in the current government, was beloved by the foreign community, the PM might actually have the balls to sack her. A stupid move it would be and, thus, not unlikely.

Sochua wondered, frankly, how she'd lasted as long as she had. Certainly, there were benefits to the prime minister of having her—the only female general ever in the Royal Cambodian Armed Forces and with an impeccable reputation for honesty—in such a high-profile position. Indeed, the prime minister's office took pains to imply to the press that she was a close friend and personal advisor of the PM, when actually they'd hardly spoken in years. But perhaps she'd gone too far this time.

It came as no surprise, of course, that Nhim Saray would use his unlimited access and formidable powers of persuasion over Thul—whose increasing senility had become the most fashionable topic of conversation in the capital—to convince him to fire her. No matter—she had plans and a weapon she wouldn't hesitate to use when the time was right.

"I want *udon*," Mai shrieked as she ran ahead of her parents through the parking lot of her favorite restaurant for Sunday lunch.

"Hey, don't run, chicken lips," Chris called after her.

Too late. Mai disappeared inside the restaurant and was no doubt already babbling to Mrs. Iwao, the indulgent Japanese who ran the place with the help of her Cambodian husband, Hun. Chris spotted Hassan Hosseini sitting by himself at an outdoor table. Hosseini worked alongside Lisa in Political, but Chris had occasion to work with him, as well, in an unofficial capacity. Hosseini's portfolio included reporting to Washington on the state of human trafficking and underage prostitution in Cambodia. As a result, Hosseini regularly shared intelligence with International Rescue Mission, and he was the only person at the embassy besides Lisa, Regional Security Officer David Finto, and Ambassador Schroeder who knew that Chris volunteered for IRM. Chris found him committed to his job and uber-competent, and it seemed as if he and Lisa ran into him every time they went out to eat.

"Well, well, if it isn't the beautiful people," Hosseini declared. "Hey, come over here. I've been wanting to talk to you two."

Chris feigned surprise. "You again? Geez, don't you ever eat at home?"

"No. Never."

"Hey, why don't you join us?" Lisa asked. "Aren't you hot out here?"

"Thanks, man, but I'm waiting for my crew."

"Crew? I wasn't aware that you had a crew, *man*."

"Of course, I do. But listen to this. Chris, you know that guy Paris was talking about Friday in the meeting—Chea Phyrom?"

"Yeah."

"Well, I knew I'd heard of him too, but I just couldn't remember where. I looked him up, and you know who he is? You turned him down for a visa last April. Consular informed Political back then because of his relationship to the PM."

"Yeah, Jim Johnson and I figured that out too. Interesting, huh?"

"And you know, I ran into him once out on the town."

"For real? Where?"

"I went out with Ram and some other guys to Desperado one night a few months ago to hear this great Filipino cover band. We used to go there a lot because the prostitutes don't hassle you, and not too many rich Cambodian punks are hanging around.

"Anyway, one night we went in there—about six or eight of us—and this guy came strutting in with a small entourage and sat at the table right next to us. He had three big, chunky bodyguards with him, and at least one of them was armed."

"How did you know it was him?"

"We had Heng Setha, one of the FSNs from Political, with us, and he recognized him because he'd seen him at parties because he's the nephew of the former governor of Phnom Penh. Anyway, we weren't too eager to advertise ourselves as being from the embassy because Heng told us that you had refused the guy's visa.

"To make a long story short, Phyrom screams at a waitress to give a request to the band. The lead vocal looks at the paper and says, 'I'm sorry, but we don't know this song.' Then Phyrom stands up and says to her in English, 'You sing the song, or you die.'

"Man, you could've heard a pin drop in that place. There must have been thirty people in there, and not one of them was talking. I certainly didn't think he was joking. The singer looked really nervous and said, 'Well, the band doesn't know it, but I guess I could try to sing it *a cappella*.' She was obviously very disturbed by the whole thing. Anyway, she regained her composure and belted out this amazing version of the song all by herself. And you know what song it was? It was the love theme from *Pocahontas*! You know—the animated, Disney version of *Pocahontas*!"

"Pocahontas? Now that's almost funny. Pocahontas. It seems he's got a soft side after all. Did he tear up when he heard it?"

"When she finished, everybody just looked at Phyrom to see what he would do. He stood up and very slowly began to clap, and we all just joined in."

"Wow. What a colossal jerk," Lisa said.

Chris's mobile rang. "Ugh. I swear I'm going to throw this thing away." He looked at his phone: George. "Thanks, Hassan. I'll talk to you later."

"See ya, pal."

Lisa excused herself to track down Mai and hurried off into the restaurant. Chris wandered toward the street and answered the call.

"George! I've been trying to reach you for days."

"I've got more bad news," George said grimly.

"How could it possibly get any worse?"

"Oh, it can always get worse."

"Yeah, I know. Stupid question. What's up?"

"Well, first of all, they fired the head of Anti-Trafficking, Sochua Nika."

"What? Really?" This was a serious escalation; according to what George had told him about Sochua, IRM would almost cease to operate without her. "So, basically, there's no chance those girls are ever going to be found—the ones taken from the shelter? They're just going to let them get away with it?"

"Yep, they're just going to let them get away with it. It's over. I mean, we'll keep trying, but, realistically…"

Chris felt his blood pressure rising. He refused to believe the nephew of the prime minister of Cambodia could make a hundred people vanish into thin air.

"Hey, bud, you still there?" George asked after a moment.

"Yeah," Chris whispered, seething. "I'm still here."

"Hey, man, there's a lot of ups and downs in this business. We'll be back. And we've done a lot of good work over the years."

Chris had rescued one girl. And now she was lost, a slave again. And no bigger than Mai. "Yeah. We'll be back."

"Anyway," George said, "there's more I need to tell you. Pete Kennedy, one of our other undercover volunteers, got beat up last night."

"Beat up?" A cold chill stopped Chris at the curb. "What happened?"

"He just pulled into his driveway, and before he could get out and close the gate behind him, four men walked in. They didn't take anything. Just beat the heck out of him and walked away. His guard took off."

"How is he?"

"He's been med-evac'd to Bangkok. A broken rib punctured one of his lungs. He's in pretty bad shape, but obviously they could've killed him if they'd wanted to."

"Shit."

"Chris, listen to me: they told him the beating was revenge for the Apsara 2."

"But—was he involved in the investigation of the Apsara 2? I thought you said that was all Cambodian."

"Exactly. It was."

"And you said he was an undercover volunteer?"

"Bingo. That's why I'm calling you. Pete didn't have anything to do with the investigation of the Apsara 2, and he was undercover—just like you. But somehow they knew who he was. They also told him if he told anyone what happened to him, they'd come back and kill him. So at his request we're not publicly saying anything about what happened, and we're not going to the police.

"I'm afraid there's not much we can do for each other at this point. IRM's basically shut down, and everybody who's able is getting the hell outta Dodge until this blows over—if it blows over. You need to keep a real low profile; although, seeing as you're an American diplomat, I don't think anybody's going to mess with you. Nevertheless, we have to assume they know who you are, and that none of us is safe, whether we were directly involved in the raid on the Apsara 2 or not."

Chris looked back at the restaurant, Mai and Lisa inside, Hosseini still sitting there. "Thanks, George. I'll be careful."

"We've told the local staff to disappear until further notice, but Mong's going to keep an eye on y'all."

"Mong? What are you talking about?"

"You've met him. He was the moto-dop who saved your butt at The Black Pussy."

"Yeah?" Chris had never even gotten to thank the man; he'd just left him in front of the Royal Palace that night and taken off. "What do you mean keep an eye on us? And wouldn't he be putting himself in danger?"

"Mong is anonymous. I'm the only one who knows him, and I'm not talking. Besides, he requested the assignment."

"Requested the assignment? Why?"

"Let's just say he believes in our mission and leave it at that."

Phnom Penh was never free of loiterers. Men hung out on every corner looking for a fare, selling something or other, shooting the breeze. The prolonged stare of a stranger prompted Chris to ask, "Can he be trusted?"

"Trust him like a brother."

"If you say so, that's good enough for me. What about you?"

"We're good. Molly and I are already at the airport. We're going to Bangkok tonight, and Jane's already there. Our flight's not for, like, six hours, but Molly was scared out of her wits."

"Alright, well, I'm glad y'all are safe. Call me when you can."

Chris hung up and wiped the sweat from his brow, suddenly aware of how incredibly vulnerable he and his family were at that moment. He pretended to talk on the phone while, under cover of his sunglasses, he studied the scene around him: a girl selling bottled drinks on the side of the road, three moto-dops in the shade of a mango tree, a parking lot attendant sleeping in a chair, light Sunday traffic. He wanted to pull Lisa and Mai out of the restaurant and go home immediately, but he didn't want to frighten them.

He checked his mobile's contacts and called the embassy's Regional Security Officer David Finto. "David, this is Chris Kelly. Sorry to bother you on Sunday, but I don't think this can wait."

Chris explained the reason for his call, and they agreed he would stop by Finto's house after lunch—it was directly across the street from the Kellies'. He hung up and headed back toward the restaurant.

Hosseini waved a newspaper at him as he walked by. "Hey, did you see this crap?"

Chris took the paper. "What now?"

The Cambodia Times
Sunday, October 2, 2016

NGO's Claims of Abduction Disputed

A statement issued yesterday by the Interior Ministry disputed claims by NGO International Rescue Mission that ninety-seven women and girls were kidnapped by armed assailants from a shelter in Tuol Kok last Friday.

The ministry stated their own investigation determined that the alleged abductees fled the shelter of their own accord with the help of concerned passersby.

The ministry claims to have numerous eyewitness accounts, including those of three IRM employees, to corroborate its version of events. A spokesperson added...

...Members of IRM's management team claim to have received numerous death threats. "I myself have been aggressively tailed by suspicious men on motorcycles. I am very worried," said one IRM expatriate employee. "We have appealed to the embassies of the US and France for protection. We have asked the police," she said.

An American embassy spokesperson denies having received any requests for protection...

...Exiled opposition leader Sambo Rithy issued a statement in which he lashed out at what he called "a complete contempt for the law" by members of the government and police, and he invited staff of IRM to seek shelter at the Sambo Rithy Party Headquarters.

"We will do what we can..."

Chris handed the paper back to Hosseini. "So that's the government's line, huh? The raid on the shelter never happened."

"Like Joseph Goebbels said, 'Repeat a lie often enough, it becomes truth.'"

"Sounds like they're in good company," he said with a wry smile. "I'll see you later."

Chris joined Mai and Lisa in the restaurant, but after George's warning call he couldn't even taste his tempura.

"What's wrong, Daddy?" Mai kept asking between loud slurps of her fat noodles.

"Nothing, noodle-head," he told her, but with his eyes he let Lisa know better.

CHAPTER 12

A S SOON AS the Kellies got home, Lisa took Mai upstairs for a nap—amid mild protest—and Chris crossed the street for his meeting with Finto. Finto had overall responsibility for the safety of the American embassy, its employees, and their family members. He managed the three-hundred-strong local guard force protecting the embassy and the homes of American staff, assessed threats to embassy security, and helped enforce the Protect Act, a law signed in 2003 that made it illegal for Americans to go abroad and have sex with children, among other things. Unfortunately, he was kind of a prick.

Finto's guard saw Chris coming and rolled one of the large metal doors inward to let him pass. "Good afternoon, sir. I have already rung the bell, sir."

"Thank you."

The guard closed and padlocked the gate, then returned to his stand. While Chris waited for what seemed like a long time, he thought of the first time he'd met Finto—on his and Lisa's second day in Cambodia. All American staff were required to attend a security briefing upon arrival at post. Chris had marveled at Finto's entirely uncluttered desk while they listened to his life story: former police officer; joined Diplomatic Security in 2003; served in Washington, Paris, Dar es Salaam, Jeddah, and most recently as assistant RSO in Asmara, Eritrea. Plaques mounted with ceremonial weapons decorated the otherwise bare walls of his office. A paperweight read "Rookie of the Year 2004."

Finto had described the grim crime situation in Phnom Penh in a confident, unbroken monotone that left little room for interruptions or second-guesses. He had all the warmth and charisma of a dead fish, and something else about him didn't sit well with Chris; he didn't like the way Finto looked at his wife.

"Did you see the way he was looking at you?" he fumed afterward to Lisa.

"I almost said to him, 'My face is up here, not between my breasts.'"

"I would've liked to have seen the look on his face. Why don't we go back?" Chris made as if to turn around.

"Come on." She pulled on his arm. "Let's go get some lunch."

"Okay, but only if you'll show me your boobs."

Lisa had slapped him playfully and scowled. "Oh my God! You men are all alike."

Chris now looked at his watch, thinking his first impression had been spot on; knowing Finto, he was just taking his sweet time getting to the door. Just when Chris was about to ring the bell again, Finto finally opened up. He was wearing a thin cotton bathrobe that was much too small for him. He looked like he might've been sleeping.

Finto didn't invite Chris in but instead nodded at a pair of plastic chairs in the shade of a mango tree. "Let's sit outside."

Chris automatically looked skyward; the daily rain would come soon. "I appreciate you talking to me today," he said.

"Frankly, I thought I'd hear from you sooner. It looks like all hell's broke loose, doesn't it?"

Chris thought he detected something smug in Finto's voice, and he didn't like it. "Yeah, you could say that."

Outside of a few polite exchanges at Jack's Bar, the last time Chris had met with Finto was to inform him of his intention to volunteer with International Rescue Mission. It had made good sense for him to inform the regional security officer for two reasons: first, the embassy would have a record proving his honorable intentions in case he ever had a misunderstanding with local law enforcement, and, second, the man in charge of keeping him safe wouldn't be blindsided if anything went wrong. Finto had listened without comment until Chris finished.

"Oh, I'm very familiar with IRM's tactics. There is no way I'm going to sign off on this," Finto had said as a matter of fact and without further explanation.

As it turned out, Chris didn't need Finto's permission, and he had come prepared. Protocol demanded that an embassy employee or family member seek the ambassador's written permission before accepting local employment or becoming involved in anything of a sensitive nature. Chris had already obtained that permission, and he presented the ambassador's letter to Finto without comment.

Finto tossed the letter back across the desk, clearly pissed. "Fine. Just understand that you are putting yourself at great personal risk. You are hereby on record as having informed me."

And that had been it until now. Until Chris came today asking Finto to get him out of the "great personal risk" he had warned him about. Finto didn't exactly say, 'I told you so,' but he may as well have.

"Actually," Finto said, "I've had the SDT watching your residence since the day IRM's shelter was raided."

"Good job. Thanks." The Surveillance Detection Team was a local guard unit employed by the embassy to see who might be keeping an eye on American diplomats. They worked in plain clothes, and their identities were kept secret. Until now, Chris hadn't even been sure they actually existed. Finto was clearly proud of himself, and Chris couldn't help but be impressed.

"That's what they pay me for. I've just assigned an additional guard to your house, and I'm going to go ahead and request a police guard, as well, for a few days. "

"Great. Anything else you can think of?"

"Well, if you've got some annual leave you need to get rid of, this might be a good time for a family vacation. Otherwise, just vary your route to and from work, and keep an eye on your rearview mirror. And don't travel alone if you can help it. By the way, your daughter goes to the French school, doesn't she?"

"That's right."

"Have you told them what's going on?"

"Not yet, but I will tomorrow."

"I think that would be wise."

Chris walked back across the street. The second embassy guard was already on duty. Good. He thought about Mong and the Surveillance Detection Team and wondered how many people were now keeping an eye on him and his family. None of it would be necessary if he'd taken Finto's advice in the first place. Maybe he and Lisa could get curtailments of their assignments for security reasons. He doubted it. Hopefully, this would all soon blow over.

He found the front door unlocked and Lisa and Mai nowhere in sight. They were probably already in bed for their Sunday afternoon naps.

"I'm home," he called softly.

The living room looked like an exploded toy store: naked Barbies, costume dress-ups, wooden train tracks littering the carpeted landscape. Every cushion had been removed from both the sofa and the love seat and lay stacked haphazardly in a corner. Mai's pink bedspread was draped over a chair rolled in from the office. The mess might have alarmed him more if the house didn't look like this on most Sunday afternoons. Still, a chill traveled the length of his spine.

"Are y'all here?"

He peeked in Mai's room. Empty. He checked his own bed. They weren't there. An inspection of the guest room provided no relief. Where the hell were they?

"Hey, are y'all here? If you're here, you need to come out *now*!"

Nothing. He dialed Finto. He heard a giggle.

"Daddy! Daddy!"

The mountain of cushions in the corner burst open. Mai raced at him and then recoiled at the glare he leveled over her head at Lisa.

"What on earth are y'all doing?"

Lisa returned the look. "Playing Gigantic Mountain of Cushions, dummy. What's gotten into you?"

"What do you think has gotten into me?"

"I don't know. You haven't told me anything yet!"

She strode away angry, and Chris tucked Mai in bed with a thick stack of her favorite books.

"Aw, Daddy, do I have to take a nap?"

"No, of course not. I just want you to read quietly in bed for a while," he said, knowing she'd be out in five. "I'll let you know when you can get up."

She pulled an exaggerated sad face. "Are you mad at me?"

"I'm not mad at you, sweetie. I just get scared when I can't find you." He kissed her on the head. "I love you."

"Well, better go make up with wifey." She opened *Cat in the Hat*. "See ya."

"Yeah, make up with wifey." He wished it were that easy. He now had to tell Lisa of the danger he'd put them in.

He found her stripping to her underwear, preparing to take a nap herself, and admired her in silence from the doorway of their bedroom.

"What?" She stuck out her tongue.

"Just enjoying the view." She crawled under the covers and turned her back to him. "Come on," he pleaded. "Don't be mad. I was worried about y'all."

She turned back over. "So are you going to tell me what's going on, or not?"

He closed the door and sat on the edge of the bed. He told her about George's call and Pete Kennedy.

"Holy shit." She looked scared to death. She sat up and leaned against the headboard. "So you think it was all because of IRM?"

"It had to be. They broke into his place and didn't even take anything."

"What did David say?"

"He said it'd be a good time for us to take a vacation. He also said the Surveillance Detection Team has been keeping an eye on the house."

"I knew something like this was going to happen. I'm scared. This is serious."

Chris took her hand. "You're right. It is serious. But everything's going to be okay."

"Well, I don't think you thought it would go this far."

That rankled. "I certainly knew it could go this far. That's why I got so upset when you started telling people that I was volunteering for IRM."

"I told my best friend. One person—and you've never let me forget it."

"Well, it was supposed to be a secret for this very reason."

"People in the political section are saying that this whole bust on the Apsara Whatever Hotel—"

"Which I wasn't involved in—"

"—wasn't well thought out, that y'all got in over your heads."

"—and I didn't know about it until it was over!"

"The director of another NGO told Paris Jefferson it was sloppy."

"Who told her that?"

"Somebody at Children's Rescue Center."

"Ouk Daravan? She was talking to Paris about this? She'll do anything to be in the spotlight. She carried the Olympic Torch with Sofia Loren, for God's sake."

Mai peeked in. "Are y'all fighting?"

Chris didn't like it when Mai saw them argue. "Fighting? Of course not. We never fight. Come on and scooch in here with us."

Chris lay down, and Mai climbed in between them.

"Anyway," he whispered, "I'm going to go talk to the school tomorrow."

"Good. Did Ouk Daravan really carry the Olympic torch with Sofia Loren?"

"That's what I heard." He gently rolled over on Mai and kissed Lisa on the cheek.

"Help," Mai squealed. "You're…squishing…me."

Chris rolled over on her three more times for good measure. "Oh, I didn't know you were there. So sorry."

Chapter 13

"**D**on't go, Daddy. Don't go!"

Mai hung on Chris's leg as he gave Sampour instructions for the night. Like virtually all expatriate families in Cambodia, his family employed domestic help—in this case a young lady who swore she was twenty-one but who Chris suspected was not a day older than sixteen. The oldest of ten children, Sampour had grown up on a smoldering mountain of garbage and begun collecting aluminum cans and plastic bottles as soon as she was old enough to walk and carry a bag. She sold what she found at two and a half cents per kilogram to the man who sat under an umbrella all day at the entrance to the dump. At first it took Sampour more than three weeks to collect a kilo of cans, but by the time she was six she could collect that much in just three days.

When she was still little her father died of some HIV/AIDS-related illness, and her mother died two years later in a similar manner, an innocent victim of her husband's unsafe sex practices. Sampour had no other adult relatives, so she and her six living siblings lived on the street for a year before they were picked up by Les Amis du Cambodge. Les Amis taught Sampour to read and to write and discovered she had a particular aptitude for math. She received practical training in cooking and housekeeping, and it had been Chris's idea to give her her first job. She wasn't the best housekeeper in the world, but she had a genuine affection for Mai, and it showed.

"Please lock the door when we leave," Chris instructed Sampour. Even with a doubling of the guard on the house, he had more confidence in the wrought iron doors the embassy had installed on every home in the housing pool. "Don't open it for anyone. Do you understand?"

"Yes sir."

"Mommy, Daddy, don't leave. Please, I'll be lost without you!"

"If someone comes to the house, just call me on my mobile phone. Do not unlock the door."

"Yes sir."

"Even for the guard."

"Yes sir. Maybe I not open door for Mr. Chris too. Ha."

He couldn't bring himself to smile. "Hmm, very funny. Good night."

"Daddy! Daddy!"

"Honey, she's playing you like a violin," Lisa called from the car, where she had been waiting for some time. "She's just being melodramatic."

"Alright, Mai, I've had enough," Chris said in his stern voice.

Mai immediately changed her tune. "Me and Sampour are going to have a Bollywood dance party," she cried, her eyes as wide as saucers. She ran into the house as if she hadn't a care in the world.

Chris waited for Sampour to lock the door and then climbed into the passenger seat of the car.

"I hate it when she does that," he said.

"When who does what?"

"Mai. I hate it when she cries like that when we leave. And I don't really like leaving her tonight."

Lisa patted his hand. "Seriously? 'I'll be lost without you!' She could barely keep a straight face. Anyway, everything's going to be fine. The guards aren't going to let anyone in."

"And I hate working on Sundays too." When they told him in A-100 that the Foreign Service was a "lifestyle more than a job" that meant that a diplomat was always on duty.

"Come on. Snap out of it. It's just dinner."

"If it's at the ambassador's, it's work. You're at something almost every night anyway. Do we have to do it on the weekends too?"

Lisa sighed and backed out of the driveway. "Can we at least try to have a good time?"

Chris didn't answer. The guards closed the gate behind them and put on the chain. Except for the light installed by the embassy in front of their compound, the street was entirely dark. The car's headlights revealed half a dozen moto-dops waiting for customers on the corner in the next block. A noodle vendor had parked his cart beside them, dishing out their dinner by the light of a cell phone. A man and a woman lay sleeping in the dirt on the side of the road. As they drove, Chris told Lisa about the indecent proposition his boss, Jim Johnson, had made on Friday.

"And what did you tell him?"

He detected a twinge of irritation. "I told him no, of course."

"Was that all you said? No?"

This was not going to make his mood any better. "I told him I wasn't interested. What else do you want me to say?"

Lisa shook her head. "I tell you, living in Cambodia has really lowered my opinion of the male of the species."

"Well, thanks a lot. Honestly, I'm sorry I brought it up. "

"Well, you didn't exactly tell him to go to hell."

Chris pounded his fist on the dashboard. "I can't believe you're actually getting mad at me because I refused an invitation to go to a whorehouse with Jim. I can't believe we're even having this discussion."

"Why didn't you tell him how you really feel about that sort of thing? Why didn't you tell him you thought it was wrong?"

"Lisa, do you or do you not understand that I volunteer to help women and girls get out of prostitution? Is that not enough for you? We've talked about this so many times; I thought you trusted me. Is that it? Do you think I get some kind of thrill going out to places like Spanky's? Honestly, the whole thing makes me want to vomit. Really? Do you think I like it?"

"Oh, please."

"Let me tell you something: first, I love you, and I'm not going to cheat on you with a prostitute or anyone else. Second, even if you didn't exist, I wouldn't pay for sex because of what it does to women. And third, even if I was the most desperate, horny teenager on the face of the earth, there isn't a condom thick enough in the world to convince me I wouldn't catch AIDS. Do you think I'm lying?"

She looked tired. "Well, I just thought you might stand up to him more."

"Hey, I know." Chris fumbled in his pocket for his mobile phone and thrust it at her. "Here. Call Alma right now. Her number's in my phone. Tell her what Jim asked me. Go on."

Lisa looked over her shoulder and changed lanes.

"What's the problem? Call her right now. Tell her what her husband gets up to. She deserves to know."

She only stared ahead.

"Well, whatever the reason is you won't call, that's the same reason I didn't tell him to go to hell. Is there anything else on your agenda tonight?"

They rode in frosty silence the rest of the way to the ambassador's residence and watched morosely while the guards checked under the hood and under the vehicle with their mirrors. Waved through, Lisa parked under a magnificent magnolia tree. Neither of them made a move. In the back of his mind Chris had been thinking the same all week; maybe he should've told Jim to f-off even if he was his boss.

"Listen," he said finally, "I'll stop working for IRM if you want me to. Is that what this is all about?" He took her hand.

Lisa didn't say anything for a long time, and when she did, it wasn't what he was expecting.

"Why?" she whispered. "Why would you stop?"

"Because I'm not being fair." What if their roles were reversed? As much as he didn't want to admit it, Chris knew what that would look like. "It's not that I wouldn't trust you if you were going into brothels designed for women—if such a thing existed in Cambodia."

"I know."

"I don't think you would ever be unfaithful to me; that's not it."

"What are you trying to say?"

"The problem is that just having you put yourself into the same situations that I'm going into is in itself more intimacy than I would want my wife to have with another man. I mean, I wouldn't even want you pretending to be interested in another man even if it were for a good cause." He let out a long breath. "There, I've said it, and I'm not supposed to feel that way because that would be a double standard, and I'm supposed to be modern and liberated. But the truth is I'd be jealous, and so if you want me to stop, I will, because I admit that I couldn't handle it if you were doing the same thing."

She examined his face. Finally, a smile.

"What?"

"So, in short, you're admitting you're not perfect?"

"Well…I wouldn't go that far…"

She kissed him. "No. I don't want you to stop. I can handle it."

"What are you grinning about?"

"Because now I know I'm stronger than you are." She winked at him and opened the door. "Come on. We're going to be late."

⅄

The American ambassador's residence, as far as ambassadors' residences were concerned, was nothing special. This suited the ambassador, as Richard Schroeder rarely entertained in his official capacity. When he did, he skimped on the hors d'oeuvres and his guests drank coffee from Styrofoam cups, prompting diplomats from other embassies to gossip about the penny-pinching American ambassador. Also, there was a standing FHB order—Family Hold Back—at Schroeder's representational events. Meaning, American diplomatic staff were supposed to reserve the food for invited guests. Chris, being a junior officer, did not often go to these events, and Lisa always came home hungry.

Schroeder did, however, have a genuine but professional affection for outgoing Public Affairs Officer Peggy Revkin, and so he'd offered to host some friends of her choosing for dinner two nights before her departure from post. The Kellies hadn't been on the original guest list, but another couple had cancelled to take their son to Bangkok for an emergency appendectomy. The ambassador's assistant had called that morning and asked Lisa if they would take the empty slots at the table, and Lisa knew the ambassador didn't like to be told no.

To Chris's surprise, Schroeder spared no expense for Revkin that night, and a good time was had by all. By all, that is, except for Chris, who had the misfortune of sitting between the ambassador and the political chief, Paul Richter, which meant he could only listen to the ambassador talk about himself and Richter's sycophantic banter and hope for an early end to his misery. He glanced occasionally at Lisa, who sat at the other end of the table conversing gaily with Christine Short, Chris's junior officer colleague from the consular section, and her partner, Eve. Paris Jefferson was there as well, sitting between Joe Lavarato, the defense attaché, and his Filipina wife, Baby, whom everybody adored.

Talk centered on the Apsara 2 debacle and the stunning event of Sochua Nika's sacking until, finally, Revkin threw her hands in the air and said, "Can we *please* stop talking about work?" whereupon the conversation turned to golf, the ambassador's passion, and, as he put it, "the reason I can't stay married." The ambassador regaled the table with tales of his exploits on golf courses of the world while Richter, whom Chris knew hated golf, appeared absolutely enthralled.

"I'm going to Da Lat next weekend, but I've never played that course. Have you been there, Paul?"

"No, I've played in Vietnam, but not at Da Lat."

"I've played it, sir," said Revkin. "It's a fabulous course. Did you know that foreign ambassadors get to play for free?"

"No kidding. I'll have to make sure I get my discount."

"Well, the only problem is, sir, they kind of think I'm the ambassador. You might have some explaining to do."

Schroeder laughed out loud. "I'm going to miss you, Peggy."

"Who did you play with today, sir?"

"Oh, the usual criminals, you know."

Schroeder listed a couple of well-known names, but Chris was busy wondering how early he could politely excuse himself. Maybe Lisa wouldn't mind if he took a moto-dop.

"…and Chea Prak, head of Brigade 70, came as well."

Schroeder's mention of Chea Phyrom's father wrenched Chris from his daydream.

Richter laughed. "Sounds like a fun bunch."

"Well, they're fun to play golf with because the only one who can sometimes beat me is Chea. He's a great guy."

"Sir," said Paris in her typical measured tone, "Chea Prak is one of the most corrupt officials in this entire country."

The room grew silent as the ambassador weighed his response.

Finally, Schroeder cracked a smile. "Paris, just because he's one of the most corrupt officials in the country doesn't mean he's not a great guy!"

He laughed heartily, and the collective sigh of relief was deafening.

CHAPTER 14

"**S**ixty-one more days," Christine Short exclaimed as she shut her window. "That's it. Sixty-one more days, and I'll never have to do another visa interview."

Chris was already at his desk, having wound up his morning interviews a minute earlier. "You just have to rub it in, don't you, short-timer?" Short was headed to a public affairs job in Paris in a couple of months, and everyone was green with envy.

Short grinned. "Well, of course." She sat down next to him and put her head on her desk. "Wake me up when slow-poke gets done," she said, referring to Jack Durrant, who was still at his window, wrapping up an interview. Jim Johnson, their boss, wouldn't let them close for lunch until the last of them was done.

Chris looked at the clock. He was anxious to leave; he had business to take care of at Mai's school during lunch. He took *The Cambodia Times* from Durrant's in-box on the desk behind him. It was a pathetic little rag—more of a newsletter, really, that had only recently become available online—but it had some good local reporting.

The Cambodia Times
Monday, October 3, 2016

Anti-Trafficking Chief under Investigation

General Sochua Nika, chief of the Ministry of Interior's Anti-Trafficking Department, is reportedly under investigation in connection with the police raid on the Apsara 2 Hotel last Thursday. General Sochua led the raid on the hotel, during which ten suspects were detained and eighty-six alleged sex workers were removed to a shelter operated by NGO International Rescue Mission (IRM).

IRM maintains that the eighty-six women and girls, along with eleven people already living at an IRM shelter, were abducted on Friday by...

...After a small number of Ministry of Interior troops were posted outside General Sochua's home Sunday morning, as many as one hundred supporters gathered in front of Sochua's residence demanding her release. The standoff came to an abrupt end when the troops suddenly left the area, giving no explanation.

Government radio described the incident as a miscommunication...

...Officials of NGO International Rescue Mission speaking at a press conference in Bangkok were visibly shaken by news of Sochua's suspension. Jane Hightower, Director of IRM Cambodia, stated, "Sochua Nika has done so much to combat the exploitation of women and girls in Cambodia. To vilify her rather than prosecute those responsible for trafficking and kidnapping these women and girls sends entirely the wrong signal. Frankly, without her we can't operate there."

Speaking at a news briefing in Washington, DC, US State Department spokeswoman Darla Evans told reporters she was "gravely concerned" by reports that Sochua had been detained in her home.

"Clearly, this raises doubts about the Cambodian government's commitment to fighting [human trafficking]. General Sochua has demonstrated repeatedly her willingness to aggressively combat..."

The Cambodia Times
Monday, October 3, 2016

Witnesses Dispute Ministry's Claim

Several eyewitnesses to the September 29 incident at a Tuol Kok shelter run by NGO International Rescue Mission, during which ninety-seven women and girls were allegedly kidnapped from the shelter, dispute the Ministry of Interior's account of what occurred.

The ministry has repeatedly claimed that the detainees fled the IRM shelter of their own accord after mistreatment at the hands of IRM staff. However, seven people who live or work nearby spoke to reporters, saying they witnessed an assault on the compound by armed men who forced the women and girls onto buses.

Srun Vireak, 34, said, "Several of the girls were crying, but they weren't trying to run away. Most of them were very quiet."

One man who, fearing retribution, refused to be identified, said, "The girls had no choice. Men were pointing guns at them and threatening them."

Another witness...

The Cambodia Times
Monday, October 3, 2016

Trafficking Suspects Released

Ten suspects detained in the raid on the Apsara 2 Hotel by Ministry of Interior Anti-trafficking Police and Phnom Penh Deputy Prosecutor Lor Mam in conjunction with NGO International Rescue Mission were released only hours after their arrest, and at least two of them could be seen entering the Apsara 2 Hotel on Saturday.

It is not known on whose orders the suspects were released, and Municipal Police Chief Sok Aun was unavailable for comment. An anonymous source within the Ministry of Interior's Anti-Trafficking Department said the decision to release the suspects was made at a very high level and that [the Department] had no choice but to comply.

Deputy Prosecutor Lor Mam denied responsibility for the release of the suspects, stating that he learned about it from The Cambodia Times. *"I can tell you it was not the courts," he said.*

Municipal Court Prosecutor...

...Meanwhile, Van Samean, a gardener working at the IRM shelter at the time of the alleged raid, claimed Sunday to have been assaulted by a member of IRM's staff.

A spokesman for Van said, "Mr. Van filed a thumbprint complaint this afternoon at the district police station against an IRM employee who brutally assaulted him in the hours following the supposed raid."

The phone rang at Chris's desk, and Short snatched it before he could; this was the kind of thing they did in the consular section to keep from losing their minds after interviewing visa applicants for hours.

"You crazy woman," Chris cried. "Give me that!"

Short shook a fist at him. "Pizza Hut, may I help you?" She frowned and handed him the phone. "Uh-oh, it's your wife."

Chris grabbed the receiver. "You'll pay for this," he growled at Short. "Hello, Wife."

"Can you get Mai today, sweetheart?" Lisa asked without preamble. She sounded harried, like she did most days.

"What? You owe me twice from last week."

"Honey, it's this stupid management conference. I'll make it up—"

"Stop, stop. I'm just kidding. I'll get her." He didn't mind; the only good thing about being a first-tour visa-*wallah* was never having to work through lunch. "Besides, I made an appointment with *la directrice* to talk about the security situation."

"Good."

When Chris left the embassy ten minutes after noon—a little late, as usual—a dense cloud ceiling loomed low overhead, the air as thick as cream. The monsoon had imposed a dusk-like murkiness on the city, whereas ten minutes before there'd been nothing but blue sky. These were supposed to be the very last days of the rainy season and its regular afternoon deluge.

"I thought you said the rainy season was over," he said, teasing a local guard.

"Maybe tomorrow, sir. Maybe tomorrow."

He stuffed his badge in his pocket, adjusted his tie, and headed toward his daughter's school located in the next block. In a hurry, he didn't immediately notice a man approach from the street.

"Excuse me. Excuse me, please."

He appeared to be Cambodian and wore crisp slacks and shirtsleeves, his eyes hidden behind sunglasses. Chris glanced at the two municipal policemen talking in a booth on the corner.

"Excuse me, you work at American embassy?"

Visa seeker—had to be. They were everywhere—waiters in restaurants, parking lot attendants, tourist guides—everybody and their cousin wanted a visa, and he didn't have time for this. "Is there something I can do for you?"

The policemen had taken notice.

"Yes. Hello. I lose my passport."

"Are you an American citizen?"

"Yes. I live Long Beach in California."

"Okay, you need to go to the far entrance between two and four, Monday through Thursday, and identify yourself as American citizen. Someone will help you." He turned away.

"Excuse me." The man persisted. "I want ask one more question."

Chris looked at his watch, not so much checking the time as hoping the guy would get the hint. "Listen, I hate to be rude but—"

The man shoved an open map at him. "Please help finding Tuol Sleng Genocide Museum. You know?"

Chris thumped the museum on the map. "I really have to go now. Good-bye."

"Thank you. I want give you something." The man reached into a satchel and pulled out a calendar. "This from my car shop." He grinned and opened the calendar to January and a picture of a topless beauty in a suggestive pose. "You like?"

Hair rose on the nape of Chris's neck—something wasn't right. He shoved the calendar at the man. "Get out of my way."

Chris exchanged a wave with the cops, threaded his way across the street, and entered the school grounds through the east gate. He encountered a steady stream of parents, nannies, bodyguards, and chauffeurs headed in the opposite direction with their charges, glancing nervously at the bulging sky. He met a number of friends.

"*Bon jour*, Chris. Say hello, Loïc."

A little boy waved his hands over his head. "'Ello, Monsieur Chris."

"*Bon jour*, Nadine. *Bon jour*, Loïc."

He made it a few steps before he was stopped again.

"Hey!"

"Oh, hi, Yoko. How is Eli?"

"Oh, he's doing much better. Thanks. Listen, I want to talk to you about next week."

"I'm sorry. I'm really late. Can I call you later?"

"Sure."

He turned the corner and walked directly into Joanne Richter, wife of the embassy pol chief. She was head of the International Women's Club and half a dozen other things, and, as usual, was dressed to the nines.

"Oh. Hi, Chris. I thought you weren't coming today. We wanted to invite Mai over for lunch."

"Oh, that'd be fine. I'll just go get her and meet you outside."

She looked puzzled. "But Madame Sandrine told me Mai already left with your driver."

"Wait—what?" Chris's body released a cascade of adrenaline so powerful, he felt lightheaded. He broke and ran, leaving Joanne Richter behind to wonder and other parents to yank their children out of his way. It had to be a mistake. Madame Sandrine stood at the end of the corridor, chatting with a parent and holding a little boy's hand.

Chris nearly ran into her. "Where is Mai?" he demanded breathlessly.

The teacher rolled her eyes. "She is already gone out with your chauffeur, and I wish you would please—"

"I don't *have* a chauffeur!" What was the point of filling out the school's goddam form?

The teacher gasped. "*Mais*—"

"Which way did they go? *Which way did they go!*"

Madame Sandrine pointed toward the west gate, and when Chris rounded the corner not yet at full speed, he witnessed the most terrifying sight of his life: his baby daughter getting into a vehicle with two men he did not know.

"Stop that van! Stop that van!"

The security guard at the gate stopped talking to his friends and eyed Chris curiously. The van spun its tiny tires and bolted.

"Stop them!" Chris screamed. Why was the idiot just standing there?

He sprinted to the gate and brusquely shoved the guard and gawkers out of his way. It was raining lightly.

"Moto!" he cried. They were getting away!

A moto-dop cranked his engine, and Chris jumped on behind. They whizzed by a startled Joanne Richter holding a pink umbrella and watching her chauffeur load her daughter in her car.

"Someone's got Mai! Call Lisa and the RSO!"

Joanne cupped a hand to an ear and shook her head. She waved as if he might be going to the grocery store and got in her car. He pointed vigorously at the white van, but she was no longer paying attention. He roared with frustration. Was there anyone without their head up their ass?

The van had almost reached Wat Phnom, but as long as he could see it there was still hope. Instead of merging right at Phnom Penh's namesake hill, it turned left into the roundabout, directly into incoming traffic, and then made another left onto Daun Penh Boulevard, heading back toward the school but on the opposite side of the wide median.

"Go across! Cut 'em off!"

The moto-dop shook his head and continued toward the traffic circle.

"I'll give you fifty dollars if you catch that van!"

The moto-dop found a gap in the curb, and they took off through the wet grass, fishtailing wildly. When they dropped off the median on the opposite side, the gap had closed considerably. The van shot past the Hotel Le Royal and took a right onto Monivong Boulevard, clipping the corner and toppling a mobile sugarcane juice stand.

Chris dug his phone from his pants pocket; his movements rocked the moto so violently they grazed two women on a scooter. He punched the embassy on "Favorites" and got the embassy operator.

"Get me the regional security officer!"

"What, sir?"

"Give me the RSO, right now!"

There was a click, and David Finto picked up almost immediately. "RSO, David."

Chris could barely hear him over the midday traffic, the whine of the tiny engine, and the wind and the increasing rain. "David, listen to me! This is Chris Kelly. I'm on the back of a moto chasing some guy who has kidnapped my daughter—"

"What? I can't hear you. Did you say *kidnapped*?"

"Two men have Mai in a white van. I'm on the back of a moto chasing them northbound on Monivong Boulevard almost to Calmette Hospital."

"What?"

"Near Calmette Hospital. I can see them. I need help *now*!"

"I'm on my way. Listen, you need to stop chasing this vehicle and give me your exact location."

Oh, shit. "Hold on a minute!"

Just ahead a road crew was breaking the pavement with picks in the middle of the busy thoroughfare. The van had to be doing more than fifty when it barreled into the crew's makeshift barricade, sending the workers diving for safety and their roadblock crashing into incoming cars.

Chris braced for impact. "Holy shit!"

The moto-dop hit the brakes, and they slid just to the right of the hole. That was close.

"David, are you there? David? We're turning left on Street 86! I see a large mosque." Static and then a fast busy signal. "Dammit!"

On Street 86, a series of spectacular potholes had slowed the van to a crawl. Chris and the moto-dop quickly caught up but were helpless to stop the vehicle in front of them, just meters away.

"Photo! Photo," the moto-dop cried over his shoulder.

"Watch the road!" What the hell was he talking about? Then it dawned on him. Chris held his phone over his head and snapped half a dozen photos of the van in quick succession.

"Okay, I got it. Photo."

The moto-dop nodded his approval.

The road ended in a T at the mosque, and the van slid left onto a narrower street bordered on both sides by crude restaurants and brick tenements. The moto-dop followed the van around ninety-degree turns into a labyrinth of hovels crisscrossed by well-trodden footpaths. The Land Rover wouldn't have fit between the walls. They went down a hill, and the chase picked up speed on a long straightaway.

The van plowed into the gap between the brick wall and a two-wheeled cart, ripping off its side-view mirrors and dragging the mangled cart into the path in its wake, where the moto-dop narrowly missed it.

The van made a hard right, and Chris and the moto-dop turned the same corner ten seconds later to find themselves in the midst of a small market of fishmongers and vegetable stalls through which the van had just mowed a path. Men and women and children stood around with their hands on their heads, not yet sure of what had just happened.

The motorcycle taxi slid through what was left of the market, trying to gain traction in the thick mud. Someone threw a rock.

"Go! Go! Go!" Chris yelled.

Too late. Several pairs of hands dragged Chris and the moto-dop onto the ground. Chris fought, kicked, scratched, and managed to get to his feet. A man shoved a board under his nose. There was a rusty nail sticking out. Someone punched him in the back. They had him.

Surrounded on all sides, Chris circled like a wild animal, daring each one of them to attack first. Every second he stood there, Mai was getting further away. He had to do something!

The moto-dop pleaded with someone in the crowd he seemed to know. It worked. He pulled his ride from the muck and beat a hasty retreat. Chris took advantage of the brief diversion and dove into a gap in the crowd. He stumbled, caught the ground with his left hand, and broke free.

He ran. The rain grew more intense, and he could barely see the liquid ground in front of him. His phone rang. He dropped it in the mud and had to stop and search for it. He found it and wiped the mud off on the inside of his shirt and answered with trembling hands.

"David?"

"Chris, where are you? What happened? Can you give a description of the van, the plates?"

Paths led off in many directions, each too small even for the tiny van. He had to keep going.

"I'm running after the van on foot, but I can't see it now. I got a picture of it."

"We've got police all over the area. You need to come out of there. It's not safe."

Fuck that. Chris shoved the phone in his pocket. Whole families stared at him from dark doorways. His feet shot out from under him in a turn, landing him hard on his hip in a foot of mud. He ran on. The mud sucked off his left shoe. A motorcycle was sloshing down the path toward him. This was his last chance; he'd either buy a ride or take it for free.

"Moto!"

The vehicle slid to a stop. Chris wiped the rain from his face and squinted at a man in a green poncho.

He couldn't believe his eyes. "Hey! You came back!"

The moto-dop shrugged. *"Vite! Vite!"*

Chris remembered that voice from The Black Pussy; it was the guy George had told him about. "Mong?"

The man nodded curtly, and Chris got on behind him. The path sloped steeply upward, and they had to push the motorcycle up the muddy incline. At the top of the hill the road met a wide paved boulevard where the rain had stopped but the lack of adequate drainage had brought vehicle traffic to a standstill. Chris had never seen so many small white vans in his life.

"Where'd they go? Where are they?"

Mong pointed at a battered van in the middle distance. It was fording deep water on the wrong side of the road.

"Let's go!"

They gave chase, but the deep water forced motos to drive double file in the center of the road to avoid submerging their engines. High-clearance SUVs passed on the right and left, sending plumes of brown water crashing down on them. The bad guys were getting away.

Chris pointed at the sidewalk on their right. "Over there!"

They carried the moto through the high water. Once on the pavement, they dodged shrubs, submerged potholes, and pedestrians but slowly gained on the kidnappers. There was hope. Sirens wailed in the distance, getting closer. They were only twenty meters behind the van on the opposite side of the boulevard and now on higher ground.

"Get back on the road!"

Mong shot off the curb with a bone-shattering crash, right on the van's tail. The kidnappers took a hard left from the far right lane down an unpaved street.

"Turn! Turn!"

They were going too fast. A child ran in front. Mong lost control. They bashed into a stand selling live chickens, sending feathery cages flying.

⅄

His cheek on the muddy pavement, his left arm pinned under him, Chris struggled to get up, to continue the chase. If he let the van out of his sight again…he couldn't think about it. He needed to move. Something heavy dug into his back. A man threw the thing off with an angry shout—a chicken coop. An unfriendly crowd was growing.

As Chris got to his knees, someone snatched his wallet from his back pocket; he grabbed for it, and a shot of pain tore through his side. Too late, anyway. He rolled over and kicked his feet under the legs of the retreating thief. The man stumbled but made off anyway under the covetous gaze of several dozen onlookers. Where was Mong? Chris dragged himself to his feet in a great deal of pain from his scraped and battered joints. He was bleeding from his left hand and his elbow.

His mobile rang. He fished it from his front pocket. It was a number he didn't recognize. He spat a dirty feather from his mouth. "Hello?"

There was a great deal of noise on the line, then, "Daddy?"

He stopped breathing. "Mai?" His knees buckled, and some stranger's hand reached out to steady him.

Chris's mind raced trying to process how it could be possible his daughter was on the phone. A man, likely the chicken vendor, poked him in the shoulder with two fingers and screamed at him in incomprehensible Khmer. Bad idea. Chris nailed the man in the chest with his free hand, knocking him backward over his coops and onto the ground.

"Mai, are you okay, sweetie? Are you okay?" *Please, please be okay.*

"Daddy?"

"Where are you, baby?" He needed something. The smallest anything that could help him find her. "Where are you?" He listened for voices, horns, music, anything that could provide a clue.

"I want to come home," she cried. "I want—"

The phone was snatched away from her.

"You won't see your daughter again," promised a vaguely familiar voice.

Despite the eighty-degree temperature, Chris froze to death. No. no. no. He knew that voice. He knew it. But where? Where? "Please, please, please, no, listen—"

"I told you I would get you. And then you fucked with me again."

He had to keep him on the phone. Just figure out what he wants. That's all. Do anything to keep him on the phone. "I'll give you whatever you want. Anything. Just don't hang up." Don't hang up.

"I got what I want."

No. no. no. Everyone wants something. *Everyone's got a price!* "No, no—wait! Anything—I'll give you whatever you—how much? How much do you want?"

"I got what I want. If you try to find her, I'll kill her." The man hung up.

"No! Let me talk to her!" The crowd pressed in. Where the fuck was Mong? "Mong, come on! Which way did they go?"

Sirens grew closer. Mong had righted his moto and was trying to straighten the handlebars.

"Which way did they go?" Chris begged the crowd. "Which way did they go!" He looked around for another moto-dop. He could still catch them. "Moto! Moto!" The people just looked at him. "I need a fucking moto!"

A police cruiser rolled to a stop, followed by a white embassy SUV.

David Finto got out. "Chris!"

"I think they went that way," Chris cried, pointing down the side street. They were losing valuable time. "Come on!"

Finto held up his hands. "Just hold on and tell me what happened."

"No! We've got to go now!" Chris limped to the open window of the SUV. He'd take it if there were keys were in the ignition. There weren't.

"Do you have a description of the van? License plate? Anything?"

Chris remembered the pictures and fumbled with his phone. His hands didn't work, and he had to enter his password three times. He scrolled through the photographs, each one blurred and useless.

"No! No! No!" He threw phone as hard as he could to the street. An adolescent burst from the crowd, grabbed it, and ran.

Chapter 15

Ambassador Richard Schroeder was at the Royal Phnom Penh Golf Club with Japanese Ambassador Gen Ishii and Brigadier General Chea Prak, waiting to tee off on the back nine, when his phone vibrated, startling him. He wiped the sweat from his face and neck with a towel and examined the phone.

"Shit." It was Deputy Chief of Mission Paris Jefferson; she wouldn't be calling now unless it was important enough to end his golf game. "Excuse me, gentlemen."

Schroeder settled into his cart. "Yes, what is it, Paris?"

"Sir, Lisa and Chris Kelly's daughter has been abducted."

Schroder jumped to his feet. "Abducted? When?"

"Less than an hour ago."

"Do we know for sure?" Cambodia had its share of problems, but kidnapping foreign children was not one of them.

"There's no question. Chris witnessed it."

Schroeder tried not to think about what that must feel like. Instead, he jumped into action, which was more comfortable. "Find out where the prime minister is and request a meeting as soon as possible with him and Nhim Saray. It'll be me, you, Finto, and Richter. Ask Esther to go ahead and draw up the dip note for the meeting and send it to the Foreign Ministry." He glanced at his watch and frowned. "It's going to take me almost an hour to get back in the office. Call the Ops Center and then go ahead and fire off a cable. Has the FBI been notified?"

"Yes. Finto told me they've already got a team on the way from Bangkok."

"Good. How are Lisa and Chris?"

"I don't know. Chris's a little banged up. I'm heading over to SOS to see them now."

"Have someone call the new regional psychiatrist. I can't remember her name. I'm sure she'll want to come out. Okay, do all that, and I want to see the country team as soon as I get there. And if they agree to it, I want you, me, Finto, the FBI people, and Richter to meet with the Kellies tonight to discuss our response."

"Got it."

Schroeder hung up and aimed his cart toward the clubhouse. "I got to go, gentlemen," he called and took off, leaving his caddy to run after him. Jefferson was a godsend.

⚔

In the third grade Chris realized other parents didn't have separate bedrooms. His father had run his own sign company in a soulless, far-flung exurb of Houston that was at the time still more cow pasture and piney woods than strip mall but developing at breakneck speed. The last time Chris visited— his father's funeral—the place was almost unrecognizable as the place of his youth. The old man hadn't believed in vacations or spoiling children with privileges, such as the right to speak in his presence. Obsessed with ensuring Chris didn't "get above his raising," his parenting style was not so much "old-school," as his father had righteously described it, as sadistic. He once locked Chris outside without a coat in the dead of winter—"this is Houston, not Canada, for God's sake," his dad had said in his defense—because he'd forgotten to put a lid on a can of paint. Chris's mother sold real estate part-time and cried (and drank) a lot. He couldn't remember her ever saying or doing a single thing to challenge his father's twisted notion of parenthood. When he was in the sixth grade his parents divorced, and he recalled thinking it was about damn time. His mother quickly remarried to a man with a modest fortune and kids of his own and moved to Edmonton, Canada. With a new life and new family, she had no need for him, and he liked to pretend he didn't care, saying "good for her," to his only teacher who would listen. On the day of his wedding, Chris hadn't seen his mother since his high school graduation—six years—and Lisa had been furious on his behalf when she found out.

"No, it's alright," he'd said, but he figured Lisa knew he was lying.

So it had taken Chris a while to believe Lisa was there to stay. On their one-year anniversary he'd jokingly asked her if he could make any improvements.

"I wish you wouldn't laugh when I tell you I love you."

He was astonished at both the answer and the quickness with which she gave it—like she'd had it ready for a while. "What? I don't laugh when you say that." He thought he was telling the truth.

"Yes, you do. You may not know it, but you do. It's more a snort than a laugh."

It took him a year of therapy to get to the bottom of that, although it wasn't rocket science: he'd been abandoned as a child.

On Mai's first night with them, Lisa had read his thoughts. She said, "We're never, ever, ever, *ever* going to leave you," and he'd cried like a baby in her arms.

Now Lisa sat with her head in her hands beside him in the Chandler Room, a mess of shock and grief, where only three days before Jane Hightower had described the raid on the IRM shelter. They were listening to Deputy National Police Chief Chet Pannha—a wide man in his late fifties who Paris Jefferson had privately described as "corrupt but competent"—offer earnest promises that every possible resource would be mustered to find their missing daughter. Chris looked at the clock on the wall; Mai had been gone for two hours.

A formidable array of Cambodian uniforms was there with Chet, and one could be forgiven for believing him sincere. Chris knew the Cambodian police could, when the top brass felt inclined, be remarkably effective. In the case of a carjacking involving the wife of a Japanese diplomat, the police cornered the offenders within half an hour. After the two men surrendered, a policeman summarily executed them in front of a large crowd of onlookers. National Police Chief Nhim Saray praised the officer for his actions, stating,

"Thanks to his bold actions, we aren't going to have any more carjackings in Cambodia." At the time, Chris had been horrified. Now he longed for such efficiency to be applied to the man who had stolen his daughter.

At Chet's request, Chris relived the entire story for the group, which included DCM Paris Jefferson, Regional Security Officer David Finto, Political Chief Paul Richter, Consular Chief Jim Johnson, Chelsea White from Regional Affairs, and Assistant Regional Security Officer Kirk Donovan. He described the chase in detail and ended with the harrowing telephone call. One of the Cambodian police officers, who introduced himself as a detective, asked several pertinent questions and took copious notes.

"Look," Chris said, finishing his account, "I know who did it. You just need to send someone out to bring him in. I'm sure you know where he lives."

Deputy Chief Chet spoke through embassy interpreter Khut Chanthy while he toyed with a wiry hair growing from a dark mole on his cheek.

"This is what we have done. We were able to determine the telephone call you received came from a mobile phone that was in the Daun Penh District at the time of the call. Half an hour later the phone was still in that area. We have set up roadblocks, and every single car going in and out of the area is being examined. We have begun a door-to-door search in the district for your daughter."

Chris didn't like that the deputy chief had ignored his accusation. "Sir, you are not listening to what I'm saying," he growled. "I know who did it. Chea Phyrom is the owner of the Apsara 2 Hotel. This is his revenge. He said so on the phone."

"Mr. Kelly, I can assure you Chea Phyrom is not the owner of the Apsara 2 Hotel."

Chris's blood began to boil. "Look. Everybody knows Phyrom was behind that whole thing. You know that."

"Do you have any proof of his involvement in your daughter's kidnapping?"

"Proof? I talked to him about it on the goddam phone!"

Chet remained as smooth as silk. "Mr. Kelly, I understand you are upset. We will conduct our own investigation. With your government's help, of course. If Chea Phyrom is responsible, he will be arrested."

"So then you'll be bringing him in for questioning? After all, he is the prime suspect, right?"

Paris put a hand on Chris's arm. "Chris, I think—"

"At this point there is no evidence to connect Chea Phyrom—"

"Bullshit!" Chris jumped to his feet, followed by Chet's men. "This is bullshit!"

"Chris! Control yourself!" Paris said.

Chris ignored Paris and pointed at Chet. Those rich bastards were all in this together, and he didn't give a fuck who they were. His daughter was *not* expendable! "You know Chea Phyrom runs brothels with little girls in them. You know he ordered the raid on the IRM shelter. And you know he's the man who took my daughter! If you won't do anything about it, then I will! I don't give a damn who his daddy is—"

Finto dragged a finger across his throat, and Khut Chanthy stopped interpreting Chris's words. Chet sat with his hands folded in front of him, his face a deep shade of red.

"Chris!" Lisa cried. "Stop it!"

He rounded on her. "You're taking *their* side?"

"I'm not taking anyone's—" and she dissolved into sobs.

Paris got up and opened the door. "Okay, it's time for y'all to go home. Now. There's a car waiting. I'll call you later."

"No!" Chris cried, but Lisa shoved herself away from the conference table and stumbled out the door, racked with sobs. He ran after her. They had to go back in there. "Wait!" He grabbed her arm.

She turned and fixed on him a look of the most heartfelt hatred. "Well, that was really stupid," she spat and pushed past him.

⋏

"Why hadn't you talked to the school?" Lisa whispered hoarsely, staring at the seat in front of her on the way home.

"I was on my way to talk to them. You know that. We discussed it this morning."

Chris caught the embassy driver watching them in the rearview mirror. "Keep your eyes on the road, please."

"Yes sir."

Lisa's face contorted with grief. "When that IRM guy got beat up," she sobbed, "why...why...didn't you go down to the school the same day and tell them? Why didn't you warn them someone might try to take her?"

Chris massaged his eyes. "Honey, it was Sunday. I went and told David Finto right away, and I was going to tell the school today."

"Didn't you think something like this could happen when you got involved with this shit?"

Of course, he'd thought about it every single day. It was the only thing he thought about. He ran nightmare scenarios through his head all the time.

"Why couldn't you go save AIDS orphans like everybody else?"

"I'm sorry. I just wanted to help—"

She punched him weakly on the chest. "You weren't trying to help anybody! You were doing it because it was exciting. Playing undercover cop is a lot sexier than changing a diaper in an orphanage!"

"That's not fair," he muttered.

She hit him again. "*Fair*? I don't give a damn about fair!"

"This is not what we need to be doing right now. We need to be supporting each other and doing what we can to get Mai back."

"Get Mai back? Are you joking? They won't even bother to waste a bullet on her. They'll knock her in the head and dump her body in some trash heap. She's not coming back! I hate you! I fucking *hate* you!"

She attacked the seat back in front of her until she tired and fell back. Chris looked at the driver in the rearview mirror. "I said, 'Keep your eyes on the damn road'!"

They said nothing for a while, interrupted only by Lisa's gut-wrenching sobs.

"Well, you sure helped things, screaming at the police like an idiot," she rasped finally.

He didn't respond. There was nothing he could say.

"We need the police," she whispered. "They might not arrest Chea Phyrom, but they might help us find Mai. It sounded like you were more interested in getting revenge on him than finding Mai."

They pulled into their driveway.

"I can't believe you said that." He got out and slammed the door hard behind him.

⋏

Minister of Interior and National Police Chief Nhim Saray was on his way back to the ministry, deep in thought after having just left a meeting with the prime minister and the American ambassador. Chea Phyrom, nephew of the prime minister and son of Nhim's archenemy, had surprised even his favorite uncle with this latest stunt.

When, as a young adult, Phyrom had frequently flouted his impunity as the only son of one of the most favored, Nhim had been obliged to pick up the pieces. When Phyrom murdered a large number of peasants in front of dozens of witnesses, the prime minister agreed only to send the boy out of the country for a while. Of course, Nhim would have loved to have taken down Chea Prak's son long ago, but over the decades the PM's two most loyal men had achieved a reasonable *modus vivendi*, whereby they could both enrich themselves at the expense of their countrymen without engaging in mutually harmful turf wars that did nothing to please the prime minister. But this time the boy had certainly gone too far, and if Nhim played the game right, he could eliminate the young Chea, strike a personal body blow to his old enemy, and further ingratiate himself with the PM—all with minimal effort.

On the other hand, the Americans acted as if Cambodia were the fifty-first state of their godforsaken country and that they had the right to inspect how he conducted every investigation of interest to them. He had already met them twice this week to discuss the raid of the IRM shelter—another of Chea Phyrom's stupid mistakes, although Nhim had to admit it was done with a certain flair—and their sanctimonious meddling made him want to retch. Irritating the Americans, however, while personally gratifying, did not serve Nhim's best interests at the moment. And besides, watching the previously impregnable Chea Phyrom go down in flames would afford him a lifetime of satisfaction. He'd cooperate with the Americans—for now.

⋏

Lisa emerged from the bedroom only at six p.m. when Ambassador Richard Schroeder arrived at their home with Paris Jefferson, David Finto, Paul Richter, and a woman the Kellies had not met. The stranger was diminutive, with shoulder-length black hair, and bounced slightly with each step as she followed the group into the formal dining room.

"Special Agent Mayela Gutierrez, FBI." She shook Chris's hand enthusiastically. "Let's get your daughter back."

Lisa waved off Gutierrez with a hand. "I'm sorry," she whispered and slunk into a chair.

Paul Richter patted Chris on the back and said, a little too gaily for the occasion, "How's it going, Chris?"

David Finto snorted derisively. "Really?" It was a well-known secret the security officer considered the pol chief a first-class moron.

"Things have been better," Chris responded dryly, Finto's smart-ass response irritating him more than Richter's unfortunate tone. Anyway, he was too tired to give a damn.

Lisa sat opposite him, shielding her eyes. "So are the police going to help us find Mai or not?" she asked, so utterly bereft that the room fell silent.

Paris looked at the ambassador. Schroeder nodded and Paris began.

"Unfortunately—and I'm sure this is no surprise to you—the police are corrupt and can't be trusted. I'm just being perfectly frank here. However, National Police Chief Nhim Saray is perhaps the most powerful man in Cambodia after the prime minister. He's been minister of the interior for fifteen years, and about six years ago he fired his own National Police commissioner and took that job for himself as well. He's certainly in a position to help us, but he'll do so only so long as it's aligned with his own personal interests."

"Now, Paris," Schroeder said, interrupting, "you're painting a bleak picture. We've had an excellent relationship with Nhim for years."

"True," she conceded.

"So how is it in this guy's interest to help us get Mai back?" Chris asked. "Isn't he tight with Chea Phyrom? Didn't the police help raid IRM's shelter and kidnap those girls?"

Paris adjusted her glasses. "Well, it's not that simple. Competing with Nhim to be the second most powerful man in Cambodia is Chea Prak, the father of Chea Phyrom, the man you're convinced is responsible for kidnapping Mai."

"He *is* responsible," Chris interjected. Why wouldn't they just call a spade a spade?

"Yes, well, his father, Chea Prak, and General Nhim hate each other with a passion, and the PM plays them off against each other to suit his needs. There hasn't been large-scale open warfare between Nhim and the older Chea in years, but everybody knows they'd love to destroy each other given the chance.

"Nhim would love to take down Chea Phyrom, and not just to hurt his father, his old nemesis. Nhim can't stand Phyrom in his own right—because for at least a decade the prime minister has forced him to let Phyrom do anything he wants, and then he has to clean up the mess afterwards. The incident we discussed a few days ago, where Phyrom shot up a crowd of people, is a case in point. It's not clear who Nhim despises more: the father or the son."

"You're forgetting," Schroeder said, "that if none of what you just said was true, it would still be in Nhim's interest to help us simply because we are the American embassy."

"Right again, sir. And as for General Nhim being involved in the raid on the IRM shelter, well, it's unlikely he was directly involved for the reasons I just mentioned, though certainly some police officers and other government officials were complicit; the loyalties are numerous and complex. I believe Chea Phyrom raided the shelter using his own people as well as people and vehicles from his father's operation, and it's likely General Nhim—and Phyrom's father, for that matter—only found out about it after the fact.

"And, Lisa, the kidnapping of your daughter changes everything. I mean, this ratchets things up many more notches, and Chea Phyrom may have tested the PM's patience one too many times. I'm certain Nhim sees this as a fabulous opportunity to take a chink out of Chea Prak's armor and get rid of the son at the same time. My guess is we're going to get excellent cooperation out of Nhim—the motivation behind that cooperation is irrelevant. He'll certainly be lobbying the PM hard to let him go after Chea Phyrom."

"And if not?" Lisa's voice was scarcely audible.

"What?"

"What if the prime minister doesn't let him go after Chea Phyrom? I mean, Nhim still has to take orders from his master, right?"

"Well, Prime Minister Thul may very well continue to protect his nephew, but it doesn't really matter. What's really important here is getting your daughter back, and Nhim can help us do that even if he can't directly go after Chea Phyrom. That's what we need to concentrate on, and, as the ambassador just pointed out, General Nhim would like to keep the American embassy as a friend. If for no other reason, Thul's not going to live forever, and someone like Nhim never knows when he might have to leave the country in a hurry. He needs allies."

"What if Thul orders Nhim not to help find Mai," Chris asked, despite having promised Lisa to let her do the talking.

"That doesn't make any sense. How could it possibly benefit the PM to have your daughter missing? And frankly, he wouldn't dare."

"And today we let them know," Ambassador Schroeder added, "in no uncertain terms, that sons of the well-connected cannot simply kidnap the children of American diplomats without repercussions."

"You stated that explicitly?"

"Yes. I stated that explicitly."

⚔

Lisa locked herself in their bedroom again after the embassy team left.

Chris tapped on the door. "You've got to eat." Vy Finto had brought over a casserole, a kind gesture even though her cook had made it.

Lisa mumbled something.

"What?"

"*I said, 'I'll never eat again!*'"

Chris turned off the lights and listened numbly to Lisa's inconsolable sobs. He should have done more to protect his family. He could have informed the school earlier about the risks. He'd lived almost all his life without Mai, but now he couldn't imagine a world without her. Right now, she was in some strange place, terrified and crying. He had promised to always protect her, but instead, all he could do was wait in silence while his wife cried herself to sleep. He would always hate this house.

Soon, anger, less complicated and more hopeful than guilt, welled up inside him. Hate opened his mind to unspeakable possibilities. He implored a long-ignored God to let him have Chea Phyrom—to torture him, to dismember him alive, to pulverize him. Please, if there is a God—do this.

Just before the first tenuous stirrings of morning, before the family sleeping on cardboard in the vacant lot next door woke, before the moto-dops began trolling for their first customers, even before the bread vendors began their rounds, the tears began to flow, and Chris fell finally into a very troubled sleep.

Chapter 16

Chea Phyrom groaned as his father, flanked by two bodyguards, marched into his dining room, interrupting his breakfast.

"How are you today, Father?"

Chea Prak put a finger in his face. "You idiot! I can't believe how stupid you are. The American ambassador was in the prime minister's office yesterday talking about the American girl. He asked him to arrest you. Is that what you want?" Prak glared at Kong, Phyrom's feckless assistant. "Get out!"

Phyrom laughed as Kong tripped over his own feet in his haste to comply. "I think you frightened Kong. Anyway, it wasn't me who took her."

"It wasn't you? Do you think I'm as stupid as you are? It wasn't you? The prime minister is ready to offer them your head on a banana leaf, and I'm not going to protect you."

Phyrom laughed again to conceal the fact that he desperately wanted to stab the son-of-a-bitch. "I didn't do it," he said calmly.

"*Do not say that to me again!* You idiot! That girl had better be back with her mother tonight!"

Phyrom smiled as the old man stormed from the room. Fortunately, his uncle, the PM, cared for him quite a bit more than his own father. He would have his revenge, and he was as untouchable as ever.

⋏

Lisa sat silently in a US government vehicle on her way to a second meeting at the American embassy—another meeting to talk about how the hell they were going to find Mai. She hadn't been able to sleep a wink. She detested coffee, but she desperately craved caffeine this morning. What was happening? Was this real? Mai had now been missing overnight. She'd spent the night away before, but this—this was something of a milestone; never before had Lisa not even known where her daughter was. And with whom?

Chris, sitting next to her in the backseat, started to speak, but she ignored him. She hated him. That's what she'd told the regional psychiatrist who had called early this morning from Bangkok.

"His family was pretty messed up, you know," she'd told her just as a matter of fact.

"Where did the two of you meet?"

"We were both going to the University of Texas. Well, actually, we met at ACC—Austin Community College—where we were both taking Calculus in hopes of getting an easier grade than at UT. It didn't really work out that way, but anyway."

She and Chris had been dating a semester when she took him to Little Rock to meet her folks, head over heels in love and already whispering of engagement.

"Your parents won't mind if you're not home for Christmas?" she'd asked him.

He laughed through his nose and said, "Are you kidding?" and she hadn't understood at the time what he'd meant by that.

When they sat down to dinner with her mom, her dad, and her brother, Todd, on the first night, he said, "Wow, I honestly can't remember the last time my family sat down and had dinner together," and they all looked askance at one another.

After dinner they went out for a beer with her dad. Chris said, "I can't imagine—not in a million years—going out with my dad and just having a beer and talking. It's unimaginable."

And Todd had said, "For real? Is he really that bad?"

Apparently, he was worse. Chris explained his father was the reason he'd chosen the Foreign Service as a career—to get as far away as possible—and "why I don't want to have children of my own."

"We actually broke up over it," Lisa told the psychiatrist, "but it turned out we couldn't live without each other, and, basically, I agreed to be patient with him about children, and he said he would try to keep an open mind."

"Well," the psychiatrist said, "obviously your strategy worked."

"And then I found out I couldn't have children." They were already living in India at the time, and she was devastated. "It was Chris who said not to worry about it, that there were so many children in India that could use a home. It was Chris who did the research and dragged me to the orphanage more or less kicking and screaming and convinced me that I could do it. I mean—and this is hard to admit—I wasn't sure I could love a child that wasn't, you know, biologically mine, and I felt really guilty about that, but Chris convinced me it was okay and that it was normal to feel that way. During that time I was an emotional basket case—kind of like I am now— and Chris took care of me and everything else, and he was the one who hadn't wanted children in the first place."

"He seems like a pretty devoted father now."

But the very day they'd brought Mai home from the orphanage, all her doubts about whether or not she could love an adopted child had vanished, and now, without Mai, what was left? No mother should live long enough to see her child's death. Never. It was the most cruel punishment God could mete out.

The driver pulled up to the bollards at the rear of the embassy compound. The local guards came out to inspect under the hood. The Marine nodded from his post. Lisa didn't acknowledge him. This was not real. Surely she had died and gone to hell.

$$\lambda$$

Agent Gutierrez, sitting between Ambassador Schroeder and Paris Jefferson, held up some local newspapers. David Finto and Paul Richter were also at the table along with two FBI agents who looked like they had arrived on the red-eye. Gutierrez had just introduced them, but Chris had already forgotten their names. Lisa wouldn't make eye contact.

"Hundreds of tips have come into the embassy and the police as a result of these," Gutierrez said.

Chris stared at the full-page portraits, unable to believe it wasn't some stranger's daughter. He remembered the black-and-white photos of missing children he'd seen on the sides of milk cartons as a kid. He once asked his dad if he thought any of them ever made it home. "I wouldn't bet on it," he'd said callously. The words echoed in Chris's head, and he zoned out for a moment. Then he thought of Chea Phyrom, and anger welled up inside of him, sharpening his focus.

"What about Chea Phyrom? Have they questioned him yet? Are we following him?"

Gutierrez's sigh gave him the answer he didn't want to hear. "Chris, the focus of the investigation is on finding Mai, not going after him."

Chris pounded the table a little too hard. "Is nobody listening to a word I'm saying? He is the only one who knows where she is!"

"The police have not yet responded to a request we made this morning to question him. We need to wait a little longer."

"How long do we wait? Is there nothing we can do to force them to cooperate?"

Lisa slammed her fist on the table. "Dammit, would you shut up about Chea Phyrom? They're not going to arrest him, so just shut up!"

"We're getting outstanding cooperation in other areas," Gutierrez noted.

"Oh," said Chris, "so I guess we should be grateful. Send them a big thank-you for not doing the one thing that can get Mai back."

"So then what do you want me to do? Tell them to go to hell and then we get no help at all? We're doing our best with what we've got to work with!"

The ambassador held up a hand. "Listen. We're already looking at options. Ways for applying more pressure if they don't comply. But we have to wait a little longer. I know it's not easy."

"Like what options?" Chris asked. "Specifically?"

"Well, we would ask the secretary of state to give the PM a call. We could put out a travel advisory warning Americans not to come to Cambodia. We could withhold bilateral assistance. We could end cooperation on a whole host of issues. We could even close down the consular section. But it would be premature to do any of these things today."

Chris threw up his hands. "Okay, fine. Okay." He was losing his mind.

⋏

In Bangkok, with only three days of meetings before fulfillment of a two-decades-long dream, Leonard Perry wandered late in the night through the Patpong brothel district only to find he couldn't keep his mind off Cambodia. He found the adult prostitutes uninviting, even disgusting, and retreated early to the Marriott, where he masturbated to the same tired fantasy.

Finally, he would be going to a place where sex with children, while not officially condoned, was readily on offer and where people understood his needs. What a relief to be in a place where he would just be another customer instead of some kind of sicko. After all, there were far worse things that could happen to a child than getting paid for a few minutes of her time. These children provided their families with much more income than they could generate begging for money in the streets. Hell, he was performing a charity of sorts.

Perry grabbed a tissue from the nightstand to clean up his mess and then lay dreaming. He recalled fondly that back in seventh grade one of the vocational training kids told him that "Chink pussy" was oriented horizontally instead of vertically. He smiled thinking that was a theory he would soon be testing out.

⋏

Chris turned the Land Rover right out of the driveway, pausing to snort at the pathetic camp set up in front of his house by the police. Two officers were engrossed in a card game under a large umbrella, their AK-47s propped against the wall behind them, while a third officer slept beneath a mosquito net in a hammock hung on an aluminum frame.

He turned right on Pasteur Street, left on Street 339 to its end at Norodom Boulevard, and there he could see it: the headquarters of Chea Phyrom Group, Ltd., crowned with a giant chrome "C." The man who kidnapped his daughter and taunted him about it, the man who knew exactly where Mai could be found, the man who had probably already killed her was most likely sitting in that building right now, gloating over his clear and total victory, laughing about what he had done. So close, and all Chris had to do was put a gun to the man's head and make him talk. No one else was going to do it. It was up to him.

Two armed guards stood at each entrance to the compound. With the pedal to the floor, he guessed he could make it to the front door before they could stop him. He would race inside and find Chea Phyrom cowering under a desk. He'd shoot him in one leg, even before asking a single question, then he would make him talk. Phyrom would grovel, plead for his life while Chris put bullets in his other leg, his feet, his hands. Then, after Chris got the information he needed, he would hold Phyrom on the ground and gouge out his eyes one after the other with some blunt instrument and then walk away feeling refreshed and exhilarated.

"Huh!"

He jerked away from the car window. A small boy and girl looked at him, smudging the glass with their grubby fingers. They pointed to their mouths and held their bellies. He looked at his watch. Five o'clock. He had been sitting in the car for almost an hour with the engine running.

He wiped drool from the corners of his mouth and studied the children next to him. Thick rivers of mucus ran from their noses into their mouths; their clothes were literally rags. They were smaller and punier than Mai, but their eyes were older. He drove away, ignoring the children as they ran alongside the car. He felt nothing.

He went straight home. Sampour was in the kitchen when he walked in through the back door.

"Someone up," she said. She nodded toward the stairs.

Alarmed, Chris ran up and found Lisa sitting in the living room with David Finto. "Hey, what's going on? Did something happen?"

Lisa's face darkened. "Where have you been? I've been calling you forever."

Chris automatically felt his pockets for his phone—the new one he'd bought after smashing his old one on the day Mai was kidnapped. Empty. "Why? Did something happen?"

"No. I just wanted to know where you were. Anyway, Sampour found your phone in the kitchen."

"Jesus! Don't scare me like that." She hadn't spoken to him all day, and now she was keeping tabs. He looked at Finto. "Hey, David. Any developments?"

Finto shook his head. "I'm afraid not. I just came by to check on you guys on my way home."

"That's not true," Lisa said. "I called him because I was worried about you, and he volunteered to come by."

Finto got to his feet. "Well, I'd better go." He took Lisa's hands in his. "I'll be in touch if I hear anything."

Chris walked Finto to the door and locked it behind him. By the time he got back upstairs, Lisa had gone in their bedroom again.

"I thought you were worried about me," he said to the empty living room.

The land line rang. Chris snatched the receiver on the end table, and Lisa answered in the bedroom seconds later: Agent Gutierrez.

"Hey, guys. I just thought I'd let you know that we told the ministry we accept their counterproposal. It could happen as early as tomorrow."

This didn't make any sense to Chris at all. "Counterproposal? What are you talking about?"

Awkward silence. "That Chea Phyrom submit to questioning by the Cambodian lead investigator on the case," Gutierrez said finally, her tone suggesting surprise at his question.

Chris pulled his hair. Why wasn't he told about this? "Wait. I don't understand. They're not going to let our side be there when they question him? They made a counterproposal? This is not a negotiation. Phyrom needs to be arrested."

"Chris, I'm sorry. I thought David told—"

"Agent Gutierrez," Lisa interrupted, "let me explain."

No way. Chris dropped the receiver and ran down the stairs. The gate was open, and the security guard was directing Finto as he backed his car into the street.

"Hey, wait," Chris yelled.

Finto pulled back into the drive and lowered the window.

Chris put his hands on the window frame. "What the hell is going on?"

Finto sighed. "What are you talking about?" he asked calmly, almost as if he were bored.

"Why didn't you tell me the police won't let us question Chea Phyrom? And that we agreed to this? You said there were no developments."

Finto cut the engine, his eyes deliberately straight ahead. "Lisa and I thought it would be best if you found out in tomorrow's meeting."

Chris the slapped the side of Finto's truck. "What the hell! You're making decisions about my daughter without even asking me? I would never have agreed to this!"

"Well, no fucking kidding, Chris. You wouldn't have agreed to it, and then what?"

"I have a right to know." It would feel so good to land a solid punch on the side of Finto's lying face.

"Yeah, you do. But what do you think the guy would say if we questioned him anyway? You think he's just going to tell us where your daughter is?"

"He needs to be arrested and charged with a crime on the evidence that already exists."

Finto turned and looked him straight in the eye. "Well, that ain't gonna happen, so you're just wasting your time." Finto started his truck and put it in Reverse. "What you need to do is go inside and take care of your wife and let us handle this."

ᐱ

So tired he couldn't see straight, Chris lay awake for hours on the surge of adrenaline coursing through his veins. He vaguely recalled the story a friend had told him in junior high of a man who had murdered a karate instructor who had kidnapped and molested his son. In a few seconds he found the grainy news footage on YouTube; the guy's name was Gary Plauche. Walked right up to the guy and put a bullet in his head, cameras rolling. Didn't even go to jail for it. Chris watched the video again and again and again. How could he get a gun? Cambodia should be an easy place to get a nice handgun. In fantasy scenario after scenario he saved his daughter and murdered those responsible.

What if Mai was already dead? This was the most likely possibility. He envisioned tracking down and murdering every single person involved in her abduction. This thinking was insane, but he was helpless to stop it, and so he continued plotting.

CHAPTER 17

onsular Section Chief Jim Johnson dropped a manila folder on the desk of junior officer LaDonna Yamamoto.

"I want you to process this visa right away."

LaDonna sighed, stopped what she was doing, and turned to her PC. She looked at the file and typed some information into the computer.

"Hey, Jim. Nhim Saray? Is this who I think it is? What's going on here?"

Johnson placed his hand on LaDonna's back and leaned too closely over her as he read the image on the screen.

His mouth dropped open. "You've got to be kidding. I honestly can't believe it." He grabbed the phone on LaDonna's desk. "Boy, the shit is going to hit the fan now."

⚓

Quynh's eighth birthday passed unknown and uncelebrated by anyone, including herself, at the Apsara 2 Hotel. She shared a small room in a dormitory behind the hotel with six other girls, two of whom she knew from the IRM shelter. She could spend her days playing with the many other girls there as long as they didn't make too much noise, and she no longer had to go to school. There were very few customers coming to the hotel, so she didn't have to do that either. Two big sisters took care of the girls, and they said the customers had been scared away by the police but that they would come back. For the time being, if Quynh succeeded in not thinking about her mother or grandmother, she was having the time of her life.

One of the big sisters shouted and slapped the girls if they had too much fun, but one of them was kind. Quynh sat on her lap when she wasn't busy and begged her to brush her hair like her grandmother used to do. Once, Quynh told the girl that she didn't want any customers to come back, that she didn't like the men, and the older girl said she didn't like them either.

"But I thought the big girls liked boom-boom. Mama told me it feels good."

The girl laughed. "Why do you think we like it?"

Quynh didn't like being laughed at, so she didn't answer. She saw the way the big sisters acted when the men came around. They dressed up in pretty clothes, painted their faces, and joked with the men before pulling them to a room, smiling.

The girl noticed Quynh's pouting face.

"No. We don't like it."

⅄

Paris Jefferson sat grimly before the Kellies and the assembled members of the Emergency Action Committee.

"Well, we have some bad news. Consular was processing a diplomatic visa for Nhim Saray this morning, and he came up a double zero hit on our system."

Lisa flinched. "Oh my God."

Chris had no idea what the hell they were talking about. "Can somebody please tell me what that means?"

"It means," said Paris, "that Nhim's been labeled as someone who absolutely cannot receive a US visa. It's typically a designation reserved for terrorists. He was trying to go to a police chief's conference in Georgia. I've never heard of it being used in this way."

"In what way?"

"Well, apparently they tagged him as a result of the raid on the IRM shelter and his perceived noncooperation in the subsequent investigation."

"And who did that?" Chris growled. He felt blooding rushing to his cheeks.

"The Trafficking in Persons Office in Washington."

"So, in other words, we just told the National Police chief to go to hell right in the middle of this investigation."

Paris was not one to sugarcoat things. "Yes. That's about the size of it."

"Don't these people in Washington understand we need Nhim's help? Don't they—"

Lisa cut him off. "What can we do about it, Paris? Can we get a waiver or something?"

"The ambassador has already sent off an e-mail to Ambassador Muller, who is head of the TIP Office, demanding an explanation, and we've also formally asked the secretary's office for a waiver due to the unusual circumstances in this case.

"To tell you the truth, I'm really irritated. Although Muller made the designation before Mai got kidnapped, we were completely blindsided. We've been communicating with him daily since the raid on the Apsara 2, but he didn't inform us that Nhim had been tagged. It's unconscionable that he would deliberately keep us in the dark on this, and he's going to hear about it."

"Oh, he's going to hear about it, all right," Chris blurted.

Paris ignored Chris's outburst. "Both of you should know that right after the raid on IRM's shelter, IRM Director Jane Hightower began calling Ambassador Muller in Washington directly, giving him somewhat exaggerated accounts of the raid and the Cambodian government's response, and she found a very sympathetic ear. Of course, she didn't have to exaggerate; the whole thing was a travesty. The people in the TIP Office are rightly zealous about their work, and it just so happens that the number two over there is Cambodian American.

"Anyway, Jane Hightower left Ambassador Muller with the impression that we at the embassy were not doing all we could to pressure the Cambodians to resolve the issue, so we found ourselves in the awkward position of Washington calling *us* up and asking if we knew what was going on in our own backyard. It appears now that Ambassador Muller decided to take matters into his own hands and didn't feel the need to let us know."

Chris shook his head in disbelief. "Well, for Muller's sake, we'd better get that waiver. When will we know?"

"Certainly by tomorrow morning."

"Tomorrow morning! Mai's already been missing for *two nights*…"

Paris pursed her lips. "Well," she said after a moment, "we won't wait until tomorrow's meeting to let you know if we get the news. And there's one more thing to remember: Nhim doesn't yet know that we can't give him a visa, and, technically, he hasn't even been denied. We can't delay forever, but we can string him along for quite some time, maybe even weeks. Hopefully, Mai will be home safe and sound long before that."

Chapter 18

US Ambassador Richard Schroeder, already in suit and tie, sat on his patio enjoying his usual breakfast of tropical fruit and a double espresso when he answered his first call of the day. The little Kelly girl had now been missing for three days. He hoped the call might be good news.

"Good morning, Paris. Any news from Washington?"

"Look at the front page of *The Cambodia Times.*"

"I hate it when you say stuff like that. Well, let's see. I have it—" He spilled piping hot coffee onto his trousers. "Ow, ow! Just a minute." Schroeder examined his stained clothes. Dammit. Dry cleaning cost a fortune in Cambodia and was touch and go at best. He snatched the paper from a pile.

The Cambodia Times
Thursday, October 6, 2016

Minister of Interior Denied US Visa

The US State Department office to monitor and combat trafficking in persons disclosed that Interior Minister and National Police Commissioner Nhim Saray has been denied a visa to the US due to allegations linking him to human trafficking.

Ambassador Dick Muller, director of the US State Department's anti-human-trafficking office, confirmed the denial of the visa last night by phone from the US. "I can say unequivocally…"

...Muller believed Nhim was planning to attend the 110ᵗʰ annual International Society of Chiefs of Police conference to be held in the US state of Georgia next month.

"Paris, are you still there?"

"Yes sir."

"I can't believe Muller sold us out like this; he didn't have to go public. Well, you'd better get on the phone and start doing some damage control. Tell Nhim's people we don't know what Muller is talking about and that Nhim's visa has not been denied." Not a lie; this was technically true—for the moment. "Do you know if Peggy's in the office yet? We need to release a statement right away—"

"Sir, Peggy's gone. Remember?"

"Oh, dang it. Of course. Well, get somebody to do it." Schroeder massaged his eyes. "Any news on the waiver request?"

Jefferson sighed. "Denied."

"Perfect. Just perfect. Well, I'm coming in now. I need to change my pants. I'll call the Kellies myself. Hopefully, they haven't read the morning paper yet."

"How's your father doing, by the way?"

"Not well. Not well at all."

"I'm sorry to hear that."

⚔

Fear. Every time the phone rang, Chris's gut clenched. Would this be the call that confirmed it? Would they talk about the location of her body and making "arrangements"? When the phone rang at eight thirty a.m., he had been lying awake in the guest room for hours.

Once, Mai had been afraid of "monsters" in her bedroom. After thoroughly checking the closets and under the bed together and having Mai certify her room monster-free, he'd tucked her in.

"Are you afraid of monsters, Daddy?"

"No, I'm not."

"You're not afraid of anything?"

"Sure, I am."

"Like what?"

He hadn't wanted to tell her that the only things in the world he feared were things that might harm her and Lisa—real monsters, like a stranger in a park who might try to lure her away, or something she might choke on, or a car going too fast as she tried to cross the street. Those things haunted him, things much more frightening and real than monsters in the closet or under the bed.

"Uh, let me think," he'd said. "A thousand little girls like you running loose in this house?"

"Oh, Daddy, you're funny."

"No, no. I'm being totally serious."

"Silly."

But now the phone kept ringing, and he had to answer it. He walked into the living room and picked up the receiver.

"Good morning, Chris. This is Richard Schroeder."

The ambassador. Why? Under normal circumstances—well, he couldn't even imagine normal circumstances. "Any news?"

"Before I start, you might want to get Lisa on the line as well."

Chris's legs gave way, and he collapsed onto the couch. They'd found her body. He couldn't move, couldn't speak. A hundred years or maybe just a few seconds passed until Lisa picked up the phone in the bedroom and the ambassador began.

"Well, I have bad news about the waiver. They won't let us give Nhim Saray a visa."

These words released Chris from his paralysis. "Why? Didn't you tell them Nhim had nothing to do with the raid on the IRM shelter?"

"Yes, but all they see is that he's not conducting a real investigation into what happened. And then when Nhim fired Sochua, head of the Anti-Trafficking unit, that was more than they could take."

"Did you explain how much we need Nhim's cooperation right now?"

"I can't defend their decision. I didn't think we had anything to worry about."

"Sir, I need to know who's making these decisions. We have to fight this!"

"The decision was made at a very high level. This administration has made fighting human trafficking a priority, and Cambodia is one of the world's hotspots."

"I get that, but Paris said Nhim wasn't involved in the raid on the IRM shelter. I swear to God, I'm going to hold these people responsible—"

"Shut up," Lisa cried, "and listen to what he has to say!"

"Thank you, Lisa. Listen. There's more I need to tell you. *The Cambodia Times* ran a front page story this morning saying that the embassy denied Nhim Saray's visa."

"What? But...I don't understand. I thought we weren't going tell Nhim anything. I thought the whole plan was to keep it a secret, to string him along for as long as we can."

"It didn't come from us. Apparently Ambassador Muller, head of the TIP office, talked to *The Cambodia Times* and told them Nhim's visa was denied."

"What? Why? Does this guy have any idea what's going on?"

"We will issue a statement to the Cambodian media saying that we are forbidden by law to discuss individual visa cases. However, we have always found General Nhim to be quite cooperative on every issue of concern to us. We will praise his efforts so far in helping to find Mai and say that Muller's comments are probably the result of a simple misunderstanding. And behind the scenes we are talking to Nhim's people and assuring them that his visa has not been denied—which is technically true—and that Ambassador Muller doesn't know what he's talking about. We can still buy quite a bit of time with this before we have to officially refuse his visa."

"Can we appeal or something? I mean, appeal Washington's denial of our request for a waiver for Nhim?"

"We can, and I will, but, frankly, I don't think it will do any good."

Chris seethed. "I need to have a heart-to-heart with Muller."

"Chris, you're crossing a line here that's very dangerous. I strongly suggest you don't try to contact Ambassador Muller. It would be a big mistake."

"Then we're screwed. We are so totally screwed. Thank you for calling. Please let us know if there's any news. I gotta go."

Anger. Anger like he'd never felt in his life. He needed to be violent, to hurt somebody. Chris swept the telephone and a stack of papers off the end table. He clenched his fists and screamed at the ceiling. He pounded on the door that had kept him locked out of his bedroom for four days.

"This is my room too! Open the door! Please!"

A muffled "no."

He drove his fist into the door with all his might—a door made of two inches of solid-core teak and equipped with a peephole, designed by the embassy to make the bedroom a "safe haven" in the case of a home invasion. It held up as intended.

Lisa threw open the door to find Chris on his knees, clutching his hand. "What the hell is going on?"

"I...punched the door. Damn. Works...fine."

"Well, that's good to know. You know, these macho displays of aggression are not very endearing."

Chris looked up and saw nothing but loathing in her eyes. "I am sick and tired—"

"And, by the way, you really shouldn't go around threatening State Department personnel."

"I didn't threaten anybody. Not yet anyway."

"There you go with that macho bullshit again."

"Go to hell! I'm leaving!" He wasn't going to stick around and put up with this shit.

"Where are you going?"

"None of your business!"

ᛉ

Lisa listened as Chris slammed the door and started the car in the driveway below. What was she supposed to do? Just hold him and tell him he didn't share some of the blame? He knew who these people were. He knew what they could do. And now...and now her daughter...how could she ever forgive him? How could they ever get beyond this? Her marriage couldn't survive it.

She felt on the verge of tears again. Maybe she'd pushed him too far. She wished he'd come back. She loved him. She didn't know what else to do, so she dialed Regional Security Officer David Finto.

"In ten years of marriage I've never seen him do anything like that. I've never seen him act so violent." He'd never looked so crazy.

"Did he threaten you in any way? Did he break anything?"

"No."

"Where do you think he's going?"

She started to cry. "I'm worried...I'm worried he might try to do something stupid."

"Lisa, I'm worried about _you_. There's no telling what he might do."

"No...no, that's not why I called." Calling had been a mistake. "David," Lisa said, exasperated, "I just want to find out where he is." She hung up, feeling even worse.

⟁

Chris again sat in the Land Rover opposite Chea Phyrom's office, plotting, when a hard rap on the window snapped him out of his reverie.

Finto yanked open the door of the Land Rover. "Jesus Christ!" Finto put a hand over his nose. "God, you stink. What are you doing?"

"Uh...I don't know." Dazed from lack of sleep and lost in thoughts of revenge, Chris wasn't quite sure.

"Did you think you were going to do something? You're going to try to hurt someone? Is that what you're going to do, buddy? Hmm?"

"Huh? No. I don't know what I was going to do." Chris wiped the beaded sweat from his face. "How did you know I was here?" His right hand hurt like hell.

Finto smiled, self-satisfied. "I told you we were keeping an eye on you. For your own protection."

Grogginess gave way to anger, and Chris got out of the vehicle. "Oh, I see. Your surveillance detection team is now keeping track of me, huh?"

Finto, already close, took a step closer. "Lisa called me, you know. You scared her. Your wife's afraid of you."

"Did she say that? I would never do anything to her, and she knows that."

"Maybe you'd better ask her again."

"Maybe you'd better mind your own damn business." He so wanted to beat this man down, to bash his face into the side of his truck and watch him bleed.

"Lisa's safety is my business, whether you like it or not. And, by the way, in case you were serious about contacting Ambassador Muller in Washington, I would advise you against making anything sounding like a threat."

"Thanks for the advice."

A small crowd of curious moto-dops and passersby had begun to gather. Finally, Finto stood down.

"Don't overstep your bounds," he called over his shoulder as he walked to his truck. "We're all trying to help you here."

"Overstep my bounds," Chris mumbled. Would breaking Finto's neck be overstepping his bounds?

Chris went home and listened to Lisa sobbing through their locked bedroom door. He knocked.

"What?" she choked. "What do you want?"

"We shouldn't be like this. This is when we need each other the most."

"David said...David said—"

"What? What did he say?"

"He said...he said, 'None of this would've happened if you hadn't been running around playing cowboy.'"

He trembled with rage.

Ambassador Richard Schroeder sat between Paris Jefferson and Regional Psychiatrist Nadine Marchan, listening as David Finto tried his dead-level best to paint Chris Kelly as a loose cannon. Political Chief Paul Richter was also there, nibbling a chocolate bar.

Schroeder was in a rotten mood. His sister had interrupted him during lunch and laid a guilt trip on him for not having already rushed to his dying father's bedside. The old man was in hospice with cancer of everything and suddenly felt the need to reconcile after a lifetime of hurting those closest to him. By his sister's account, the end was nigh, and Schroeder needed to get on a plane to LA before it was too late. He struggled to concentrate as Finto made his case.

"Sir, I'm concerned. I understand the man is under a lot of stress, but sitting in front of Chea Phyrom's office? What if he had tried to go in there? And he's making threats. And trying to break down doors. We have to consider Lisa's safety."

Paris Jefferson tapped inch-long purple nails on the table. "What do you suggest we do, David?"

"At this point we should ask him to leave the country voluntarily, for his own safety and the safety of those around him."

"And he'll refuse, of course, and then what?"

Schroeder didn't let Finto answer. "Nadine, Paul, do you have anything to say?"

Richter had a mouthful of chocolate. He shook his head.

"Well." Marchan sighed. "I haven't talked to him. I've called several times, and he refuses to speak to me."

"I think a stern warning will do," Schroeder concluded. "And I'll make visits with Nadine mandatory."

"Ambassador," said Jefferson, "I know Chris well. You want me to give him the talking-to?"

"No. This needs to come from the ambassador. I'll do it myself."

A positively euphoric Chea Phyrom relaxed in the back of his Toyota 4Runner on his way to a very late lunch with a Chinese investor. He could not believe how stupid the Americans could be. Just when they needed Nhim Saray the most, they pissed in his face by denying him a visa. This had been his week: that foreign NGO had been shut down; Sochua Nika had been put in her place; the strength of his close relationship with his uncle, the prime minister, had been demonstrated for the benefit of both General Nhim and his father; and he now had eleven more girls working for him at the Apsara 2 than he'd started with.

But best of all, he'd gotten his revenge on the American. Maybe when the girl was old enough, he'd make a special trip down to Sihanoukville to break her in himself, although he suspected she wouldn't live that long. It felt good to be the best.

CHAPTER 19

It was not yet nine in the morning when Yen, the Kellies' regular daytime guard, opened the gate with a crisp salute. Chris was dead tired. He'd barely slept at all—it was the fourth night without Mai—fuming about yesterday's run-in with Finto across the street from Chea Phyrom's glistening headquarters.

He surveyed the scene in front of his compound. As usual, men from the construction sites next door and across the street stopped their work and stared at the foreigner. Mai was gone, and yet life was normal: barefoot children begged for aluminum cans; the policemen played their games of cards; a man ate noodle soup out of a plastic bag; a girl carried a basket of shellfish on her head; and a saleswoman walked a bicycle overloaded with brooms, whisks, baskets, pails, mops, stools, bowls, chairs, pots, pans, spatulas, and knives.

He hailed a moto, trying not to think about what he was about to do.

The driver asked, "Okay. Okay. Where you go?"

Chris looked around at the dozen or more people on the street and wondered which one was a member of the embassy's Surveillance Detection Team. He climbed on behind the moto-dop.

"You know Spanky's?"

"Okay, okay." The man laughed and hit the gas.

Spanky's looked much different in the daytime. The prostitutes and their patrons were nowhere in sight, and the only thing greeting him at the door, which was propped open with an irregular chunk of concrete, was the smell of stale beer. Bright sunlight poured in through the large east-facing windows, and a Cambodian love song could be heard over the muffled noise of the traffic below. A balding man sat alone at the bar nursing a beer and eating what looked like pancakes. Chris found a table, and a woman approached with a menu.

"What you want?" She almost smiled.

"I'm looking for Arthur. Is he around?"

With her tongue probing the inside of her cheek, the woman sized him up for a moment. She then turned without a word and glided to the back of the bar. She returned a few minutes later.

"He say he no got nothin'."

"Huh?"

"He no got nothin' today. You come back tomorrow. Maybe he have somethin' tomorrow." She shooed him away with her hand.

"Listen. I'm looking for something else. Tell him I'm a friend of George's. I need to talk to him. It's very important."

The woman threw her head back and sighed loudly, demonstrating her distaste for playing messenger. She disappeared again into the back.

He waited. After several minutes he gave up and went after her through a dark hallway and into a room where Arthur sat hunched at a desk smoking a cigarette. The woman squatted on a baby-blue plastic step stool, her knees at her chest, smoking pot and watching *Knight Rider* dubbed into Thai with Khmer subtitles. A young girl was asleep on a lime-green sofa cratered with cigarette burns.

Arthur dropped his cigarette on the floor and stomped it. "God, I wish you'd turn that shit off!"

"Fuck you! *Baywatch* come on next!"

Arthur turned to Chris. "Do I know you?"

"Yeah, I came in here once with George Granger. I really need to talk to you."

Arthur flicked off the TV. "Come on." He lumbered out the door amid expletives shouted at him in Khmer. He led Chris to the bar and plopped himself unsteadily on a stool, squinting against the sunlight. "That was Barbara. Lovely, isn't she? Anyway, how the hell is George? I haven't seen him lately."

"He's gone to Thailand for a while."

"No shit? Why?"

"Well, it's kind of a long story. He had to leave because of the raid on the IRM shelter in Ang Keo."

"Aw, man, I heard about that. That was fucked up."

"Yeah. To say the least."

"Yeah, I remember you. Craig, right?"

"Chris."

"Yeah, yeah, yeah. Chris. That's it. What can I do you for?"

"Listen, Arthur. I need some help."

"Anything, man. Whatcha need?"

Chris lowered his voice. "I need to get my hands on a gun."

"Holy shit! A gun!" Arthur clapped his hands to his head. "What the hell did you come to me for?"

"Not so loud, okay?" He wanted to say, 'Shut the fuck up'—that's how on edge he was—but he needed Arthur's help. "George told me you knew how to get your hands on things."

"Yeah, but a gun? I can't get you no gun. I mean, if you needed some pot or something, maybe some yama or some heroin. Damn, dude. This ain't friggin' Texas."

"My daughter was kidnapped by Chea Phyrom."

For maybe a full minute Arthur was speechless. When he spoke again his eyes were welling with tears. "You're shittin' me, man. That was your daughter? Aw, man, I saw her picture in the paper. This is too fucked up!"

Chris wiped tears from his eyes, too, and took a deep breath. Maybe Arthur was decent after all. "Tell me about it." They laughed awkwardly.

Arthur reached for a napkin and blew his nose. "Dude, do you know what you're doing? What the hell you think you're gonna do with a gun? Man, you're gonna go and get yourself killed."

"It's just for protection. No one's ever going to know I have it."

"Awright, man, it's your ass that's gonna get killed. What kind of gun you want?"

"I don't care."

"Nine millimeter, forty caliber? What do you want?"

"Something that shoots bullets would be nice."

"That's funny, man. That's really fucking funny."

"Something small I can hide easily. And I'll need some bullets too."

Arthur dropped his head on the table, cursing quietly under his breath. Finally, he sat up and exhaled powerfully into Chris's face.

"Fine. Give me fifty bucks and come back tomorrow. I got some shit going on later, so you have to come before ten. But don't come before nine!"

Chris handed him the money. "Got it. Thanks."

"Hey, you know who you gotta go see, don't you?"

"Who?"

"If I was you, I'd go see that lady general, Sochua. She hates Chea's guts. They fired her because of him, and I bet she knows every friggin' single thing about him. She's a sharp ol' gal, that one. If you ask me, they ought to let her run the country."

Interesting. "How do I find her?"

Arthur scratched his head. "Well, she's got a big-ass mansion right on Sihanouk down from the prime minister's house. I'd just go the hell over there if I was you."

⚔

"I was about to leave you," Lisa said coldly. There was an embassy sedan in the driveway, and she was standing next to it in a T-shirt and jeans. "Where have you been?" She looked like she might be on her way to a soccer game instead of to another briefing on the investigation into their daughter's kidnapping.

Chris had hoped maybe Lisa would soften a little today, but it seemed she was as hard as ever. "Just needed to get out for a bit," he said, figuring the truth—that he'd just ordered a gun at Spanky's and then stopped by the home of General Sochua Nika to ask for an audience—wouldn't do. He paid the moto-dop for the ride and walked inside the compound.

Lisa snorted. "Well, we're about to be late." She got in the backseat of the sedan and shut the door. Yen and the extra guard—Chris didn't know his name—looked at their feet.

Chris got in the front of the car. "I'll ride up here with you," he said to the puzzled driver.

"Yes sir."

Chris closed his eyes, and they rode in stony silence to the embassy. He wondered if Sochua—the famous general—would see him. George certainly had a high opinion of her, and maybe Arthur was right. Maybe she did have some information about Chea Phyrom that could help him find Mai. Her guard had simply taken his written request and disappeared without a word. Would they guy even give it to her?

When they got to the embassy, Ambassador Richard Schroeder was waiting in the hallway outside the Chandler Room.

"Chris, could I speak to you alone for a moment?"

This was a surprise; the Chandler Room was already full of people. "Uh, sure," Chris said. He noticed Lisa just kept walking as if she knew what Schroeder had in mind.

Schroeder patted him on the back and ushered him down the hall to the executive suite like they were the best of friends. There was a woman standing in Schroeder's office. She was tall and pale with red curly hair.

"Chris," Schroeder said, "this is Nadine Marchan, our regional psychiatrist out of Bangkok. I believe the two of you have been playing phone tag."

The presence of the psychiatrist confirmed Chris's suspicions: Finto had ratted him out.

"Yes," he said, wondering what Marchan would say if she knew about his visit to Spanky's this morning. "It's nice to meet you." He shook her hand.

Marchan smiled thinly. "Thank you. You too."

Schroeder closed the door. "Have a seat."

"I know this is a hard time for you," Schroeder continued, "and I know you're under a lot stress. We all understand that, but you're actually making it more difficult for us to help you find Mai."

Damn right he was under a lot of stress. "I have no idea what you're talking about, sir."

"What you did yesterday—going to Chea Phyrom's office—is unacceptable. It's dangerous for you and dangerous for your family. If you persist in this kind of behavior, I'll have no choice but to do some things I don't want to do."

Chris had already decided his course of action; the only thing to do now was maintain calm. "What does that mean?"

"Every member of this mission is here at my pleasure," Schroeder said pleasantly. "If I deem that you are a danger to others or are impeding this investigation, then I'll have to ask you to leave the country."

"So, basically," Chris said belligerently, "you're saying you'd force me to leave." So much for maintaining calm.

Schroeder stopped smiling. "If you did not leave voluntarily, your diplomatic status would be revoked, and the Cambodian government would cancel your visa. If you continued to stay, then you would be in Cambodia illegally and subject to prosecution under Cambodian law. And this doesn't just pertain to you. Lisa would have to leave as well. But," he continued, softening his tone, "we're getting way ahead of ourselves here. Revoking your status would be disastrous, and nobody wants to see it happen. Nadine's come here for no other reason but to help you and Lisa get through this. I want you to schedule some time with her daily. That's not negotiable."

Chris managed a smile; he couldn't let himself get kicked out of the country. "Thank you, Ambassador. I apologize for my behavior."

Schroeder stood. "The apology is unnecessary but accepted. I'll let you and Nadine work out when you two can meet. Now, let's join the others in the Chandler Room and see what Agent Gutierrez has to say."

⚔

Lisa Kelly waited in the Chandler room for the meeting to get started. The members of the Emergency Action Committee—minus the ambassador—were there, maintaining a respectful silence for her sake. Or maybe they just didn't know what to say. They were all waiting on Chris and the ambassador to finish their talk with the regional psychiatrist. God, what if Chris lost his temper again? She missed him so much. She wanted him to wrap his arms around her. She wanted to do the same for him. As crazy as it sounded, she wanted to make love to him. She hated this cold war. But she was just so angry. She wanted to forgive him. But she just…couldn't.

Lisa traced with a trembling finger a scratch in the new conference table. Before the table arrived, the Chandler room had briefly stored some pieces of the playground equipment that were now installed on the embassy grounds next to the Marine house. She could just see the end of the tube slide from the window.

On the Saturday after the playground went in, she had squeezed with Chris and Mai into a single cyclo and headed to the embassy for a picnic, because, as Chris had put it "a swing set that won't give you tetanus is a *huge* deal." It was the middle of the cool-dry season, a perfect day. They could barely hear the traffic rushing by the front of the embassy on Christopher Howes Avenue. There, on the manicured lawn, in the shade of two enormous beng trees and out of the public eye, Lisa wished it could last forever.

"Why do the Marines get a playground?" Mai asked innocently.

"Silly, girl," Chris said, "the playground's not for the Marines. It's for the embassy kids like you."

"No," Mai said, shaking her head vigorously. "I don't think so. This playground is for the Marines. They get up in the middle of the night and play on it so no one will see them."

"Lisa?"

Lisa opened her eyes, and she was back in the Chandler room.

Paris Jefferson gently patted her forearm. "Are you okay, honey?"

Lisa took a tissue offered by Agent Gutierrez. Everyone was looking at her. "Oh, I guess I nodded off for a second."

Chris and the ambassador came in. Chris had deep circles under his eyes. He needed a shave.

The ambassador rubbed his hands together. "Alright. Let's get going."

Gutierrez grimly admitted to the group that the investigation was going nowhere. The lead Cambodian investigator had been suddenly and inexplicably removed from the case and an incompetent rookie assigned to replace him. Calls of complaint to the ministry were not returned.

"We've received more than two hundred leads and investigated many of them, each one a dead end. We had a walk-in this afternoon. A Mr. Dou Pranam, who says he saw Mai on day two."

"What? Where?" Chris cried.

Lisa couldn't believe her ears. "A walk-in?"

"Well, don't get too excited. He says he saw some guys walk out of a shop and shove a little girl into a white van, and she shouted at them, 'Stop it! Leave me alone," in English and that he didn't think much of it until he saw her picture in the paper. We can't be sure if he's for real; he's kind of an Americaphile, and he wants to know if he can have a green card. Anyway, when we went out with him, he couldn't seem to really remember where he saw them, but we're still working with him."

"Okay, so what's the game plan?" Chris asked impatiently. "Nhim's not going to cooperate with us on the investigation anymore—and, frankly, I don't blame him—and the only lead really worth investigating is still off limits. What do we do now? Well?"

Retired Brigadier General Sochua Nika contemplated from her balcony the endless stream of motos circling Independence Monument. The traffic resembled an enormous wheel in constant motion that eternally peeled off its outer layer even as another was added to it. She looked beyond the monument at the soaring roofs of Wat Lang Ka. She'd come outside to ponder a most interesting request for a meeting. What exactly did the American diplomat think she could do for him? Yes, everyone knew Chea Phyrom had kidnapped the girl, and yes, she had a vendetta against him, but she knew nothing that would help Kelly find his daughter. Too bad.

She looked again at Wat Lang Ka and its crumbling stupas. Novice monks walked in and out of the monastery's northern gate in their saffron robes. The Buddhist temples provided the country a useful safety valve in tough times, absorbing many thousands of young men who might be otherwise idle. The temples fed the poor. And they also…provided a place to hide. Yes.

An idea dawned on her that was so beautiful, so perfect, that she rushed to write it down lest she forget. What a pleasant and wholly unexpected surprise! Mr. Kelly's request for an audience made possible a simply marvelous scheme to tie down a troublesome loose end that might otherwise complicate her ambitions. His unique predicament presented an opportunity that must not be missed. And best of all, she could let Chea Prak and his half-wit son, Phyrom, do all the dirty work for her. Because she knew what Chea would do anything for. A little girl would be a trifle to pay.

Sochua examined her plan from every angle, considering every possible outcome, however unlikely, formulating in her mind worst-case scenarios until, confident there was a significant chance of success—or at least little chance of a disaster in which she shared a part—she ordered her assistant to invite Mr. Kelly to her home the following morning and then admired the young man's backside as he hurried away to do her bidding.

As far as Chea Prak was concerned, Phnom Penh's vast Pur Senchey district contained merely two things of note: Potchentong Airport and the headquarters compound of Brigade 70, where he sat at his desk having just been informed of an entirely unexpected caller on the line. Chea, commander of Brigade 70—the prime minister's personal bodyguard unit—could think of no reason for Sochua Nika, of all people, to be calling him, although it certainly could not herald good news.

He picked up the receiver. "Good afternoon, General. How have you been lately?"

"Do you mean how does forced retirement suit me? I've been very fine."

"What can I do for you, Nika?"

Chea had once considered Sochua valuable in that she was a persistent thorn in the side of his nemesis, Minister of Interior Nhim Saray. The prime minister had forced Nhim to tolerate Sochua in the National Police despite her outspokenness because her great popularity with international donors allowed the PM to demonstrate he was serious about the problem of human trafficking. Of course, in the end—and what a delicious irony—it was that very popularity with the international community that convinced the PM to fire her just to prove to the world that he, not Washington or Paris, was still sovereign in Cambodia.

The spectacular crash of Sochua's rising star meant she had also lost any practical value she might have once held for him. However, he and Sochua had a long and colorful history and had always been more or less on speaking terms, despite her personal crusade to ruin his only son, Phyrom. And, besides, it was always refreshing to speak with someone who loathed Nhim Saray as much as he did.

"I got an interesting request today," she said.

"Oh, yes? Please tell me about it."

"The father of the American girl your boy kidnapped is coming to see me."

"Really?" Chea wouldn't bother denying the charge, and he tried to sound neither alarmed nor too interested. "What about, I wonder?"

"I was hoping you could tell me."

"Well, perhaps he's going to ask you to help him find his daughter. After all, it was you who made that whole thing possible by antagonizing Phyrom in the first place."

"Yes, perhaps I should have known better than try to enforce the law. I admit that I underestimated the prime minister's affection for his nephew. I thought he had tired of his antics."

"Apparently not." What did she want? "Is there something else you want to say?"

"I thought you might be interested in making a deal."

Now this was the Sochua he had known and tussled with for years. "Bun?" Chea said to his senior aide-de-camp, sitting at his desk across the room.

"Yes sir."

"Get out."

"Yes sir." Bun left and closed the door behind him.

"Alright. I'm listening."

"I understand you're still looking for Yun Naren."

Chea froze. Mention of the man who destroyed his daughter took his breath away. He recalled the hospitals, the surgeries, the botched suicide attempts...the successful one. He couldn't begin to imagine what would motivate Sochua to make such a statement. Why? What did she hope to gain?

"I'm still listening," he whispered.

"I can give him to you."

Chea Prak did *not* like surprises. They cost lives. And this...for the first time in a very long time he found himself caught utterly off guard. His daughter's disfigured face flashed before his eyes. "Assuming this is true," he said as casually as he could, "what's in it for you?"

"I want Phyrom to release the American girl."

Anything. Chea would do anything to get his hands on Yun, and Sochua would know that. His men had scoured the country for him, bribed and threatened anyone who might have information. People had died. Sochua's price was far too low. "I don't understand."

"Have you forgotten that I have a conscience?"

"Yes, your greatest weakness."

"I can't help but feel somewhat responsible for what's happened."

Sochua was a terrible liar. "Yet your conscience will let you sacrifice Yun for the girl."

"Yun Naren is of no use to me. Sooner or later you're going to find him and kill him anyway. I may as well use him to help the girl."

"Hmm. Where is he?"

"I'll make sure the girl's father goes to see him. He'll lead you right to your prey. After all, I suspect you're having him followed already."

"True," conceded Chea, struggling to contain his anger at having to play this game on Sochua's terms. "But if you know where Yun is, why don't you just tell me? I can make sure the girl is released. Why get the American involved?"

"It's not that simple."

"It never is."

"I don't know where Yun is, but the American is going to find him for us."

"This is absurd!" Chea shouted. "My men have been searching for Yun for a year! What makes you think your American can find him? And why would he?"

"You've got to trust me, old friend. All you've got to do is have him followed from my home tomorrow. Do we have a deal, or not?"

"Trust! There is no such thing as trust!"

"If the American succeeds—do we have a deal?"

"Yes!"

Chea Prak hung up, fuming. Yun Naren might be in hiding, but Sochua lived her life in public. And if this was a trick—if she was lying—*nothing* would stop him from making her pay!

$$\blacktriangle$$

Chris pressed his forehead against the bedroom door. God, what a day: Spanky's, Marchan, another pointless meeting in the Chandler Room. He wondered if he'd ever hear from Sochua. "Lisa, how much longer? Huh?"

No answer. "I can't be alone tonight," he whispered. "I'll lose my mind."

He went out on the street and hailed a moto. The night was as dark as coal. The moto-dop asked him something, but it didn't register.

"He wants to know where you want to go, sir," Bunroeun said.

"Oh...yeah." Chris couldn't think of anything but "not here." Finally, he sought refuge at Land & Sea, where Chenda would know nothing of Mai's disappearance. He sprawled on a raised platform near the roof's edge. The railing was dangerously low there, and he made a mental note to sit somewhere else if he ever came back with Mai.

Chenda traipsed toward him, smiling brightly until she saw his face. "What wrong?"

He couldn't bear to tell the story again. "Nothing." It felt like a betrayal.

"Okay. Nothing."

She sat down and dangled her legs off the platform. He hoped she might graze his leg or bump his shoulder, just so he could feel something.

"What you want eat?"

He shook his head, too sad to answer.

"Okay, I make something special for you make you happy."

He gazed at her lithe body as she walked away. It entered his thoughts that tonight, instead of bringing his order, she might guide him to one of the guest rooms on the second floor and quietly close the door behind them. What would he do then? Would he resist? To gently hold her and feel her soft feminine body beneath him and smell the jasmine in her hair, to caress her and be caressed, to forget the present for just a moment and lose himself in her body would be irresistible. She returned with a mug and a bottle, and he discreetly positioned a cushion across his lap.

Sometime after midnight Chenda turned off the lights. "We close now. You gotta go home to pretty wife."

Aroused from a stupor, Chris looked for his wallet. "Oh shit. I left my money at home." He owed her for several bottles.

"Okay, you pay me later. No problem."

"I'm sorry." He reached for her. "You gotta help me up."

She obliged. "How you gon' go home?"

Good question. Had to think about that a sec. "Uh…oh, I know! I'll take a moto!"

"Not so much loud, okay?"

Was he shouting? He'd show her he could be a good boy. "Shhh." He put a finger to his lips for emphasis. "I'll be very, very quiet."

She didn't look convinced. "How you ride moto? You got no money. You forget?"

"Fuck it. I'll walk." But first he'd have to crawl down the stairs because they were gently swaying.

"No, no. Too dangerous walk late in night. I give you ride my moto."

"Naw, Chenda, it's okay." He desperately wanted to ride with her.

She laughed. "You think I want wash dishes with Sinan? Go down stairs, but don't hold on this." She shook the loose railing. "Maybe it fall off, and then you fall off too. How I explain you pretty wife?"

She went down ahead of him, and by the time he reached ground level she was waiting on a scooter at the bottom of the stairs. He climbed on behind, her beautiful body between his thighs, the lure of her skin so near.

"You got tell me where we go. I don't know where you house."

He closed his eyes and let his head drop on her shoulder. He could so easily wrap his arms round.

"Hey, you! You so drunk you forget you house?"

He pointed. She drove. He basked in the caress of her hair on his face.

Lisa looked at the clock when she heard the door open downstairs, surprised to see she'd been talking on the phone with David Finto for almost half an hour.

"He's home." She wiped her eyes. "I have to go."

"Are you going to be alright?"

"I'll be fine."

"You call me if you need me," he said sweetly.

"I will. He's coming. I have to go."

Chris picked up the phone in the kitchen. "Hello? Who's this?" He sounded drunk.

"Please, get off," Lisa begged.

"Lisa, do I need to come over there?" Finto asked.

"David? Yeah, why don't you come over here," Chris slurred. "You son of a bitch!"

"If you don't want to find yourself on a plane back to the States real soon," Finto growled, "you'd better control yourself!"

Lisa hung up; she couldn't bear it. She locked the bedroom door and listened to Chris pace the living room, cursing drunkenly to himself. The black cloud descended. Marchan had called it "situational depression" and said it was a common response to stress. It wasn't entirely unwelcome. In a way, it was a comfort to plumb the depths of her despair. The darkness could be peaceful, gently swallowing her up. The risk was surrendering to it entirely.

Years ago, when she learned she couldn't have children, the black cloud had nearly smothered her. She'd been unable to move—even think. Chris had rescued her that time. But there was no chance of that now.

Just before surrendering to a tormented sleep, she dreamily acknowledged a desire to call David back, and she didn't care if Chris found out.

Chapter 20

Chris awoke in the clothes he had slept in, his mouth full of cotton and his eyes crusted with sleep. What happened last night? Had he yelled at David Finto on the phone? He winced at the pounding of his pulse in his ears.

"Mai is coming back?"

"Huh? What?" He squinted at Sampour standing in the doorway of the guest room. He looked around. Dried chunks of vomit decorated the sheets. "I don't know," he croaked.

"Why you not go find her?"

"I don't know where she is. How can I find her when I don't know where she is?" There was something he was supposed to do. What the hell was it?

She just stared at him.

He remembered: Arthur! "What time is it?"

"Nine and half. Come. I give you *baa baa* to eat." She dropped her mop, and the crack of the handle on the tile floor reverberated painfully in his head.

"No!" He held up his hands, imploring her. "Just save it for me. I got to go out."

Sampour mumbled in Khmer as he crept gingerly down the stairs, clutching the rail, his head exploding. He stumbled out the back door and cursed the daylight.

Yen stepped out of the guard shack. He looked concerned. "Everything okay, sir?"

"Yeah. Open the gate."

Yen hurried and did what he was told. On the street, Chris hailed a moto-dop—he didn't feel in any condition to drive—and rode to Spanky's in a daze.

The moto-dop poked him in the shoulder. "Eh! Spanky's."

Chris opened his eyes and realized the ride was over. What the hell? It was a wonder he hadn't fallen off the back. He paid the man and paused at the foot of the stairs. What was he doing buying a gun? Had he lost his mind? Yes, that must be it.

Arthur greeted him with a wide grin and a slap on the back. "Man, you look like shit!"

Chris groaned agreement.

"Seriously, dude, like frickin' death warmed over. Naroat, hand me that takeout bag."

A woman brought Arthur a white paper bag printed with "Spanky's" and a graphic of a nearly naked fantastically buxom nymph holding a paddle and suggestively tonguing her middle finger.

"Here you go, pal. Hope you enjoy it." It could have been a burrito to go.

"Thanks, man."

"Wait. You got some change." Arthur handed over fifteen dollars. "I got you a good deal. For your daughter."

Trudging down the stairs, an empty stomach and the realization of what he'd just done made Chris feel weak, almost faint. He collapsed on the filthy bottom stair and leaned against the spattered wall with his eyes closed, unable for the moment to stand. He remained this way for a while. He might have even fallen asleep.

A tall silhouette hovered over him. "Moto?"

"Yeah, just give me a minute."

The moto-dop broke off the end of a baguette. "Eat."

The bread settled his stomach, and he let the man drive him home, where he went directly to the guest room, now his room. He locked the door behind him. Thankfully, Sampour had changed the sheets. Inside the Spanky's take-out bag was another bag wrapped with three wide rubber bands. Inside that he found an oily handgun wrapped in a bundle of newspaper and another bag knotted at the top and holding a dozen 9mm bullets.

He removed the gun and tested its weight; it had been a long time since he'd held a gun, and he found its mass comforting. He turned the pistol over in his hand. It appeared in good condition. Its ferrous odor reminded him of the taste of blood.

There was a knock on the door. "Sir, it's me, Sampour."

Chris hastily rewrapped the gun and put it back in the bag with the bullets. "Just a minute." He opened the closet and grabbed a tool box off the top shelf. It was pink and labeled "Ladies' Mate." Lisa's father had given it to her for high school graduation. Chris laughed at the name every time he saw it. He put the gun in the box and put it back in the closet.

He let Sampour in. "Yes?"

She held out a small cream envelope. "This come for you." Her eyes darted to the closet door and back.

He opened the envelope and pulled out a folded card inscribed in handwritten Khmer. He handed it back to Sampour. "What's it say?"

She studied it a moment. "Uh—it say somebody want meet with you."

"Who? Who wants to meet me?"

"Lady."

"A *lady*! Is it Sochua Nika?"

"Yes. It say she want meet you in her home on Saturday, October 8, time eleven o'clock."

Chris fished his phone from his pocket in a panic. "Sampour!" he cried when he saw the time. "That's, like, in fifteen minutes! When did you get this?"

"I put on desk for sir yesterday when I go home, but you don't see because you so much drinking last night."

Chris shooed her out of the room. "Okay, okay. Go out! I need to change."

"Yes, I think that good idea." She pulled the door shut on her way out.

⋏

A woman in her mid-thirties offered Chris a fresh lime soda. "General Sochua will be with you in a moment."

Chris took a sip and looked around the enormous sparsely furnished room. On opposite ends were grand marble fireplaces—ridiculous in the tropical setting—and above them gilt-framed mirrors pocked with black spots. The floor was of a magnificent but neglected hardwood parquet. Cobwebs floated in the corners, and patches of white paint had here and there peeled from the walls, exposing a mustard ocher beneath. Purpose-built ornamental bars decorated open windows that looked down upon Sihanouk Boulevard. The once elegant mansion, like the French imperialism that inspired it, exuded a palpable aura of faded glory.

General Sochua Nika entered, and Chris thrust his hand at her in greeting. She ignored his hand and placed her palms together in front of her, leaving him to gracelessly follow suit. She was trim and tall and plainly attired in a floral print dress that was much too old for her and reminded Chris of his grandmother. She wore her entirely gray hair in a single braid that she'd pulled over her right shoulder. She looked about fifty, and was not unattractive. The self-assurance with which she carried herself suggested she was a woman long accustomed to operating in a man's world.

"Please, sit down, Mr. Kelly."

He took a seat on a sofa with a floral print not unlike the general's dress. On an end table was a colorized framed photo of a serious man in a short-sleeve white shirt and tie, a woman in a pink dress, and a squinting girl in front of them.

Sochua must have followed his gaze, because she picked up the photograph. "My father was a low-level official in the Lon Nol government. He worked in Phnom Penh and was taken to Tuol Sleng by the Khmer Rouge and executed. His picture is on display there in the museum now. Number 45193. My mother starved to death in a Khmer Rouge labor camp." She placed the photo back on the table.

Chris swallowed hard. She would have been a child. "How old were you then?"

"Too young," she said. "I went with my cousin to a refugee camp in Vietnam. That is where I learned to speak English. At the age of fifteen I ran away from camp and joined General Thul's forces. I had no shoes and no gun, and because I was a girl they made me carry water for them—until I proved myself."

Sochua spoke slowly and conservatively, carefully enunciating each word, pausing often to consider the correct term or phrase. Though heavily accented, her English was grammatically without fault.

"What can I do for you, Mr. Kelly?"

The woman who had served him a drink and whom Chris had presumed to be a servant took a seat at Sochua's side and placed a hand on the general's knee. At first Chris thought the woman had come to interrupt for some matter of business, but Sochua did not acknowledge her, and the woman did not speak. In vain, Chris waited a moment for an introduction before answering.

"Chea Phyrom has kidnapped my daughter."

"Yes, I have heard." Sochua cocked her head. "How is Mr. Granger?"

"George?"

"You work for the same organization, do you not?"

"I'm just a volunteer for IRM. Anyway, he's in Bangkok. He didn't think it was safe to stay."

The general looked at him blankly, unspeaking, and he wondered if she'd heard him.

"General?"

"Oh, yes. Pity he had to leave—but prudent."

There was another awkward moment of silence while Chris waited to see if she would continue.

"General, please—"

"Ah, you wish to talk about Chea Prak's troublesome son. We have many like him in this country."

Sochua stared out the window past him. One eye twitched slightly. She sighed.

"There is no reason Cambodia should be as poor as it is today. We have abundant natural resources, we have great tourism potential, we are not plagued with natural disasters, we are at peace. Yes, education of the young must improve, but that is not our greatest problem."

She paused for a long sip of her drink, which had sweated a great amount of water onto the table in front of them. Chris waited impatiently. Clearly, Sochua expected to be indulged. Maybe this was just a waste of time. He didn't come here to play games.

"Cambodia is so poor," Sochua continued, "because of its governing elite. They are thieves who steal everything from their countrymen and leave them with nothing." She sighed again. "I am not optimistic."

The young woman patted Sochua's knee gently. Chris tried again.

"General, is there anything you can do to help me find my daughter?"

"Do you have a picture of her?"

"Yes, of course."

Chris unfolded a photocopy of an enlarged print. Mai smiled at him from her first school photo. Sochua found her reading glasses on an end table and fastidiously placed them on the end of her nose. She tilted her head and studied the picture.

"Your wife is Cambodian?"

"No."

"Your daughter does not look like you."

"Mai is adopted. She was born in India. Listen, General—"

"You adopted an Indian girl?" She eyed him over her spectacles with what almost looked like reproach.

"That's right." He massaged his tired eyes. This woman was a nut case.

"She doesn't look exactly Indian."

"Mai is from Manipur near the Burmese border."

"Yes, I know where Manipur is. That would explain her unusual features. She is quite beautiful."

"General, please. Can we talk about—"

"He has almost certainly killed her by now."

Sochua's abrupt change of subject and her assertion, so confident and matter-of-fact, felt like she'd suddenly knifed him in the gut, and what made him want to reach across the table and slap her face was that he couldn't tell that she wasn't enjoying herself.

"Why do you think your daughter is still alive?"

"Well, I can't just give up, can I? Besides, Phyrom said if I ever tried to find her he would kill her, which leads me to believe she may still be alive."

"Hmm. It is possible he may want to keep her alive, but unlikely; she represents a risk for him while she lives. Let me ask you something, Mr. Kelly: Do you *hate* Chea Phyrom?"

"Hate him? Absolutely."

"Then you can begin to understand him, to think like him. Ask yourself this question." Sochua leaned forward and looked him directly in the eye as if she had rehearsed the move. "If you were Chea Phyrom, what would be your perfect revenge? Even better than ending your daughter's life. I know what I would do. Don't you?"

He didn't like the way she'd said that. It almost felt like a threat. "Yes. If I were him...I would..."

"What? What would you do?" She slid to the edge of her seat. "You know now, don't you?"

"Yes."

"Tell me."

"If I were a scumbag like Phyrom, I would put her in one of my brothels."

The spell was broken. Sochua leaned back, once again the harmless eccentric.

"There is a man named Yun Naren. He worked for me in the Anti-Trafficking Police. He was a most unusual officer. He believed like me on many things, and he dreamed of arresting men like Chea Phyrom. Yun knows more about Phyrom and his operations than anybody alive. He may be able to steer you in the right direction, as they say. You should speak with him."

"Where can I find him?"

"I don't know. Unfortunately, Mr. Yun was not capable of understanding certain political realities, and I was eventually forced to fire him. He went into hiding, entered a monastery—that's what men do in Cambodia when life becomes unbearable or they want to disappear—but *The Cambodia Times* interviewed him last year. They might know where he is. Good luck, Mr. Kelly, and please be careful."

⚔

As the American left the compound, Sochua Nika's daughter finished what remained of their guest's lime soda and laughed.

"You are truly evil," she said.

Sochua smiled, playfully biting her bottom lip.

⚔

Chris dialed Agent Gutierrez on the way home. He'd always made it a point not to talk on the phone and drive—to set a good example for Mai. Voice mail. Damn. He waited for the stupid beep.

"This is Chris Kelly. I've got an interesting lead for you. Please call me on my mobile as soon as you can." He swerved to miss a moto driving down the wrong side of the road. "Idiot! Oh, sorry, not you. Uh…it's a long story. Please call me. Bye."

He found Lisa at the kitchen table, still in her pajamas at noon. "It's good to see you again."

She stared into her milk, her eyes puffy and bloodshot. "Where have you been?"

Sampour stopped washing vegetables and fled the kitchen.

"Out looking for my daughter. Does this mean you're going to start talking to me?"

She ignored his question. "Are you going out again?"

"What do you care?"

"Well, you can't take the car."

"Why not?"

"Not unless you tell me where you're going and what you're up to."

"What is your problem? I don't need the car, and I don't like your line of questioning. Is there something you're trying to say?"

She hesitated, trembling. "If I tell David Finto you've bought a gun, they're going to force us to leave the country."

Something like hate welled up inside him, and it tasted of bile. "Did you take it?"

"Chris, why did you—"

He jabbed his finger in her face. "*Did you take my gun?*"

She recoiled at his outburst. Finto was right; she *was* afraid of him. If anger hadn't taken precedence, Chris would have been overwhelmed with sadness at how low they had sunk—*he* had sunk. He ran up the stairs and into the guest bedroom, threw open the closet door, and pulled his toolbox from the top shelf. He released the metal latch, flung open the lid, and found only tools.

"Lisa!"

Halfway down the stairs he heard the door slam. Sampour shrieked as he burst past her and into the driveway.

"Where'd she go?" he shouted at the two security guards. They just stared at him with stupid looks on their faces. "Where did she go?"

"Across the street," Yen answered. "Mr. Finto's house."

Chris raced back inside. He snatched a military surplus duffel from a hall closet and ran to the bedroom and crammed it with clothes. In his office he unlocked their emergency stash of money—important in a country with only two ATMs—about five hundred dollars. He grabbed a large stack of photocopies of Mai's picture off the desk. From the toolbox he took a flashlight and box cutter and shoved them in the duffel. He ran outside; Finto would be there any second. Mai's T-ball bat—he'd been coach—was leaning against the wall, and he shoved it in the bag as well.

"Everything okay, boss?" It was Yen, the guard. His radio crackled loudly, and he hastily turned down the volume.

Chris strode past him. "Open the gate, please."

"Yes sir."

On the street he raised a finger. "Moto!"

The policemen didn't look up from their card game; construction workers paused to stare; a man sat on his haunches eating noodle soup from a plastic bag. There was movement inside David Finto's compound directly opposite.

"Moto!"

A moto-dop on the corner jogged to his vehicle. Chris studied the man eating noodles.

Yen grinned obsequiously. "Where you go today, sir?"

"None of your business, but nice try."

The moto-dop rolled to a stop. Chris pounced on the man slurping noodles and sent him sprawling onto his back, covered with hot liquid.

Chris thrust a fist in the man's face. "Don't try to follow me! You understand?"

"Yes sir. Yes sir."

He climbed on and tapped the moto-dop on the shoulder. "See y'all later."

Yen looked grave. "Be careful, sir."

They took off toward Monivong Boulevard.

"Turn right."

At the corner he looked back and saw Lisa standing in the street in her pajamas next to David Finto, his hands on his hips. No turning back now.

"Shit!" He realized he'd left his phone on the kitchen table.

The moto-dop looked over his shoulder. "Where would like to go, sir?" he asked in Khmer.

Chris had no idea how to say *"The Cambodia Times"* in the local language. "Uh—it's—uh—"

"You can speak to me in English, sir, if you prefer."

"Yeah, okay. Take me to *The Cambodia Times*. The newspaper. You know where it is?"

"Bat."

⋏

David Finto watched Kelly ride out of sight on the back of a moto. "Well, that was damn stupid." What a dick. He looked at Lisa Kelly trembling next to him. She hadn't said a word since she'd come running to his door in her pajamas with a gun in hand. At the moment, her state of dress was attracting a great deal of unwanted attention from the crowd that had gathered to gawk at the foreigners.

He placed his hand on Lisa's back; she wasn't wearing a bra. "Let's get you home." He steered her to the safety of her housing compound. "You did the right thing coming to me. I'll check on you later." Damn, she was hot.

He waited for her to go inside and lock the door, then called Ambassador Schroeder. He hated to say "I told you so," but Schroeder should've listened to him.

Schroeder answered right away. "Hi, David. You got, like, one minute. I'm about to go on stage."

"What are you doing, sir?"

"I'm about to hand out backpacks to underprivileged school children. What's up?"

Schroeder listened to Finto's account of what had just happened at the Kelly household. "Damn it, this is exactly the kind of situation we were trying to avoid. Well, I guess we have no choice but to revoke his privileges."

"Yes sir."

Finto hung up. He didn't like this situation—not at all. He'd told Kelly to hold his shit together, but then he went and got a fucking gun. Stupid son of a bitch. And if Kelly had listened to him in the first place—he'd tried to warn him off from engaging in this kind of stupid volunteer shit—none of this would've happened. What did Kelly think? That these people were just going to let him run them out of business? He had no idea who he was fucking with. What an idiot. And now they'd made him pay alright; there was no way in hell he was going to get his daughter back. His best chance was to see if they would ransom her. Sad. Stupid son of a bitch. And Kelly was going to lose his wife too, and she was such a MILF. And one way or another this was going to reflect badly on him too, before it was all over. Goddam it.

Chapter 21

The offices of *The Cambodia Times* occupied a rambling two-story monstrosity on an unpaved alley a few blocks south of the American embassy. When Chris arrived on the back of a moto, soaked with sweat, a motley circus of noodle vendors, moto-dops, disfigured beggars, and deliveries all but blocked access to the country's only English-language daily. Two dozen or more motos were parked haphazardly inside the open gate of the compound, occupying every available inch of space in the small paved forecourt so that Chris spent some time wending his way to the front door, which was propped open by a chair.

A Cambodian man sitting at a battered desk closed his book, a ceiling fan swinging like a pendulum above his head.

"Can I help you?"

"Yes, please. I'm searching for an article that appeared in *The Cambodia Times* last year, and I don't think you have your back issues—"

"Database upstairs," the young man said, gesturing toward an open door before returning to his book.

Chris entered a dark stairwell. Dozens of half-collapsed file-storage boxes labeled with black marker, scratched out, labeled again—some of them half a dozen times—were crammed beneath the stairs and stacked to the ceiling against the walls. More boxes were piled two or three high on the stairs themselves. Chris clutched the metal balustrade to help him negotiate the narrow path to the second floor, and it wobbled frighteningly. An enormous cat with a stunted tail passed him on its way down without so much as a curious sniff.

The stairs opened into a large rectangular room where several people sat at a long wooden table staring at their laptops. No one paid any attention to Chris as he entered. He examined each of four small offices off this main room and found them all empty but one.

Behind a desk sat a harassed Caucasian man in his thirties wearing a loud shirt and busily typing away on a prehistoric desktop computer. His eyes darted to Chris and back to his work.

"Excuse me," Chris said.

"Yeah?" The man shook his head as if to clear it. "What can I do for you?"

"I was hoping I could use your database. The guy downstairs told me I could find it up here."

The man laughed. "Database? Heng has got a great sense of humor. Come here."

He led Chris across the lobby to a shoddy metal shelf leaning away from the wall. He slapped one of several cardboard boxes, and dust filled the air. He gave a little cough and waved his hand in front of his face.

"This is this year. The bottom two shelves are last year. Everything older is on shelves in that back room there or under the stairs. It's all more or less labeled. More or less."

"Is there an index or anything?"

"Sorry, mate. And don't get it out of order."

Chris sighed and grabbed a dusty box labeled "Jan.–Feb. 2015."

"Why don't you tell me what you're looking for? Maybe I can narrow your search."

"Well, what I'm really looking for is the person who did an interview with a police officer named Yun Naren."

"Doesn't ring a bell. What's it about?"

"I'm not entirely sure. I just know that y'all did an article or interview with him last year."

"Sorry. Don't remember."

"Don't worry about it. Thanks. I'm Chris, by the way."

"Dunc."

Beginning with the first day of January, 2015, Chris thumbed through each issue, hoping to find something about an ex-cop named Yun Naren. Half an hour later, he had just finished May–June 2015, when Dunc interrupted him.

"Hey, man. Did this guy you're looking for get in trouble with the son of Chea Prak?"

"Maybe. He worked for the Anti-Trafficking Police under Sochua Nika."

Dunc placed his forehead in his right hand and shut his eyes tight. "Okay, I'm getting a vision." He massaged his temples. "I remember this guy. Let's see. He called us up and said he had a story. I don't remember who wrote it up though. Try looking at about…mid-December of 2015. It was after Pchum Ben, I remember that."

Chris eagerly went for the box labeled "Nov.–Dec. 2015." He soon found exactly what he was looking for in the National News section of the December 24 issue.

The Cambodia Times
Thursday, December 24, 2015

VIP Sends Man into Hiding
Susan Reid

Speaking by telephone from an undisclosed location, Yun Naren, formerly second deputy chief of the National Police's anti-trafficking unit, told of a heated argument with Chea Phyrom, son of Chea Prak, head of Brigade 70, the prime minister's personal bodyguard brigade.

Yun said he went into hiding out of fear for his life and the safety of his extended family as a result of a roadside run-in with Chea Phyrom in August during which Yun claims to have been brutally beaten by Chea and his companions.

According to Yun, he was driving…

…"I went to the local police station, but they refused to help me. They said, 'Chea Phyrom is untouchable.'"

Commenting yesterday, Kandal District Police Chief Pich Sum said he did not recall receiving a verbal report of the incident and that there was no record of any written complaint having been filed. "If Yun had filed a proper report, of course we would have investigated the incident," said Pich.

Another police official, however, who requested anonymity, said he vividly recalled Yun stumbling into his office in early September bleeding from his head and begging for help. "He said he was a police officer, so we were very concerned for him. But when he told us who did it, we told him there was nothing we could do."

A spokesman for Chea Phyrom refused to comment on the alleged incident on Monday. Chea Prak also declined to comment.

Yun said he had gone into hiding and would no longer attempt to hold anyone responsible for the incident. "I just want to be left alone. But if something happens to me, now the world will know the truth."

This was it. Chris took the paper with him to Dunc's office.

"Hey, where can I find Susan—"

Dunc held up a finger to shush him. "Give me a minute, chief."

Chris waited while Dunc talked casually on the phone about his plans for the holidays. Finally, he gave up and walked over to the long table in middle of the main room, where a number of foreigners were still on their computers.

"Excuse me. Do any of you know where I can find Susan Reid?"

A tanned woman with straight blond hair turned abruptly. Her jaw was square, masculine.

"Who wants to know?" She wasn't smiling.

"I'd like to talk to Susan Reid about this article written in 2015." He waved the paper in front of her.

She looked appraisingly at him. "What do you want to know about it?" The woman was fit and athletic. A pink sports bra was visible under a tight tank top.

A man with square glasses and curly unkempt hair glared at them from the next computer. "Would you please go somewhere else?"

"Jesus, Larry. Shut your ass!" The woman shut her laptop and beckoned to Chris. "Come on over here."

She led him to a room with a rattan table, its glass top smeared with greasy fingerprints and remnants of lunches. A lime-green refrigerator hummed in a corner.

"Sit down." She took a seat and leaned back on two legs. "Well, what do you want?"

"Are you Susan?"

"No. She's a friend of mine."

"Do you know where I can find her? I want to talk to her about this article."

"Sorry. She left Cambodia a few months ago. No forwarding address. What do you want to know about the article?"

"What can you tell me about this guy Yun Naren?"

She shook her head. "Nothing."

"Well, I'm looking for him."

The woman snorted and made a lengthy show of lighting a cigarette and enjoying a drag.

"Well, you won't find him. Dropped off the face of the earth, you know."

Chris's temperature was starting to rise. "But I need to find him."

"Well, I don't know where he is."

"Do you have any idea?" She knew more than she wanted to tell. He was sure of it.

"Not the slightest. And you know what? Even if I did, I wouldn't tell you. You know—journalistic ethics and all that jazz."

She was lying. "Look," he said in a growl, "my daughter has been kidnapped. Her life is in danger. I have good reason to believe Yun could help me find her. If you know where he is, I need to know."

"His name rhymes with moon, not sun, asshole."

"Holy shit. You're that Kelly guy, aren't you?" It was Dunc, standing in the doorway, an eyebrow raised.

"Yep. That's me. Do you normally print stories in this paper that are just called in by someone claiming to be beaten up on the side of the road?"

"No, we—"

"Then Susan Reid must have met Yun or verified his identity somehow. Where can I find her? My daughter has been missing for five days now, and I'm running out of options!"

Chris took from his back pocket a photocopied picture of Mai and unfolded it and showed them.

"Shit." The woman kicked a chair in angry surrender. It fell over backward.

Chris frowned. "Wait. Are you——?"

"Yes, I'm Susan Reid," she said dismissively. "My real name is Karen Galindo. We have to take precautions around here."

"So what can you tell me about Yun?"

"Where do you want me to start?"

"At the beginning."

"How much time have you got?"

"As much as you need."

"Well, you see, Yun——he fucked with the wrong people. Well, really they fucked with him first. He was driving down the road one day, and Chea Phyrom——that's the son of the commander of the prime minister's body-guard unit——well, Phyrom and some of his buddies ran him off the road into a ditch or something. He screamed at them, so they got out and beat the hell out of him.

"After they beat him up, he tried to get the police to do something about it, and they told him he could forget it. He tried to get his boss Sochua Nika to help——she was the head of the anti-human-trafficking police——and she'd have none of it. She told him to drop it. By the way, Yun claims he and Sochua were in a romantic relationship, and——"

"What? For real?"

"People say Sochua likes her younger men, but that's the kind of shit you can expect men to say about women in power, right?

"Anyway, Yun tried to file formal charges against Chea, but that wasn't going to happen. Then he went out to Chea's house once, drunk and scream-ing for him to come outside, and so Chea's bodyguards beat the hell out of him again. I'm not sure why they didn't just kill him then. After that, Sochua fired him, most likely on orders from the prime minister himself. Did I men-tion that Chea Phyrom is the prime minister's nephew? Anyway, when Yun lost his job, his fiancée dumped him because she didn't want to be married to a washed-up former cop with a death wish, and then he just went nuts."

"And so he went into hiding?"

"Shut up. I'm not finished. Well, Chea Phyrom's sister, who he supposedly adored, was supposed to get married, not too long after Yun's downfall. Just before the wedding, she was coming out of a photo studio on Monivong getting her pictures made, when Yun walked up to her and threw acid on her face. Almost killed her. They say she looked like the Elephant Man, but worse. Blinded her in one eye. She eventually killed herself. I think her name was Nimol, or something like that. Then Yun shaved his head and joined a monastery."

"Wow. Why didn't you talk about the acid attack in the article?"

"I didn't know about it at the time. Yun didn't want me to know about it. He's very ashamed of what he did. I only found out later he was the same guy. He claims that he doesn't really remember doing it. Like he was in a daze or something. No complaint or anything was ever made by the Chea family; these people like to take care of this kind of stuff themselves."

"What else do you know about his relationship with Sochua Nika?"

"Well, not much. Just that they were reportedly an item until he decided to get married—to someone else. But I didn't give a shit about any of that; I was concerned with the story of his run-in with Chea Phyrom. Anyway, I don't get it. What on earth makes you think Yun can help you find your daughter?"

"Because he knows where Chea Phyrom is, and Phyrom's the one who took my daughter."

Galindo's mouth dropped open. "Hold on a minute. Chea Phyrom was the one who kidnapped your daughter?"

"That's right."

"And you think Yun knows where to find him?"

"Exactly."

"And who told you that?"

"The good general herself. And she said y'all might know how to find Yun."

Galindo and Dunc exchanged looks. "Seriously? Just hold on one fucking minute. You're telling me that Sochua Nika sent you over here?"

"What part of this don't you understand? I need to talk to Yun, and I need to talk to him now."

Galindo leaned in close. "Well, that's not going to happen, so you can just forget it."

"No. You don't understand. I—"

"No, *you* don't understand," she said, jabbing a finger in his face. "It ain't happenin'!"

Dunc put a hand on Chris's shoulder. "Would you let me and Karen talk privately a moment?"

He shrugged. "Fine."

He lurked outside the lunchroom and tried to snatch pieces of their furious whispering.

"I will not—"

"It's him—"

"We have to do—"

Galindo noticed him listening and slammed the door. The voices within grew louder but less comprehensible. A minute later Galindo stormed out, bumping Chris hard in the shoulder as she passed.

Dunc's face was red. "She's going to take you herself to see him."

"What? But I—"

Dunc held up a hand. "Don't say anything else. She wants to be there when you talk to him. That's the only way she'll do it."

"Why?"

"This guy went into hiding because very powerful people want him dead. She made a promise to keep his whereabouts secret, so she feels she needs to go and explain the circumstances to Yun. I wasn't sure until now that she even knew where he is."

Chris pursed his lips and said nothing.

"The only reason she's helping you at all is that she also wrote the story of your daughter's kidnapping. It had a real effect on her. You'd better go talk to her before she leaves." He nodded toward the door.

Chris found Galindo frantically stuffing books into a maroon backpack. "Well?"

"Meet me here at eight o'clock in the morning" she snarled.

"No. We have to go today."

Galindo shoved the last item in her bag and jogged down the stairs with him on her heels.

Chris implored, "Listen to me. I can't wait until tomorrow."

"Moto," Galindo shouted.

"Every minute could make a difference. We have to go now."

Galindo climbed on behind the waiting moto-dop and placed a middle finger in Chris's face as they drove away.

In the late afternoon Quynh streaked down the hall of her dormitory looking for her friends. Her handlers never allowed the girls outside except when they were led from the dormitory through a narrow alley into the hotel proper in order to be shown to customers, a few of whom had begun to return. She found some of the older girls squatting in a circle playing a game. Curious, she approached the group and watched them pass around a brown jar.

"What are you doing?"

The older girls all laughed at once. Quynh turned away and crossed her arms. She hated to be laughed at!

"Come here, little sister." One of the girls reached out her hand to Quynh. "Try this."

Using her finger, the girl dabbed what looked like a white, almost clear, honey on the palm of her hand. She beckoned Quynh closer.

"Sniff it. Like this." The older girl put her nose near the substance and inhaled deeply. "Come on. Try it. You'll like it."

"What is it?"

"Glue."

Quynh didn't know what glue was, but she came closer. She put her face near the girl's hand but found the smell offensive and recoiled. She was too slow; a hand grabbed her neck.

"Inhale! Inhale!" The bigger girl was too much for her. "Inhale!"

She took a quick breath over the glue. Maybe then the girl would let her go.

"Through your nose, stupid!"

Quynh sniffed hard. The goo singed her nostrils.

"Again, again!"

The older girl rubbed her hand into Quynh's face, forcing glue into her nose. She let go, and Quynh stumbled away crying and coughing.

She sneezed several times, and glue and mucous oozed out of her nose; she wiped it on her forearm and shirt. She zigzagged to her room and fell onto her mat with the room spinning around her. She had a strong urge to vomit. Even when she closed her eyes the starry blackness behind them re-volved slowly.

After a while she discovered that if she lay on her side the dizziness sub-sided a bit and didn't seem so bad after all. She felt hot and drowsy and began to giggle and think about her mother and grandmother. They felt so close and so real.

Once, some people of her village decided after the rice was planted to make a trip to Oudong to visit the ancient temples there. Most years, she was told, friends and family would make a trip like that, if times weren't too bad, but she didn't remember any previous or subsequent journeys. She had no memory of her father, but she recalled her mother packing their two cooking pots, some rice, and a few other items before the trip, driving her mad with anticipation. On the appointed day, her mother, grandmother, and grandfa-ther climbed, along with perhaps as many as fifteen other people from her village, onto a moto-pulled wagon the group had hired together for the jour-ney. They moved slowly. Ungainly top-heavy palms swayed above the endless paddies of rice ripening under a perfect sky, and even Grandfather seemed to be in good spirits. She loved being crammed together, sitting on her mother's lap all the way to Oudong, a journey that took two days.

After the first day's rain, they drove two more hours before stopping for the night at a pagoda. The women made fires while the children, with the monks' permission, gathered lotus root and morning glory in a shallow swamp on the monastery's grounds. The women prepared a delicious meal of stuffed frogs—an expensive delicacy they had bought on the roadside along the way—rice, and the freshly picked vegetables. Everybody shared and laughed, and food had never tasted so good.

After supper they rolled out their straw mats on the floor of a pavilion and listened to the old men tell stories—for the entire night, it seemed! At one point Grandfather took his turn with the story of Hanuman, the Monkey King, and she'd never been so proud of him. She lay close to her mother and let her play absently with her hair, something that normally drove her crazy but on that night felt wonderful. That was her last happy memory and the one remaining memory of her mother. She played it back in her mind, again and again.

"Shut up," someone hissed from across the room.

Quynh's hair and face were soaked with tears. She rolled over and tried not to think of those impossible things anymore.

Chris left *The Cambodia Times* and went to Land & Sea because he didn't know what else to do. He found one of the cooks sleeping in a hammock, a lit cigarette dangling between two slack fingers. It was five thirty and almost dark, but there were no customers yet. Chenda stood at a basin, peeling mangoes and smiling at some pleasant thought. She didn't notice him right away, and he seized the opportunity to catch his breath and watch her.

Eyes still on her work, she giggled as if she had known he was there all along. "What you doing?"

"Nothing."

She brought some iced artichoke tea and sat on a bench opposite him. She laid her head on her folded arms and closed her eyes.

"Oh, I so tired today."

"Chenda, listen. I need a place to stay."

"What wrong? Problem with honey?"

"Yeah, we got in a little fight."

"You foreign people so strange. Come with me."

Shaking her head reproachfully, she led him downstairs to one of the three rooms she let to tourists. She handed him two white bedsheets and a padlock.

"You stay here. Just don't bring back girl tonight."

"Thanks, Chenda."

"See you later, okay? You come up eat something." She grinned broadly and left.

What a day. The room, which had absorbed hours of fierce tropical sunlight, must have been at least a hundred degrees, maybe more, and a spindly overhead fan provided no relief at all. He left the door open, since the air outside was considerably cooler. In the mirror he saw an unshaven lunatic with dark bags under his eyes who looked as if he'd just been for a swim with his clothes on. He cast one sheet over the bed and lay down on the warm mattress.

He'd lost his daughter, his wife, and his home, and now he was sure his visa was about to be revoked, forcing him to leave the country. He might even go to jail. He should call Lisa, he should just go back home, but he simply couldn't stay awake.

Chapter 22

A door slammed, and Chris heard footsteps amid the early morning light in strange surroundings. He lay awake for almost a minute before he could remember where he was and why, and when the realization dawned on him, he was the more miserable for it. Someone had draped a mosquito net over him—probably Chenda. His watch read 7:27 a.m. He'd slept almost fourteen hours.

Where was the bathroom? He stumbled from bed and tried the door. It wouldn't budge. He didn't even remember closing it. He tried it again, and it held fast. What the hell was going on?

What sleep was left in him dissipated rapidly. He reached between the bars on the window and felt the door: padlocked on the outside. A quick search of the room revealed the contents of his pockets among the bedsheets, including the key. He could just reach the lock and free himself.

He trudged upstairs and found Chenda serving breakfast to a couple of scruffy backpackers. "Chenda, what the hell—"

"You sleeping very nice. I put mosquito net and lock door so nobody stealing you." She looked him up and down. "You no look so good. Maybe you take shower?"

He scratched his head. No time for that. He had to get back to *The Cambodia Times* to meet Galindo. "What time were you going to let me out?"

"I don't know. But you don't smile, maybe I lock you in room again."

▲

Karen Galindo looked daggers at him as he climbed off a moto. "You're late."

"Not by my watch," Chris lied. It was 8:10. As many as two dozen bored moto-dops watched their exchange with interest on the nearest corner.

"Man, you look like shit."

"People keep telling me that."

"What'd you do? Sleep in your clothes or something?"

"As a matter of fact, yes." Galindo had on tights and a bikini top. "What about you? Trying to dress as culturally inappropriate as possible?"

Galindo shook her head in disgust. "Sexist pig." She climbed on a tall motorcycle with knobby off-road tires and raised the kickstand. "Well, are you going to get on or not?"

He silently slipped on behind her, feeling slightly repulsed, trying to avoid a touch. They drove south on Norodom Boulevard through central Phnom Penh via Independence Monument. Just opposite Chris's own neighborhood they passed Chea Phyrom Group, Ltd., then the imposing walls of the Thai embassy, redesigned after the anti-Thai riots of 2011, and finally the Japanese embassy. Soon the trappings of a modern city began to slough off, and they found themselves in another place, the real Phnom Penh of tiny home-based shops and informal economy.

At the roundabout where Norodom Boulevard met Monivong Boulevard they joined the majority of cars, bicycles, motos, trucks, vans, tractors, horses, wagons, and hand-pulled carts and headed east to cross Monivong Bridge, also known as Vietnamese Bridge for the ethnic minority living in ramshackle huts in its shadow.

The bridge deposited them on the east side of the river almost on top of the lively Chbar Ampov Market. Here the road became not so much a highway as a bazaar, transit hub, and pedestrian mall through which they carefully wended their way. After a few minutes Galindo abruptly left the highway on a red-dirt road that hadn't dried from the previous afternoon's rain. Chris knew they were near the monastery when he saw a white tiered chimney, its top stained black from the smoke of countless cremation fires. They drove through a gate and parked under a magnificent banyan tree.

"You wait here," Galindo ordered, striding off toward a group of white buildings.

Chris shrugged and sat on a broken concrete bench. He watched a train of black ants journey purposefully between his feet and straight up the trunk of the banyan tree and out of sight. What could he expect here? It seemed unlikely Yun would be able to help him much, but what else did he have to go on? If the monk gave him some useful information, he would go straight to Agent Gutierrez. If not, he wasn't planning to go back home and let Finto have him booted out of the country. He needed a plan badly, but he had none.

After a long time Galindo came marching in his direction, and she didn't look happy. She barreled right past him and mounted her motorcycle. She was about to leave him!

"Hey!" He snatched the key from the ignition. "I've been waiting out here for twenty minutes, and you can't even tell me what he said before you drive off? What the hell is wrong with you?"

"Give me that key, you bastard!"

He dropped the key in his front pocket. "You're not going anywhere until you tell me what he said."

"Well, he was really pissed off we came out here to see him."

"He's a monk! I thought they weren't supposed to get pissed off." Galindo cracked a smile in spite of herself while he continued his rant. "I'm sick of your crap! My daughter has been kidnapped! I don't give a damn if he's ticked off!" He threw her key in the mud. "Go on! Get the hell out of here if you want to. I'm going in there to talk to him myself!"

"You will not!" Galindo jumped off her bike, and it toppled over into the muck. She ran after him. "You will not go in there!"

He kept moving. "Why the hell not? He's going to tell me what he knows."

She ran in front of him and put up her fists.

"You'd better get out of my way," Chris snarled.

Galindo didn't move. "Yun doesn't know anything, goddam it! And now we've come out here—" She yanked at her hair, mute with frustration. "Damn it! Why the hell did I listen you? And now we've put his life in—"

"Please, stop," someone said, putting an abrupt stop to their argument.

They both turned. A Buddhist monk stood looking down upon them from the steps of a nearby building. He held up a hand. It had to be Yun. He looked much older than Chris had imagined. Maybe it was the shaved head. He came down the steps but stopped at a distance.

"I already tell Karen I know nothing. Yes, I one time know much about Chea Phyrom's business. That was long time ago. I don't have information anymore. You must speak to General Sochua."

Chris pushed past Galindo on his way out. "Shit." Sochua must have known this guy would know nothing. What was she playing at?

As he walked away, he heard Galindo pleading with Yun.

"I'm sorry," she said. "Please forgive—" and then he could hear no more.

Chris stepped over Galindo's fallen bike and hailed a moto. What the hell was he going to do now? The moto-dop pulled his scooter alongside and cocked his head, waiting for direction.

Chris threw up his hands. "I don't know. I don't know where to go." He had no fucking idea.

The moto-dop looked at him expressionlessly.

"Just go. Just drive."

They drove back into the city center, passing within a few blocks of the house where Lisa was doing—what? Crying? Cursing him? Or maybe she was standing in the yard where Chris had built for Mai a castle that was nothing more than a few dollars' worth of bamboo poles lashed together with twine but that to Mai was "the best thing ever." He should just go home where he belonged. But for what? Lisa hated him, and without her and Mai what was the point?

He directed the driver to Sochua's compound and motioned for him to wait. He rang the bell. A guard opened a tiny window in the gate, looked him up and down, then closed the window. When the man didn't open the gate right away, the moto-dop offered Chris a seat on his scooter and stepped away to smoke. After a couple of minutes, Chris couldn't take it anymore and got up to pace. He noted the high walls of Sochua's compound were topped with a great deal of concertina wire. In fact, it looked like a prison.

After a few more minutes he rang again. Nothing. He held his finger on the bell and listened to it ring within the compound. He pounded on the thick metal with his fists.

"Hey! Open the door!"

He crossed the street so he could see over the wall to the second floor of the general's home. There was movement at a window.

"Hey, Sochua," he shouted, cupping his mouth, "I need to talk to you again."

A latch lifted, and a large man opened the gate. Finally! Chris jogged across the street, but when he tried to enter the compound he got a powerful openhanded blow to the chest. He tripped backward off the high curb and fell hard on his back in the street, traffic whizzing dangerously close.

"Asshole!" he yelled as the guard closed the gate again.

The moto-dop stubbed his cigarette out on the curb and put it in his shirt pocket. He got on his moto and drove off without a word.

"Well, thanks for nothing," Chris mumbled, getting up. Now what was he going to do? He'd done what Sochua said, and it had gotten him absolutely nowhere. Now what? He had no idea.

Chris slogged up the stairs at Land & Sea, defeated, deflated, and heartbroken. He removed the padlock—he didn't feel like talking to Chenda—but the door stuck stubbornly. Stupid piece of crap. He shoved it hard as he could, and it flew open with a crack. There was a grunt behind him, and two hairy arms encircled his torso, lifting him off his feet. He had no chance.

"Gotcha!"

George? His assailant let go, and Chris dropped to the floor. He rounded on his friend, fists balled. "You jerk!"

George laughed. "Man, you're slowing down. You walked right past me up the stairs and didn't even see me."

"I'm not in the mood," Chris said testily. "I've got a lot on my mind."

"So I've heard. Sorry. My bad."

Chris ran his hands through his sweat-drenched hair. He took a couple of deep breaths to calm down from the shock of being attacked from behind. "Well," he said finally, trying to ease the tension with as much wry humor as he could muster, "another second, and you would've been a dead man. You're lucky I didn't kill you."

George smiled and patted him on shoulder.

"What are you doing here?" Chris asked. "Are you back?"

"Well, not really. We went to Koh Samet for a week, and as soon as I got back to Bangkok I heard about Mai. I called your house, and Lisa told me everything. And she said you'd gone frickin' AWOL, completely off the deep end, and, from the looks of things, I'd say she's right. I caught the first flight over this morning. Lisa told me they're going to revoke your diplomatic status and cancel your visa. Congratulations, you're practically PNG."

"PNG? What the hell is that—Papua New Guinea? Don't screw with me, George. I told you I'm not in the mood."

"*Persona non grata*, man! I thought you knew all that diplomatic lingo. They're going to kick your butt out of the country."

"Yeah? Well, they're going to have to find me first. Is Molly still in Bangkok? Did she come with you?"

"Don't worry about Molly. She's fine."

"Good. Have you heard from Mong?"

"Nah. Mong gets in touch when he wants to. Why?"

"When we lost Mai, we crashed into a bunch of chicken coops, and the crowd looked like they were about to lynch both of us. Then the embassy people showed up and began paying for all the damage, and by the time I looked around for him, he was gone." Chris sat on the bed and put his face in his hands. "You didn't have any trouble finding me, I guess."

"I figured you'd probably turn up here sooner or later. Of course, I didn't tell Lisa that."

"Is she okay?"

"No. She is definitely not okay. Her daughter's been kidnapped. Her husband's run off. To be honest, she's completely hysterical. She wants you to come home."

"She didn't want me when I was there."

"Well, of course not. Women are nuts under the best of circumstances. I told her I'd take care of you."

Chris couldn't help but smile. "I'm really glad you showed up."

"Me too. You look like you could use some help." He grinned. "First bit of advice—you might want to take a bath."

Chris sniffed a fistful of shirt and grimaced. "Hmm. Yeah, I guess you're right."

George's smile disappeared. "Listen to me. Go home. Right now. Let's just take you back home and let the police handle this. This is insane. I'm telling you, as your friend, this is totally nuts."

"You said it yourself. If I go home, they'll force me to leave, and I can't leave here without Mai. I'm not. I'm just not. I'm going to find her one way or another or die trying. I've made up my mind."

George hung his big head. "Well." He sighed. "Then I'm going with you."

"Bad idea."

"Doesn't matter. I'm going."

Chris started to protest, but his heart wasn't in it; they both knew he couldn't go it alone, and George wouldn't take no for an answer anyway. "Fine. Thanks, man."

He brought George up to speed on everything since he left home, including his visit to Yun Naren.

"The monk doesn't trust Sochua. He says he doesn't know anything about what Phyrom's up to these days and that Sochua knows that. I think there's something fishy about the whole thing."

George twirled his moustache thoughtfully. "I don't know, man. It seems hard for me to believe that Sochua's got anything up her sleeve. It just doesn't make any sense."

"I wonder if she's the saint everyone thinks she is."

"She's been with us since day one. I can't tell you how many girls she's gotten off the streets. You know, I met Yun once. He was a good guy. I guess that's why he didn't last very long."

Chris was only half listening. He was thinking of his conversation with Sochua. "We've got to get inside the brothels," he said. "That's the only way we're going to find her."

"Dude, there've got to be at least three thousand brothels in this country, and, anyway, it doesn't make a whole lot of sense that he would keep her in one. It's too risky."

"Man, I'm telling you, when I was at Sochua's house—well, I just realized that's what he'd do with her. We've got to get in the brothels, and we've got to do it without anybody knowing who we are."

"That's impossible; too many people know me. Even with a disguise they'd recognize me."

"Right. You're like frickin' Bigfoot."

"And whoever's got Mai has probably got your picture."

"Right."

"And you're still sure this is what you want to do?"

"Where do we start?"

George crossed his arms and pondered this a moment. "Let's go see Arthur."

⊼

Arthur kept Chris and George waiting at the bar for ten minutes while he engaged in a clearly audible knockdown drag-out with Barbara behind the scenes. Every now and then he stuck his head through the beads to say he'd be with them in a minute.

"Sorry 'bout that. Women. Y'know what I'm sayin'?" he said when he finally joined them.

Chris nodded. "Yeah."

Arthur pulled up a chair, flipped it around backward, and took a seat facing them. "Alright. What's up?" He held up a hand. "No! Hang on! I gotta tell you something before I forget. One of my boys knows some people, and they know some people who told me that them girls of yours— the ones that got stole from your shelter—are all doing tricks over at the Apsara 2 now."

George smiled sardonically. "So Phyrom got them all back and then some."

"I swear," Chris said, "I'm going to kill that piece of shit."

Arthur laughed. "Well, good luck with that. I'll be the first to congratulate you. Now, what brings you gentlemen in today?"

"You tell him, George. I'm too tired."

"Sihanoukville," Arthur told them after George explained their reason for coming. "That's where I'd go if I was you."

Sihanoukville was where Chris took the family to the beach. Mai had learned to swim there. "Why?" he asked.

"Well, people say Chea Phyrom practically owns the place, which means you'd better be *pret-ty fuck-ing careful.* I wouldn't go waving that gun around if I was you."

George gave Chris a playful punch. "Uh, his wife has already disarmed him."

"Thanks, George," Chris muttered.

Arthur grinned. "No shit? That's pretty damn funny, Rambo."

"Yeah, that's what I was thinking: funny."

"Chea the Younger," Arthur continued, "has several whorehouses down there—but Sochua would've known that. Kinda makes you wonder why she didn't mention that to you."

Chris looked askance at his friend. "Yes, it does."

"Anyway, since you people shut down Svay Pak, that's where all the pedophiles are going. One of my girls now has her own place in the Chicken Farm next door to the Busy Bar, or whatever they're calling it this week. Anyway, people will know it. Her name is Srey Ni, and she owes me. She knows shit, and she ought to be able to help you narrow your search. Watch out for her mean-ass dog."

"Chicken Farm?"

"Don't worry. Your buddy George knows what I'm talking about."

George nodded. "Lovely place."

At that moment, Barbara stormed into the bar wearing a leopard-print miniskirt and thigh-high leather boots. She was carrying several designer bags—likely fakes—and eye makeup ran in wet tracks down her cheeks. She marched straight up to Arthur and slapped him across the face.

"I hope you die first! I hate you!"

"Barbara, wait."

"My name not 'Barbara,' you stupid, dumb person. How many time I tell you?"

They watched her tromp out the door.

"Yeah, go on and get the hell out! I'll be dancing on your grave!" Arthur yelled.

"I do sex with your brother," she screamed from the stairwell. "And he better than you!"

Arthur massaged his temples. "She's full of shit, man. There's no way my brother's better than me." There was awkward silence. "I found out I have fucking HIV, man," he said, finally. "She's got it too."

Chris slumped forward. Apparently, he wasn't the only one with problems. "Wow, Arthur, I'm sorry to hear that."

Arthur got up and put an arm around Chris's shoulders. "Oh, it doesn't matter, man. Just go find your daughter."

⋏

Chris and George walked one block east to Sisowath Quay and sat down on a bench with a view of the river. With the steady breeze the weather was perfect, and a large number of Cambodian families and Western tourists strolled on the palm-tree-lined promenade under the flags of many nations. A golden lion statue gazed across the river under the flag of Argentina, and Chris thought of a game he and Lisa used to play with Mai to identify the flags as they walked along the quay to a favorite restaurant or to pass the time on a weekend. Eventually Mai had memorized them all. Chris felt a fresh stab of pain, that happy memory a distant mirage.

"So do you think Arthur has any idea what he's talking about? I mean about Chea Phyrom and Sihanoukville?"

"Yeah, I figure he probably does. Granted, even if he's right, it's not a whole heck of a lot to go on."

"Nope."

"But it makes sense he'd want to get her out of Phnom Penh."

"Yep. Well, come on. Let's get on the road."

George grabbed his arm. "Hey, you know we can't make it to Sihanoukville today."

"Why? It only takes three and a half hours to get there."

"Then you obviously haven't seen my car, and you know as well as I do it's way too dangerous to drive that road at night."

Chris yanked his arm away. "Six nights, George! She's been gone six nights! Do you know what it feels like to wait one more?" Torture. Every single second was torture.

George looked at his hands and then back at him. "Even if we hired someone to take us, by the time we got it all arranged, we couldn't make it before dark."

Chris hated to admit he was right. By day the trip to Sihanoukville was harrowing and dangerous—farmers dried their crops on the roadway, herders drove their cattle to and fro, and children played on the pavement with utter disregard for passing vehicles—but by night it was suicide. David Finto liked to tell the tale of a French diplomat who'd tried to make the trip at night alone from Sihanoukville to Phnom Penh after getting in a fight with her boyfriend at a seaside resort. She'd hit a water buffalo being driven across the road in the dark and rolled her car. She was beaten and robbed and left for dead on the side of the road until she was found by a contractor for World Vision in the morning. No, they couldn't drive after dark.

"Well, shit." Chris numbly watched the boats on the Tonle Sap. After a minute he said, "Last year we had some friends visit from home, and Mai and I took them down here for a boat ride. When we got finished, we were walking along the river just over there, and a lady with a tiny baby came up to us and asked us for some money to buy formula. I thought that was a little strange, and I asked her why the baby was drinking formula instead of breast milk, and she claimed to have found the baby under a tree.

"You should've seen that thing. Cutest little baby I'd ever set eyes on. I held her, and she just grinned the biggest toothless grin. She had some terrible scalp condition and a rash on her face, but she seemed so happy. Anyway, the woman said she had no money to feed the child and that she wanted to find a good home for her. I told her I could help arrange for an orphanage to take the baby, but that they weren't going to give her any money for her. When I said that, she stopped playing games and offered to sell me the baby outright for a hundred and fifty dollars.

"Well, we just took Mai and left, and the lady just kept shouting at us while we were walking to our car: 'Okay, a hundred and twenty-five. A hundred. Alright, alright! Seventy-five.' Like she was just selling tourist crap. By the time we got in the car, she was down to fifty bucks. And after we got out of there, you know what Mai said? She said, 'Daddy, you probably could've gotten the baby for even less.'"

They sat in silence.

"I wonder where she is now," George whispered after a minute.

Chris was about to say something, and then he realized George could be talking about the baby girl—*or* about Mai. His throat got tight, and he had to turn away to hold it together.

The sun had dipped behind the riverfront façades of Sisowath Quay, meaning the night's revelry would soon begin in earnest. Touts in cheap suits chased tourists, exhorting them to try their fried frogs' legs or happy hours or live nude shows; moto-dops were out in droves; children ran alongside better vehicles promising to find parking spaces for a small fee. Something among the havoc in front of the Foreign Correspondents' Club caught Chris's attention, and it momentarily took his breath away. He turned back to the river.

"Hey, George?"

"What?"

"Talk a walk with me."

George didn't hesitate. "Aright."

Trailing a small retinue of juvenile panhandlers and trinket vendors, Chris led them south along the riverfront. "Try not to be obvious, but take a look across the street at that moto-dop right there on the corner in front of the FCC. Standing next to the white sign."

George paused and ostensibly examined a vendor's wares. "There's like six of 'em. Which one?" He dropped some coins in the salesman's hand and took a pack of gum. He resumed walking and offered Chris a piece. "Chiclet?"

"No thanks. The one with the blue hat pulled down over his eyes. He's wearing a red T-shirt."

"Yeah, what about him?" George handed the gum to an adolescent girl, and she shared it among her peers.

"He's the same moto-dop who drove me back from the pagoda this morning."

George raised an eyebrow. "From Yun's pagoda? Really? Are you sure?"

"Look. Tons of foreigners are walking right past him, and he's not even trying to get a fare."

"Now that *is* weird."

"I swear it's the same guy. And you know what? Now that I think about it, he might've been out front of *The Cambodia Times* when I met Galindo there this morning. But I'm not sure." Chris stopped and turned his back to the street. The riverine scene before him was bathed in a rich sepia. It should've been beautiful, or at least exotic, but it just pissed him off. "You think he's following me?"

"It's possible, but—"

"So who would be following me?"

"Could be the embassy's Surveillance Detection Unit, or whatever they're called."

"Could be. But if it was the SDT, why wouldn't they just send the cops to come arrest me?"

"Good point. Well, Chea Phyrom or his father might want to know what you're up to. He's got to know you'll be hunting for him. Or…"

"Or what?"

"Or maybe Phyrom's decided to come after you." George considered this a moment and continued. "But then, I guess if that were the case, you'd already be dead by now."

"Right." Chris crossed his arms, contemplating the same thing that had been gnawing at him all afternoon. "Do you think—and I know this is crazy—but do you think it's possible that Sochua and Phyrom could be working together?"

George snorted. "What? No way. Anyway, why? Why on earth would they be working together?"

"I don't know. It's just weird, you know? I mean, Phyrom would do anything to get his hands on Yun because of what he did to his sister, right?"

"Yeah…"

"And then Sochua sends me out to see Yun, and Yun doesn't know anything."

George chewed thoughtfully on a thumbnail. "So?"

"So—I don't know. It's just weird. And then I go back over to Sochua's, and she won't see me."

"She probably wasn't even there. I'm still waiting for you to say something that makes any sense."

"Maybe she told Phyrom where I was going. So he could get to Yun."

"What? That doesn't make sense on, like, so many levels. First, Sochua didn't even know where Yun was. You found him yourself. Second, even if she could help Phyrom, why would she? Like Arthur said, she hates his guts."

"I don't know. Money? Sex? Power?" Chris glanced over his shoulder at the Foreign Correspondents Club. The moto-dop was still there, apart from the others. "Just seems strange."

George shrugged. "Don't know what to tell you, bro. Anyway, if Phyrom just wanted you to lead him to Yun Naren, why would that guy still be following you? Tell me that."

"Well, I don't know, but we have to get rid of him before we go to Sihanoukville."

"How you going to do that?"

"I've got an idea."

⋀

Chris distributed pictures of Mai on the riverfront until dark while George left to run errands and check on his house. They reconvened for a late supper at Land & Sea. There was a nice breeze, and the small restaurant was busy with young backpackers from the hostel across the street drinking beer and telling travel tales under the strung lights.

"God, I'd give my good knee for a decent burger," grumbled George. "The meat is always too lean."

"Have you seen Cambodian cows?"

"Hmm. Good point." George thumped his menu. "What do you think the difference is between Australian-style Fish & Chips and British-style Fish & Chips?"

"I don't give a damn. Just order me something, okay?"

"Fine. I'll get the British and you can have the Aussie, and we'll compare."

"Whatever you say, man."

Chenda took their food order and turned a battered fan on them. She directed a reproachful look at Chris. "No beer for you tonight," she said and took their menus without further comment.

"I think she's mad at you."

"Well, she'll have to get in line."

Chris brooded in silence until the food arrived. Rectangular plates of pressed palm leaves held generous portions of battered deep-fried fish, fries, and small green salads topped with shaved carrot.

George chuckled. "They're exactly the same."

Chenda glared at him and switched the two plates. Chris couldn't recall having had lunch, but he only picked at his fish. He just wanted Mai back. And Lisa.

Momentarily, feminine giggles came up the stairs. A Cambodian girl—to call her fifteen would be generous—playfully slapped away the hands of a balding Westerner as he chased her into the restaurant.

"Come on, baby! Give me a piece of that ass." He sounded American.

"Naww, my hungry now. I give you ass later," she teased.

"You betcha you will."

The man kicked a chair from under a nearby table and pulled the girl onto his lap, where they continued their flirtatious tussle. Chris began to see red.

Chenda confronted the man, hands on hips. "We no got girlfriend menu here."

"Huh?"

"No sex tourists in my restaurant."

"Don't get your panties in a wad, sweetie. What's the problem?"

Chenda addressed the girl kindly in Khmer.

The girl smiled and took her man by the hand. "Come. We go to one more place."

"No. Fuck that. I want to eat here."

"No. I no like here. We go," she pleaded, pulling.

"I am not moving," he snarled, yanking away his hand.

"No. You need go now," Chenda demanded.

The john looked at Chris and George and shrugged. "What the fuck's her problem?"

"You make her sick coming in here with a child like that," Chris remarked coolly. "That's the problem. You ought to be ashamed of yourself."

The rooftop became very still. The stranger scratched his chin in silence as his face noticeably reddened.

"Ha," he boomed at length, slapping his knee. "That is rich! I ought to be ashamed of myself. What are you—my fucking mother?"

The man got suddenly to his feet, no longer smiling. His chair fell over and slapped the floor. "Maybe I don't want to leave. What then?"

"Well, Chenda wants you to go, so I don't think you have a choice."

The man pounded a meaty fist into his palm. "And who's going to make me?"

Chris stood. A week ago the idea of getting in a fistfight in a restaurant— or anywhere—would have been laughable; now he was dying to off-load his pent-up rage on the guy's ugly face.

"Well, I guess that'll have to be me," he said, amazed at the words issuing from his own mouth.

George pushed the table away and got to his feet. "And me," he said.

The man's mouth moved, but nothing came out. He cursed under his breath and retreated down the stairs, the girl close on his heels and trying to salvage the situation.

"Don't worry," she said. "This place food no good. I show you better."

"Just shut your mouth!"

When the pair could no longer be heard, Chris turned to George. "Girlfriend menu?"

"These foreigner restaurants always keep a menu of local food for Cambodian 'girlfriends' that don't know what cheeseburgers are."

"Hmm. I learn something new every day with you. Boy, I scared the hell out of him, didn't I?"

"Looked like he'd seen his own ghost. Sure did."

After George had finished all of his food and most of Chris's, he said, "You're welcome to crash at my place tonight."

Chris shook his head. "Nah, I'll just stay here." He wanted to be alone.

"Suit yourself. I'll see you bright and early." George gave Chenda a fist bump and his share of the check and left.

Instead of going right away to his room, Chris plodded down the stairs and into the street, where a host of moto-dops offered him a ride. He ignored them and set out on foot across Sihanouk Boulevard. On the corner of Pasteur Street he found one pay phone stall still open. A woman with no legs offered him a plastic stool and dialed a number he wrote on a scrap of paper. When Lisa answered, the woman handed him her mobile phone and started a digital timer.

"Hello?" She'd been crying. He could tell.

"How are you?"

"Okay," she whispered. "I was hoping you'd call."

So now she wants to talk? "Why?"

"I want you to come home. I don't want to lose you."

He'd wanted to say hurtful things; they were on the tip of his tongue. Instead, he apologized.

She began to softly cry. "I'm sorry too. I don't blame you for what you did or for what happened to Mai."

The hard knot in his stomach relaxed a little. "It's good to hear that."

"I'm worried about you. Where are you? When are you coming home? I want you here with me."

He tensed again at the thought of going back home and dealing with Finto. "I can't come home now. I'm not going to let them kick me out of the country."

"We'll figure out something. Just come home."

"I can't."

"What are you going to do? Hide out forever in the Cambodian country-side? That's crazy. Please come home."

"I'm sorry. I can't. Listen, I'll be okay. George and I are just going to do some looking around for Mai."

"So he found you, then? That's makes me feel a lot better. Please don't do anything stupid."

"Since when have I ever done anything stupid?"

"No comment. Sweetheart, you've got to come home."

"I love you. I'll call you soon."

Something muffled was whispered, as if she had put her hand over the phone, then, "Wait. You left a message about a lead on Agent Gutierrez's voice mail. Everybody's been wondering what that's about."

"Forget it. It was nothing. A false alarm." He paused. "He's there, isn't he? David's there with you now."

"He's just—"

Jealousy stung him hard. "Bye." He barely resisted the urge to smash the phone on the pavement.

The woman punched the timer. "One thousand five hundred riel."

Chris handed her the money and bought some beer before heading back to Land & Sea.

$$\text{\Lambda}$$

Before the atrocities of the Khmer Rouge, Yun Naren lived with his mother, father, six brothers, and three sisters in a narrow shop-house in Phnom Penh. His father, a policeman, worked long hours and often came home in a foul mood. His mother, to supplement her husband's meager policeman's salary, sold fresh pork in the market. Though only five—the youngest of his family—when it all ended, he could still recall being with his mother in the market all day, running breathless and barefoot among the stalls with the other children. He remembered rounding a corner once and, slipping in the mud, flying sideways into a fishmonger, sending her two large catfish rolling through the dirt. The toothless hag had castigated him so ruthlessly and at such frightening volume that he'd peed his pants on the spot. He didn't know why he remembered that incident, but that's what he was thinking about when he heard men in the monastery courtyard speak his old name.

"Good evening, *lōōk sang,*" they said to the senior monk. "We are looking for Yun Naren."

Expecting these visitors, Yun had been unable to sleep and instead had lain awake thinking of the past. He'd known sooner or later they would find him, and when the father of the kidnapped girl showed up this morning—sent there by Sochua—he suspected it wouldn't be long. Because if Sochua knew where he was—well, she wouldn't simply keep that information to herself. She'd find a way to use the knowledge to her advantage with those who wanted to see him pay for his sin. Indeed, he *was* guilty, and he could never forget.

It was a year ago, September. He he'd been tooling slowly down the highway, a wide grin on his face, passing restaurants where the rich ate frog legs and drank Tiger beer in pavilions built over the water. Roadside workshops fashioned oversized fauna and fantastical beasts that would adorn temples and pagodas. Hopeful women waved handkerchiefs at passing motorists, hawking coconuts, painted gourds, charcoal, lotus flowers, insects, bamboo tubes of sticky rice, and unglazed pottery of every shape and size.

He couldn't stop smiling because he was on his way from Phnom Penh to pick up his fiancée, Theary, who was visiting her parents in Kampong Thom. He'd be able to tell her he had just received a promotion to second deputy chief of Sochua Nika's anti-trafficking squad. She'd be so proud of him, and she adored Sochua—although she'd certainly change her mind if she knew the extent of his relationship with her.

Yun also had to hide from Theary the fact that his promotion was, in truth, something of a mixed blessing. In his old assignment, he could and did supplement his income with small bribes and fines—nothing outrageous, only reasonable amounts, and when it was well deserved—and he often came home with more than fifty dollars for the month. Sochua, however, didn't tolerate her officers extorting the even greater sums that under any other commander would be a perquisite of his new position. Even though he'd now get a gasoline ration, which he could sell for a bit on the black market, he would hardly be able to feed himself on his new salary of thirty dollars per month, much less a family, and he had hoped that Theary would be able to quit her job as soon as she had a baby. He'd come up with something.

Yun wore a checkered *krama* over his nose and mouth and a scratched pair of bootleg Ray-Bans as protection against the tremendous amount of fine dust suspended in the air. He had plans to make it to Kampong Thom before the afternoon rain came and then return to the capital with Theary in the morning, but the wind had already whipped up, knocking over lightly loaded tables and flailing wind chimes. Enormous thunderheads raced from the horizon, full and powerful. In a great spectacle of sound and light, they would soon exhale all at once in a furious torrent that would fill every street and pathway and hole and bring all progress to a temporary standstill. But the fields were already to their brim with water, which meant the rains would soon stop, leaving the country without another drop for six months.

Away from the city the traffic got lighter, and Yun was able to overtake many older, more cantankerous motos. It'd taken him four years to save four hundred dollars to buy a second-hand Honda, and he'd waxed its black skin until it shone like a mirror. Some distance behind him he heard the blasts of a high-pitched horn growing rapidly closer. He didn't have to look to know that another arrogant government or military official was gaining on him, driving too fast down the center of the road, honking and expecting motos and other smaller vehicles to cede the pavement and take to the red-dirt shoulder.

He hated them. Those "untouchables" gang-raped the country while policemen were relegated to arresting only chicken thieves and other petty criminals.

He sighed and slowed to pull off the road, but the car approached faster than anticipated. A silver Toyota Land Cruiser burst past him only inches from his elbow, horn blaring. Without thinking, he shook a fist in protest. To his horror, brake lights immediately burned red, and the vehicle skidded to a dramatic stop in the middle of the highway.

The pounding of his heart drowned out all other noise. How could he have been so stupid? He pulled onto the unpaved shoulder and drove slowly past, deliberately avoiding eye contact. The SUV matched his speed, inching slowly closer. The road, built higher than the surrounding countryside to avoid inundation during the rainy season, was flanked on both sides by planted rice fields under several inches of water. If the vehicle got any closer he'd be forced off the shoulder and down the steep bank.

Yun hated what he had to do. He now had to bow and scrape—apologize for daring to shake a fist at a member of the privileged class of foul *nouveau riche* that exploited the country and its rapidly dwindling resources.

He stood his moto and approached the imposing vehicle with head deeply bowed, his palms steepled at his forehead. A tinted window slid down.

"I am deeply sorry I offended you, sir. It was my mistake. Please accept my most humble apology."

When at last he raised his eyes, it was into the barrel of a handgun. Terrified, he stumbled backward to raucous laughter.

Two somber men in gray uniforms got out of the front of the vehicle. Two men in jeans jumped from the back, clearly amused. Yun instantly realized the one with the gun was the mafia celebrity Chea Phyrom, the prime minister's thuggish nephew and number-one target of Sochua's anti-trafficking unit. He dropped to his knees to beg for his life.

"Please, sir. I—"

"Shut up." Phyrom kicked him in the small of his back.

A moto-pulled wagon loaded with gawking peasants stopped in the middle of the road to watch the show. Phyrom brandished his gun at them, inciting a general panic that caused a woman to fall off on her head as the wagon took off with a jolt. He had a good laugh over that and turned again to his captive.

He suddenly pelted Yun in the head with the grip of his gun. Pain tore through Yun's head, and he fell to all fours. His ears buzzed with a deafening whine.

Another man circled excitedly. "Do it!"

Phyrom pressed the barrel of the gun into Yun's temple. "Do you know who I am?"

Of course Yun knew! Chea Phyrom, son of that bastard general, Chea Prak, Thul's lackey. But he must beg to live. "Please. I'm...a...police...man."

Phyrom laughed. "Do you think I care? The egg doesn't hit the stone! Now don't move." He reared back and planted a boot squarely in Yun's ribs.

Yun collapsed, screaming, clutching his side. The pain...the bone...he could feel it...moving. Each tortured breath felt like his guts were being massaged through a hole in his side. "Please—"

"You shouldn't have fucked with me!" Phyrom gloated. "That's where you fucked up!"

Yun didn't care. He didn't care. Didn't care. *Just do it. Do it.*

"Hey, watch this," Phyrom said. He made a running start and gave Yun's Honda a good shove with his heel.

Helpless and choking, Yun watched his moto topple.

"Come on! Let's get out of here," Phyrom said to his entourage. They abandoned Yun on the roadside as the day's monsoon rain began to fall.

Yun's new moto. He found it on its side at the bottom of the embankment, half submerged in a rice paddy. Watching that rich scum destroy his pride and joy hurt him more than his broken ribs. He vowed revenge, but his anger and pride had blinded him to a practical reality: Chea Phyrom was above the law. Yet, something snapped inside him besides his ribs that afternoon, and he intended to get noticed.

Two months later Yun had watched a pair of bodyguards talking next to two late-model SUVs parked on Monivong Boulevard in front of Ya Tep Photo. He had no idea how long he'd been standing there waiting for the wedding party to emerge. He wasn't even sure where he'd slept the night before or how he'd wound up on the street with a jar of concentrated sulfuric acid. But he recalled he'd been aware of one sensation: regret that Chea Phyrom wouldn't be there to watch his sister die.

Now, of course, more than a year later, being of sound mind and having put the outside world behind him, Yun regretted his attack on the innocent, but regret was irrelevant. What was done was done. He got up and looked out the window. He could make out five men standing in the yard, one in monk's robes. If the monk's face showed any expression, it was obscured by shadow.

"Please wait. I will bring him," the monk said.

Yun took the cap off a plastic bottle. He hurriedly poured a small amount of a salt-like substance into the water; the combination would need almost five minutes to become lethal. When the elder monk whispered in his ear, he was ready. He was resigned.

"Little brother, there are men outside who want to see you."

"I need a few minutes."

The monk nodded in accord and left.

Carrying the liquid, Yun stole through a back door into an open pavilion. At the far end, an image of Lord Buddha sat serenely, barely visible in the dark. He approached the image and knelt before it. He removed the cap from the bottle and placed it next to him on the tile. His hands were shaking. He closed his eyes and took a deep breath. He began to weep—for the girl he'd disfigured; for his one-time fiancée, Theary; for his own wasted life. He'd expected much more. But...no time.

He wasn't afraid to die. No. That would be just like going to sleep—peace at last. That's not was he was afraid of. He picked up the poison. Would they call him a coward?

There was a sudden commotion behind him, a blow and a ringing in his ears. A sweaty body tackled him. A sack was pulled over his head.

Yun panicked, shrieking. He struggled. This was the nightmare he had night after night! This is what he feared the most! *Of course* they would take him alive!

CHAPTER 23

Chea Phyrom teed up next to his father on the second floor of the Senate driving range. He hooked another shot into the net.

"I hate this stupid game."

Chea Prak nailed the bull's-eye at the end of the range, only one hundred and twenty-five meters. He teed up another ball, his back to his son, his bodyguards expressionless.

"The father of the American girl has talked to Yun Naren." A satisfying crack sent his ball straight to the limit of the range again.

"What?" Phyrom dropped his Callaway. It didn't matter; it was a Chinese fake anyway. "How do you know?"

He waited while his father casually readied another ball and swung. A perfect shot, just over the bulls-eye. The game, the waiting, the feigned non-chalance—there was not one thing his father did that wasn't calculated, a power play, orchestrated to unnerve and infuriate him.

"We've been tailing him ever since you took her," the elder Chea replied, shielding his eyes to follow his ball. "I don't like it here. Next time let's go to Parkway."

"Why?"

"The range is too short. I hit the net every time." He teed up another ball.

Phyrom cracked his knuckles. "Not 'why do you want to go to Parkway,' but 'why have you been tailing the American?'"

Another beautiful shot. "You see. That ball would've easily gone two hundred and twenty-five meters."

Prak handed his club to a bodyguard and took a cool towel offered by a young hostess. He wiped his face and turned to his son.

"Don't be an idiot. Did you never think Mr. Kelly might do something stupid? Did you know he bought a gun? Did you know he sat in front of your office on two separate occasions watching the building? What if he attacked you and your bodyguards killed him? What then?"

Phyrom would someday get even with his father for the humiliation he had endured over the years. He dreamed about it day and night—fantasized about it. "Why did he go see Yun? How did he find him?"

"Sochua. She told the American Yun could help him find his daughter."

Phyrom drove his fist into his palm. "Ah, that whore! And what did Yun tell him?"

"What could he possibly know?"

"So you know where Yun is now? Tell me. I'm going to rip his head off!"

"You'll do nothing."

"What! But why? After what he did to Nimol?"

"Yun was picked up and brought to me."

"Let me have him!"

"Stop shouting, you imbecile. This is why I will take care of him. You can't control yourself." He smiled.

"So then why are you telling me this?"

Chea Prak removed his glove and took a long drink of water. "I made a deal with Sochua. She gave us Yun in exchange for the girl's freedom."

"What? She gave us Yun for the American girl? Why? What does she care about her? And, anyway, I told you I don't have her."

"What, Son? You don't think the great General Sochua Nika could be motivated simply by a desire to help a little girl return to her family?"

"Not for a second." Sochua could be expected to drive a much harder bargain.

"That's exactly what I thought. Maybe you're not as stupid as everyone thinks you are."

"No. I'm not as stupid as *you* think I am. So why did Sochua really help us find him? What does she really want?"

"I don't know, but I'm going to find out. And that, Son, is the reason I have not killed him. That is the reason I will not let you 'rip his head off.' That is what I intend to force him to tell us before I kill him for what he did to your sister. Now, do you finally understand?"

"Yes, but why should I release the girl if you already have Yun?"

"Because I made a deal with Sochua."

"We have what we want. Screw Sochua!"

Prak stepped into his son's face. "You *will* release the girl," he snarled. "Do you understand?"

Phyrom bit his lip, very aware of the two men in the shadows.

"You've disobeyed me long enough," his father continued. "Have your people drop her at the nearest police station tomorrow. When I'm finished with Yun, I'll let you have him." He nodded to his men. "Let's go."

Phyrom noticed the girl cowering in the corner. "Get the fuck out of here!" She shrieked and ran down the stairs.

He would never release the American girl, even if it meant he could get his hands on Yun.

He picked up his driver and flung it onto the grass. It landed near the twenty-meter marker. He'd kill her if he had to, but he would never let her go. Not for his father, not for Sochua, not for anyone. They'd learn their lesson alongside the American diplomat: he was *not* to be fucked with.

⚔

Chris wolfed down the English breakfast at Land & Sea and hailed the nearest moto-dop.

"Moto! Take me to Big S."

Big S, the first and only building of its kind in Cambodia, rose incongruently adjacent to the old Central Market, towering several air-conditioned stories above its surroundings and capped with a dome of blue glass. At night its side streets became a drive-through sex market where young pimps negotiated with motorists before ushering a girl into a backseat. On slow nights the pimps blocked traffic and simply shoved girls in unlocked cars without asking.

At nine o'clock in the morning the mall was already filling with shoppers, touts, families out for a stroll, and primping teenagers traveling in packs. A crowd of Cambodian tourists posed for souvenir photos on the front steps. Chris pushed his way through and checked to make sure he was still being followed. The moto-dop in question had parked his scooter with an unencumbered view of the front door and appeared content to wait for him to return.

The last time Chris had been in Big S—the day after it opened—thrill seekers had stood at the base of the escalator daring one another to give the newfangled contraption a try. Mai had amused herself by riding up and down the escalator, waving to the crowd below, while Chris and Lisa watched from a table in the food court. By this time the novelty had worn off.

Chris took the escalator to the eighth-floor observation platform and looked for a minute at the best view of Phnom Penh. He took in the entire city, fantasizing that his gaze might touch Mai somehow and she'd know he was looking. Maybe he'd feel her presence in one quarter or another.

But he felt nothing. To the south was Wat Koh and Olympic Stadium. Then Independence Monument, and, beyond it, Boeung Keng Kang, where Lisa would be at absolute rock bottom—like he was.

Chris put his head against the glass and closed his eyes. He'd been strung out on adrenaline and anger and grief for days, a bundle of raw nerves. How much longer could he take it? He didn't know. But he had to get to Sihanoukville.

He took the elevator down to the second-floor parking garage and jogged down the textured ramp and onto the street at the back of the mall. His tail was nowhere in sight. That was easy. He hailed a motorcycle taxi to take him back across town.

He had never been to George's, and so it took him and the moto-dop a while to find his place between numbers seventy-nine and four. It was just like all the other expatriate houses—enclosed by a high wall topped with razor wire. He pounded on the compound door and, finding it unlocked, pushed it open.

George looked at him from under the hood of a vintage military jeep. "I was beginning to get worried about you."

"Did you know there are three number twenty-fours on this street?"

"Oh, I guess I should've warned you about that. Any trouble getting rid of your tail?"

"Like giving candy to a baby." Chris pointed at the jeep. "What's this?"

"1945 Willys. And they say the Americans were never in Cambodia. Ha! They were still using these suckers in the seventies. Got it for three hundred dollars. Do you have any idea how much collectors would pay for this baby back in the States?"

"Haven't the slightest." Cars were not Chris's thing. "Where are the doors?"

"You know," George said, letting the hood drop, "this jeep won World War II. Funny thing, though. Willys was bought by Kaiser, Kaiser was bought by AMC, AMC was bought by Chrysler, and then Chrysler was bought by Daimler-Benz. I guess the Germans got their revenge, after all."

"That's nice, George, but can it get us to Sihanoukville?"

"Of course it can. Don't be such a friggin' pessimist."

Chris circled the vehicle, appraising it critically. He poked the stiff canvas roof. A long tear in the material focused a wide arc of sunlight on the passenger seat.

"What about the rain?"

"Rainy season's over. It's not gonna rain."

"It rained the day before yesterday."

A loud creak of hinges startled them and they spun around, tensed for action. A slight Cambodian man slid inside George's compound and quickly closed the gate behind him. He wore dark sunglasses and a floppy hat pulled low on his head. A *krama* covered his face.

Chris would have been alarmed if the man hadn't looked so ridiculous. "What the hell?"

The man shuffled silently to the jeep and climbed in the back.

"Well, I guess this means Mong's coming with us."

"You very help," Chris said in Khmer. "My daughter. You help. Thank you."

Mong stared at him, blinking.

He tried a second time. Mong remained expressionless.

"Doesn't talk much, does he?" Chris asked.

Mong said something and George chuckled. Chris had learned his Khmer from a professor in a classroom at the Department of State's Foreign Service Institute in suburban Virginia, and this definitely was not the same Khmer spoken by Mong.

"What? What did he say?"

"He says he can't talk to you because your Khmer hurts his ears. But I can assure you he said it in a nice way."

"Sure. Whatever. Can we go now?"

▲

On the phone in Los Angeles, exiled dissident Sambo Rithy listened to Kep, his most trusted advisor, repeat a familiar refrain.

"People here are calling you a coward. Those who were arrested for criticizing Thul on Human Rights Day last year have captured the headlines by remaining in jail. They've become martyrs, and you've become a memory."

Sambo had no intention of returning home to face the music. He'd sampled a Cambodian jail once before, and it had not suited him well; in fact, he'd contracted tuberculosis.

"Not yet," he said. "Now's not the time."

Sambo conceded that there were those both within and without his party who'd begun to question his relevance. A prominent journalist and one-time supporter asked on the front page of the widely read *Rakusmei Kampuchea*, "Has Sambo Rithy Lost His Taste for the Fight? Opposition Leader Fears Jail Time." But even when he couldn't hear himself think over the noise of those who would have him change the name of the Sambo Rithy Party—his party—Sambo refused to accept that he had made a grave strategic error by remaining abroad for so long.

"You are out of touch with the reality here," Kep insisted. "It's been more than three years."

"I'm well aware of how long it's been!"

In 2013, with arrest imminent, Sambo had borrowed his security guard's uniform and sneaked to the American embassy. The next day a special legislative session was convened to lift his parliamentary immunity. When it became apparent the vote would succeed, Paris Jefferson, the Americans' newly arrived deputy chief of mission, escorted him directly to the airport in an official vehicle, flying two American flags on the front.

"Technically, I'm not supposed to do this," Jefferson had said in fluent Khmer. "Only the chief of mission can fly the flags."

"Well, maybe by the time I come back to Cambodia, you'll be ambassador, and we won't be breaking the rules."

She'd assured him he wouldn't be gone that long. The US granted him political asylum, and within days he'd joined his wife and two boys in the immodest Brentwood estate they'd been living in for more than a year, tired of harassment back home. Thul's kangaroo courts convicted Sambo in absentia of criminal defamation of character and sentenced him to two years in prison for remarks he'd made on Honeybee Radio. Three years had passed quickly.

"Well," hissed Kep, "if you don't come back, Sochua takes over the movement."

"A woman? Never!"

The advent of Sochua had been a surprise to Sambo—even though it was now apparent to anyone with half a brain that she'd been slithering into position for years. She'd remained unquestionably Thul's man until she'd landed in the perfect spot to establish her populist bonafides and a credible reputation for giving a shit. But then she overplayed her hand when she disrupted the livelihood of members of the PM's own family—even if it was the PM's disgraced nephew, Chea Phyrom. So the PM fired her and created the monster that "reluctantly" agreed to breathe life into a popular opposition movement that Sambo had created. She was loved, but, still, the people that mattered would never accept her. No, she would never take over.

"You're a fool," Kep said.

"That's enough!" Sambo, unapologetic, uncompromising, and untainted, had been the undisputed leader of Thul's only serious opposition since the death of Prince Chhun in 2002, and he wasn't going to yield to some *arriviste* moll overnight! "You just keep them in line! I will figure out something!"

Sambo hung up. It was damn late, and he was tired. Sochua! Ridiculous. He would bide his time, and sooner or later—when Thul was gone and the country was ready—he would become prime minister and the architect of Cambodia's modernization.

▲

Deliberately dressed down for the occasion, General Sochua Nika joined the twelve people already assembled in her formal dining room.

"Please, please, be seated. I am so sorry to keep you waiting, gentlemen." This was a lie; Sochua had kept the group waiting unnecessarily. Nevertheless, her guests were all smiles, if not fawning. She waited until everyone had taken a seat. "Now," she asked kindly, "is there room for me?" She took her seat at the head of the table. "Charya, tea please," she called.

There was not a man in the room—and there were no other women present—who did not resent the fact that he was now obliged to accept that Sochua had unquestionably usurped leadership of their popular movement—and she knew it.

"Thank you for agreeing to meet here today. I don't seem to know from one day to the next whether I am under house arrest or not." Everyone laughed politely.

The men at the table represented nearly every local human rights and labor organization that planned to take part in the International Human Rights Day Rally on Wednesday in Olympic Stadium, and she already knew which ones had reluctantly accepted her much-needed support for their flagging cause and those who could hardly stand the sight of her out of their own selfish vanity. Representatives of the Sambo Rithy Party, a major sponsor of the rally, were conspicuously absent.

"I wonder, my friends, if we are making any progress," Sochua said wistfully.

Charya served tea, and Sochua let the men talk. The truth was that the Cambodian radical opposition was not radical at all—especially after the arrests at last year's rally—and in reality was a self-censoring group that repeatedly shied away from confronting the government. Cowards. She required a significant change in tactics.

When finally there was a lull in the discussion, Sochua's old friend, Ngor Samnang, from the Cambodian Independent Workers' Federation, leaned into the center of the table and turned to her. "What is your opinion, Nika?"

Of course, Sochua had made certain Ngor knew her opinion and was already in support. "I believe we should lead a march from the International Human Rights Day event to the Ministry of Justice."

Panh Bunchhoeun, also of the CIWF and Ngor's rival, almost choked on his tea. "For what purpose?"

"To demand the release of the leaders of your organizations who were detained last year."

The room erupted with several simultaneous heated discussions. "It is illegal," said Seng Sovan. General Seng had earned a name for himself—and jail time—in 2000 for refusing to participate in a brutal crackdown on "terrorists" who were nothing more than peaceful protesters.

Sochua nodded. "Indeed."

"This confrontational approach," sputtered Norodom Nath, minor royalty, "it's not the Cambodian way."

"Of course," said Sochua, "I submit to your greater authority and experience in the matter."

Norodom gave a polite nod and grunted.

"But," she went on, "seven men remain in jail. We have already lost our dear friend Pang Sokkruen. With due respect, it is the prime minister who has been confrontational. Yet, in detaining the leaders of your movements, the prime minister has united you like never before. He has always conquered us by dividing us."

"General, you have come late to this movement," said Norodom. "Forgive me, but you speak as if you've suffered as we have."

Sochua lowered her gaze and said nothing. Suffered? Norodom spent half of each year on the Côte d'Azur!

"Yet you cannot deny General Sochua's popularity among the masses," said Ngor. "With her popular appeal and a united front, we can succeed. We must march now, united and purposeful."

Sochua bowed her head slightly. "I humbly offer myself as an instrument to achieve our goal, but only if we are all in agreement."

It would be the largest demonstration in Cambodian history—far larger than Sambo Rithy's undeniably impressive march in 2013—and virtually every man in the room had initially opposed the idea. Yet Sochua had met with each of them personally over the past several days, working her formidable charm. She extolled the great contributions and sacrifices they had made to the cause, stroked their egos, issued but a few handsomely veiled threats and a great deal more promises, and at the end of the day they could not deny her untainted image and clear popular support. There remained among them a small number of holdouts, but before they adjourned, the group unanimously, with some reservations, agreed to support a march. Sochua graciously accepted their decision, marveling at how easily men could be manipulated.

⚔

In happier times the Kelly family had driven the road to Sihanoukville to stay at Rose Beach Resort, hands down the best hotel in town, their days of backpacker hostels having ended with the advent of Mai. Built with a grant from the US Agency for International Development, the highway was decidedly the best and most important road in Cambodia, linking the capital with the country's only deep-water port. On no other road in the country could Chris reach speeds close to sixty miles per hour, and on a good day the family could make the trip in little over three hours. George's jeep wasn't capable of such high speeds, though just how fast it was moving wasn't clear since the speedometer remained stuck on zero.

Progress was slow. George stopped to pee in the grass, top up the oil, pee on a tree.

"I swear, I've never seen a little girl go to the bathroom as much as you do."

Mong unfolded a poncho and pulled it over his head, and within minutes the rain began. The hole in the roof funneled water onto Chris as George struggled to see without a functioning windshield wiper.

"I thought you said the rainy season was over," Chris shouted over the din.

"Yeah, but this here," George shouted back, "is what you call a nonseasonal rain."

Five hours into the journey Chris awoke to a crack followed by a rhythmic slap.

George pounded the steering wheel. "Damn it! Damn it! Damn it!"

"You got a spare, don't you?"

"Of course I got a spare. Just don't have a jack."

"Great." At least the rain had stopped.

They pulled off the road onto a dirt track near a small cluster of huts and a drink stand. A group of men sat in the shade playing cards. Mong walked away toward them.

Chris kicked the offending tire. "Son of a *bitch*!" At this rate they would never get to Sihanoukville. He kicked the tire again. "Hey, you know what today is? Do you know? It's been exactly a week since Mai was kidnapped. A fucking *week*!"

"Hey, man, I know it's been—"

"And what were we thinking? Trying to drive halfway across Cambodia in this stupid piece of shit antique! What the hell were we thinking?"

George screwed up his mouth and looked away.

Chris strode into the highway. "I'm going to try to flag someone down." He waved his arms at a white SUV with diplomatic plates. The vehicle drove around him, honking, and sped on.

"Fucking Brits! So much for the 'special relationship!'"

"Hey, Chris. You gotta see this," George said, pointing.

Mong directed as eight men lifted the rear end of the jeep off the ground. Chris watched in awe as two more shoved a tree stump under the axle. Within minutes the tire was changed, and, for the cost of a round of drinking coconuts, they were on the road.

"Mong saves the day again," Chris muttered gratefully, recalling the night in The Black Pussy.

In another hour they were on the outskirts of Sihanoukville, where they stopped to buy gas. It was almost four o'clock; a drive that normally took three and a half had taken six. The gas station consisted of a clapboard shelter and a wooden stand holding several glass bottles of dubious petrol. A young woman poured all six liters of her stock in the tank while George relieved himself in a ditch behind the building.

Mong sat on a stump, drinking a Coke. He pointed at a tree and began to talk.

George climbed up the slope, zipping his pants. "What's he saying?"

"Something about that tree over there and when he was a boy."

"He say," the woman said, "in time Khmer Rouge he job—" She said something in Khmer to George.

"'Bark,'" he said. "The word is *bark*."

"He job," she continued, "take bark from tree for make all clothes black. Khmer Rouge say make all clothes black that time. He job find bark for make clothes black."

Mong really got going. He pointed at horrific scars on his ankles and wrists and gestured as if he were placing something on his head. The gas station attendant looked expectantly at George.

"He says that one time while he was out gathering bark he tried to eat a cricket, and he got caught, and so they tortured him. They chained him up and, well, basically, they water-boarded him."

"Damn."

"Yeah, Mong's been through some shit. Last year he made a pilgrimage up to Anlong Veng to piss on Pol Pot's grave. That bastard died peacefully in his sleep, you know."

Mong took from the stall owner a pack of cigarettes and handed her his empty bottle. He grabbed his spare cloth sack from the jeep and began walking in the direction of town, sandals flapping.

Chris watched him for a moment, utterly bewildered. "Where's he going?"

"No telling. Come on."

"We're just going to leave him?"

"Looks like *he* just left *us*."

The woman touched Chris's arm as he got in the jeep. "Hey, mister. You need pay for he cigarettes and Coca-Cola."

George laughed and climbed behind the wheel.

"I was at the rally all day," Allison Rosenburg said, "and I didn't see any banner. Nobody did. Then a couple of days later all those guys were arrested in the middle of the night, and nobody had any idea what Thul was talking about. Then Thul puts some banner on prime-time TV, citing it as 'an example of the underhanded tactics of dangerous radicals.' The whole thing was just stupid."

Rosenburg, USAID senior Democracy and Governance officer, and Paris Jefferson had simultaneously received word from their contacts within the human rights movement that General Sochua Nika planned to lead a march on Wednesday from the International Human Rights Day rally to the Ministry of Justice in order to demand the release of seven political prisoners. The two women now sat in the office of American Ambassador to Cambodia Richard Schroeder, along with Political Section Chief Paul Richter, junior officer Hassan Hosseini, and the new Public Affairs officer, Matt Hernandez.

"Or quite brilliant," Schroeder said, "depending upon your point of view. What do you think, Paris?"

"I think we should issue a statement supporting Sochua's plan." On Schroeder's orders Jefferson had wasted a good deal of her past year badgering the Cambodian government to release the eight activists—seven, now that Pang Sokkruen had died in custody—who had been arrested for their involvement in last year's rally. Schroeder was naïve, in her opinion, to think Prime Minister Thul would ever negotiate in good faith and let the activists go without a great deal more pressure. After all, Thul had created the entire crisis out of thin air as an excuse to lock them up—some hard truths about the PM were supposedly seen on a protest banner, and then he arrested the leaders of virtually every local human rights group.

"What did the banner actually say?" asked Hosseini.

"Well," said Jefferson, "the one they showed on TV said that Thul was a Vietnamese lackey who had received a kickback to settle a border dispute in Vietnam's favor."

Hosseini smiled sardonically.

Ambassador Schroeder addressed his new public affairs officer. "Don't make a statement, but if anybody asks, we, of course, support the release of the activists, something that we have been calling for all along."

Jefferson went back to her office feeling deeply depressed. Although she supported Sochua's march, Prime Minister Thul would likely use it as an excuse to crack down even further on dissent. After all, he had a new benefactor in the Chinese, and they provided their aid with no questions asked—or at least no uncomfortable questions regarding human rights. But what tore at Jefferson's heart was that Mai Kelly had been missing for over a week, and the investigation was at a standstill. National Police Chief Nhim Saray hadn't returned her calls since the published reports that his US visa had been denied. The prime minister had assured the ambassador that investigators were leaving no stone unturned, but she wasn't stupid. The idiots Nhim had reassigned to the case amazed her only in their lack of competence.

On her desk was a small stack of photocopies of Mai in a soccer jersey. She took a thumbtack from her desk drawer and tacked one on the wall to her left. This brought a tear to her eye that she dabbed with a Kleenex. Mai was a special child. Jefferson had once wanted to have kids of her own, but that ship had sailed and gone. The truth was that the Foreign Service didn't lend itself to dual-career families—although the Kellies had been able to pull it off—and few men were willing to be trailing spouses. This had changed some, but it was too late for her. She'd met someone once, but that was more than a decade ago. It hadn't worked out.

She packed up her things. She planned to leave early and visit Lisa. Maybe she'd stop by the happy hour at the Le Royal afterward—but she hated to drink alone.

Chapter 24

The jeep crested a hill, and Chris could see below them the shimmering Gulf of Thailand and a number of container ships awaiting their turn to unload. He and George headed for Sihanoukville's port since its environs included the infamous Phum Thmei—New Market or "Chicken Farm," as it was known to foreigners. George had given him the scoop on the place; it was an isolated stretch of primitive brothels and short-lived nightclubs staffed by as many as a thousand mainly ethnic Vietnamese and widely known to employ underage girls. The Cambodian government periodically made a show of cleaning up the area—the names changed, the sex workers stayed out of view for a few nights—but at the end of the day it was business as usual: any brand of sex for as little as five dollars, plus tips, day or night.

The principal street of Phum Thmei was quiet at five p.m. No working women were in sight, a few bored moto-dops chatted on corners, two bone-thin dogs fought over a soiled condom, and barefoot children barely registered their presence. The Farm reeked of decay and raw sewage, but all was quiet.

George stopped in front of a two-story cinder-block-and-glazed-tile bungalow. The red lights were off at this time of day. A sign read "Foot Massage For U One Dollar."

"This is the place. Don't forget what Arthur said about the dog."

"Dog?"

"He said she's got a mean dog."

Chris followed as George, in flip-flops, ducked through the open door. Several young women slid off a pink vinyl living room set and greeted them warmly. If they were surprised to see customers so early, they didn't let on.

"Hello," one purred. "You need full-body massage? You want virgin?" She tapped the shoulder of a young colleague. "This Samnang. She virgin for you."

George dropped onto the sofa, sinking deeply and catapulting two women off the opposite end and onto their feet. They giggled. Chris preferred to stand. A woman put two bottles of water on a coffee table.

"Cold water you like?" she asked with a flourish of her hand.

"We're looking for Srey Ni," George said.

The women looked at each other. "Mama," one called.

A fortyish woman appeared, drying her hands on an apron. She sported a purple punch perm and batted inch-long false eyelashes at them, an angelic smile plastered on her powdered face. Then she looked at George hugging his knees on her couch, and her jaw dropped.

"You? You?" She shook a fist in George's face. "You get fuck out now!"

"Oh, shit. Chris, help me get up." He thrust out his hand. "We need to go."

Chris grabbed and pulled with all his might; George actually looked frightened, and that didn't bode well.

Srey Ni snatched a broom from a corner. "Go! Now! And you friend too. You no welcome here."

George rolled off the couch onto all fours. Srey Ni whacked him on the head with the broom.

Chris grabbed for it. "Stop it!"

Srey Ni rounded on him, wielding her weapon like a broadsword. She swung and missed. She tried again, and Chris dodged backward. He tripped over George's feet and landed on his rear on the coffee table. The table wobbled and collapsed in pieces beneath him. Srey Ni stopped, her face frozen in horror. The other women gasped, their eyes agog.

George yanked Chris to his feet like it was nothing. "Run!"

"I kill you!" Srey Ni screamed, giving chase.

Outside, a salt-and-pepper mutt dashed from the back of the building and latched on to the hem of Chris's shorts.

"Holy shit!" he cried. "Help!"

George limp-jogged past him to the jeep with Srey Ni in hot pursuit, broom raised to strike.

"George, look out!" Who *was* this woman?

She nailed George on the head again. "Go! And no come back!"

George wrenched the stick from Srey Ni's grasp and broke it over a knee. He hurled the pieces down the street.

She attacked him with her fists. "You motherfucker!"

Fending her off with one hand, George climbed in the jeep and started the engine. "Chris! Get in!"

"Well, I'm trying, but there's a dog attached to my leg!"

George reached across the car, grabbed Chris by the belt, and pulled him mostly into the vehicle, dog and all. He stabbed the jeep into gear and the shift knob came off in his hand. The dog was scratching the hell out of Chris's leg.

"Goddang it!" George threw the shift knob over his shoulder. "Hang on!"

He did a doughnut, slinging off the dog and scattering a family of chickens. Srey Ni picked up the discarded knob and threw it. It bounced off the hood with a *thunk*. The men raced downhill in the opposite direction from which they'd come and slid to a stop where the road ended at the beach. Chris sat staring out at the ocean in the cloud of dust they'd raised, his mind a total blank.

"Uh, sorry 'bout that," George offered finally.

"I take it you know her."

"You could say that. We shut her operation down in Phnom Penh a few years back. Looks like she's moved her business down south. Didn't recognize her at first...but, uh, I guess that's her."

"Well, that's just great. She was our only lead." Chris needed a minute. He got his feet tangled trying to get out of the jeep and nearly fell onto the ground. "Goddam it!" He could just make out Srey Ni at the top of the hill shaking her fist at them, her unkind words lost on the wind. "I'm going for a walk."

He trudged across the sand and threw off his sport sandals. He waded into the water up to his ankles and screamed into the wind just for the hell of it. A lone vendor watched dispassionately. Seven days. Mai had now been gone seven days, and he was no closer to finding her than on day one. There wouldn't be any big thing. There wouldn't be any showdown or dramatic rescue. It would be just like this; nothing at all. Mai would just fade away, and they would never know. For the rest of their lives they would never know what really happened. There would never, ever be peace. Ever.

"You want buy?"

Chris nearly jumped out of his skin. He whirled around. A man offered a carved shell in each outstretched hand.

"Get away from me!" He slapped the shells out of the vendor's hands. "Get the hell away from me!"

The vendor stoically collected his wares from the shallow surf.

George caught up to them. "Chris, come on."

The three men in the water faced one another in a circle; it looked some sort of odd ceremony.

"What are we going to do, George? What the hell are we going to do? We got nothing. We got no plan, we got no contacts, we got nothing. This is not fucking working!"

"Listen, we'll find an Internet café in town and figure it out. People blog about this stuff; they brag about it online. Give me an hour and a half of decent Internet connection, and I'll know where we need to look. We'll find her."

"Yeah, but we can't get inside the brothels. They'll be looking for me, and you're like a walking billboard."

"You want girl," the salesman ventured.

"Yeah, I want a girl!" Chris unfolded Mai's picture and shoved it at the man's chest. "This girl. I want this girl. I'm looking for *this* girl!"

The vendor took the paper and ran his fingers over Mai's face. He shook his head. "No."

Chris handed him two thousand riel and took a shell. He threw it as far as he could to the horizon. The three of them stared after it.

"Man, Mai can throw, like, twice that far," George said finally, shaking his head.

"Shut up."

"No, seriously. That was some wimpy-ass throw." He turned to the vendor. The man shrugged.

"Well, I never was very good at sports," Chris mumbled.

George shook him by the shoulders. "Come on. Let's go find somewhere to spend the night, and then we'll figure out a plan."

Sihanoukville, a low-slung port town and Cambodia's largest seaside resort, boasted a fair number of paved streets and a well-earned reputation as Asia's cheapest sex tourism destination. The city's renown for freewheeling sleaze attracted a multinational clientele, as well as fugitives of diverse backgrounds—an unknown number of reclusive Russians maintained a fortified compound with an airstrip overlooking the town—who could settle down and even open a brothel or bar as long as they had enough cash to keep the police happy. Despite land grabs by wealthy Cambodians that had resulted in a scattering of flashy hotels, Sihanoukville, a sister city of Seattle, maintained a tumbledown desperate feel that undoubtedly held charm for wannabe pimps and hard-core sex tourists.

For this very reason Chris and family had normally steered around the city unless it was to go to the Alligator Ranch—an open-air restaurant run by a cryptic Ukrainian that kept an alligator chained in a shallow pool an arm's length from diners—for excellent "beef" stroganoff. Instead, they spent their time on the private beach of Rose Beach Resort at the same time as they disdained the exclusive nature of their vacation. The Kellies had invited George and his wife, Molly, to join them on their next trip at New Year's.

Chris's last visit to Sihanoukville had been in official capacity to attend a reception aboard the *USS Gary* on the occasion of it being the first US ship to dock in a Cambodian port since the Mayaguez Incident. The last official battle of the Vietnam War, the incident was fought by US Marines not in Vietnam against the Vietnamese but in Cambodia and against the Khmer Rouge. The *USS Gary* had arrived on a humanitarian and public-relations mission, renovating a local clinic and providing medical care, and while diplomats hosted local dignitaries on deck, the sailors took over the town for one night of shore leave, a boon for local sex workers.

Chris put that out of his mind as he and George rolled into town in baking heat in front of the long-distance bus terminal—headquarters of the local moto-dop mafia and point of entry for low-budget travelers down from the capital. Within stumbling distance of the terminal, the longtime tourist mecca of Victory Hill—twenty-four-hour bars with names like Sin Central, Motherfucker, and Pussy Galore—had seen its better days. Still, with plenty of bamboo thatch huts in which grunge backpackers, seasoned expats, and sex tourists looking for what Thailand used to be could stay for only the price of drinks and food, it managed to hang on.

Sucking dust on the garbage-strewn main thoroughfare, Ekareach Street, they continued past the dreaded police commissariat. If the police, as a professional force, did not entirely meet international standards in the capital, Sihanoukville by comparison had no functioning municipal police presence at all and was, rather, at the mercy of a criminal gang got out in official uniform. Chris had witnessed this firsthand—he'd once had to interrupt the family's beach vacation to deal with an urgent Am-Cit case.

A vacationing American couple had been robbed and beaten with a metal pipe by two men on New Beach on the night of Victory over the Genocidal Regime Day the previous January. Bleeding and traumatized, the pair begged a moto-dop to carry them to CT Clinic, but instead he dropped them at Sihanoukville Hospital, a public institution, because it paid a higher commission. The hospital, however, wouldn't treat them since they had been relieved of all their money. Finally, a sympathetic Russian paid the hospital to stitch up the man—done without anesthesia—and then carried them to the police station in the wee hours of the morning. The officers on duty, when they discovered the pair had no money to pay for their services, arrested them for disturbing their sleep.

The Russian fled and called the American embassy, which ordered Chris to investigate. A surprise visit by an American diplomat alone was enough to make the police back down and release their prisoners. The couple demanded the police investigate the crime, but when Chris privately explained that would require facilitating payments and was unlikely to achieve a positive outcome, they took his advice and money and caught the next bus back to Phnom Penh. On his current visit to Sihanoukville, Chris intended to avoid the police at all costs.

As he and George neared the Vietnamese consulate, a moto-dop honked past carrying no fewer than five passengers: two toddlers in the arms of a stoic mother and a man on the tail-end holding in the air a dark-red intravenous bag attached to an elderly woman in the middle. A tattered billboard advertised a shooting range—for a hundred bucks tourists could blow up a live cow with a rocket-propelled grenade—and another, newer sign reminded passersby of the prime minister's patronage of a local public works project. Plastic bags floated gently on the sea breeze.

They entered downtown and the chaos of Psar Leu Market, just south of the Blue Mountain red-light district, dubbed, George told him, "simply *the* place to shag" by a sympathetic Royal Mail retiree from Liverpool proudly blogging of his Southeast Asia sex holiday.

Chris shook his head. "You think this is what hell looks like?"

"Not far off, I reckon."

By the time they found a place to stay on Champion Beach, which was no more than a raised platform with a thatch roof, a pair of hammocks, and mosquito netting, it was almost dark. Champion was a barang ghetto of beachfront bars with marijuana-laced "happy" pizza and fifty-cent beer where painted "taxi girls" strung out on highly addictive methamphetamine-like *yama* traipsed through the sand in high heels and short skirts. A didgeridoo-playing hippy and an amateur fire juggler danced around a bonfire of beach trash and scrap, providing free entertainment for an unimpressed party of scruffy backpackers. A two-man band played Lynyrd Skynyrd to empty seats in a bar powered by a diesel generator rumbling in the distance.

"You want girl?" the hotel owner asked. "Yama? Pot?"

George shook his head. "No thanks. Something to drink."

"Whiskey? Beer?"

"I'll take a ginger ale if you got it."

Their congenial host's young son shimmied up a nearby coconut palm, brought down two nuts, and deftly opened them with a rusty machete. He presented them with a straw and a smile. George collapsed into a plastic chair with a groan, and its hind legs buckled under his weight. Chris didn't even laugh at the sight of him on his back in the sand, covered with coconut water; instead, he headed down the beach.

"Hey, where you going? Can't we rest just five minutes? Pressing that clutch was hell on my knee."

Chris ignored him.

"Well, try not to get shot."

Chris approached a scrawny tourist with pierced nipples lying in a hammock reading pornography by the fading light.

"Excuse me."

"'Sup?"

He held up Mai's photo. "You haven't seen this girl, have you?"

The man didn't take his eyes off the magazine. "Nope."

"Would you mind taking a look? It's real important to me."

The tourist took the sheet and gave it a cursory glance. He shook his head. "Nope. Haven't seen her."

"My name's Joe, by the way." Chris wasn't sure why he'd lied.

"Hey, Joe," the man sang, "where you goin' with that gun in your hand?" He put his cigarette in his mouth, leaving his hands free to do a lazy air guitar.

"Oh, I get it: Hendrix. So, you been around here for a while?"

"Cheapest pussy on the planet."

Chris's blood began to boil. "You like to do it with little girls too?"

"I think you better get your ass out of here."

He could've done it. God, he wanted to do it. Break this asshole's nose with one swift uppercut.

George tapped him on the shoulder. "Yo. This is not the battle you need to fight right now."

Chris let George put his arm around his shoulders and steer him away.

"Hey, fuck you," the man yelled after them, "and the horse you rode in on. Fuck you."

Back at the hut, George put a finger in his Chris's face. "Dude, we have got to keep a low profile. Phyrom's people are going to be on the lookout for us, and have you forgotten that you might be in Cambodia illegally? There might be a warrant out for your arrest? What the hell's wrong with you?"

Chris shoved him off. "I think you know what the hell is wrong with me!" He walked away and sat down against a palm tree. He let his head fall back against the trunk. How the hell was he supposed to keep a low profile when Mai was missing? How?

The palm tree shook hard. "What the—"

George had sat down against the opposite side. He was massaging his knee.

Chris looked up at the coconuts hanging high above their heads. "I'm sorry about all this, George."

"No need to apologize."

"Lisa'll never forgive me, you know. I'm going to lose her too."

$$\lambda$$

Chea Prak grimaced at the rank smell in the room. The tropical heat didn't help. "So we finally meet face-to-face."

Yun Naren lay naked on the wire mesh of a rusty bed frame, his face a swollen pulp, a pool of urine on the checkerboard tile. Chea was impressed; his boys had softened him up nicely. Yun's split lips twitched.

Chea drew close. "Got something to say, have you?"

Yun spat weakly into his face. Chea calmly removed a handkerchief from his trousers pocket and wiped it off. This was going to be fun.

"Ah, I see you haven't given up yet. Good. That leaves me something to work with." He circled the bed. "Actually, this can be very painless. You see, your good friend, Sochua Nika—oh, wait, she was more than just a friend, wasn't she? Excellent taste, I might add; tried her myself once a long time ago." He paused to let this sink in. "Yes, that's right. I knew about you and

Sochua. I make it my business to know who people in power are sleeping with. It makes my job easier.

"As I was saying, it was your former lover, Sochua, who sent the American to you and then told us to follow him. In this way, we easily found you. But why? Why would General Sochua hand you over to us like this?"

Yun's breathing became agitated.

"She said," Chea continued, still circling, "she did it in exchange for the kidnapped American girl. She made me a deal. She sacrificed you to save the girl's young life. This made some sense, given that you so rudely dumped her for another woman. That must have just been too much for her, you see, because that's exactly what *I* did to her twenty-five years ago. You and I have that in common, at least. Oh, by the way, I'm sorry you lost your fiancée— what was her name? Theary? But you did ask for it, didn't you?"

He gave the cot a swift kick, eliciting a moan.

"Don't you fall asleep on me! I need your help figuring this out. I need your help, because it doesn't make any sense. The Great Brigadier General Sochua Nika motivated by her desire to help a little girl and avenge a broken heart? I find it hard to believe she's gone that soft in her old age. And besides, she doesn't have a heart."

Chea sat on a folding chair and put his boots up on the bed.

"Now here's what I'm thinking, and you tell me if you agree: I'm thinking that Sochua wants you out of the picture for some other reason. I don't think she cares enough about the girl to want to save her, and I don't think she cares enough about you to want revenge. I think she wants you dead for another reason." Chea twisted Yun's bloody ear. "Well, what do you think?" Yun cried out. "I thought you'd agree."

The prime minister's chief bodyguard wiped the blood from his hand and began circling again.

"Sochua's an ambitious woman," he said. "Not only ambitious but popular. Some say she has political aspirations. So, what do you know? What is the reason she wants you dead?"

Chea prised open one of Yun's eyes with a thumb and index finger and brought his face close enough to smell the man's dank breath.

"I don't...I don't...know."

Chea resumed his pacing. Yun would talk. They always did.

"Look. We can do this the easy way or the hard way. You can tell me what that reason is, and I'll let you go. Or—and I honestly don't want to do this—I will begin cutting parts off your body until you die or tell me. It's really up to you how we proceed."

Yun began to cry.

"So, tell me." Chea studied his victim's mutilated face upside down from the head of the bed. "What do you know about Sochua Nika that would make her want to kill you? Wait!" He held up a cautioning finger. "Don't answer at once. Think about it for a minute. Get it right the first time."

Yun shivered despite the heat and humidity. "If...I...knew, I would tell... you."

Chea laughed. "You know what? I believe you. I mean, why would you protect Sochua after she's betrayed you? You wouldn't, would you?"

"N-no."

"So that means, you're *not thinking hard enough*!"

"Please!"

"Shut up!"

The only sound was Yun's irregular gasps for air.

Chea sat down on the mesh, his voice once again calm. "Look. You've suffered enough already. I'm willing to forget the past and let you walk out of here if you help me. Even after what you did to my daughter. You never got to see Nimol after your handiwork, did you? Her teeth permanently exposed, her nose melted, that evil eye."

"I'm sorry," Yun sobbed. "I'm...*sorry!*"

"Yes, you owe me. Think carefully. Is there something Sochua told you she did? Is there something she is planning to do? Is there something she told you about herself that she wouldn't want anyone else to know? Is there something you overheard that you weren't supposed to? Think!"

Chea had already begun to doubt himself and his intuition. Perhaps it was no deeper than the face of it: a jilted lover gets revenge and does a good deed in one fell swoop. Maybe that's all there was to it. Well, at least he would get to kill Yun. His efforts wouldn't be entirely wasted.

He stood and sighed, ready to end the interview with one last question.

"Do you know anything that could stop her from one day becoming prime minister?"

Yun closed his eyes. He seemed to be summoning the strength to say something. "I...yes. I know...what it is."

Chea couldn't believe his ears. "What?"

"If...if I tell you...you'll let...me...go?"

"Tell me, and I will let you go. I made you a deal, and I'm a man of my word."

"She's Vietnamese."

Chea froze. *Please, Lord Buddha, let it be true.* "Say that again."

"Sochua. She's...Vietnamese."

That was it. That had to be it. That would be an instant deal killer for her. This would immediately obliterate any chance, forever, she might have of becoming prime minister. Cambodian enmity for the Vietnamese resulted not only from the national disgrace of a decade of occupation that ended the Khmer Rouge era but also from centuries of humiliating vassal relationships ending only in the nineteenth century with the protection of colonialist France. If there was anything the Cambodians hated more than the Thais, it was the Vietnamese; the people would never stand for it.

Chea stood and crossed him arms. "How do you know this?" Yun didn't answer. "*Can you prove it?*"

"Yes. Yes...I can."

This was even better than Chea had thought, beyond his wildest dreams. Now Sochua was at his mercy, and he could play both sides of the game until it became clear which way the political wind would blow.

⚔

George led the way across the sand to a sad little restaurant festooned with a single string of lights attached to what looked like a car battery. "Sit down," he said, taking a seat at a bamboo table. "We gotta eat."

"I can't," Chris mumbled, but he did as he was told. He stared out toward the darkness of the sea.

"What amazes me," George said, "is that there's not a single hospital within a hundred miles I'd send my dog to, but I've got a perfect five bars on my cell phone. Can't get any data though." He shook the menu at him. "Looks like you can have anything you want, as long as it's fried rice."

Chris couldn't bring himself to smile. "I guess I'll take the fried rice," he mumbled.

"Yeah, I think I will too." George waved at the waiter. "Two fried rice, my good man."

The waiter wrote this down on a scrap of paper. "Two...fried...rice. Okay."

Two Cambodian women in bikini tops and skin-tight jeans approached. "You want date tonight?" one of them cooed. "We have good time."

Chris dropped his forehead on the greasy table. "Oh my God, George. Make them go away. I can't take it anymore."

George waved them off. "Sorry, ladies. Kind of you to offer, but not interested."

The waiter returned. "Sorry. No fried rice today."

Chris lifted his head. "But fried rice is the only thing on the menu."

George tapped himself between the eyes. "Uh, Chris, you got a piece of rice stuck to your face. Right here, buddy."

"No fried rice today. You want fried egg?"

"Sure," George said. "Bring us some fried eggs."

The waiter hustled off.

"George. Right now. This moment, I want you to remember it, because this is the moment that I lost my mind."

"You got to hold it together, bro."

"Sir?" Their server grinned. "Sorry, no egg today."

Chris took the man's hands in his. "Listen to me, please. I'm having a really, really bad day. I'm begging you. Go into the kitchen and see if there is any food. Anything. Please."

The waiter didn't move.

"Please."

A boisterous group of ex-pats laughed their way to the restaurant's other table, and the waiter went to retrieve more menus. The burliest of them loudly explained the way of the world to his slimy friends: "It's the free market, you see. Raw, pure capitalism. We have the money; they have the product. And it used to be a buyer's market. But now you got all these arseholes and morons come in here waving around money and distorting the market, paying twenty bucks even for those used-up Vietnamese skanks, and it makes it hard on the rest of us. But, fuck that. I tell those bitches I'll just give my money to the next girl.'"

Chris stood.

"Chris? Whatcha doin'?"

The foreign men stopped talking. They'd taken notice. One of them elbowed another.

"I'm going to go find some damn food."

Instead, he found a phone stall and called Lisa. He didn't know what he was expecting. He just knew he'd give anything in the world to have her and Mai in his arms again. Would it make a difference if he told her that? He doubted it.

"Come home," she implored.

"I can't. Not yet."

⋀

Private citizen Sochua Nika gave the first of what would become nightly addresses on the nation's most popular radio station.

"Radical action is required to make radical change! On Wednesday we will march from Olympic Stadium to the Ministry of Justice and remain there until the heroes arrested during last year's rally are released."

Chapter 25

Leonard Perry, not one for mosquitoes and hammocks, slept in town at the adequate Cambodia Palace Hotel, but on the advice of a fellow traveler he hung out on the garbage-strewn sands of Alaska, Lucky, and Champion Beaches during the day. The few foreigners there were mostly male, society drop-out types with long skanky hair and tattoos who looked like they'd been off the grid too long. Those bums made him sick, and he ignored them, as well as the army of hawkers who harassed him every minute. But it was on these beaches he discovered, to his great delight, he could negotiate openly for what he wanted, and no one would give him a second glance.

On his last morning in Cambodia he lounged on Champion Beach under an umbrella of reeds, his toes in the sand and his eyes on two lily-white foreign girls of around three or four frolicking in the safe edges of the surf while their mother sat nearby hugging her knees. These children had caught Perry's eye because they weren't wearing any clothes—the sort of thing these dirty Bohemian types let their kids do—and on them he trained the telephoto lens of the camera he'd bought just for this trip, zooming in when they remained still for a brief moment. He'd snapped a dozen photos and was scrolling through them with glee, when an angry voice startled him.

"Excuse me. What are you doing?"

He'd been so engrossed he hadn't noticed the mother approach. She sounded English. He rolled out of his low chair onto his knees.

"Uh…" He should've had something prepared.

"Why are you taking pictures of my children?"

"I'm a photographer for the Bangkok Post. I'm taking pictures of the beach."

She reached for his camera. "Do you mind if I see them then?"

"I don't have to let you see my photos."

She looked like she might slap his face until something over his shoulder caught her eye. "Fine."

She made a beeline for two shirtless tourists standing at a beachside bar. Time to leave. Perry packed his bag and hurried in the opposite direction toward a group of moto-dops waiting at the edge of another string of open-air restaurants. It took like fucking forever to get there.

"Hey, taxi!"

The first in line started his engine. "Where to, boss?"

"Go! Just go," Perry managed, breathless, climbing on the back of the moto.

"Where? You want girl?"

"Yeah, whatever. Just go."

"Okay, okay. I know good place."

They took off. He was safe, but what a shitty way to end his trip.

Chris rolled out of his hammock, feeling like he hadn't slept at all. George was already up. "Sorry about last night. I think I'm going crazy."

"Of course, you are."

The sun had just risen above the hills behind them, but the temperature was already in the eighties.

Chris hooked a thumb toward the water. "I'm going take a quick bath."

George chuckled. "I'm never seen you in a wife-beater before."

"Huh?"

"I said 'I've never seen you wear a wife-beater.'"

"You want to explain?"

"Your shirt, man. It's called a wife-beater."

"This kind of shirt? It's called a wife-beater?" Chris asked.

"Are you culturally illiterate, or what? That kind of shirt you're wearing is called a wife-beater.'"

"Is this some term, like, your average person is going to know, or did you just make it up? I swear I've never heard that in my life."

"Man, I'm telling you ninety-five percent of Americans would know that kind of shirt is called a wife-beater. Have you never seen Marlon Brando in *Streetcar Named Desire*? 'Stella! Stella! Come here and let me beat you, Stella!' It's a wife-beater, man—that's what it's called. I don't know what planet you've—"

Chris stopped listening. He was watching a foreign woman, clearly agitated, waving her hands and trudging toward them across the sand as fast as she could drag two little girls.

"Help! Can you help me?"

"Hey, George. Look."

The two men jogged to her side, and she breathlessly explained her encounter with some weirdo taking pictures of her kids. "Can you help me get that camera?"

She pointed, but the guy in question was already on the back of a moto.

George shook his head. "Ma'am, I'm really sorry this happened to you, but, uh…"

Chris stared after the moto heading up the slope from the beach, the foreign passenger looking desperately over his shoulder at them again and again. Desperate. Absolutely desperate not to get caught.

"Don't you worry, lady. We'll get that camera. Come on, George!"

George looked at him stupidly. "Hey, I'm sympathetic, but are you sure this is a good idea? You know, keeping a low profile and all…"

"Man, this is it. That guy's our ticket to get inside the brothels."

"I don't follow."

"I'll explain in the car. Come on!"

The woman tried to grab Chris's wrist. "Hey! What the bloody hell are you talking about?"

"I'm sorry. We don't have time to explain. Come on, George!"

"No! Wait! I want an explanation," she cried, running after them.

They climbed in the vehicle. "I'm really sorry. I promise you, no one will ever use those photos. George, haul ass!"

They left the woman cursing on the beach, her children crying beside her.

"I'm really sorry!" Chris yelled over his shoulder.

⋏

The conference room doors opened and Colonel Son, the prime minister's longtime personal secretary, entered. "Gentlemen, the prime minister," he announced flatly.

Prime Minister Thul Chorn entered the room and took his seat in the center of the table without comment. "Sit. Sit," he said impatiently.

Two dozen official advisers took their seats at a long conference table, Brigadier General Chea Prak and Minister of Interior and National Police Chief Nhim Saray—on Thul's left and right, respectively—among them.

Thul was bitter. In a simpler time, International Human Rights Day had been little more than a benign celebration of officially sanctioned speeches held annually in Olympic Stadium and suitable for live broadcast. The Cambodian government's official human rights watchdog had been the sole presenter at the event, and there were never any surprises. At the turn of the century, however, attendance at the rally had fallen so low that the event had become a liability, only serving to underscore what the radicals described as "the dismal human rights record" of his administration. So he'd given them exactly what they wanted and turned the organization of the event over to a committee of local human rights groups with the *single* condition that his official human rights office remain a voting member of the committee. But they were never satisfied; the event quickly became much more strident in its criticism—due mainly to interference of the international community—and was now the radicals' favorite platform for lampooning him and his government. No one appreciated stability.

If he could just throw out all the foreigners and start over! This was his and Cambodia's greatest curse: every charity, NGO, and this-or-that watchdog in the world scrutinizing his every move. Since simply shutting down the rallies was not politically expedient, he'd opted for containment of the damage, allowing the event to take place but limiting it always to the grounds of the Olympic Stadium and keeping the stadium half full, citing "safety concerns." Of course, he made sure that paid government supporters were always assured a seat. Human rights people had complained, but not too loudly until last year.

Last year radical activists had demanded unlimited access to the rally and with no warning urged their supporters to go to the stadium *en masse*. They caught security forces totally off guard—Nhim Saray's fault—and before reinforcements could arrive they had pushed down the fence surrounding the stadium, and the gathering became a true public event. Ten thousand people had watched as the activists unfurled a banner accusing him of numerous human rights abuses and acts of corruption. They'd gone too far; if he allowed this sort of defiance to stand, there'd be no end to their demands. He ordered the security forces to arrest the leaders—the international community shouldn't have encouraged them—and now they were paying the price.

After the activists spent five months in jail awaiting trial, he secretly offered the eight their freedom in exchange for a written apology and agreement not to incite unrest in the future, a face-saving gesture for all. Despite their promises to the contrary, the activists immediately leaked the news of his offer to the press, and instead of receiving accolades for his efforts at reconciliation, he had been lambasted on all fronts. A lesson needed to be taught; now they would receive sentences ranging from eighteen to thirty months with no credit for time served. Except, of course, for Pang Sokkruen, whose death, though unfortunate, was no fault of the government's.

And yet this year they planned further defiance. He had reorganized the organizing committee to include more government supporters, but hardliners, egged on—according to sources within the movement—by Sochua Nika, planned to leave the stadium and march to the Ministry of Justice to demand the release of their comrades. Sochua, traitor and erstwhile defender of the rights of mankind, would lead the group, and this was the reason he was in his office in the Peace Palace this morning.

Thul rapped the table. "Well?"

"Sir," began Nhim, "Sochua's intentionally trying to provoke a crisis. The march is her idea—I'm told she had to overcome quite a bit of resistance among her own people—and she will be leading it. We can't allow it."

"Of course we're not going to allow it!"

"Let me arrest her now. Without her, the will of the others will evaporate instantly."

"And martyr her further? And what if they march anyway?"

"Sir, these people are cowards. They wouldn't dare march without her. And you can rest assured my men are ready for anything."

Thul steepled his fingers in front of him, thinking. Maybe Nhim was right.

⁂

Chea Prak saw his opening. "Like they were last year?" he asked rhetorically in response to Nhim's assertion that his men were "ready for anything."

This allusion to Nhim's most humiliating moment, when Ministry of Interior forces had been overrun at last year's International Human Rights Day rally, was designed as much to rile Nhim as it had been to play on the prime minister's greatest fear.

Chea continued. "Arresting Sochua would be a mistake. I suggest a much less risky option. Release the prisoners on the eve of the rally as a gesture of 'goodwill and desire for national reconciliation.' Take away their reason to march. Sochua will have no choice but to call it off. And if she doesn't, well, she provokes us unnecessarily."

Nhim addressed his response to the PM. "Then they will know they can get away with saying anything they want. We can't just let them lie about you and get away with it!"

"It's a unilateral gesture of our willingness to cooperate," Chea argued calmly. "Not an admission of wrongdoing."

"And what if—"

The prime minister held up a hand. "Enough. We'll release them. But if the demonstrators still try to leave Olympic Stadium"—he nodded at Nhim for emphasis—"it cannot be allowed."

Chea Prak left the room astonished and congratulating himself over the ease with which he had manipulated the prime minister. Since learning Sochua's secret, he had given considerable thought to the question of where his loyalties should lie. If Thul were ten years younger there would be no doubt, but given that the old man's days were now so obviously numbered, Chea would be remiss if he didn't consider his own best interests.

His archrival Nhim, on the other hand, had everything to gain from the long-expected orderly succession of the prime minister's son, Thul Ly, who would soon wed Nhim's daughter. Ly, a weak political debutante, would be easily controlled by his new father-in-law, and Chea couldn't expect to last long under such an arrangement. But if Sochua were able to turn her significant popularity into a true political force—not a foregone conclusion, by any means—Chea could count on the information he'd gotten from Yun Naren to protect him. Blackmail was not the best way to ensure long-term job security, but he could live with it, and while a little jail time for Sochua Nika might increase her popularity, it was risky. One never knew what might happen in the course of an arrest and incarceration—especially when it would be Nhim Saray's troops that would nab her. And, if Sochua ended up accidentally shot dead, that would mean the end of him too once Thul's son took over. Whether he liked it or not, Chea was already playing the role of Sochua Nika's chief bodyguard.

Ambassador Richard Schroeder presided over Tuesday morning's regular Country Team meeting in the Chandler Room. All State Department section chiefs were in attendance—including the new public affairs officer who had replaced Peggy Revkin and whose name he could never remember—as well as the other agency heads. Allison Rosenberg from USAID also was there.

"Where do we stand?" he asked. All eyes turned to Deputy Chief of Mission Paris Jefferson.

"Sochua was interviewed by Khak Vanrith last night on Honeybee Radio and repeated her call for a general strike and her pledge to speak at the Human Rights Day events and then lead a march from Olympic Stadium to the Ministry of Justice to demand the release of the activists."

"Anything from the prime minister?"

"Nothing new. His position is that the march remains illegal and will not be allowed to take place, and he's issued a statement to that effect."

"What are your contacts on the inside telling you?"

"The same thing," Jefferson said. "That he's going to crack down hard if they try to march. They say he's not going to budge."

PAO Matt Hernandez held up a sheet of paper. "He said in this morning's *Rakusmei Kampuchea*—quote: 'If radical elements urged on by the international community threaten public order by holding an illegal march, then we will be forced to make more arrests.' He then was asked if that included General Sochua Nika. He said, 'Of course.'"

Schroeder nodded. "Looks like we got us a showdown then. Prepare a release saying something like 'The American embassy recognizes Cambodians' right to peaceful assembly and urges restraint on all sides. To make further arrests of nonviolent protesters would be a step backward.' I'd like to see it on my desk ASAP."

"Hold on a minute," interrupted Jefferson, looking at her mobile phone. "Hassan, turn on CTN."

They all turned to the TV mounted on the wall. "What is it?" Schroeder asked.

"Thul is about to hold a press conference. It looks like he's going to release them."

On the screen, Thul walked to a podium. He cleared his throat and adjusted his glasses, smiling broadly. He began to speak.

"Well, what's he saying?" Schroeder didn't speak a lick of Khmer.

"Hang on. He's just blabbing."

Thul joked on camera with the small crowd assembled on chairs before him.

"Okay, here we go," Jefferson said. "He says that...uh...'when Khmer talk to Khmer and don't listen to the voices of outside interference, anything is possible. I have spoken today with the seven detained friends,'—his words—'and based upon those conversations, I have decided to drop the defamation cases against them. They will be released immediately. I hope this will be interpreted as a demonstration of my desire for reconciliation and as a gift to the country on the eve of International Human Rights Day.'"

Thul Chorn left the stage, still smiling, without taking any questions.

"He didn't even mention Pang Sokkruen. But I guess it's too late for him anyway."

Schroeder clapped his hands together; Thul had made a wise decision. "Well, at least it's some good news—a step in the right direction. Looks like he's trying to take the wind out of Sochua's sails, huh?"

Jefferson gave him a wry smile. "I would say he's succeeded."

"What about Sambo Rithy?" asked junior officer Hassan Hosseini. "Do you think he'll let him come back from the US? Why didn't he mention him?"

"Well," responded Jefferson, "he's a whole different ball game. First of all, he's already been convicted, and so the PM can't easily drop the charges. He would have to ask the king to pardon him. Second, Sambo actually leads an organized political party and therefore is probably seen as a much greater threat. But what I find interesting is that Sochua only demanded the release of the activists detained last year. She never even mentioned Sambo. In fact, if you believe the rumors about her wanting to start her own political party, the last thing she'd want is Sambo back in Cambodia."

Schroeder cleared his throat. "Matt, prepare an appropriate statement. We need to include something about Sambo too. And express regret that this release happened too late for Pang Sokkruen, who died awaiting trial."

"Got it."

Jefferson stayed behind as the others filed out. "Richard?"

Schroeder expressed mock concern. "What? You're giving me that look."

"Go see your dad. You'll regret it if you don't."

Schroeder stroked his mustache. "With all this going on?"

"It looks like the political crisis has resolved itself, and—"

"You know it's not the stupid political crisis I'm thinking about."

"Yeah, I know. Look, we're already doing everything we can for the Kellies."

Schroeder looked at his feet. He did want to go, but...

"Lisa and Chris would understand. You've done a great job, but you being here now is not going to change anything. I can keep things going."

He nodded, unsmiling. "Alright. I'll think about it."

Jefferson dialed an extension on the conference phone. "Esther, please have Travel make reservations for the ambassador to go to Los Angeles tonight."

Schroeder breathed a sigh of relief. "Thanks, Paris."

⚓

Chris and George watched the pale mustachioed tourist, who was sitting on the sand, surrounded by ragged children. They'd followed the man back to his hotel—where he stayed for about an hour—and then to Joy Beach on the opposite end of town from where he'd met with the English mom earlier in the morning. He was a little on the plump side, bald, early middle age. He habitually adjusted his eyeglasses while children climbed in and out of his lap. Once in a while he snapped a picture.

"Alright," said George, "we've cut off his escape route. You ready?"

"Let me go. You might scare him off."

"Remember," George warned. "Low profile."

"Gotcha. Low profile. But if he tries run, you grab him, okay?"

Chris sauntered across the sand and sat down on the beach next to the man. "Hey."

The guy shooed the children away. They were filthy with no shoes or sandals, wearing a mishmash of well-worn clothing gleaned from the rejects of the garment factories.

"Can I help you?" he asked coldly. His eyes darted about the sand, the water, anywhere but Chris's face. His T-shirt read "I'm Too Sexy."

"Hey, man, cool shirt."

"Thanks. What do you want?"

Chris leaned closer. "Listen," he whispered. "My friend and me, well, we just got here, and we were wondering if you knew where we could get some girls."

"Is that a fucking joke? Man, they're all over the place. Just ask any motorcycle taxi driver. Just ask your hotel. Hell, you can probably ask the police."

"No, I mean, we're looking for, like, virgins. You know what I mean."

"I don't know anything about that."

"Man, come on. People like us, we got to help each other out."

"Fuck off. I got to catch a plane." The man struggled to one knee.

"Hey, hang on. I just want you show you something."

Chris held up a photo of Mai sitting in a kid-sized rocker with her elbows on her knees and her chin resting on her hands. She was wearing her favorite shirt—an electric-blue soccer jersey with the number twelve—her hair in pigtails. He had taken her to a photo studio near the house where for a couple of dollars she'd spent the afternoon playing movie star. They'd dressed her in traditional Cambodian costumes, her Snow White dress, and an Indian *salwar kameez*, but she always liked her picture in her jersey the best.

"Have you seen this girl?"

The guy shrugged. "No."

"Really? Are you sure?"

He held up a second picture, one he'd taken himself. Mai's hair hung loose and wild on her shoulders. She was out of doors and barefoot, wearing the same yellow sundress she had on the day she disappeared.

"The American government is offering a substantial reward for information about her. No questions asked."

The stranger looked like he was about to loose his bowels. "No. Now leave me alone."

Chris watched him get to his feet and head for a group of moto-dops. Let the pedophile think he's getting away.

"Moto? Moto, sir?"

George stepped in the man's way. "Uh-uh. We're not finished with you yet."

The man tried to walk around, and George wrapped a tattooed bicep around his neck and marched him back to Chris.

"Hey! This is kidnapping. You can't do this."

"Kidnapping? Did you hear that, Chris?"

"Yeah. Kidnapping. Real funny."

George released his catch with a shove, and he stumbled into Chris. Chris shoved him back.

"So, what'd you say your name is?"

The man whimpered and came up with "Uh…John."

"Yeah, right," Chris said, cracking his knuckles. "Okay, John-Boy, let me see the camera."

"But…but…"

"Now!"

The man cursed under his breath and handed it over. Chris scrolled through far more lurid photos than the ones taken on Champion Beach, some involving sex acts with minors. "Hey, this is some crazy shit, man. George, you want to take a look?" George shook his head, arms crossed. "So what were you going to do with these?"

"I was going to delete them!"

"Oh, no, no," Chris said, wagging a finger, "you're not going to delete them. You see, these are evidence. Did you know, John, that it's against the law to have sex with children in Cambodia? Not only that, but it's against American law for Americans to have sex with children in Cambodia. So you can go to prison for it here or there. Personally, I hope they put you in prison here. They say conditions are excellent." He poked the enormous fanny pack around the pedophile's waist. "Give me the bag."

Chris put the camera around his neck and dumped the contents of the fanny pack onto the sand: a limp chocolate bar, half a dozen Trojan-enz, sunscreen—SPF 50—wadded tissues, a hotel key on a ridiculous wooden chain, and an American passport.

He picked up the passport. "Well, let's see…Leonard Perry. This picture just doesn't do you justice at all." He handed it to George, who had a look and laughed. "Does your wife know what you get up to in Cambodia? Your kids? What do you think they're going to say when they find out?"

"Listen. I don't know anything about that girl. I—"

"That girl," Chris snapped, "is my daughter, and you're going to help us find her. You're going to go into every brothel in Sihanoukville posing as a scumbag pedophile—that part should be easy for you—and you are going to look for my daughter until we find her."

"No way! I haven't done anything!"

Chris grabbed a fistful of Perry's shirt and pulled his forehead to his. "I don't care what you've done," he said, snarling. "You are going to help us, or I'm going to beat you to death on this beach right now."

"If—if—" Perry sputtered.

George tapped him on the skull. "I think he means it."

"If—if I help you, you'll let me go?"

Chris released him. "Of course. If you help us, we'll hand you back your passport and give you a ride to the airport."

Perry dropped his head. "Well…"

"Well, what?"

"I think maybe I saw her."

George and Chris looked at each other.

Chris lifted Perry's chin to face him. "What do mean, 'you saw her'? Where?"

"I think I saw her. In a hotel."

"Bullshit. You got a picture?"

"No, I don't have a picture!"

"I think you're lying to me. What hotel?"

"I don't…um…I don't know."

"You don't know? You don't know? Do you hear that, George? He doesn't know."

George began to massage Perry's shoulders, towering over him from behind. "If I were you, pal, I'd figure it out real quick."

"I don't know the name," he whined, "but I know where it is."

"Great," Chris said genially, "you're going to take us there right now." He pointed at the jeep sitting in the shade of an enormous casuarina. "You ride shotgun."

Perry hesitated. George put a vise grip on his trapezius, and he got the message.

"Okay, okay! Ouch!" Perry cried, his knees buckling.

"Are we going to have any trouble from you?"

"No! No!"

George let him go. "Good. Now get in."

Perry limped to the jeep, massaging his neck, and got in the front seat. George gave a thousand riel to the man who'd been guarding the car. Chris climbed in the back and leaned over Perry's shoulder.

"Well, where're we going, big boy?"

Perry sighed hard and pointed the way.

⋏

Sochua Nika flung the remote on the table. She got up and opened the French doors leading to the garden. It wasn't grand. The walls of her compound seemed as much to pen her in as to keep out the riffraff.

"Are you surprised?"

The general glared at her daughter, Charya. "Not at all. It's what I would've done. Makes perfect sense."

Sochua pursed her lips. No, this was not unexpected. Now, with Thul having freed the human rights activists, there was no obvious reason for the march. She would have no choice but to publicly call for the cancellation of the general strike and the march to the Ministry of Justice. Her phone began to ring with calls of congratulations.

"Tell them I'm not available," she said sharply. "I need time to think." She walked into the garden and sat on a stone bench. She looked at her orchids.

After a moment Charya joined her outside. "Well, I'm happy the march to the ministry will be canceled," she said. She stroked the general's hair. "The prime minister said the police would use force. You may have gotten hurt."

"Stop it!" Sochua slapped her daughter's hand away like swatting a mosquito. "Hurt me? Thul's not that stupid. The people would riot."

Charya smiled. "The people do love you," she said kindly.

"Yes, I suppose. But what good does that do me now?" She had to come up with something.

⋏

Perry directed them to a dilapidated colonial-era bungalow on Blue Mountain, a district of entirely male-oriented businesses renown for the youth and vigor of its painted ladies. "Lady Massage," a wooden sign announced. A bedraggled man working for tips shouted at some children to move their curbside game to make a parking space. Freelancers beckoned to the trio from a corner.

Chris pointed over Perry's shoulder to a hotel down the street. "Is that it?"

"Yeah. Can we get out of the car?"

"Shut up and tell us exactly what you saw."

"They brought in a bunch of girls. They said I could take my pick—but I told them no because I don't go for the really young ones!"

"Admirable of you," George remarked.

"And where was my daughter?" Chris asked in Perry's ear. "You better be telling the truth." He could see sweat running in rivulets down Perry's fat neck.

"She was—"

"She was what?"

"Well, she was—"

Chris grabbed Perry around the chin and yanked his head back. "You're lying to us, aren't you? You're making all of this up."

"Ow! Let go!"

"Goddammit, George! He's lying to us. I can see it in his ugly face."

"Ow, you're breaking my neck!"

"Yes, that's right. If you don't tell me the truth, I will break your neck! Was she in there?"

"Well...well...ow!"

"Yes or no?"

"Well, they all kind of looked the same! I'm not sure."

The rage that had been building up in Chris all week came to a head at that moment. He wrenched Perry's head back as hard as he could—and then an image of Mai flooded his mind. He let go. "Damn it! You stupid, lying son of a bitch."

"God! You almost broke my neck!"

Prasidh Veng, daytime manager of the Apsara 2 Hotel, felt pleased to have dispatched a discreet car and driver to the Sunway to pick up one of the Apsara 2's regulars, Henry Ung. Ung came often to Cambodia to look after business interests, and when he did he always managed to make at least one visit. He liked to have oral sex performed on him by little girls, a craving difficult to satisfy in Singapore without outrageous expense and unacceptable risk, and, Veng suspected, Ung would've gladly paid a lot more for it than the going rate at the Apsara 2. At any rate, Ung's singular tastes were of concern to him only to the extent that he could profit from them; Ung tipped, and he tipped *big*.

As usual, the chauffeur brought Ung in through the secure back entrance, out of sight of any prying eyes. Foreigners had taken to photographing visitors to certain hotels and splashing their faces on the Internet, and Veng's livelihood depended upon ensuring that didn't happen to the customers of the Apsara 2.

A guard opened the car door, and Veng greeted Ung warmly in Mandarin. "Welcome back, sir. It's very nice to see you again so soon. May I prepare the usual, sir?"

Ung grunted agreement.

"Of course, sir. We have your room ready."

"*Ow!*" the Chinaman cried. "You stupid *yuon!*"

Quynh hadn't meant to do it, but the Chinaman wouldn't stop. She started to cry. The man called Veng ran into the room. He looked crazy.

"What happened?"

The Chinaman was buttoning his pants, and he was really mad. He shoved Veng. "The little bitch bit me! That's what happened!"

Then they started speaking in the Chinaman's language, and they went out of the room. Veng came right back. Qunyh could tell he meant to hurt her.

"He kept pushing my head down on it! I told him to stop! He was choking me!"

Veng made a fist. "So you bit him?" He locked the door.

"Sorry," Quynh cried. She hadn't meant to do it! It wasn't her fault! "I'm sorry! I'm sorry!"

"Shut up!" Veng took off his belt. "Shut your mouth!"

Quynh knew what Veng's belt could do. He'd used it on her friend Sethiya. "No! Please! I'm sorry!"

He came for her, and she scrambled over the bed. "Please! *Please!*"

"Shut up!"

Veng swung the belt at her. He hit the light above the bed, and it broke into pieces. This made him even madder. He swung the belt back and forth. It made a terrifying whooshing sound.

"No!" she shrieked.

Veng hit her on the neck.

"*Ow!* It stung like a thousand needles—burned like a hot coal. "Stop!" She threw up her arms. "Stop!"

Veng hit her on the legs. "Shut up!"

Oh, it hurt. So. Much. "I— I— Please! I'm sorry."

"Shut up! Shut your mouth!"

Quynh crawled away, and Veng brought the belt down again and again on her back.

It sizzled like a burn. Her skin was on fire. "Please!"

"I'm not going to stop until you shut up!"

Quynh curled into a ball. "No…"

"Stupid *yuon*! I'm not going to stop until you're completely broken!" Veng whipped her again and again.

Then he stopped. "I hope I've made my point," he said.

The door slammed, and it was quiet. She hadn't meant to do it.

⋏

The environs of Psar Leu, Sihanoukville's principal market, buzzed with the energetic chaos of people making money. While George waited in the jeep a block and a half down the street, Chris sat cheerlessly in a grimy café abutting an unpaved lane crowded with men and a few old women involved in the transport of every imaginable good that could be piled, strapped, or stacked onto a moto, cyclo, wheelbarrow, bicycle, donkey cart, or truck, each loudly jockeying for advantage. He watched Leonard Perry enter Lucky Massage

Parlor at the opposite end of the block. All Perry had to do was go in, ask for little girls and see if Mai was among them. What were the odds he wouldn't screw it up?

A teenager in flip-flops dropped some silverware and a greasy menu in front of him. *"Chum riep sua."*

By the way she looked at him, he must have made a scary sight with his wild hair and crazed look. "Coffee, *saum.*"

The girl collected the menu and disappeared.

A quintessentially Cambodian scene unfolded in front of him: an incomprehensible tangle of power lines cast an odd shadow; three young policemen smoked on the opposite corner as if they lacked a care in the world; a cyclo driver stood on his pedals above the tumult looking for a path; a shirtless man unloaded bags of rice from a tumbrel; a toddler with a naked bottom wobbled like a drunken sailor; a half-dozen young women pedaled their sewing machines in silence in a tailor's; vendors' wobbly stands displayed rubber sandals, questionable Gauloises, kids' backpacks in gaudy colors, purses from "Lois Vitton" and "Guci"; dense smoke billowed from an alley; shared-taxi minibuses inched by, their barkers announcing destinations far and near.

The toddler teetered and fell forward onto the buckled sidewalk. He didn't cry but instead began to diligently examine some filth at close range. Chris thought of Mai and her strange sereneness as a baby just arrived from the orphanage. Put in her crib, she would only sit and blink at her new parents and then lie down on her side with her thumb in her mouth as if accustomed to being left alone. She rarely cried. What had her earlier months been like? Had she been loved? He and Lisa had tried to give her so much love, and now...

"Mr. Man. Your coffee."

Chris took a sip so scalding he got angry, and then tears welled, and he found he couldn't stop them. The girl stood close by staring, open-mouthed.

"Please stop watching me," he croaked, and she left.

He closed his eyes, willing the caffeine to help organize his thoughts after an almost sleepless night.

After several minutes Perry emerged from the massage parlor looking ridiculously foreign against this backdrop. He stood for a moment on the corner—harassed nonstop by touts and moto-dops—until he saw Chris. Instead of hailing a moto as per the plan, he waved off the mob and gingerly stepped into the street, making a beeline for the café.

"No," Chris mouthed, but Perry kept coming. "Stop."

Disrupting traffic and eliciting impatient shouts, Perry attracted a great deal of attention, including that of the policemen, who laughed at him and seemed to casually remark upon his trajectory.

Chris looked away as Perry, huffing, sat down. "What the hell are you doing?" he hissed. "You were supposed to take a moto back to the beach."

Perry grinned. "Kiss my ass. I'm thirsty."

"You're thirsty? Listen to me," Chris growled through clenched teeth, "you are going to do only what I tell you."

The policemen were watching.

"Give me my passport back," Perry said, "and I'll think about it."

"Listen, asshole—"

"Dude, chill out and let me get a drink. You got any money?" To the waitress, he said, "Hey, sweetheart, over here."

"Chill out? I'm going to rip your face off. What if the cops come over here?"

"So what? I'm not breaking the law. I'm just sitting here with a friend having a drink."

Perry waved his fingers at the policemen across the street. He straightened and gave an exaggerated salute.

"You stupid idiot! I swear to God I'm going to kill you."

Perry smiled sweetly. "Oh, you're just all talk, aren't you, sugar?"

Chris wrapped his fingers around his fork. "You're going to pay for this." He pictured himself jabbing it into Perry's throat, his throbbing jugular. But at the moment, he was more concerned about the cops.

The police officers appeared perturbed that their casual smoke had been intruded upon by Perry's cheeky gesture. One of them tossed his butt into the street and languidly gestured to the other two officers. He took a folded paper from his pants pocket and showed it to his colleagues. They looked from the paper to Chris and back again. Discussion ensued, and they seemed to reach a conclusion. The leader stepped off the curb, stopping traffic with a hand. They headed toward Chris's table.

"Shit!" Chris pretended to ignore the cops even as he desperately looked for avenues of escape.

"What's your problem?" Perry demanded. "We're American. They can't fuck with us."

"Shut your mouth now. Just shut up!"

"Geez, would you calm down?"

Chris couldn't imagine how this was going to end well. The police were closing in and at the very least would extort a small bribe for their troubles. If they somehow had identified him—what was on that paper?—they might arrest him, and he'd be deported for sure, ending his hope of remaining in Cambodia to find Mai. George watched him helplessly from the jeep, surrounded by heavy market traffic, offering no chance for escape. There was only one way to go.

"Hey, Leonard. Stand up."

"Huh?"

"Just get up for a sec. I want to show you something."

Perry complied. "What?"

Catapulting hot coffee, Chris shoved the pedophile backward off the curb. He landed on a cart hauling bananas and lotus flowers, and the street erupted. Chris sprinted for the labyrinth of the covered market. High close stacks of jeans and T-shirts and countless bolts of silk and cotton muted the angry shouts of the three men in hot pursuit. He made a hard right and bolted past motorcycle spares, brass bowls, musical instruments, and coiled wire. A tourist stepped in his way, and he knocked him into a shelf of bootleg DVDs. "Hollywood for Famous" read the sign.

"Stop!" a policeman shouted.

The aisle narrowed, and Chris left a wake of angry shoppers as he shoved and jostled them out of his way and into the shops on either side. Shopkeepers in his path poked their heads out to see what the ruckus was about. They hurled insults at the police, demanding an arrest. On a long straightaway a burly man blocked the way; Chris detoured through a jeweler's into the next aisle, tripping over a plastic stool and frightening two young saleswomen to screams. He crashed headlong through a tarp wall into the fresh produce section of the market.

Vendors of lemongrass, jackfruit, papayas, bitter gourds, coriander, and guavas stood staring open-mouthed at this commotion in their midst. An old woman pushing a wheelbarrow full of *longans*—Mai had nicknamed these "eyeballs" because that's what they looked like when peeled—froze like a deer in headlights. Chris inexpertly hurdled her wagon, catching his trailing foot on the edge. He stumbled, arms flailing, and smashed into piles of *rambutans*— labeled "hairy eyeballs" by Mai—dragon fruit, and soursops. A box of tamarind pods slid off a broken counter and poured its contents on his head.

On hands and bruised knees in the dirt and surrounded by angry citizens, Chris scrambled between the legs of fruit and vegetable stands and came up for air in the "food court" directly under a table holding a giant jar of quails' eggs. Its owner just managed to catch the jar but was sloshed with a face full of the brackish liquid within. Diners of grilled fish, frogs' legs, and noodles stopped to watch as this crazed foreigner stained with tropical fruit juices tried to figure out which way to go. Police came around the corner, hastening Chris's choice.

He flew past mounds of beetles, deep-fried tarantulas, and grasshoppers, and slid across the fat- and blood-slicked tiles of the fresh meat aisle, nearly losing his footing several times. A butcher brandished a bloody cleaver. Aisles intersected, and daylight could be seen to the left.

Chris squeezed past browsing tourists in this section of the market where they bought stone carvings, wooden Buddhas, compasses, opium weights, betel-nut boxes, and *kramas*. He knocked a backpacker into a display of faux antiques, and she cursed him loudly. He didn't care—sunlight lay only fifty meters dead ahead, and he intended to get there, where he could at least make a better run for it.

The throng thinned toward the exit, and he was gaining speed. Heads ducked into stalls. In just a few seconds he would burst into full daylight. The light at the end of the tunnel stood almost within reach, but then that light diminished, blocked by a lone silhouette, arms akimbo, waiting for him.

Chris froze. Behind him uniformed men were rapidly closing in, and here the stalls of vendors were of cinder block; he couldn't crawl under tables or burst through walls. He was cornered.

He snatched a large woven basket and ran at the man blocking the exit, shoving it hard at his chest. The policeman stumbled backward and fell into a bookseller's table. Chris clamored over him, stepping on his face. Dragging his legs free of the man's grasp, he managed to stumble a few steps before he was knocked to the ground by a blow from behind, his ears ringing. Three men tackled him, then a fourth and a fifth. He raised his head just enough to see the shadow of the club descending . . . and then nothing.

On Tuesday morning in Los Angeles, Sambo Rithy sat on his white leather sofa with his head in his hands while his two boys played in the pool under the watchful eye of their full-time nanny, Dulce. A few hours ago he had live-streamed Honeybee Radio and listened to General Sochua Nika wax triumphant on the eve of Human Rights Day: "The government has seen the power of the people! All our demands have been met. The people can take the power from the oligarchs, if only we will stand up and do it! I am asking you: come out tomorrow to Olympic Stadium and celebrate our victory!" Bitch.

It was now almost midnight in Cambodia, and he had just gotten off the phone with the nearly hysterical Sambo Rithy Party General Secretary, who had voiced his long list of emergencies: Sochua had secured the release of the detained human rights activists; Sochua would address three times as many as Sambo had in his last address in Cambodia; Sochua planned to announce the formation of a new political party; two prominent SRP members said they would join any party formed by Sochua; etc., etc.

Far more than Thul ever could, Sochua threatened his long-term political prospects. All the years of deprivation, all the hard work, the potential riches he had forsaken for the good of the country—all of this sacrifice would be wasted if he didn't act now. He'd been blind. He needed to get back to Cambodia right away, but for that he needed the help of the prime minister. He had a feeling that, for once, he and Thul might see eye to eye on something: Sochua had to be stopped.

CHAPTER 26

A converted rice *barge chugged downstream from the sleepy town of Kampot. Mai bounced on a foam cushion in the bow, holding hands with her mother as the heavily forested banks fell away on each side as this finger of the delta reached the silty edge of the Gulf of Thailand. They continue toward the void, the sun already low on the western horizon. Presently, the young captain in the stern cut the engine, and they floated in silence. Though they were half a kilometer from the shore, the water was as flat as soup in a bowl. With a playful yelp, the Cambodian jumped from the boat, and the Kellies laughed to see he was standing in water only to his ankles. He bowed with a flourish, and they clapped. Chris looked over the side and realized they had been traveling in a narrow channel in the delta. He lifted Mai and then Lisa onto the silt. In places the water was only inches deep, but it looked as if they were standing in the middle of the ocean.*

"Look, Daddy. I'm running on water," Mai shrieked.

Their guide pointed out starfish—hundreds, thousands of them, just below the surface of the water. He gently picked up a two-foot-long intestine-like creature and offered it to Mai. Lisa grimaced, but Mai, never squeamish, took the slimy thing in her hands. The animal released the fecal contents of its body into the water, and an empty sausage casing slid from her hands.

"Oooooh, cool," Mai drawled, utterly impressed.

Eventually, the mute captain nodded toward the west, but even he looked reluctant as they weighed anchor and headed toward the river's mouth. Darkness was almost complete as they docked on the riverside promenade in front of the Kampot Riverfront Lodge. Starving and giddy with the day's excitement, Mai devoured an enormous plate of fettuccine carbonara, of all things; it was delicious, and she now had a new favorite dish. She barely protested before falling into the deep sleep of a kid having spent a day in the sun. But when Chris went to check on her in the middle of the night, her bed was empty.

"Mai?" The sheets were cold. "Mai!"

"*Mai!*" Chris awoke in agony. His abrupt start had cracked the plasma-hardened scrapes on his knees and elbows. Had he yelled out? His head felt as if it had been crushed in a vise; on the back was a knot the size and feel of an orange half.

He remembered the chase and had some murky recollection of a bright light in his face and men's laughter. It actually hurt to blink; he figured he had a concussion. Wincing with pain, he lifted his head and looked around a dark room. Where the hell? Vague shapes on the floor did not stir. He softened with his tongue the crusted blood on his split lower lip. He was wearing only his underwear. None of it made any sense until he saw the bars.

Stiffly, slowly, he rose and crept toward the far end of the cell as light began to grow. It was slow going; sleeping prisoners were spooned together on every inch of the floor. A concrete lip separated the sleeping area from a shattered urinal and two hole-in-the-ground toilets splattered with liquid feces. A ladle floated in a plastic bucket. He held his nose and squatted over the toilet, but the stench was too much; he vomited instead and slipped to the floor. The jolt ricocheted terribly in his brain. Someone laughed quietly.

Men woke and spat where they could. They peed into empty water bottles and ladled brown water over themselves until the bucket was empty. Those with tattered mosquito nets tied them in knots where they hung. Most of them only wore underwear or *kramas* tied up like diapers between their legs. An inmate with normal clothes made an announcement in Khmer that Chris didn't understand and was met with indifference by the others.

No one paid any particular attention to Chris. He counted his cell-mates: thirty-three. Some of them began heating water for coffee or instant noodles on tiny stoves fueled with cans of gas. Others cooked stinking offal in pots or tin cans. They bought this from women with large aluminum pots of the stuff, who ladled it to them between the bars of the cell. Others bought bottles of water. Chris had no money, and so he waited.

Music started in the street outside: a single Khmer pop song blasted over and over. Flies crawled everywhere. Morning had arrived.

Policemen came and shouted commands, and the trusty who had made the earlier announcement slapped Chris on the shoulder. A decorated officer pressed a thermal fax paper against the bars. In the midst of large Khmer lettering, Chris saw an image of himself.

"U. S. A.," the officer said, tapping the paper. He grinned.

That's it: they knew who he was. His search for Mai was over.

⅄

"Come."

Quynh shrugged and followed a man to a white van parked under a *neem* tree at the back of the Apsara 2 Hotel. He and the driver of the van talked through the open window. Money changed hands. The driver spat on the ground.

"Get in," he said. He opened the door, and she climbed in. She didn't think about or even care where they were going.

She watched the driver chew, chew, chew, then spit out the window. That reminded her of her grandmother; she liked to chew *slaa* and spit the blood-red juice. They drove a long time in the city and stopped on a busy street. The chewing and spitting man opened the door and grabbed her elbow with a wet hand. He stopped to spit on a tree growing right up out of the sidewalk. He said something, but Quynh couldn't hear over the noise: impatient horns, bells, competing shouts of "moto! moto!" He pulled her past TVs, food smells, and gold jewelry behind glass. Past trussed hens, pink dresses, and toys shaped like guns. They stopped at a shop house.

"*Chum riep sua,*" the man said.

"*Chum riep sua,*" responded a woman lying in a hammock hung from another tree growing up through the sidewalk. A red paper lantern hung above her. The man slipped off his sandals and disappeared inside.

"You're going to stay here now, little sister," the woman said, getting out of her hammock.

"Yes, Auntie." Quynh wasn't sure how she felt about that. She liked the Apsara 2 Hotel. She had friends there and a nice room to share that stayed dry even when it rained. And plenty of food to eat. She liked to play dice with her friends Pilavai and Daosadeth, the only boys at the hotel. Best of all? No school.

"You can call me Auntie Oanh. Come."

Auntie Oanh examined the welts on Quynhs's arms, face, and legs and grasped a handful of filth from the base of the tree and rubbed it on her clothes. She mussed her hair and put dirt in it and spat on her own dirty hands and rubbed them on Quynh's cheeks and forehead. She regarded her with approval.

"Go beg for money in front of the shopping mall." She pointed at a cavernous building across the street. "Foreigners only."

Quynh was confused.

"I told you to go across the street."

"I don't know what to do, Auntie. Is it yum-yum?"

She laughed. "Not yum-yum, stupid. Just ask them for money."

Quynh's cheeks began to burn. "And they give me money for nothing?"

"Just go over there and watch what the other kids do. Now go!"

"Brothers and sisters, I give you the hope of Cambodia, Sochua Nika!"

In The Queen Bee, Honeybee Radio's mobile broadcasting van, Khak Vanrith beamed as the general was introduced by one of the seven political prisoners released by Prime Minister Thul only the day before. Sochua took the podium with a slight bow, her palms pressed together in front of her face. Ten thousand people roared their approval from inside the stadium complex while at least twice as many cheered outside the perimeter fence. Khak swelled with pride that thousands more would listen to Sochua's speech live on Honeybee Radio, *his* station.

A decade ago, Khak, wanting desperately to get his children away from his ex-wife and the drug- and crime-ridden streets of LA, had sold his successful donut-shop franchise and returned to his native Cambodia, where he got rich in the restaurant and nightclub business. He'd eventually tired of that too and opened Cambodia's first privately owned radio station—he'd spent a fortune on bribes to make that happen—and in just six years he'd made Honeybee Radio a household name. He hadn't come home to be an activist, but he abhorred what the kleptocrats were doing to his country as much as he hated lining their pockets to ensure his businesses ran smoothly.

Khak had despised Prime Minister Thul Chorn even before the Sambo Rithy incident in 2013, and he used his station—now at 105.1 FM—to sow discord on a daily basis, something that had landed him in hot water on several occasions. He'd even been the target of an assassination attempt: three shots fired at point-blank range while he sat waiting in front of his girlfriend's house. Amazingly, he'd survived unharmed and lived to hire a small army of personal bodyguards and send his kids to boarding school in Leysin, Switzerland. The government denied any involvement, of course, and an investigation yielded nothing.

No less than three laws regulating the airwaves had been passed as a result of his broadcasts, and he knew he walked a very thin line. He intended to continue his work as long as he was able, but he had enough money squirreled away in the US to live comfortably for the rest of his life if things ever got too hot. He considered himself a Cambodian patriot, and he was willing to accept some personal risk to change things.

This morning Khak sat in his like-new mobile broadcasting van—the only one in Cambodia—broadcasting live from Olympic Stadium. When he announced his intention to air the International Human Rights Day rally, the government warned him that under current law broadcasters could be held criminally liable for any defamatory comments made live on the radio and that this would be strictly applied to his unprecedented broadcast. Khak ignored the warnings and went ahead with his plans, including those to broadcast in its entirety the speech of the Conscience of Cambodia, General Sochua Nika.

"I am only a humble woman," Sochua began. "I have no interest in politics. I am only interested in justice and freedom for the Cambodian people." Applause. "And I will tell you this: the elites can no longer deny you justice!" Applause.

Khak delighted in the knowledge that at this very moment Prime Minister Thul Chorn would be in his official residence greeting Lieutenant General

John Sanderson, the visiting former head of the United Nations Transitional Authority in Cambodia. The roar of the crowd in Olympic Stadium would provide the backdrop as Thul shook hands with Sanderson and welcomed him back to Cambodia. Likely, Sanderson would tactfully make no mention of the noise as, a kilometer to the east, Sochua took her victory lap.

"Last night, the prime minister said he gave us a gift. He released seven heroes from prison and called it a gift to the Cambodian people. Well, let me tell you something, Prime Minister: freedom is not yours to give!"

Khak saw mothers, fathers, and children inside and outside the stadium cry out her name. Peanut vendors and souvenir hawkers stopped what they were doing and cheered for this woman who inspired them to dream.

"Freedom is the right of every human being!"

Thanks to his broadcast the police listened; the elderly listened in their homes; shopkeepers turned up their radios and angled them toward the street; workers in government offices would listen where they could get away with it.

Sochua raised a fist. "Democracy, Mr. Prime Minister, is not yours to give! Security is not yours to give! These things belong to all of us, and you have stolen them from us! Prime Minister, you have stolen these things from us, and you have stolen them from Pang Sokkruen!"

Khak watched captivated, tears streaming down his face—then something went wrong. Sochua, exultant, flinched. Several thousand people—those close enough to see their hero—gasped collectively. Shots were fired, and she ducked. Large men rushed on stage. Sochua looked suddenly terrified and frail. Khak tore off his earphones and rounded on his technician.

"What the hell's going on? Are we off the air?"

The man nodded. Khak looked out the window. A number of plainclothes thugs were tampering with his generator. When he turned back to the stage, Sochua was gone.

"Let's get out of here right now!"

⋀

Prime Minister Thul Chorn slouched behind his desk, staring at a distant spot on the floor. Whispered in his ear during his lunch with Sanderson were these words: "Violent confrontations at Olympic Stadium; something has happened to Sochua."

Thul's secretary, Son, entered the room. "Sir, I have General Nhim on the line."

Thul snatched the mobile phone from Colonel Son's hand. "What is going on?"

"There was an explosion near the stage," Nhim explained, "and Sochua was taken to her residence by her own people. Then the crowd started throwing bottles and rocks at my men."

"Did you do this?"

"Sir, I—"

"Did you order the assassination of Sochua?"

"I did nothing. Those were not my orders."

"Then who did it?"

"I don't know," said Nhim, "but I'm going to find out."

"You're not going to lose control of the streets again, are you?"

"I'll crush them."

"Keep it under control, but we don't want a bloodbath."

"Yes sir."

Thul ended the call and looked again at the spot on the floor. This was not good. Not good at all. Somebody once said, "Only a crisis—actual or perceived—produces real change." He was certain the observation had been made in an entirely different context, but, well, this needed to be contained—and quickly.

⋏

Minister of Interior and National Police Chief Nhim Saray didn't believe it for a minute. He had to hand it to Sochua: orchestrating her own assassination attempt, while unoriginal, had been brilliant. Yet, he would carry out his orders from the prime minister and put an end to her movement.

At the moment, however, he paused to consider a distraction. His deputy, Chet Pannha, had just informed him the American diplomat, Chris Kelly, had been arrested in Sihanoukville. He didn't wish to attach to this news undue significance—he certainly had enough on his mind—but he would be remiss if he did not consider what gain might be had by taking one course of action or another or, indeed, no action at all. Kelly, his diplomatic visa revoked, was in Cambodia illegally, and the Americans would be pleased if Nhim had him gently deported. But he was not in a mood to cooperate with the Americans. After all, what kind of cooperation could they expect from a man not worthy of a travel visa?

It would not do, on the other hand, to simply keep Kelly locked up, because sooner or later word was bound to get out, and then how would he explain his inaction to both the American embassy and the prime minister? No. That would please no one. If he were to release him, where was the harm in that? Kelly might even make some trouble for Chea Phyrom, and that couldn't be a bad thing. And if Phyrom tired of the game and killed the American or his daughter, the PM might, in the face of the death of an American diplomat, have no choice but to act against his nephew. Yes. The best thing was to simply get Kelly off his hands.

⏶

"You betrayed me." Chea Prak's voice quivered with anger. "I told you to release the girl."

Chea Phyrom had rarely seen his father this agitated. The general's entourage had stopped in front of Chea Phyrom Group, Ltd., and Phyrom had been "invited" to join his father in the back seat of his SUV. Civilians had stopped to gawk. Men in uniform surrounded the vehicle, their weapons at the ready. Apparently, there'd been some unrest at Olympic Stadium.

"Let me explain."

"My sources in the National Police have just informed me that the American girl's father has been arrested in Sihanoukville. What was he doing there? Why was he looking for his daughter there?"

"I can take care of it."

"You don't understand. I made a deal with Sochua. The girl must be released—*now.*"

"We have Yun. Fuck her!" There was something his father was not telling him. "Were you able to find out why Sochua turned Yun over to you? You know it wasn't just to save that little girl. Were you able to find out why she wanted him eliminated? Well?"

"*Do not question me!*"

"You told me you would let me have Yun when you were finished with him. After you extracted Sochua's secret."

Chea Prak's nostrils flared. "And you told me you would release the girl! Do it and you will have Yun! I will not ask you again. Now get out of my sight!"

Phyrom opened the door and stepped out of the vehicle feeling strangely calm. His father knew how to make men talk. If Yun knew something about Sochua—something that could wreck her plans—you could bet the old man knew. But what? He and Sochua were planning something big, and Phyrom intended to secure his place.

$$\lambda$$

"Madam! Madam," Sampour cried.

Lisa Kelly covered her ears; how many more crises could she handle? She had been lying in a fetal position on the sofa when Sampour placed in her hand their embassy-issue two-way radio, which had been emitting loud bursts.

"Attention! Attention!" The voice of David Finto could be heard clearly. "Please stand by for an important security announcement to be followed by a check of all units."

"How long has that been beeping?"

"Few minutes, madam."

"Attention! Attention! The following is an official security announcement. Due to violent civil unrest in central Phnom Penh, particularly in the area of Olympic Stadium, all Mission employees and family members are advised to stay in their homes unless there is a critical need to leave. This announcement will be followed by a check of all units."

Finto repeated this message and then a guard supervisor took over.

"Eagle Two, Eagle Two, radio check."

Paris Jefferson answered immediately. "Eagle Two to Eagle Base, I read you loud and clear. How me?"

Lisa turned down the volume. At Eagle 47, it would be a while before her turn.

"What's problem, madam?"

Lisa shrugged. "I haven't the slightest idea. I haven't read the news in forever. Thul or some of his buddies probably decided to bulldoze another slum to build a casino. Scumbags."

Sampour's brow furrowed. "Don't understand, madam."

"It's okay, Sampour. I'll call Hassan and see what's going on."

And she would have, but she got a "Network Busy" message on her mobile. She looked through the ornamental bars on the windows but could see nothing over the high walls surrounding the house. Where were they? Mai. Chris. What were they doing now? Why didn't Chris call her? She thought she'd try to call Hassan again—to see what was going on in the outside world. Her phone's background photo was of Mai cavorting on the playground at BB World. Just two weeks ago. Just two weeks ago. Un-fucking-believable.

CHAPTER 27

Quynh found it easy enough to pretend she was hungry; she hadn't eaten a single thing all day. She rubbed her belly. *"Nyam, nyam?"*

Like most of them, the woman didn't look at her and pushed on into the building. She touched her leg as she passed. She liked to do this. She played the game to amuse herself—see how many foreigners she could touch in a day.

"Hey, look," other beggar children exclaimed.

Another barang, a giant with straw-colored hair framing his mouth, got out of a *tuk-tuk* carrying a boy child and holding a girl by the hand. Quynh and her compatriots raced to him.

"Nyam, nyam," they cried.

The little girl was like a skittish animal, clinging to her father's leg as he paid the tuk-tuk driver. Her skin, almost transparent, glowed as if lit by white lights from behind. She was luminous. She had blue marbles for eyes, and her hair was like a doll's. Quynh reached out to touch her hair, having forgotten her purpose. An enormous hairy hand pushed hers away.

"Nyam, nyam," she whispered at the marble-eyed pair.

The man pressed something into her palm. Then they were gone. Quynh opened her hand and saw the green money that made the adults so happy— the same green money Mama had given Chinh for her.

"Wow, look what you got," one of the other children said.

"What is it?"

"It's one."

"One what?"

"Just one. It's better than riel."

Quynh sat on the curb and pondered her good fortune.

"Get out of the way!" a tuk-tuk driver cried, startling her. She moved to let him park. "Got lucky today, I see," he said, eyeing her money.

"Yes, Uncle."

"That's a dollar. If I were you, I'd keep it for myself—go around the corner and get me one of those rice cakes." The man pointed to the far end of the parking lot. He had a twinkle in his eye.

His words stunned her: keep it for herself. Her mouth dropped open at the very idea. She could keep the money for herself. They would beat her. She looked across the street to where Auntie Oanh lay asleep in the hammock under the tree. She wasn't moving.

The man followed Quynh's gaze. "Hurry. Before she wakes up."

Quynh walked to the end of the parking lot. Auntie Oanh didn't move. She walked out of the parking lot and around the corner into the irresistible smell of grilled rice cakes. A vendor's mobile kitchen stood parked in the street, surrounded by eager customers.

Mesmerized by the practiced movements of the woman as she flipped her treats for policemen, moto-dops, and shopkeepers, Quynh forgot all about her money. She wiped the drool from her mouth.

"One rice cake, Auntie?"

The busy cook batted away her outstretched hand. "Tssst! Go away!"

Quynh waited and watched the delicacies sell, three for five hundred riel. How she wanted to reach out and grab one!

A moto-dop smiled at her. He had three cakes and handed one to her.

"*Aakun*, Uncle."

The vendor threw her a nasty look, but she was much too hungry to care. The steaming rice burned her tongue as she sank her teeth through the browned crispy outside and into the soft center. Delicious.

Savoring her prize, she turned another corner in case the other children might see her and get jealous. She'd go back in a minute. She wandered unpaved side streets, gaping at her new surroundings, her mind free of any organized thought. She remembered her money and noticed she didn't know the way home. She noticed she didn't really have a home.

⋏

Paris Jefferson, now *chargée d'affaires* in the ambassador's absence, didn't know what to make of it all. She had gotten the official story from Regional Security Officer David Finto. A lone man had approached Sochua from backstage with a Russian-made hand grenade. Sochua's bodyguards shot him before he could pull the pin. No one besides the assassin was seriously injured.

The news was a shock. Yet it was the same thing Thul had done to Sambo Rithy in 2013, so why should it come as a surprise? The tactic worked very well for him the first time. Unlike in 2013, however, this time Thul's people had phoned her immediately to deny they'd had any involvement. Was that possible? Could it have been anyone else? Sochua's side insisted she'd been the target of a Thul-backed assassination attempt. Unfortunately, Sochua's bodyguards shot and killed the only man certain to know the truth.

Jefferson's mobile beeped. It was a text from Allison Rosenburg.

"Multiple sources say Sochua about to be arrested."

⋏

Sochua Nika spoke live on Honeybee Radio via telephone from her residence.

"I will not run and hide. If they want to arrest me, they can come and get me."

"Close your shops, leave your work, and protect Sochua," Khak Vanrith shouted ebulliently over the airwaves.

Phnom Penh's heavily oversubscribed mobile phone network shut down.

⋏

Hours later food was brought for those who had no money: a ladle of clear fish broth over rice. Chris couldn't keep the flies away, but he drank it all nevertheless. For the first time, he noticed a boy of about ten among them. Some prisoners again heated water for instant noodles; a lucky few received parcels packed by family members who had the wherewithal to bribe the guards to deliver. After lunch they gambled for money and cigarettes; the boy did well. Two men briefly fought over a spoon. Business was conducted: a guard rented a flip phone, drugs were swapped and sold. One man lay on the floor all day without moving. Liquid crept across the bathroom floor as the prisoners relieved themselves or poured the contents of their plastic bottles into the broken urinal. The fetid liquid reached the concrete lip and was held in check for the moment.

"Do you speak English?" a man asked, scooting across the floor to where Chris leaned against the wall. "My name is Hun. What your name?"

"What do you want?"

"How much for this book?" The man proffered a dog-eared Penguin Classic copy of *Jane Eyre*.

Jane Eyre. Chris vaguely recalled reading it in high school and wondered if that was the one where the man locked his crazy wife in the attic.

"How much you give me?"

"I don't have any money."

"Why you don't have money?"

"I guess the police took it."

"You don't know?"

"Nope."

Hun considered this in silence for a moment and then shuffled off.

The temperature rose. It would be in the high eighties by now, but the oven of the jail felt much hotter. Chris hoped it wouldn't rain in the afternoon; the tin roof was peppered with holes. In the late afternoon another man approached and stood looking down at him.

"Come on, man. It can't be that bad."

Chris looked up at a foreigner with long hair and beard, speechless at the suggestion that "it can't be that bad."

The man snorted. "Alright. So it sucks in here." He slid down the wall and sat next to him. "What'd you do?"

Chris shook his head. Didn't feel like talking.

"Alright. Not talking, huh? Yeah, that's the problem, see. These fucking Cambodians think every foreigner is a fucking pedophile. If you so much as look at a kid, they lock you up so they can get money out of you. I didn't do shit. They framed my ass. That bitch's mom told the police I fucked her daughter, and I didn't do shit." He paused. "Come on, man. What'd you do?"

Chris stared at the floor. He would've strangled the guy, but he was too tired.

"Well, this is what they do next. They'll tell you got to pay to go to your own fucking trial. That's what they did to me. They told me I couldn't go to my hearing unless I paid them five dollars! Well, I don't got no damn five dollars because they took all my money when they brought me in here! And I ain't got nobody on the outside who's going to send me any money. I mean, the guards brought a girl in here the other night for one of these guys—she couldn't've been no more than thirteen—and he just fucked her right there on floor while everyone watched. I wonder how much he had to pay for that.

"Listen, man. You tired of living on instant noodles? Ha! Do you think that Japanese dude who invented instant noodles ever would've thought that thousands of fucks like us all across Cambodia would be living on nothing but that shit? You can starve to death on it, but it's still better than the shit they give you for free in here!

"Listen, I got this, and I'll sell it to you." He held up a canned good. "Yeah, I bet it's been a long time since you had something like this. It's expired, but it's still good, let me tell you."

Chris reached weakly for the can, and the man snatched it back. It was corned beef hash. In some other universe he would've smiled at the notion of reading *Jane Eyre* and eating cold corned beef hash out of a can with his hands in a Cambodian jail.

"Shit looks like dog food, but, if you heat it up, it's damn good. Ten bucks and it's yours."

Chris would've traded a foot for a couple of Advil. "Leave me alone."

"Come on, man. I just need to get to my trial. How about a pack of cigarettes?"

Chris put his middle finger in the man's face. He just didn't give a damn.

"Alright. Have it your way, you stupid son of a bitch." He got to his feet with much groaning. "Hey, you know what they did when they brought you in here? When you were passed out on the floor, they all looked at your dick to see how big a foreigner was. They do shit like that. Crazy motherfuckers."

⋏

Quynh entered a wide thoroughfare crowded with people walking in one direction. Curious—and frightened a little—she followed. Along the edge of the procession vendors hawked every conceivable treat: flavored ice, grilled pork belly, roasted insects and spiders, durians and jackfruits, *sumlar mjew*—sour Vietnamese soup—and her favorite: *chook*, or lotus seeds. The vendors had smiles on their faces. People and more people, all walking, laughing, crying, shouting. One man was talking to himself and wiping blood from his face. She heard some nasty words. "Calm down," others exhorted.

What was this festival? Through the forest of adult legs she caught glimpses of pink stone: a building shaped like a bamboo shoot—a giant, pink bamboo shoot. That's where she would go. The forest thickened, and she had to squeeze through to get there.

She threaded her way up the steps of the monument and joined a few other children on a narrow ledge. They paid her no mind. From her vantage point she looked over a sea of black heads that stretched to the horizon. On her left, men with helmets and shields stood six deep behind a metal fence. It was all very interesting.

She grew hungry again and wandered back into the throng. She held her dollar in front of a noodle vendor.

"One please, Uncle."

He was very busy. Without a word he took her money and handed her a piping hot box fastened with a rubber band.

"Hey, wait for your change!" he called to her as she turned to leave.

He gave her three one-thousand *riel* notes. Stunning.

She sat on the grass in the shade of a stone bench and raked the steaming noodles into her mouth. No one paid her any attention. No one would take her back to the shop house. Maybe she could find her way back to her village. She scooted under the bench and lay on her side. She counted the cracks on the heels in front of her. She yawned and soon drifted to sleep with a full belly.

▲

Four mansions west of the home of Sochua Nika, troops of Brigade 70 had secured the perimeter of the prime minister's residence. From the Tonle Sap in the east to Monivong Boulevard in the west, from as far south as the office of Chea Phyrom Group, Ltd., to the American ambassador's residence in the north, tens of thousands of citizens danced, cheered, sold souvenirs, chanted slogans, taunted the police, and ate their midafternoon snacks. A troupe performed traditional dance in the center of the grand esplanade in front of Sochua's and the prime minister's homes. The shops along Sihanouk Boulevard remained open, doing brisk business.

Prime Minister Thul Chorn looked out the window of his office at the crowd and shook off a chill. "How is this happening?" He glared at General Chea Prak and then at National Police Chief Nhim Saray. "What is going on?"

"The radio spread a rumor that Sochua is about to be arrested," said Nhim. "Thousands of people gathered in front of her house while my men were still being attacked in front of Olympic Stadium. I believe it was carefully coordinated."

"I don't need any excuses!"

Chea stepped forward. "Sir, I have it from a credible source that she had her people initiate the rumor of her arrest."

"Of course she started the rumor!"

"She intends to make another radio address at six o'clock. Some say she's going to announce the formation of a new political party. Others say she is going to demand your resignation."

"And what do you suggest we do?"

Nhim cut in. "Sir, there may be as many as fifty thousand people out there, and a lot more are on the way. We will need to use live ammunition to clear the streets. And we need to arrest her. Say we're taking her into protective custody."

"No," Chea said. "That would be a mistake. Let me talk to her. Sochua and I have always had a more or less cordial relationship. Let me find out what she wants. She's not unreasonable."

"Negotiate with her? Never! Sir, let me take care of this now before it gets completely out of control."

Thul sat down, calmer. "No. You've already let this get completely out of control." He placed his elbows on his desk and steepled his fingers, as lucid as he ever was. To Chea he said, "Tell her this: if she agrees to get the people off the streets now, within one month I'll make a public announcement that I won't stand in the next general election, and I give her my word that she won't be arrested. She has until six p.m. to respond."

"But, sir," Nhim cried. "Why?"

"Why not? Haven't you heard what everybody else already knows? I wasn't planning to run for reelection anyway. This discussion is over."

"Well, congratulations."

Chea Prak smiled at the former Anti-Trafficking chief. The street behind the prime minister's and Sochua's residences and the North Korean embassy had been sealed off for security reasons for years, and so after the meeting with the prime minister he'd simply walked to her back door and rung the doorbell. It was all rather peaceful.

"Congratulations are a bit premature, don't you think?"

"Why? Thul is all but history, and I would imagine Sambo Rithy is despondent about his prospects. They say he's on a plane back from Los Angeles now."

"I wouldn't know. What did you come here to talk about?"

Charya entered the room carrying a tray.

"Ah, Charya. How are you? You look wonderful." Chea took the tray from the young woman and set it on the coffee table. He took her hands in his. "Still not married, I hear."

Charya smiled without meeting his gaze.

"Coffee?" Sochua interjected.

"Yes, please. By the way, this so-called assassination attempt. Brilliant. I'm just angry I didn't see it coming. It's a shame your people had to kill the poor man. I guess he didn't know that was part of the show."

Chea helped himself to a seat on the low sofa where he imagined the American diplomat had sat just days before on his own visit to General Sochua. The two women took chairs opposite him. Sochua stared at him blankly, giving nothing away.

"I can see you wish me to get to the point," he continued. "First, as you requested, the American girl will be released."

"Excellent. When?"

"And the prime minister, aware of our longtime cordial relationship, has asked me to come here on his behalf to try to defuse the current situation."

"What, specifically, is on offer?"

"Your job. An apology. Whatever you want. The prime minister wants you back in the government."

"Not interested."

Charya took her coffee with her and left the room.

Chea laughed to disguise his irritation. "I'm not surprised to hear you say that." He sighed, pausing to add sugar to his coffee. He stirred the liquid and took a careful sip before continuing in a low voice. "He's willing to guarantee you won't be arrested, and he'll announce within a month that he will not run in the next election. Just tell the people to go home."

"No thanks." Now it was Sochua's turn to engage in the protracted coffee ritual. "I'm not interested. Surely you can see why." She waved a hand toward the window.

"Nika, listen. You underestimate Thul's resolve. The elites are united against you, he still has the National Police—not to mention the Army—and he's going to order Nhim to empty the streets if you don't agree to his terms. And Nhim will be brutal. He must be; without Thul in power he cannot survive. Have you forgotten that his daughter will wed Thul's son in June? A lot of people are going to die."

Sochua looked him steadily in the eye. "No."

Chea Prak moved to the chair next to his one-time lover. "You have my support," he whispered. "But not like this. It's too risky. You might not win. *We* might not win."

She turned away. "I'll win."

"You strike me as very confident. Why, I wonder?"

⚔

Sochua took a deep breath and shuddered with memory. "Strange that you should wonder. You knew everything."

It was 1975. She was only thirteen when the Khmer Rouge took her. She considered herself one of the lucky ones, really; most of her relatives were dead. She became the personal slave of the commander of the Eastern Sector, Pech Borin, a twisted man responsible for the deaths of thousands of innocent civilians, who never once looked at her face and spoke to her only in the imperative. She fetched his water, cooked his food, bathed his feet before bed, and slept on the floor beneath his cot in case he might have needed something during the night.

As she cooked just beside them, Pech spoke freely with many men. He spoke of his plans for genocide, he spoke of torture, plans to "purify" the country. Later, he spoke with two of his men of plans to escape to Vietnam, obviously thinking his servant incapable of understanding. Pech had to escape because Sar Saloth had sent an emissary to bring him to the infamous death camp, S-21.

While she lay curled up on the floor too frightened to breathe, Pech cut the throat of Pol Pot's messenger and disappeared into the night with his two comrades. She was questioned. Did she help Pech escape? They shackled her ankles—she still had the scars—and placed a plastic bag over her head. They asked her questions she couldn't answer. She lost consciousness again and again. Finally they stopped. Pech was no longer talked about. They said he was dead, killed by the Vietnamese.

Two years later, Sochua escaped across the border. She wound up in a refugee camp, where she volunteered for the Cambodian resistance, several thousand refugees training to be the vanguard of a Vietnamese-funded invasion to rout the Khmer Rouge. Who did she find leading this small army? Pech Borin. But going by a different name.

She could see Pech was greatly respected; he saw many high-ranking visitors from the Vietnamese Army. He spoke fluent Vietnamese, itself a crime punishable by death under the Khmer Rouge—a sentence she saw him carry out many times with her own eyes.

Pech's two deputies were also in the camp. They did not remember Pech's shy, silent servant from before, but they noticed her now because she had become a woman, something of a beauty. They competed for her attention like adolescent dogs, and she foolishly fell in love and gave herself to one of them. After that, the two men became bitter enemies.

When the Vietnamese invaded Cambodia in April of 1979, Pech Borin and his small force of Cambodian freedom fighters led the charge. Pech let himself be installed as prime minister, a position he held throughout the subsequent decade of rule by Hanoi. Sochua distinguished herself in the fighting and, with the help of her lover and her lover's rival, who still hoped to steal her away to his own bed, she was made a minor officer in the new Cambodian army a few months after her seventeenth birthday. Her lover, having already promised to marry her once the war was over and knowing full well she was pregnant with his child, thrust her aside when the opportunity arose for him to marry the new PM's sister. Once she was discarded, her lover's rival lost all interest in her as well.

A much wiser Sochua now looked at Chea Prak, her first love, sitting next to her. It was time she used the weapon she'd been hiding for almost forty years.

"No. I don't trust him. You go back and tell *Pech Borin* to call for a general election and announce his immediate resignation, or I'll expose everything. I'll give him until nine a.m."

⚔

Chea, who had been casually stroking his chin, froze. This name—Pech Borin—was one he hadn't heard mentioned in decades, and to hear it from Sochua now was unfathomable. He remained outwardly calm while his mind raced madly to discover one thing: how this would affect *him*. He had planned to keep his secret a little longer, but this forced his move. He clasped Sochua's hand in his. She bristled at his touch.

"You've got no evidence. No one will believe you."

"They will. I have spent a lifetime in preparation. The moment I lead them to a mass grave, they will believe."

"Let me give you some advice," he said with a snarl. "Whatever you intend to say on this subject, well, you'd just better make sure it doesn't include me."

"In case you were wondering, I've made arrangements for evidence to be distributed widely in the event of any 'accident' involving me. Now take your dirty hands off me!"

She tried to pull away. He crushed her fingers in his and held fast. She winced.

A heavy click startled them both. Charya stood several feet away at an open desk drawer aiming a pistol at Chea's chest. The chief bodyguard released her mother's hand.

He laughed. "Come, girl. You wouldn't kill your own father. Put that thing away before you hurt somebody."

"I'm ashamed to have you as my father."

As he rose, her aim followed him. "I'm unarmed! Put that away."

Charya's eyes darted to her mother. Sochua nodded. Charya lowered the gun.

Sochua pointed at the door. "Now get out!"

"Not yet. I have something I want to say." Time to use his own greatest weapon. "But should I say it in Vietnamese? After all, that is your native tongue, isn't it?"

Sochua's mouth dropped open slightly as he continued.

"Yes, that's right, and I can prove it. And you don't have to worry about any 'accidents.' After all, I need you around to make sure I always have a job. So I don't care what you say about the prime minister, but, like I said, you'd better keep me out of it. Oh, and how did you put it? 'In case you were wondering, I've made arrangements for evidence to be distributed widely in the event of any *accident* involving me.'"

Chea marched toward the door. He paused in front of his daughter and brought the back of his hand across her face. Blood spewed from her lip.

"If you ever point a gun at me again, I'll have you cut into pieces!"

Sochua rushed to her daughter's side. She lifted her chin and dabbed her lip with a tissue.

"Why are you smiling?" asked Charya, crying.

"Because," Sochua said, holding Chea's gaze, "now I understand how much your father needs us to win."

"I'll see myself out." Chea Prak turned on his heel and left, confident Sochua understood she needed him too.

Prime Minister Thul Chorn felt every one of his seventy-four years. He sat silently at his conference table, the corners of his mouth quivering, between Nhim Saray and Chea Prak. Outside, a helicopter landed within the residence compound; it would be carrying General Phann Phalla, commander in chief of the Royal Cambodian Armed Forces, as well as the Deputy Commander in Chief and Army Commander Meas Sophea.

"Sir, Sochua's got no proof, no evidence," said Nhim. "She's bluffing."

"Perhaps." Maybe there *was* proof. Pech Borin *did* exist.

It was during December of 1976. Pech Borin, a fit man of thirty-four in a black pajama-like uniform lay awake, waiting. Another man snored on a raised wooden platform. The few months of the cool-dry season were upon Cambodia, and in the Eastern Mountains the night was chill. The jungle and a crescent moon spared little light for Pech as he studied the regular rise and fall of his comrade's chest, not yet daring to make a move.

Long after midnight, Pech examined a child soldier sleeping on the floor. Satisfied he would be unnoticed, he slithered from his cot and crouched beside it, listening. He analyzed the sounds of the forest: the frantic chirp of cicadas and katydids, the careful movement of animals, the steady hum of decomposition. He strained to hear above the din the arrhythmias of man-made noise. Nothing. Creeping to the entrance of the hut, he peeked at a boy sleeping against a mango tree, a rifle cradled in his arms. He knelt at the head of the sleeping man and slid a knife out of the red *krama* tied at his waist.

Pech examined the face of the man who had certainly been sent by Sar Saloth—known to the outside world as Pol Pot—to bring him to S-21, Democratic Kampuchea's most efficient torture chamber. Fingering the blade, he pondered the irony of his fall from favor. Granted, he and Sar had never been personally close, but Pech's revolutionary credentials were impeccable.

While Sar, an undistinguished student with a privileged background and palace connections, learned his socialism studying in France on scholarship, Pech had risen from a family of desperately poor rice farmers to become a secondary-school teacher by the age of sixteen. He was already a hard-core member of the Indochina Communist Party when Sar was still drinking Beaujolais in chic Left Bank cafés talking politics rather than armed struggle.

In the beginning Pech had been an efficient administrator of the eastern sector, carrying out Sar's dubious social reengineering programs and diligently silencing enemies of the Revolution. He had followed Brother Number One's leadership with true revolutionary zeal and had honestly believed they could succeed in building a classless agrarian utopia. The people would one day forgive what he had done for the greater good. However, as he began to see the revolution for what it was—nothing more than the twisted megalomania of one paranoid despot—he realized he also had been overzealous. One day someone would dig up all the bodies, and the nation might not be so forgiving after all.

Word of Sar's internecine purges had reached Pech long before the unexpected guest sleeping before him. Official propaganda had recently begun describing the party as full of traitors and infected by "disease-ridden microbes" under which the heat must be turned up to save the greater body. Pech, certain Sar had marked him for death, began making plans for his escape. He would shed his revolutionary pseudonym and flee to Vietnam, where he was well known from his pre-revolution days. There he would reestablish ties with the Vietnamese Communists, join the Cambodian resistance, and be well placed when the current regime fell. His plan was not perfect, but it was his best chance—his only chance—for both physical and political survival. He had placed one hand tightly over his comrade's mouth and slit his throat from ear to ear. Yet, there was still the matter of the mass graves...

Nhim cleared his throat. "Sir?"

Thul snapped out of his reverie. "Well, that's it then." Proof or no, Sochua had to be brought to heel.

"What is your order, sir?"

"Empty the streets," Thul responded without conviction.

"Yes sir."

"Wait until early morning. Just before dawn."

Nhim smiled thinly. "And what shall I do with Sochua?"

"Prime Minister," interjected Chea, "I think it would be a mistake to arrest her now—"

"Why are you always protecting this woman?" Nhim demanded.

"Let me finish!" Chea roared.

"Perhaps you still have feelings for her after all these years."

Chea pounded his fist on the table. "How dare you question my loyalty! If she does have evidence, the prime minister could face charges of genocide. We all could."

"All the more reason to get rid of her now."

"Enough!" The confrontation had energized Thul. "No. I've already been too lenient. That's where I went wrong."

"Every hour she's free, we appear weaker," Nhim said.

"Yes. That's right. This is a coup attempt, and that's what she'll be charged with," Thul said.

"Yes sir."

Thul rose and opened the door, ushering in his armed forces chiefs himself.

⋏

George Granger rested his head on the steering wheel, utterly out of ideas. Chris was in jail, Mai was just as missing as she had been on day one, and, realistically, he couldn't hold Leonard Perry against his will forever. Chea

Phyrom and his folks were bound to have heard by now that Chris had gotten himself arrested, and they would be moving Mai from Sihanoukville—if she had ever been there—or worse. The only thing to do was call the American embassy and tell them everything, which meant Chris would be kicked out of Cambodia without his daughter.

He got a text message from Jane Hightower: Where RU?

"Sihanoukville"

"WTF?"

He hadn't told Hightower he was leaving Bangkok, but he couldn't explain here. "Long story"

"Hear about Sochua?"

"No"

"Assassination attempt."

Granger was intrigued but up to his eyeballs in trouble already. He tried to use his phone's voice to text to say, "Well, right now I've got bigger fish to fry," but the message came out, "we'll fight now I've got the Christopher eye". He sent the text anyway. "Stupid piece of junk," he said, and tossed the phone in the passenger seat.

Leonard Perry had emerged from Cabaret, a popular blow-job bar, a block and a half away and was loping in his direction. He gave a thumbs-down. Granger cranked the engine. Well, that was it. This had to be the last.

Perry, instead of continuing to the jeep, stopped and pointed at something. What the hell was he up to? Granger shook his head. Perry pulled his earlobe, dragged a finger across his throat, and twisted the tip of his nose as if he were giving some sort of signal. Perry laughed at his own joke and held up a finger indicating he should wait.

Granger watched impatiently as Perry made several timid attempts before crossing the busy garbage-strewn avenue to a stall selling cigarettes and lottery tickets. Moto-dops shooting the breeze with the cigarette vendor moved aside for a paying customer. A minibus stopped in front of the stall, took on some passengers, and moved on. Perry generated much interest as he dug at length in his pockets, proffered some cash, and retrieved a pack of cigarettes. A second customer approached. Perry and the man briefly made eye contact before another minibus blocked Granger's view. Perry crossed the street, giving wide berth to a noisy pack of mutts roiling down the center of the avenue. He climbed in the jeep with some difficulty, his purple face beaded with sweat.

"How long are we going to do this?"

Granger paid him no attention. He was watching the cigarette stand.

"What is it?"

"Shut up."

The second customer had made his purchase and now surveyed the area as he tapped out a cigarette. Granger looked away.

"What's your problem?"

"The big guy in black at the cigarette stand. Is he looking at us?"

"No."

Granger eased the jeep into first gear and grimaced at the noise. He drove a block and parked, adjusting his side mirror to observe his subject.

Perry looked over his shoulder. "Who was that?

Granger kept his eyes on the mirror. "That is none other than the infamous Mao Vannak. He works for Chea Phyrom, the man who kidnapped Chris's daughter."

Perry shrugged. "Alright. If you say so. Does this mean I can go?"

"No. It means we're going to follow him and see where he goes."

"I hate this place. Oh, shit, I forgot to get a lighter."

"Since when do you smoke?"

"Starting now."

"You're even dumber than I thought."

A

Even nominal Commander in Chief General Phann Phalla had to admit the Royal Cambodian Armed Forces was something of a joke. While officially the combined forces stood at just over one hundred thousand souls, the actual number was somewhere around thirty thousand, though it was impossible to be sure, and no more than twenty thousand had the kit and training to put up any kind of a fight when they weren't busy smuggling drugs, humans, or timber. The best of the twenty thousand effective troops belonged to Brigade 70, the prime minister's two-thousand-strong personal bodyguard unit based in Takeo under Chea Prak, who theoretically reported to the commander in chief but in reality took his orders directly from the prime minister.

This left General Phann with roughly eighteen thousand trained troops under his command with which to protect the capital, divided more or less equally between Region 2, based in Kampong Cham, and Region 3, headquartered in Kompong Speu. Included in Region 3 was the special case of the 911 Parachute Regiment, which operated more or less independently from its regional command.

The 911's independence was a legacy of the coup attempt of 2002, during which the Region 3 commander, a royalist loyal to Prince Chhun, led a surprise attack on the capital following Thul's ouster of Chhun from the People's Party of Cambodia and the government. The attack from Region 3 took everyone by such surprise that the prime minister had to flee the Council of Ministers to avoid being captured, and the rebellious troops might still have gotten him if the 911 regiment hadn't disobeyed the orders of its traitorous regional commander and come to the aid of the PM. Thul duly rewarded the loyalty of the Parachute Regiment, whose support raised many eyebrows given that its commander, General Hem Bora, was also a known royalist, and since that date the regiment had maintained a tradition of quasi-independence from the Region 3 command, a tradition implicitly supported by the prime minister.

The same regiment had also been responsible for some of the greatest abuses in the aftermath of the short-lived conflict, summarily executing many hundreds of rebellious officers and troops, some of whose bodies had lain on the street in front of the regimental headquarters for days, their eyes gouged out, and others whose decapitated bodies decorated the Tonle Sap. Still, General Phann didn't trust Hem Bora and his 911 regiment, but, to be fair, he didn't trust anyone.

It was also subsequent to the coup attempt that Thul created the bodyguard unit under his brother-in-law Chea Prak and hired twenty thousand additional National Police troops under his oldest ally, Nhim Saray. Phann himself had been promoted to Thul's inner circle and made commander in chief after Thul sacked Phann's three immediate superiors for being surprised by the coup attempt. Phann relished this current opportunity to prove his worth, yet he couldn't dream of ever penetrating the ruling clique he jokingly referred to as The Gang of Three. That much was clear.

He had his plan ready for Thul. Units from Region 2 would control access to the capital from the east and north; Region 3 would do the same in the west; Chea's bodyguards not already in the capital would control access from the south; the 911 Parachute Regiment would secure the airport and shut down Honeybee Radio; and the National Police, under Nhim Saray's command, would then wipe the city clean.

CHAPTER 28

A grim and unapologetic prime minister addressed the nation on TV1, TV3, and TV5, the red and blue Cambodian flag, with its image of Angkor Wat, serving as a backdrop.

He issued denials. "This government was in no way involved in the apparent assassination attempt of General Sochua Nika. Furthermore, there is not and never has been any plan to arrest General Sochua. This rumor is entirely unfounded."

He talked tough. "I assure the citizens of this country that I will not allow a gang of ruffians to threaten the stability of the nation with unlawful and violent demonstrations."

He made meaningless concessions in an attempt to divide his opposition. "In the interest of national reconciliation, I will request His Majesty King Norodom Sihamoni to pardon our brother Sambo Rithy, and I invite Mr. Sambo to return to Cambodia and engage in civil debate over the future of our country. He has nothing to fear.

"My fellow citizens, the forces that oppose the will of the Cambodian people have organized against us. Those who are favored by the imperialists and the colonialists insult me, wrongly accuse me, and vilify me in the press and on the radio without shame. I do not care for myself, but I will continue to defend the people as I always have. I will not surrender!

"In the darkest hour of Cambodian history I willingly gave you my blood. Now the country requires sacrifice again. I am not afraid. Outsiders do not want us to be an independent and prosperous nation, but we will prevail!"

But the crowds stayed in the streets.

⚔

At dusk all prisoners—except for the man who still lay unmoving on the floor—were lined up and counted by the trusty as he menaced them with a rubber hose. Chris wondered if food would be brought again; it was, but this time only for those who could pay.

Darkness came. Bare bulbs hung at opposite ends of the cell, but they never so much as flickered. Some detainees sat quietly talking; those with mosquito nets crawled under them. Money changed hands, and a guard gave a portable DVD player to a man who played porn featuring a woman having sex with a chimpanzee. The others crowded around the spectacle in open-mouthed silence. Chris thought of canned corned beef hash and Lisa and Mai and staggered sick to the edge of the wet bathroom, poisoned by his lunchtime meal.

⚔

Khak Vanrith couldn't sit still for a moment. Intoxicated by events of the day and the sense that his radio station had played an important part in them, he worked tirelessly to put eyewitness accounts of the morning and the scene in front of Sochua's house on the air. Tucked away in his soundproof box, he didn't hear the shouts until a young woman threw open the studio door and interrupted his live broadcast.

"You've got to come see this!"

He cut to music.

A convoy of trucks and armored personnel carriers rumbled toward them down both sides of Boulevard de la Confederation de la Russie led by a single T-54 battle tank. For the first time in recent memory, Khak was speechless.

The tank passed directly in front of The Beehive, turned abruptly, and drove onto the grass median. Its steel track crushed a concrete park bench. The tank's dome-shaped turret rotated and aimed its gun at the center of Khak's modest radio empire. Still, he didn't believe it. Armed men poured into the building.

Programming resumed, consisting entirely of uninterrupted repetitions of the Cambodian national anthem.

⋏

At seven p.m., Sochua stood among the orchids and potted palms on her balcony and raised her hands to heaven.

"I. Am. Alive!"

She waited five minutes for the crowd to stop cheering.

"They have taken our radio station, but we cannot give up now! We must stay in the streets until the prime minister calls for new elections and steps down from his office!"

⋏

General Hem Bora, commander of the 911 Parachute Regiment, answered the phone with one word: "Impressive."

"Are you going to keep your end of the bargain?" Sochua asked.

"We can't win," he stated flatly. "It would be suicide."

Sochua Nika suppressed an urge to scream. "You filthy coward! I knew you would betray me. Just like you betrayed Chhun in 2002."

"Yes, and the odds were much more in my favor then. But we still would have lost, and I had no interest in losing. And I don't now."

Sochua contemplated the risk and made a decision. "We have Chea."

Hem laughed through his nose. "I don't believe you. Chea would never do it. Never. He's playing you."

"Believe it. Thul Ly will marry Nhim Saray's daughter within weeks. Chea knows he can never let Ly succeed his father. Nhim would destroy him."

"I'll believe it when I see it."

"Fine. And then I'll count on your support."

⋏

Throughout the years, though they were favored sons—perhaps because they were—Nhim Saray and Chea Prak had found it expedient on a handful of occasions to meet in secret to discuss matters in the prime minister's best interests but without his full knowledge. Sometimes it was just easier that way.

For this purpose, the two rivals maintained a discreet couple in a home on the northern edge of town. The couple ran the home as a brothel so that the two men might maintain plausible deniability if anyone ever questioned their reasons for being there.

When Chea arrived at 11:10 p.m., Nhim's entourage was already outside. Husband and wife stood bathed in pink fluorescence in the doorway, palms together in front of their faces.

"Your room is ready, sir."

Chea nodded and made his way to the second floor. He knew why Nhim had called this meeting. He'd expected it and had already decided not to meet him. In the end, however, he couldn't resist the opportunity to meet his old enemy and flaunt his victory. He wanted to see the look on Nhim's face when he realized his ruin. His two best men took their places outside the room next to Nhim's men. He opened the door and went in alone.

The windowless room was long and unfurnished but for two simple chairs and a square table. Nothing on the walls, nothing on the floor, nothing on the table. Nhim, in battle dress, was already seated and clearly impatient. He didn't rise or acknowledge Chea in any way until they were both sitting down.

"I think it's time we agreed upon what happened in the seventies," Nhim said.

"Oh?"

"We have to assume Sochua's going to implicate us, as well. But she has no proof we knew anything. So as long as our stories match and we put forth a united front, we—you and I, I mean—can survive this."

"But she only threatened to expose Thul," noted Chea. "Perhaps she's sending us a signal."

"Perhaps. But we need to be prepared, in any case."

Chea scratched his chin. He allowed a smirk. "No, Minister. You do."

Fear, something he hadn't felt in a long time, cut Nhim. What was this about? Clearly, Chea had a plan, and it must be good. He hated the waiting, Chea being in control. He braced himself and asked the obvious question.

"What do you mean?"

"I mean that I have taken out a little insurance policy to ensure my safety. Sochua would not now dare speak ill of me in the least. You, on the other hand, well…"

Nhim swallowed dryly. Chea was bluffing.

"What's wrong? Got nothing to say?"

Nhim waved a hand dismissively. "What 'insurance policy'?"

"Let's just say that Sochua has her own little secrets, and I've made it my business to know them."

"This is ridiculous!" Nhim was losing his cool. "No matter what you think you may have on Sochua, nobody's going to believe anything you say. Our only chance is to—"

"No, you're wrong," interrupted Chea. "They will believe this. It's the *only* thing they'll believe. The only thing that could destroy her."

"What is it that you could possibly know that the people would not forgive her for? There is nothing. We must stick together!"

"You may as well face it, Nhim. I've won. When Sochua takes power, you'll be ruined. After all these years, I've finally won."

"You've won nothing. No one will believe you, and Sochua will never take power. Ly must succeed his father. This is treason!"

"It's over." Chea stood as if to leave.

Nhim jumped to his feet, dangerously lightheaded. He let his hand brush against his trousers leg; he'd recently upgraded his private piece to a Kel-Tec P32, a low-caliber worst-case-scenario mouse gun—nine ounces, fully-loaded—which he kept in a pocket holster.

"Listen to me!"

Chea smiled. "Good-bye." He turned and headed toward the door.

"Stop! *Stop!*"

Chea continued walking. Nhim yanked the gun from his pocket. He aimed unsteadily at the back of his one-time fellow student, comrade-in-arms, and best friend. And fired.

The door burst open and bodyguards rushed into the room, weapons drawn. Chea staggered backward, gaping at the growing stain around the exit wound in his chest. Nhim laughed. He won. He closed his eyes and willed the bullets come.

Chapter 29

Chea Phyrom hugged a hostess at the Long Beach VIP Karaoke Club.
"Love me tender, love me true," he sang over her shoulder.

His phone vibrated in his pocket. He pushed the hostess away, and she killed the music for him.

A bull. That's what he imagined he looked like minutes later when, shoulders back and fists balled, he burst through the double doors of the Emergency Room at Calmette Hospital. One door hit a nurse pushing a trolley of supplies, and the other crashed into the yellow wall. On his heels were a distressed receptionist and a beefy man in black, his sidearm in plain sight. Patients and their families and friends waiting on the floor scrambled to get out of the way.

"Where is he?" roared Phyrom, scanning the chaos in front of him.

"In the VIP wing," the receptionist stammered, pointing the way to a corridor of closed doors where no patients had to sit on the floor. "At the end of the hall."

Phyrom saw it. A dozen of his father's men stood in front of a door, both in and out of uniform.

"Move!"

Inside the room, white uniforms were everywhere. Phyrom bent over his father.

Chea Prak's lips moved. "Son," he sighed.

A foreigner entered the room, pulling on surgical gloves. "Clear this room! If you don't need to be here, get out now!" Several people scurried toward the door.

Phyrom grabbed the man's forearm. "Is he going to live?"

The doctor shouted something in French and began to cut open the victim's shirt. "Not if I don't stop his internal bleeding. Who are you?"

"I'm his son."

"Well, you need to get out of here now and take that gun with you." He nodded at the bodyguard at the foot of the bed.

"I need to talk to my father."

"Sorry. He's going to the operating room *now*."

"Not until he talks to me, he's not!"

Phyrom gave a nod. His man grabbed the doctor's right arm and pinned it to his back. He yanked him away from the patient and pressed his face into the wall.

Phyrom rounded on the horrified Cambodian staff. "Get out!"

They complied in haste.

"Father," he said in his father's ear.

"Phyrom?"

"Yes, Father."

"I'm sorry."

"I need to know. What did Yun tell you?"

"I'm...sorry. Forgive me."

"What did Yun tell you about Sochua?"

Prak's mouth worked, but no sound came out. He smacked his lips several times, then lay still.

"Father? Father, tell me."

Prak's eyelids fluttered. "Phyrom?"

"I need to know what Yun told you about Sochua."

"Uh...he...I..."

The doctor struggled behind them. "He's going to die if you don't let me operate!"

"Tell me. What did he tell you?"

Phyrom examined his father's bare chest. In one pectoral was a small round hole. No blood, just a breach in the skin, black around its edges. Phyrom touched the cold skin of his father—the father who had never loved him. The man he'd spent his entire life trying to please and make proud. He touched the small hole with his index finger.

"Tell me Sochua's secret."

He dug his finger deeply into the wound, twisting it to and fro. His father's back arched off the bed, but there was no scream, just a liquid wheeze.

Phyrom probed the wound further. "What did he say?" He put his ear on his father's lips and heard the old man's last words. He smiled and turned to his man. "Let's get out of here."

The bodyguard released the doctor.

"What the hell is wrong with you?" the doctor screamed at them. "Are you crazy?"

Phyrom drove his fist into the unsuspecting man's chin, laying him flat on the tile.

Sochua couldn't sleep. A loud knocking on her bedroom door startled her. Was this it? Surely not. When they came, they would come blazing. Still, this couldn't be good news. She slid open the drawer of her nightstand and took out her old .45, her hands not as steady as they ought to be.

"Mother?"

Sochua put the gun away and opened the door.

"You're not going to believe what I'm about to tell you."

Sochua listened, and her balance failed her. She felt behind her for her mattress. Charya had been right; this was too much to believe: Nhim Saray and Chea Prak dead at each other's hands.

She looked in the mirror and saw an old woman with her hair down hunched on the edge of the bed in a tired satin nightgown. She could have been anyone's grieving mother.

"What is it?"

"It's just…it's just…well, there were times. Things could have been different. Should have been different."

"What's wrong with you?"

"Don't be ridiculous." She just needed to clear her throat. "I'm fine."

"Then what is it?"

Sochua held her head in her hands. "We're lost."

"But—"

"Let me think!" The general said nothing for almost a minute.

"I wonder," said Charya finally, "who shot first."

Sochua studied her daughter. She already had the same wrinkles around her eyes as her mother. Yes. Who shot first? That gave her an idea.

"What?" Charya asked. "What is it?"

"Did you hear that men loyal to Nhim and Chea have begun fighting each other in the streets?"

"No, I haven't heard that."

"You will. Hand me that phone."

Sochua called General Hem Bora, who, having also just learned the news of his rivals' spectacular demise, listened to Sochua's second plea of the day with renewed interest.

"I need Honeybee Radio," she said. "I need it back on the air."

Hem was no fool; he knew the risks he faced. "What's in it for me?"

⅄

Chris awoke to cold water thrown in his face. Darkness was complete, and he knew nothing of where he was or why. The lights came on, blinding him and then revealing the trusty wielding a pail and exhorting him in an incomprehensible staccato of alien words. Disoriented and wasted, he offered no resistance as two uniformed men dragged him out of the cell where he had spent the last thirty-six hours. Some clothes were thrust into his hands, and he staggered, bent, into the moonless night outside the jail.

Hunkered relatives of the imprisoned opened their eyes and raised their heads to stare at him squinting into the darkness. A lone noodle vendor didn't look very open for business. Chris careened into the black with a vague notion that he needed to get back to the beach and find George, without considering the danger of staggering through Sihanoukville alone in the wee hours or even the direction he was headed. He stepped on a sleeping dog's tail—it yelped and scattered—and tumbled to the ground, rolled onto his back, and lay still, too weak from dry heaves and dehydration to care.

Presently, a hand raised his head and bottled water reached his lips, a vaguely familiar voice meeting his ears. He drank the entire bottle.

"Mong?"

How long it took them to get to Champion Beach or how he managed to stay on the back of a moto, Chris had no idea.

"Well, look what the cat dragged in," he heard George say as he lifted him into a hammock. He remembered nothing else.

⋏

Inside his official residence, Thul Chorn, prime minister still, sat at his desk in his night clothes, accompanied by his loyal secretary, Son. Only a small table lamp was on, and the room was in shadow. He heard something. He heard it again. Like a voice from the bottom of a well.

"Sir?"

"Huh? What is it?"

"Honeybee Radio, sir. What are your orders?"

Thul Chorn grabbed the man and shook him.

"Get Hem and find out what's going on. Now!"

There it was again. The pressure. Thul pressed his palm just below his rib cage and leaned back in his chair. He needed his nitroglycerin. Nobody knew about that—not Nhim or Chea, and especially not his wife—except for his doctors in China, where he'd gone for his "routine physical." But where were his pills?

⋏

For a decade and a half, Deputy National Police Chief Chet Pannha had waited for his moment. He should've been made chief years ago when Interior Minister Nhim Saray fired his immediate superior. But instead of promoting him to the job, Nhim took the position for himself and had remained in both positions ever since. So Chet had to pretend it didn't bother him. He had to smile for the cameras and act as if rage at being publicly emasculated by a man ten years his junior didn't burn within him at every waking moment. He contented himself with the not entirely unfulfilling cause of personal enrichment, having given up any hope of moving into the top job.

Nothing, absolutely nothing, could have prepared him for the news he'd received tonight. Chea Prak and Nhim Saray had gunned each other down in a whorehouse. Whatever the real story behind that one was, he couldn't begin to imagine, but it worked out well for him. The prime minister had ordered him to end the insurgency that had brought the capital to a standstill. Not a problem. He would do it, and he would not hold back. He wouldn't allow this kind of public defiance as long as he was in charge. And Sochua? Well, he would just go ahead and quietly end her life. The PM could thank him later. For fifteen years he'd been waiting for this.

"Sir?"

Chet looked at the young colonel in the doorway.

"Honeybee Radio is back on the air."

"What? How?"

"General Hem's regiment, sir, has apparently joined the rebels.

Chet froze. General Hem. Joined the rebels. This complicated the situation significantly. "Are you sure?"

"Yes sir."

⚔

Sochua Nika listened in her living room as Khak Vanrith of Honeybee Radio read on the air news reports she had prepared.

"Ministry of Interior troops loyal to the late General Nhim Saray continue to clash with members of Army Brigade 70, the prime minister's bodyguard unit, at locations throughout the city. These revenge attacks are apparently the result of a shootout that took place around midnight involving Nhim and chief bodyguard Chea Prak, who later died in hospital. A witness said..."

Charya brought tea. "Frankly, I'm surprised he agreed to do it."

"Khak will do anything I ask of him."

"Yes, but broadcasting fake news?"

"He will be generously rewarded."

"I don't think he cares about those kinds of rewards."

"Then he does it for the good of the country," Sochua snapped. "Who cares why!"

Charya sat and poured tea for her mother and then herself. "Do you think it will work?"

"I do." Sochua imagined an Army troop transport approaching a National Police roadblock. The Army driver waves the police aside. The police motion for the vehicle to stop. Men on both sides are heavily armed. "Relations between the Army and the National Police are fraught under the best conditions. We've just provided the match."

⅄

A radio crackled at Paris Jefferson's bedside; it was the encrypted channel. Groping in the dark, Jefferson knocked the handset onto the floor. Eyes still shut, she rolled off the bed and homed in on a tinny electronic version of David Finto's voice.

"Yes, David, what is it?"

"I've just heard from a credible source that both Nhim Saray and Chea Prak are dead."

She took a few seconds to process what Finto had said. It must be a mistake. "What happened? Is it a coup?"

"Apparently they shot each other—in some kind of argument."

Unbelievable. "Is it confirmed?" If true, this would decimate Cambodia's four-decade-old ruling clique. Real progress might be possible.

"Hassan is on his way to the hospital right now to see for himself, but my source has never been wrong before."

"Okay. Keep me informed—and tell Hassan to be careful."

"There's more. The radio's reporting that Army and National Police troops are fighting it out in the streets."

Then it's true; Nhim and Chea would never have allowed such a thing. "Issue a mandatory stay-at-home order right away."

"Will do."

Jefferson placed the radio in its cradle. She opened the blinds and could see the residence of Nhim Saray in the yellow glare of sodium lamps across the street. Groaning, she turned on her bedside light. All hell was about to break loose. "Maybe that's what's needed," she said to herself in the mirror.

Thul Chorn waited for the pain to subside and beckoned for the phone. Judging by the look on Colonel Son's face, he must appear on the verge of death.

"Are you alright, Prime Minister?"

Thul ignored him and dialed a three-digit number. Thul's new National Police chief, Chet Pannha, answered immediately.

"Sir!"

"You need to control your men now!"

"Sir, I—"

Thul couldn't listen. The pain was back. This time worse than the last. A tightness, a weight in his chest, had moved up into his left arm and his neck.

Son rushed to his side. "Are you okay, sir?"

Thul waved the man away. "I'm fine."

He would be fine if these idiots would just leave him alone. He clutched his chest. "I want…that radio station…off the air. Get me the commander in chief."

"Yes sir. Are you okay, sir?"

"Hurry!"

Quynh awoke with a start and couldn't sort out day from night. In all directions the ground wiggled, alive, as citizens woke and small huddled groups stood to see what was the matter. She squeezed her way onto the bench to witness the action: at the far end of the esplanade, vehicles and men clashed under streetlamps, near enough for her to make out pops and faint shouts. She was afraid and wanted to go back to Auntie Oanh's. But how? At once the crowd began to move, and she was soon swept up in it.

Paris Jefferson was on the fast track to an ambassadorship, but what she was about to do would certainly scuttle those plans; Washington would not approve. Yet even with the police momentarily in disarray, Sochua wouldn't last the night. Chet Pannha would soon regain control of his National Police troops, and then the crackdown would begin. Sources told her Prime Minister Thul had already given the order to empty the streets and eliminate Sochua. If Chet proved unable to end the unrest, the Army was more than capable. But Jefferson had a unique opportunity to influence events, and she'd come to care for Cambodia too much not to try.

She couldn't ignore the irony, however, of risking her career on behalf of Sochua. One could be forgiven for thinking that a natural affinity might exist between the two most high-profile professional women in the country, but that was not the case. Jefferson had found Sochua dismissive, if not downright hostile, on the numerous occasions they had met, and she got the impression the general preferred the company of men—or, at least, took them more seriously.

It was 4 a.m. Five minutes earlier Jefferson had dispatched a trusted courier with a message to Khak Vanrith at Honeybee Radio. She needed not await his response; she was committed to her course of action in any event.

Several men jumped to attention when she stepped outside into the cool, dense humidity. On a normal night there would be only two local guards on duty within the compound. She quickly counted six. The high walls did not entirely muffle the unrest without, but otherwise the dark serenity of the compound belied the chaos in the streets outside.

"Sokh, I'm going out."

"Yes ma'am."

Ousaphea, her chauffeur came running and opened the car door.

"No, I'll be driving this time."

"Ma'am?"

Jefferson explained her intentions. "And I don't want you involved."

"Ma'am, if you go, I want to drive you."

"Ousaphea, I will drive myself."

"Get in the car, please, ma'am. It is my responsibility."

"Fine. You drive. But uncover the flags first." This time, as *chargée d'affaires*, she had the right.

"Yes ma'am!"

Jefferson watched as Ousaphea removed the sleeves and unfurled the small flags on the front of the vehicle.

Pidour, a guard supervisor, rushed to the scene. "Ma'am, are you going outside?"

"Yes, open the gate, please."

"No, madam, cannot. It is not safe."

"Open the gate, please."

"Yes ma'am." He turned away and mumbled into his radio. Asking David Finto what to do, no doubt, and Finto would tell him to keep her there. Technically, as regional security officer, he had the authority.

Jefferson held out her hand. "Could I borrow your radio for a sec?"

Pidour didn't hesitate. "Yes ma'am."

She turned off his radio and tossed it onto the backseat of the car. "Thanks. Now open the gate." She got in the back seat and closed the door.

Pidour loosed a rope, and counterweights raised the long gate arm. He directed his subordinates to lower the bollards to street level. Guards removed a padlock and rolled the massive steel doors open on their track to reveal Norodom Boulevard filled with Cambodians of all stripes marching south.

"Madam?"

"Lock the doors, Ousaphea."

"Yes ma'am."

The car crept out of the compound past two dozen municipal policemen in riot gear, interrupting the flow of the dense crowd moving toward Independence Monument. People pointed and pressed their faces to the windows—curious, not hostile. The doors of the compound clanged shut behind.

"Slowly, Ousaphea. Slowly."

"Yes ma'am."

Ousaphea matched the direction and speed of the crowd. Pidour, the guard supervisor, was, with some difficulty, jogging alongside, shouting into another radio and waving people out of the way. Finto would call this "a potentially explosive situation." He would be right. Jefferson cracked the window.

"Go back, Pidour."

"No ma'am," he shouted.

A teenager climbed on the hood and danced, to the great delight of the crowd. An older man scolded and pulled him off, but the idea had taken hold; half a dozen boys jumped on. Pidour brandished his nightstick.

"Pidour, no!" Jefferson yelled.

Ousaphea stopped the car. "Cannot see, madam."

"Turn on Honeybee Radio."

Khak Vanrith was on the air: "…American ambassador is on her way to the home of General Sochua Nika. As we speak—"

"I'm not the ambassador," Jefferson muttered, "just chargée."

Protestors began to cheer and clap and urge one another to clear a path for the vehicle. The young men were coaxed off the hood, and the car began to roll again. It took five minutes to make the quarter mile to Independence Monument. On the northwest corner of Sihanouk Boulevard, heavy machine guns were mounted behind sandbags in front of the prime minister's residence, but it was Sochua's mansion that dominated the esplanade, lit up like a beacon by monument lights on the grounds of the general's estate. That's where they were headed.

Ousaphea eased the car at a snail's pace through the crowd and stopped the vehicle, almost touching the crowd-control barriers behind which National Police troops with shields and helmets stood guard. High white-washed walls topped with concertina wire ringed the compound. Jefferson was not perturbed.

"I'm getting out."

"Madam?"

She opened the door, and the people, curious, surged forward into the vehicle and forced the door shut again. She simply slid across the seat and got out on the opposite side. A great cheer went up from the crowd. She had left Cairo in January of 2011 on the very cusp of the uprising that became the

Arab Spring, and the violence of that movement stood in stark contrast to what she saw now. Many thousands of Cambodians—men, women, and children—crowded together as far as the eye could see in all directions, cheering, congratulating one another, hopeful. The atmosphere was festive, not unlike the city during Pchum Ben, but with water cannon and bullhorns instead of the fireworks and floating barges.

With Pidour by her side, Jefferson confronted the police. Up close she could see they were young, barely adults, and these, at least, did not wear sidearms.

"Please move and let us pass," she shouted over the noise. No going back now.

The mob surged forward, and the police, as a unit, began to beat their shields with their batons. The tactic caused the crowd to surge in the opposite direction, and Pidour and Jefferson, who had been pinned by the wave of people against the metal barriers, were suddenly released.

Pidour tripped over his own feet and fell to the ground. Jefferson reached down and helped him up. There was a heavy clang behind her. She turned to see, and the thick steel doors of Sochua's compound opened inward, revealing a half-dozen of Sochua's men backlit by flood lights. They were armed with rifles. A police officer shouted orders. His men moved two barriers aside. He waved the car through. Ousaphea gunned it and then slammed on his brakes inside the compound. Jefferson and Pidour walked through the gap past Sochua's men.

"Thank you," Jefferson said. The men closed the gate, and she threw her head back in relief. "We did it!"

⋏

At 4:45 a.m., Khak Vanrith got a call from a friend at the Ministry of Defense: the Cambodian Air Force's only helicopter gunship, a Soviet-built Mi-24, had just taken off from Potchentong Air Base with orders to destroy Honeybee Radio and the Council of Ministers building, which had been seized by the rebel 911 regiment. Within seconds the radio station would be well within range of its S-5 rockets.

Khak cut to the National Anthem and threw open the studio door. "Everybody out of the building! Get out now!"

He scrambled for the stairs like everyone else, but instead of going down he ran up and onto the roof. The sky had not yet turned light blue in the east. The pilot would have seen him waving his arms like a madman on the roof of the building before veering south toward Independence Monument. Khak watched in awe as the helicopter circled the monument and headed northwest, where it landed behind rebel lines.

Khak wiped tears from eyes. "The Air Force has joined us!"

⋏

At 4:50 a.m., Prime Minister Thul Chorn flung his phone at the wall.

"*How did that happen?* How did that dirty African get into Sochua's house?" He sat down so he wouldn't fall. "Nothing changes! Tell Chet my orders remain the same! *And get me a new phone!*" He doubled over and clutched his knees. "Pills…"

"Sir?"

In a minute he would be able to answer. In just a minute. But it was different this time.

"Sir? Sir! Get the doctor!"

⋏

At 6:15 a.m., tanks parked at the Ministry of Defense began to move in the predawn pink. They rumbled north on Norodom Blvd. Commander in Chief Phann Phalla had issued orders, and soon the northwest quadrant of the city would be taken from the rebels. The loss of the Air Force had been a surprise but by no means a fatal or even very serious turn of events. Everything was under his control.

Two kilometers east of the ministry, Sochua Nika had heard the news and listened without emotion as Khak Vanrith of Honeybee Radio realized his finest moment.

"The armed forces are coming from the south. We must resist, but do not resort to violence! Do not attack our Cambodian brothers. Enough

Cambodian blood has been spilled by Cambodians. Chop down trees! Park your vehicles in their path! Stand in their way! But do not fight! That is what their leaders want! They want excuses to kill you!"

Tanks led, followed by armored personnel carriers, followed by troop transports. The convoy turned west on Mao Tse Tung Boulevard and then north on Monivong Boulevard.

"Look," someone shouted at the intersection of Sihanouk and Monivong Boulevards. Four hundred meters down the hill, a man stood in the path of the Army. An officer standing in the hatch of the lead tank waved him aside. The man stood his ground. The officer aimed a weapon, the man crumpled, and the sound of the shot reached the spectators. The man hit the ground, and the tank accelerated over his body.

People began to run.

Three blocks to the east, the Venerable Lon Bhut stepped out of Wat Lang Ka, followed by two hundred and twenty-three monks, one hundred and two nuns, and seventeen *ta-chees* in a single file. He silently led his followers west on Street 278. They crossed Monivong Boulevard and stopped, forming three more lines behind the first, blocking the entire width of the boulevard. At a gesture from their leader, they sat as one.

Citizens returned and stood behind them. The tanks slowed and finally clanked to a stop twenty meters away. One of them continued forward. The monks began to chant, their eyes closed. The tank inched forward, monks directly in its path. Its engine roared, diesel fumes floated away, black on blue background. The tank grunted forward. Stopped. Inched forward again. Stopped. Nobody moved. Silence, but for the low chanting.

The monks continued their meditation, but the people swarmed around the tanks and beyond. Thousands surrounded the troop carriers and shook hands with the young men, gave them tokens of something or other, and smiled at them. On the corner, employees of BB World handed out French fries, and girls offered flowers. The troops broke ranks *en masse* and joined the celebration.

⚊⚊⚊

"Sir, the American embassy is calling, sir."

'Nothing changes. Arrest Sochua.' This was the order new National Police Chief Chet Pannha had received from the prime minister's office despite the American's presence in Sochua's compound, and so it was with some trepidation that he took the phone from his subordinate.

"The American embassy?" Then Chet saw the call was on the government's private cell network: Sochua. "I don't understand."

Chet's deputy eyed him gravely. "I don't know, sir."

Chet scratched the mole on his cheek. An American on this network was an extraordinary breach of protocol at the very least. What could this be? "National Police Chief."

"Good morning, sir. This is Paris Jefferson, chargée d'affaires, American Embassy Phnom Penh. I've called on behalf of General Sochua Nika to negotiate the terms of your surrender."

Chapter 30

George gave the hammock a shove. "Hey, man. How long has it been since you had a bath?"

"Huh," Chris rasped. "What?"

"It's time to get up. We got business to do."

"Oh my God, George. Make it stop, or I'm going to be sick."

George mercifully stopped the ride. Chris rolled out of the hammock, still in just his underwear.

"I said, 'When was the last time you had a bath?'"

Chris clutched his knees, waiting for unsteadiness to pass. "What?" He thought for a minute. It was broad daylight. "I...I forgot. What day is it?"

"Then it's been too long. It's Thursday. How about you go jump in the water?" George tossed him a plastic bag. "And you probably ought to burn these."

Chris looked in the bag. "These aren't my clothes. These aren't my clothes! They gave me the wrong frickin' clothes! Listen, I...I've got to have some food. I need to put something in my stomach, or I'm going to puke."

"Here." George handed him half a stale baguette and a bottle of water.

Chris sat for a minute with his legs hanging off the edge of hut, leaning against a post and nibbling the bread. Thursday. Fuck. A whole day wasted. A day and a half really. He noticed George was busy packing up. "What are you doing?"

George grinned. "I said we got work to do."

"Yeah. When I find Leonard Perry, I'm going to kill him."

"No, that's not what I—"

At that moment Perry waddled around the corner of the hut in his track shoes, tucking his shirt in his shorts. Chris lunged for him, but George easily arrested his friend with a shove that sat him back down.

"Hold on there, cowboy. Don't kill him just yet." Turning to Perry, he said, "Tell him. I can't hold him back forever."

"Tell me what? What? Tell me!"

"It wasn't my fault you got arrested," Perry whined indignantly, cowering behind the trunk of a coconut palm. "It—"

"Shut your trap, Leonard, and sit down." George indicated a wooden lounge chair.

"Tell me what happened!"

George grabbed Chris's shoulders and gave him a shake. "We found her, Chris. We know where Mai is. She's okay!"

Chris jumped to his feet. "What? For real? Wait! Why didn't you tell me?"

"Dude, when Mong brought you in here last night, you couldn't even speak in complete sentences."

"Well? Where is she?"

George relayed the story of following Mao Vannak to the Sihanoukville Hotel.

"It was right on friggin' Main Street. And then I sent Leonard in there to look for Mai."

The two friends looked at the pedophile.

"Well, go on," George prompted. "Spill it."

"Well, we found her. Your daughter. Now when are you going to let me go?"

Chris grabbed George's bicep. "Is he telling the truth? How do we know he's not lying?"

"I swear I'm not making it up," Perry protested. "She was in there. They took me to a room where there were a bunch of little girls sitting around that I could pick from. That girl in the picture—your daughter—kept looking at me, and she looked different from the other girls. Then the Mama-san said something in Cambodian to another girl, who got up and took your daughter out of the room—in a hurry. And she sounded angry."

"How did she look different?"

"Well, she wasn't as skinny as the rest of them. She looked kind of, you know, fat. I mean, compared to the rest of them."

"That's all you got? She wasn't skinny?" He was full of shit.

George scratched his beard. "Hear him out, Chris."

Chris put a finger in Perry's face. "Are you telling the truth? You'd better tell me now."

Perry leaned back in his chair and dragged his fingers through his greasy hair. He smiled from one corner of his mouth.

"Listen, I've kept my end of the bargain here. If you're going to get any more cooperation out of me, you're going to have to start treating me with some resp—"

Chris dove at Perry and wrapped his fingers around the salesman's fat throat, carrying both of them and the chair backward onto the sand.

"You son of a bitch! If you're lying to us, I am going to kill you. Kill you! Do you understand?"

Perry eyes bulged in his red face. George looked at his nails.

"I will strangle you to death with my bare hands if you are lying."

"Alright," George drawled, "I suppose that's enough." He peeled Chris's fingers from Perry's throat. "Let's don't kill him yet."

"Shit! What is wrong with you?" Perry bawled. "You didn't need to do that!"

Chris got up and dusted off sand. "On the contrary, I think I showed remarkable restraint."

"I was trying to tell you about her glasses."

Chris shook off a chill. Ever since she'd been diagnosed with nearsightedness, Mai had cared for and protected her glasses with a fastidiousness that bordered upon obsession. Every night before bed she would insist on cleaning them with a special cloth and placing them in a hard case that she tucked with care in her sock drawer. Otherwise, she rarely took them off unless she was going to roughhouse, and then she would again squirrel them away for their protection.

"What color were they? The glasses."

"Pink. Hot pink."

Chris turned to George, his mind racing to figure out how Perry could be tricking them, how he could have known.

"None of the photos we showed him had her wearing glasses," George confirmed before he could ask the question.

Chris poured out the contents of his duffel. He opened a manila folder and spread out on the floor of the hut the photocopied pictures of Mai.

"Did we ever tell him she had glasses?"

George shook his head. "Nope. And, like I said, we saw Mao Vannak walk in the door."

"Then it was her," Chris said finally. He began to frantically stuff the papers back in the duffel. Knowing where Mai was made every second of delay even more excruciating. His strength returned on a pure surge of adrenaline; he felt like he could run a marathon. "Well, come on! Let's go!"

Within a minute they were ready to roll. Perry hung back. "I guess you won't be needing me anymore, so I'll just—"

Chris grabbed Perry by the shirt and shoved him along. "Get your ass in the car!"

The pedophile minced across the sand to the vehicle.

George snickered. "So how was jail?"

Chris took a bite of hard bread. "Food sucks."

⼈

"Calmly, I take the first step toward eternity and leave life to enter History." This is what the Brazilian fascist Getúlio Vargas wrote before shooting himself rather than resign his presidency. Chilean Socialist Salvador Allende blew a hole in his chest with a gift from his old friend Fidel Castro. Thul had seen Allende's bloodstained shirt on display in a Santiago museum. That's how he would go out. Not like Ferdinand Marcos, sneaking out the back door to exile.

It was over. Defeated by a mere woman, where armies could not succeed. He had done too much for his country. There was no greater patriot than he. He'd fought in the sixties against the corrupt royalists—Sihanouk had killed thousands—and he'd fought in the seventies against the CIA-backed Lon Nol government. All he'd ever wanted to do was give Cambodia back to Cambodians, to end *eight hundred years* of foreign domination—half the people living in Phnom Penh when Lon Nol fell were Vietnamese or Chinese!—and save the nation from corrupting Western values. Independence! That's what they'd wanted. They would usher in the new age of Angkor, a pure Cambodia. But Pol Pot had ruined it all. He'd destroyed the dream with his purges, by making his own people his enemy.

Thul had shed blood for his country and brought stability, twenty years of steady economic growth and peace. Cambodia now treated with its neighbors as equals! But no one appreciated what he'd done.

He looked around his private quarters in the Peace Palace, his official residence: cold, stale, state gifts on silly doilies. Better to die here than at home, his private residence where he spent much of his time. He cradled the means to his death and tried to steel his resolve. "Oh, poor Cambodia, what will you become without me?"

He placed the gun to his temple, his hand shaking. *Pull the trigger. Pull the trigger. Now.*

▲

The three men parked on a wide boulevard opposite a whitish building labeled "Sihanoukville Hotel." Across a side street from the hotel was another trashy rent-by-the-hour sort of place with windows on the west side of the building that overlooked the Sihanoukville. From that vantage point they would be able to watch everyone going in and out the front door, as well as the back door, which opened onto a weedy lot parked with a few cars and one tourist van. They rented two rooms: one for Perry on the opposite side of the hall and one with a view.

"Just one double bed that room," protested the front desk clerk.

"It's okay. We like to be real close," George boomed, putting his arm around Chris's shoulders and giving him a rough squeeze.

"Okay, okay. As you like. You pay now."

They went to Perry's room. George pulled a pair of handcuffs from his bag and dangled them in front of Perry's eyes with a twisted smile.

"Something told me these would come in handy."

"What? Why are you handcuffing me now?"

George grabbed one of Perry's wrists and snapped a cuff on it. He attached the other end to the grid of bars on the window.

"I just want you to stay put. No monkey business from you."

"When are you going to let me go?" whined Perry. "I've kept my part of the bargain. You're not going to turn me in to the cops, are you? You told me you'd let me go."

Chris grabbed his face. "See, the thing is, Leonard, if you're telling us the truth and my daughter is really in that hotel, then we're going to let you go with all your stuff. But if you're lying to us, we're going to turn you over to the cops. So, I'm going to ask you one more time: Is my daughter in that hotel?"

He held Mai's picture in front of his face.

"The girl in that picture—I'm sure I saw her there. But she might not be there now! She might have—"

"Shut up," George said. "Now, just sit tight. For your sake, she'd better still be there."

The look on Perry's face strongly suggested he wouldn't be vacationing in Cambodia again anytime soon.

⅄

Sochua Nika took a call from Hem Bora, commander of the 911 Parachute Regiment, the man she had promised to appoint commander in chief of the Royal Cambodian Armed Forces.

"Thul's asking for safe passage."

"Give it to him. Immediately."

She hung up the phone. Charya looked askance at her mother.

"You could have had him tried for war crimes. For what he did for Pol Pot."

"War crimes?" She laughed. "With what evidence? Just my word against his."

Sochua went downstairs to join the American diplomat, Paris Jefferson, for breakfast and at ten a.m. turned on the television as she had been advised.

Thul Chorn sat in front of the Cambodian flag. "Fellow citizens, by the time you see and hear this message, I will have already left the country. His Majesty King Norodom Sihamoni has agreed to accept my resignation as prime minister so that I may seek medical treatment in the People's Republic of China. Long live Kampuchea. Religion. Country. King."

⚔

George turned from the window. They'd been watching the hotel next door for an hour and seen no activity of any kind.

"Chris, it's time to get the police involved."

"The police? Are you out of your mind? Those same yahoos who locked me up?"

The Cambodian police had nervous trigger fingers, and Chris figured they would likely end up killing everyone involved, including the innocent. Furthermore, it was highly probable that once the police were informed, the entire mission would be compromised, and word of an impending raid would quickly make its way to the hotel.

George threw his hands up. "Alright, boss. What's your plan? We just waltz in there armed with a knife and a T-ball bat and ask them to give up?"

Chris looked at the building across the street. That's what he wanted to do. He wanted to go in with a bat and start hurting people. "Give me your phone."

"Who you going to call?"

"Gutierrez, the FBI agent. She'll know how to handle it."

Both men froze at a knock on the door. Chris motioned for George to get against the wall. He opened the door.

"Yes?"

Two hopeful young women smiled at him from the hallway.

"Oh, Jesus Christ! Go away," he moaned, closing the door.

"You handsome man," one woman said, pushing into the room. "You want long time or short time? Full-body massage? Boom-boom?"

"I want you to get out. That's what I want," Chris said, gently shoving her out.

Both women pushed back surprisingly hard. "We make good love for you."

"Not interested. Get out." Chris put his shoulder into the door and shoved with all his might without much progress. George covered his mouth, laughing.

"Dammit, George! They're stronger than they look."

George burst into loud laughter.

A feminine hand caressed Chris's cheek through the opening. "You want yum-yum?"

Chris slapped her hand off. "Out!" He tried to pry the women's fingers off the doorjamb. "George, this is not fucking funny!"

"I need money go back Vietnam. Please, mister."

George walked over. "Sorry. We've got our own problems. Best of luck." He closed the door in their faces and locked it.

Chris put his back to door and breathed a sigh of relief. George offered his phone with a raised eyebrow.

"Times are tough all over, looks like."

Chris snatched the phone from his friend's hand. "No doubt."

He dialed the American embassy, but the call didn't go through. "Dammit! Will nothing in the place work?" After several tries he left George to keep an eye on the Sihanoukville Hotel and went downstairs to find a land line. Thankfully, the two women were nowhere in sight; he was not in the mood to be polite. The front desk clerk was snoring loudly on a stuffed chair in the lobby.

Chris poked him on the shoulder. "Hey! Wake up! I need to use your phone." The man didn't budge, so Chris picked up the desk phone and dialed, not giving a damn.

"Mayela Gutierrez, please." The phone was transferred with a click.

"Finto."

"Where's Gutierrez?"

"Out in the field looking for your daughter, asshole. Where are you?"

Chris bit his tongue; he could deal with Finto later. "Listen, I know were Mai is."

"What? Are you sure?"

"I have a witness that claims he saw her at close range at the Sihanoukville Hotel in Sihanoukville. He identified her from her photo. He also identified the color of her glasses even though he didn't know she wore glasses."

"Who is this witness?

"A man named Leonard Perry from LA."

"Listen, we can call out the cavalry on this, but I'm going to need to speak to the witness first."

"No! It's too dangerous to get the local police involved. They'll—"

Finto cut him off. "You think I'm stupid? I know the people to contact to get it done it right. This is what I do. Now let me talk to the witness, and then just stay out of the fucking way!"

With great difficulty, Chris remained calm. *Focus.* He didn't have time to drag Perry into the lobby. And who knew what the hell he might say? "Alright, give me a minute," he growled, still without a plan. He looked at the snoring front desk clerk. Shook his head in disgust. Then it dawned on him—George!

He ran back upstairs and found George looking out the window. "Hey! Have you ever met David Finto?

George cocked his head to the side. "I mean, I was introduced to him at the meeting we had at the embassy to talk about the raid on Shelter 4. Why?"

"But you don't know him well? He wouldn't recognize your voice?"

"No. He wouldn't recog—"

"Great! I need you to go down to the lobby. There's a phone off the hook on the front desk. Finto's on the line. I want you to pretend to be Perry. Tell him everything Perry saw."

George got a pained look on his face. "But—"

Chris grabbed his friend's shoulders. "Finto won't pull out all the stops with the National Police until he has a witness that Mai's in the hotel." Chris pointed at the building across the street.

George processed this for about a second. "Gotcha!" He got up and limped out the door. "Pretend to be Perry."

Chris sat on the bed and stared at the Sihanoukville Hotel. That was it. The wheels were in motion. Mai's life was now in Finto's hands—his and the hands of whatever corrupt police officials Finto thought he could rely on. He wondered if he'd just signed Mai's death warrant.

⋏

New National Police Chief Chet Pannha stood before an ascendant Sochua Nika. Despite the fact that Sochua held no political office, there was no question who was giving the orders now.

"I want this to be done right—do you understand? Go to Sihanoukville immediately and take charge of the operation yourself, not Soun. This absolutely must be kept quiet; inform only those who need to know. You will personally give the order to move on the brothel, and I will hold you responsible for the outcome."

"Yes ma'am."

In less than twenty minutes the American security chief and the mother of the kidnapped girl arrived in a police escort at the newly vacated prime minister's residence, where Chet ushered them and Paris Jefferson onto a Ministry of Interior helicopter. The American deputy chief of mission understood, Chet was assured during the flight, that he was a friend of the Americans, that the Apsara 2 debacle was not of his making, and that his assistance during the kidnapping investigation and at this critical juncture would be remembered and appreciated.

⋏

Chea Phyrom's mobile vibrated in his pocket: 10:45. His new Hummer H1, a first for Cambodia, had just arrived, and he stood in his driveway admiring its mighty metal presence. The interruption irritated him.

"What?"

"They know where the girl is," announced a familiar voice within the Ministry of the Interior. "And the Americans and Chet are already on their way."

This raised concern but not alarm; Phyrom had prepared for this. "How much time do we have?"

"An hour."

Phyrom smiled. More than enough time. Mao could handle this.

⚔

His elbows propped on the windowsill, Chris Kelly watched two Asian men walk out the front door of the Sihanoukville Hotel at eleven o'clock. The two men turned and gestured angrily back at the hotel. Chris thought he could hear shouting in return, but he couldn't see anyone in the doorway from his vantage point. The men rode off on motos.

The heat was incredible, the humidity unbearable, and his T-shirt was transparent with sweat. George lay on the bed, his mouth open, snoring loudly. How could he sleep at a time like this? He looked at the time on George's phone. It had been forty-five minutes since he'd called that knuckle-dragger Finto.

"Don't do anything stupid. Wait until we get there," Finto had warned him.

By now he'd be with Lisa on a helicopter provided by the National Police, and the *federales* would be on their way. Finto'd found Gutierrez. She was in Prey Nob and already on her way to Sihanoukville by car. Chris gazed intently at the hotel across the street. An easy stone's throw away, and he couldn't grab her. Couldn't do anything about it.

When Mai was a toddler the family had gone swimming at the Little Rock YMCA while on home leave visiting Lisa's parents. They were out of the pool and packing up to leave when Lisa asked, "Where's Mai?"

Chris turned to her with alarm. "I thought you had her." Then they saw it: Mai's sun hat floating on the surface of the water, a dark blob on the floor of the pool beneath it—on the other side of the pool.

Screaming for help, Chris sprinted around the pool and dove into the water. But the teenage lifeguard had been paying attention and got there first. She pulled Mai out of the water, and no harm was done. But what still gave Chris nightmares was the memory of those few seconds racing to save Mai, with her right there under the water and knowing that he might not get there in time. That's how he felt now.

George made a particularly loud snort, turned on his side, and resumed his buzz-saw snoring.

"George, wake up! Would you get up? Go check on Leonard or something. Your snoring's driving me crazy."

George muttered something and stumbled out the door and across the hall. Chris checked the time on George's phone again. A push notification popped up from the Bangkok Post: Prime Minister Thul Chorn flees Cambodia amid violent unrest.

"What the hell?" Thul fled the country? Violent unrest? In panic, he realized this meant help from the National Police might not come. And Lisa?

Again, there was movement on the street below. A third man left the hotel by the front door, followed in quick succession by a fourth. At the rear of the hotel, a man got in a small white Toyota sedan and drove away. Chris watched this procession with heightened interest but not alarm, until the back door of the building slammed open again and a pair of women walked out squinting in the sunlight, then another, then two more.

"George. Come over here and take a look at this."

"Just a minute," George called from across the hall in Perry's room.

Across the street, some women got in a second white car, and a gray van pulled into the lot. More women sauntered out of the hotel and got in the van, urged on by a man in black who seemed to be directing things.

"George! They're clearing the place out! Come, look."

George joined him, lucid, at the window. Another van drove into the lot, and more women began to crowd into it.

"Wow. Didn't take long for the word to get to them, did it?"

"I don't see Mai."

Just then, a file of little girls emerged at the back door. Chris zoomed in with Perry's camera.

"Okay, they're moving out the little ones, but…let's see…Mai's not with them. No. Where the hell is she?"

Chris's neck ached with tension. This was worse than seeing her taken away. Where was she? Had she ever been there? The last girl hopped in the van and disappeared.

"You didn't see anybody go out the front while I was watching the back, did you?

"No, but I was looking for my knife."

"Watch the window for a minute." Chris jumped across the bed and headed out the door.

Perry winced when he saw him coming for him. Chris grabbed Perry's chin and slammed his head against the bars on the window.

"Tell me the truth! Was she in there? Tell me the truth or—"

"Chris!"

Chris released Perry and ran back across the hall. What was it?

George handed him the camera. "Look!"

Chris focused the camera across the street. A little brown girl in a blue dress walked out of the back of the Sihanoukville Hotel between two men. Mai! It was her! Still wearing her hot pink glasses. She was alive! Then his heart stopped: Mai was holding the hand of none other than Mao Vannak, Chea Phyrom's trusted henchman.

Chris threw the camera on the bed. "Let's go!"

The two men raced for the door, George wielding the knife and Chris hefting Mai's bat. Chris ran down the stairs and took the last flight in one leap, generating a cloud of dust in the lobby. George was several seconds behind. When Chris flew around the corner he saw two men moving Mai toward an SUV parked at the far end of the lot. They didn't hear him until he was almost on them.

The two thugs spun around at the same time. One of them reached for a sidearm, but Chris had already put the bat in motion. The full force of the swing met the side of the man's head. Chris could feel the crack of his skull. The goon's eyes rolled skyward, and he slumped to the ground in a heap.

Mai shrieked and covered her eyes.

Chris reached for her. "Mai!"

Mao snatched her first. He clutched Mai to his chest with one arm, her feet kicking in the air. His other hand held a knife under her throat.

Chris let the bat drop to the ground. *No, no, no, no. Please. Don't.* He held up his hands in supplication. "Okay, okay, just hold on," he pleaded. "You don't have to hurt her." *Anything. I'll give anything.*

Clutching Mai, Mao backed slowly toward the vehicle behind him, his eyes articulating his threat. He yelled something in Khmer that Chris couldn't catch.

"He says he's going to kill her if we don't back off and let him get in the car."

"You know we can't let them get in that car."

"Yeah, I know," said George.

"Daddy! Help! He's hurting me!"

"I'm going to save you, sweetheart. I promise."

Mao reached the car door. *Stop!* Mai cried out in pain. *Stop!* There was only one way.

"I'm going to jump him," Chris explained, his eyes on the knife under Mai's throat. "He can't cut me and Mai both. He'll have to stop me first. When he does that, you grab her and run like hell and don't look back. I'll tell you when I'm ready."

It ends here.

"Chris?"

"Yeah?"

"That's not the way it's going to happen."

"Wh—"

George lunged at the would-be killer with his arms spread wide as if to crush him in a great bear hug, leaving himself completely exposed.

"George! No!"

Mao reflexively met the incoming attack, necessarily releasing Mai. George wrapped his arms around Mao's torso, lifting him off his feet and sending them both falling. Mai ran. Mao plunged his knife into George's lower back.

"No!"

The two men landed with a thump on the ground. Mao stabbed again. With a sickening lump in his throat, Chris tucked Mai under his arm and ran.

⅄

Chris raced around the corner in front of the Sihanoukville Hotel carrying Mai.

She was crying. "Daddy! Daddy!"

He ignored her. He couldn't let her in yet; Mao was too dangerous—a trained killer. But he knew this: he would die before he let him take her again. He scanned the streets for a moto—nothing. At any given moment there should've been a half-dozen moto-dops waiting for fares on this corner.

"Dammit!"

He couldn't outrun his pursuer with Mai in his arms. He only had seconds before Mao, presumably now armed with his partner's gun, would catch up. Their only chance was to hide until help arrived.

The hotel desk clerk was sleepily rubbing his eyes when Chris ran into the lobby carrying Mai.

"Call an ambulance," Chris screamed, bounding up the stairs. "To the Sihanoukville Hotel!"

He lost his grip on Mai's legs and stumbled over her. She cried out in pain. He threw her over his shoulder and ran to the third floor. There were angry shouts below.

He ran into his room and locked the door. George's bag lay on the bed. George! He glanced out the window. Two bodies lay facedown in the lot across the street, their hands almost touching. He looked frantically about the room. A thick grid of bars was on both windows. The tiny bathroom offered no means of escape. He would have to fight, and for that he would need a weapon.

He grabbed George's bag and upturned it on the bed. Nothing! He would hide Mai under the bed and then resist all he could until Mao killed him. Mao would then find Mai and...

Bam! A loud report from downstairs was not a gunshot; it sounded like a door slamming—or being kicked in. Good. Mao didn't know where they were. That gave him a few more seconds to figure out what to do. Perry's room. He unlocked the door and pulled Mai with him across the hall into the other room.

"Come on, sweetheart."

Perry let out a cry and cowered against the window. "Oh, it's you," he said with obvious relief. "What the hell is going on out there?"

"Shut up."

"Let me go," Perry cried, looking at Mai. "You told me you would let me go when you got the girl."

"Shut up!"

Chris scanned the room for something useful. Attached to the wall near the one barred window was a crude lever with a ceramic ball on its end.

"Hang on, baby. I'm going to get you out of here."

"Let me go," Perry pleaded. "You got what you wanted! We had a deal."

Chris examined the window. "Yeah, well, you like to have sex with children. I lied. Sue me."

A two-by-two square cutout of the window bars was mounted on hinges so that it could swing into the room. Chris pulled the lever, and a cascade of dried paint fell to the floor as it rotated on its fulcrum for the first time since many paint jobs, stretching what looked like the cable of a bicycle's hand brake. The cable pulled a spring mechanism until, with considerable effort, he could yank open the primitive fire escape.

"Please," Perry cried.

There was a loud commotion in the hallway.

"I'll deal with you later. Shut your mouth."

Below the window, a wide ledge jutted from the wall. Just beyond this ledge was the peeling side wall of the building next door.

"Mai, come here."

She obeyed silently. He held her little face in his hands and really looked at her for the first time since her rescue. She was shaking uncontrollably. He touched her cheek. "Mai…" He almost lost it. *Focus!*

"Mai, listen to me very carefully," he said sternly. "I'm going to lower you out the window. There's a place for you to sit down. You have to be very quiet and very still."

He picked her up. She buried her face in his shoulder and held tight.

"Mai! You have to do what I say. If you don't, that man is going to get us. Do you understand?"

Mai nodded, but she began to kick and struggle as they neared the window.

"No, Daddy! No!"

He clapped his hand over her mouth. "Stop. Stop!" Mao could burst in any second.

"Mai, do you trust me?"

She nodded.

"Remember that time in Vietnam when we jumped off the big rock together into the water?"

"Uh-huh."

"And you were really afraid, right? But I told you to trust me, and everything was okay, wasn't it?"

She nodded, her eyes terrified, tears streaming down her face.

"Then you have to do exactly as I say. I know you're scared, but you have to do what I tell you." Loud voices in the hall.

"Okay, Daddy."

Chris picked up Mai and sat her on the windowsill, facing the building opposite. She began to struggle again.

"Mai. Trust me. Daddy came and found you, didn't he?"

"Yeah," she squeaked.

"Okay. I'm going to put you on that ledge down there. When you get down there, just sit down and don't move, okay?"

"Okay, Daddy."

They were running out of time.

Chris took Mai's hands and lifted her off the windowsill. He leaned out the window as far as he could. Her feet hung in the air several inches above the ledge.

"Okay, sweetie. I'm going to drop you to the ledge now. Just lie down and close your eyes."

"No, Daddy, no."

No time to argue. Chris leaned out a little farther, held his breath, and let go. Mai dropped to the ledge, tottered for a moment, and then leaned against the wall.

"See. It was okay. Now, baby, just sit down. That's good. Okay. Now just lie down and close your eyes if you want to."

"I'm okay, Daddy."

"Okay. Listen, baby. Just sit right there and don't move for any reason. Do you understand me? Don't move for *any* reason. Do you promise?"

"I promise."

"I'm going to close the window now. But you have to stay there and be quiet. You can't cry or call me for any reason until I come back. Do you understand, sweetie? Even if you have to wait a long time, you have to sit there and be quiet."

"Okay, Daddy."

"Okay, I'm closing the window. Remember. Sit there and don't make any noise. I'll come back for you when it's safe."

"Okay, Daddy. I got it, already. You can go now."

Chris smiled. "Good girl." Tears welled in his eyes—he loved this little girl—but he choked them back.

He pulled the casement window shut and slammed closed the bars. Movement was right outside the door. Mao! He clutched the lever of the fire escape and ripped it sideways off the wall.

"Hello! They're in here," Leonard Perry shouted, *sotto voce*, his hands cupped to his mouth. Triumph creased his face. "Uncuff me, or I'll scream. I'll tell him where she is."

With a roar Chris grabbed Perry's sweaty face in his hands.

"Hey!" Perry screamed. "In here!"

Chris pounded Perry's head into the bars. "Die, you piece of shit!" He would've killed him but for the rapid approach of footsteps in the hall.

He rolled over the bed, snatching a large glass ashtray, and flattened himself against the wall. The door flew open and crashed into the wall, removing a large chunk of plaster.

Mao crossed the threshold, his eyes and gun trained on Perry. Chris swung the ashtray at his head. Mao dodged. The ashtray hit the pistol, knocking it to the ground. The ashtray crashed to the tile and shattered into a million pieces.

Mao gave a terrible roar and lunged, carrying Chris over the bed and onto the floor. He pinned Chris's shoulders to the ground, his sweat dripping onto his face. Chris kicked him as hard as he could in the groin.

Mao didn't flinch. Nostrils flaring, he dragged Chris to his feet. He flung him headfirst into a shoddy vanity. *Crash!* Hurt like hell. Glass fell in large pieces. Chris looked at his hands. Lots of blood. *His* blood. He was not winning this fight. Not even close.

Mao tossed him at the window. Perry swung out of the way. Chris hit the bars with his right shoulder. His legs gave way, and he dropped to the floor. He opened his eyes, and there it was. The gun. His only chance. On the floor on the other side of the bed.

Mao dragged him upright again and buried his fist in his stomach. *Ouch.* That really hurt. Chris gasped for air. The room began to darken. Something hit him somewhere, and he fell to the floor again. He heard Mao's ragged breathing. *Killer.*

Chris opened his eyes. He lay on the glass-strewn floor, the gun an arm's length away. Mao threw the bed against the wall like it was Styrofoam. Chris reached for the gun. Mao kicked it away. It spun across the floor and into the hallway. Mao smiled. He strode out the door. Chris struggled to his feet and stumbled after him into the hall. *Mai.*

The gun was at the top of the stairs. Mao bent over to pick it up. Chris tackled him, and they flew into the stairwell.

Mao hit the stairs first. They tumbled to the second floor in a tangle. Mao landed on his back, Chris on top of him. Chris pushed off and scrambled up the stairs toward the gun on the landing. Mao grabbed his ankle and dragged him down. Mao pulled himself to his knees and tried to crawl up. Chris punched him in the gut, and Mao rounded on him with a roar. Face-to-face on the stairs, they began to pummel each other.

Mao nailed him in the nose. Blood began to gush. Chris landed a fierce uppercut, and Mao was dazed. Chris hit him on the side of the face. And again. Mao stumbled. Chris kicked him in the back of the knee, and he fell.

He jumped on Mao's chest and let loose—for Mai—for Lisa—for all the others. He pounded Mao's face faster and faster. He busted his lip. Mao spit out a tooth. Chris grabbed Mao's face in both hands and banged his head against the concrete stair again and again. It got easier and easier. Finally, Mao stopped resisting at all.

Exhausted, Chris crawled to the third-floor landing. He picked up the gun and leaned against the wall. *Mai.* He had to get up. Mao stirred and opened his eyes. Chris could barely lift his arms to point the gun at him.

He pulled back the hammer. *"At-tay,"* he said. "No."

With a groan, Mao rolled onto his side. Grimacing, he got on one elbow. He looked up at Chris, his swollen eyes pleading. Very slowly, he got to his knees. He held up his hands. *"At-tay."*

Chris didn't flinch. Suddenly, Mao lunged. Chris pulled the trigger.

The shot reverberated painfully in the narrow stairwell. Mao twisted, screaming, clutching his leg. Chris fired again. Mao rolled headfirst down the stairs. Chris waited, ears ringing, gun leveled. Mao stopped moving.

There was a cry from above. "Hello! Somebody?"

Perry. Chris dragged himself to his feet, not feeling very steady. Wincing, he pulled a piece of glass out of his cheek. His nose—he felt pretty sure it was broken. He gingerly traced a long gash on his head. *Mai.* Crouched, he limped into Perry's room.

"Oh, thank God it's you," Perry said, breathing a sigh of relief. "Goodness, you look terrible."

Leaning against the wall for support, Chris pointed the gun at Perry's face. "Leonard, I'm going to kill you now." He'd killed once already; it wouldn't be so difficult.

"I—"

"Shut up!"

"But…but…Mai's safe!"

Chris stumbled forward and jammed the muzzle into Perry's neck. "Don't ever say my daughter's name again! Do you understand me? *Don't ever say it again!*"

"Okay, okay! I won't!"

Mai. Chris put the pistol in the small of his back and shoved Perry aside. With shaking hands, he pried open the fire escape with his room key. He thrust open the casements and looked down. Oh, God. There was Mai on the ledge, just as he'd left her.

She craned her neck to look up at him. "Daddy, is…that…you?"

"Yeah, baby. I told you I'd come back."

In great pain, Chris climbed onto the windowsill. The drop onto the ledge made his head feel like it was being bounced on the concrete. He slumped against the wall, breathless.

Mai gave him the strangest look. "Daddy, are you okay? You've got blood *all over* you."

"Yeah, yeah, I'm…okay."

He took Mai in his arms and was finally able to feel again. She squeezed him tight.

"Careful, careful," he said. "Not too tight. I'm kind of bunged up."

Her hair tickled his face. He breathed in her smell—something he thought was gone forever—as if she'd died and come to life again.

"Don't let them take me again," she sobbed. "I didn't like that."

With tears in his eyes, he reassured her. "I know. I know. I won't let them," he said. "Here, let me look at you." Her glasses were nearly opaque with tears and dust. He took them off and set them on the ledge. "Are you okay?" *Please.*

Mai cast her eyes downward and stuck out her bottom lip. He pushed her lip in with a finger, playing a little game of theirs—one that his grandmother had played with him. "You better put that lip back in. What if a freeze comes, and your face gets stuck like that?"

The faintest hint of a smile appeared on her face. He smiled too. Then he realized he still had George's phone in his pocket. He hastily pulled it out: no service. George…

Mai tensed suddenly. "Daddy!" she shrieked, pointing behind him.

Chris pushed Mai off, his hand going for the gun. He turned, and—it was Mong, watching them from the roof of the building next door. He sighed with relief, pins and needles of adrenaline subsiding.

Mai buried her face in Chris's shoulder. "Who is it, Daddy? Who is it?"

"Oh," he said as calmly as possible, "that's just my friend. He's been keeping an eye on us all along."

Mai peeked up. "Oh, I didn't know that."

Chris cupped his hands to his mouth. "George?" he yelled at Mong.

Mong slowly shook his head. He touched two fingers to his floppy hat. He climbed onto a rusted ladder bolted to the side of the building and disappeared below without a sound.

"I miss Mommy," Mai said after a moment. "Where is she?"

"She's on her way. She'll be here soon."

"You know," she said, "I wasn't just being mellow-grammatic."

Chris looked at her, utterly confused—no idea what she was talking about. "Huh?"

"You know, when you and Mommy went to the fancy party at the ambassador's house, and Mommy said I was being mellow-grammatic."

Tears welled again in Chris's eyes, and this time he let them go. He had no idea what Mai was talking about, but *this* was Mai. She was okay. He shook his head. "No. I...don't...know," he stammered.

Mai touched the tip of his nose. "Well, I said, 'I'd be lost without you.' Do you remember? I said, 'I'd be lost without you,' and y'all thought I was just making it up, but it was true." Here her bottom lip poked out again. "I *was* lost without you. I really was. And I didn't like it."

Chris pulled her close. "Yeah. We were lost without you too. Really. We couldn't do anything right at all." And that was the truth.

They stayed there on the ledge holding each other until help arrived.

CHAPTER 31

It was almost noon. The police car had barely slid to a stop when Lisa bolted from the front seat and ran up the hospital steps. She knew what they said—Mai safe and unhurt, Chris with minor injuries—but she couldn't yet believe it. FBI Special Agent Mayela Gutierrez was waiting by the front door, smiling.

She hooked a thumb over her shoulder. "All the way down at the end. You can't miss it."

Lisa sprinted down the corridor toward a crowd of uniformed men. She felt strangely disembodied—as if she were watching herself in slow motion. The men hushed and moved aside. There was an open door. She may have shouted. Mai poked her head into the hall.

"Mommy!"

Lisa's heart fluttered at the sight of her, and she melted to her knees. Mai ran into her arms. She was okay! She was alive!

"Oh, honey, I love you," Lisa sobbed. "I love you so much." She took Mai's face in her hands. "I thought...I thought I'd never see you again."

"I love you, too, Mommy." The corners of Mai's mouth turned downward. "I missed you."

"No, no, no, don't cry." Lisa begged. "Did they hurt you? Are you okay?" She touched the tiny scar under Mai's chin; you wouldn't notice it, but it was there if you knew where to look. Lisa felt Mai's arms and hands and fingers. It couldn't be! "Are you okay? I love you. I love you so much!"

"I'm okay. But you better check on Daddy. He had to save me, and it was kinda difficult for him."

Lisa's heart sank. Chris. Was he hurt? What if she gained one and lost the other? "Is he okay?"

"Yeah. Come on. I'll show you." In a whisper she added, "He's all bloody. It's kinda gross."

Holding her breath, Lisa let Mai lead her by the hand into the hospital room. When she saw Chris, her mouth dropped open in spite of herself. He lay awake in bed looking at her: two black eyes, swollen nose, hair matted and crazy, his shirt stained with what could only be blood. There where dried trails of blood down the side of his face and into his ear.

"Sweetheart, are you okay?" She clasped her cheeks. "Are you?"

"It's not as bad as it looks," he said softly.

"Well," she whispered, tears running down her face, "I...hope not."

He smiled weakly. "Yeah, they could've cleaned me up a little bit."

Mai squeezed Lisa's hand. "He's going to be alright, isn't he?"

Lisa looked at her. Now Mai was crying too. Lisa wanted to reassure her, but her voice failed her.

"Y'all stop it now," Chris said, frowning. "You're really bumming me out. I'm fine."

Everywhere Lisa looked there was blood or scrapes. "Can I touch you? Where are you hurt?"

Chris turned his head, wincing. "Ow."

Lisa gasped. On the top of his head were two long rows of stitches painted orange with Mercurochrome. "Oh my God. What happened?"

"I got about three dozen stitches."

She gasped again. "Are you going to be okay?"

"Yeah. I just want to go home."

Lisa sat on the bed and took his hand in hers, her other hand still holding Mai's. "I'm sorry, sweetheart. I'm so sorry." She'd promised him that she would never abandon himand then . . . "I should've—"

He pursed his lips and looked away. Not angry but sad, like he did when he heard sad news. She knew all his expressions, every contour of his face, when he needed her and when he wanted to be left alone.

"Will you forgive me?"

Paris Jefferson knocked on the doorjamb. "Hello. Can I come in?"

"Hey, big sis!" Mai cried, running to the door. She gave Paris a high five.

"Hey, little sis. How are you doing?"

"Peachy!"

Lisa felt dearly the absence of Mai's hand, but she needed this moment with Chris.

Paris seemed to understand. "Hey!" she said to Mai. "Guess what we get to ride home in."

Lisa turned back to Chris. "I'm really sorry for the way I treated you." All the promises she'd made to him, when put to the test, hadn't amounted to much.

Chris's eyes welled with tears. "I thought..." His mouth twisted with emotion. "I thought...I was going to lose...both of you."

"I'm sorry."

"No. It's not your fault. I should never have put y'all at such risk. I was stupid. I...just...I just wanted...to help. There are so many of them, you know."

"I know. I know."

"And they're just children—just babies—some of them, and, you know, when I saw those little girls...I just thought...I just thought...well..."

Lisa placed a finger on his trembling lips. "Shh. I know. You wanted to save them all."

"Yeah." He sighed. "But in the end, I couldn't even save one."

"No," Lisa said. She nodded at Mai in the doorway, who was listening intently to Paris. "You did save one."

He looked at Mai and choked back a sob. "But...but...she almost...she could've..."

"No, silly. I mean six years ago in India. If it hadn't been for you, we would never have adopted Mai. She might never have had a family. *We* might never have had a family." She kissed him on the forehead. "You're my hero. Did you know that?"

He blinked a few times, and a glimmer of a twinkle returned to his eyes. "Yeah," he said, "I know."

She giggled a little. "Where's George?"

Mai tugged Lisa's arm. "Mommy! Guess what Paris told me?"

Chris fixed Lisa with another expression she recognized, one that sent a chill up her spine. "They didn't tell you?" he whispered. He bit his lip.

Lisa shook her head. *Not George.* "Is he...?" Grief twisted her insides, and she couldn't go on. Not George.

Mai pulled again. "Are we really going to get to go home in a helicopter? Really?"

"That would be cool, wouldn't it?" Chris said, still holding Lisa's gaze.

CHAPTER 32

On Friday morning, the day after their reunion in Sihanoukville, Chris and Lisa Kelly lay in bed with Mai between them. They'd slept in, gone downstairs to eat breakfast, and gone back to bed together. Yen patrolled the yard, while four members of the prime minister's personal bodyguard—assigned upon orders of General Sochua Nika—sat inside a black Toyota Land Cruiser blocking their driveway. The family's plan was to sleep all day, but a thought of work crept, unwelcome, into Chris's mind.

"I suppose we should go in at some point and clean out our desks and stuff." He and Lisa had been granted a "compassionate curtailment" of their assignments in Cambodia, for obvious reasons.

"Yeah, but nobody would blame us if we didn't. But I did want to say good-bye to some people."

Mai squirmed and sat up. "Alrighty then. Y'all are boring me now, people, with this work stuff." She rolled over Lisa and off the bed. She put her hands on her hips like her mother and Sampour always did. "I'm going to go get some books. I'll be right back." She paused in the doorway and turned on all the living room lights. "Daddy, will you come check on me?"

"I promise, pumpkin. If you're not back in two minutes, I'll come check on you."

"And you too, Mommy? Do you promise?"

"Yes. I promise."

"Okay, well, here I go then. Faster than a speeding bullet!" Mai took off.

Lisa rolled on her side and looked at Chris. "You want to hear something interesting?"

"Sure." Chris didn't really care. He just wanted to lie there and watch the ceiling fan's slow whirl.

"Allison told me that she and Vy Finto and Alma Johnson and a couple of other ladies went out for drinks to the Cambodiana that Thursday night I was in Kep and, well, it seems they all got a little tipsy, and they got on the subject of marital infidelity—"

Chris sighed. "Really?"

"—and Alma Johnson said she didn't mind if Jim went out on the town because she knew he couldn't be unfaithful."

Chris felt like he was missing a point. "I don't get it."

"Pay careful attention to what I'm saying here: it's not that he wouldn't be unfaithful, but it's that he couldn't—if you know what I mean."

"Oh, now I get it," Chris drawled, considering the irony of his consular section boss's invitation to join him for a night in a brothel.

Chris's mobile rang on the dresser. He looked at the screen and frowned. "It's the embassy."

Lisa spoke through a yawn. "Answer it. It could be about our tickets."

Chris was surprised to hear the voice of Jim Johnson, the smarmy chief of the consular section about whom he had just learned a great deal.

"Good morning, Chris. How is everybody?"

"Wonderful. Just wonderful."

"I hear you're staying until your pack-out."

"Yeah, three more days, and then we're out of here."

"Fabulous. Listen, there's something you ought to know about your friend George Granger."

"Yeah?"

"Well, we tried to notify his next of kin—his wife—and we found out that, well, his wife is dead."

"What? Are you sure? His wife, Molly?" So many times George had promised to introduce her, but it never happened.

Lisa sat upright on the bed. "What is it?"

Chris put the phone on speaker.

"Yeah, that's right," continued Johnson. "I talked to his brother back in the States this morning. Molly Granger died of liver cancer several years ago. He said it was a really drawn-out and terrible death."

Chris reached for Lisa's hand. "Did you talk to anyone at International Rescue Mission?"

"Yeah. I called Jane Hightower. She was just as shocked as you are."

"I don't believe it." Why would George lie? "Are you sure?"

"Yep. I checked. There's a death certificate on file in the system, and her passport was cancelled. And there's more."

"What?"

"His brother doesn't want to have him brought home. He wants him cremated here and his ashes scattered."

⩓

"A toast, ladies and gentlemen."

Sochua Nika stood in the center of her *grand appartement*—hastily spruced up for the occasion since a party of this magnitude had not been thrown in the old house for years—flanked by the American chargée d'affaires, Paris Jefferson, and General Hem Bora, glowing with the expectation of power. Powerful men lined up to shake her hand. Suddenly, it were as if Thul's supporters couldn't be found, as if the whole world loved Sochua and Thul had not had the loyalty of the elites, the Army, the royal family, and the clergy for forty years. As if everyone had supported the uprising before its success was assured. Now it seemed everyone was a democrat and a patriot. Hypocrites—they would sell her out in a second if they had half a chance. But, for now, *she* was in charge.

Everyone in the room raised a glass. "To the end of tyranny. To Kampuchea. Religion. Country. King."

Sochua's speech was carried live from her balcony to television and radio.

"Deputy Prime Minister Pov has agreed to ask His Majesty Norodom Sihamoni to dissolve parliament immediately so that new elections may be held on April first." The people roared their approval. "I invite progressive elements within the country to contest this election with me under the auspices of a new political party."

⚹

Late Friday evening, seventeen Sambo Rithy party supporters waited outside Potchentong International Airport to greet their party's namesake upon his triumphant return from exile in the United States. *The Cambodia Times* sent a reporter, but the story didn't make the front page.

CHAPTER 33

Chris, Lisa, and Mai Kelly, preceded and followed by an entourage of plain-clothes bodyguards, inched across a narrow plank to a rustic tourist boat waiting just off Sisowath Quay. Lane Connelly also came on board, along with a few other people from IRM; Chenda from Land & Sea; Arthur from Spanky's; Jack Durrant, the junior officer in whose bar George and Chris first met; and Durrant's latest Cambodian girlfriend. Chris looked back at the crowded bank, not really expecting to see Mong among the chaos even if he was there. The diesel engine coughed to life, and the boat chugged away from the polluted shore with Mai clinging to her mother and father. Chris squeezed her hand, and she squeezed back. He would never, ever, take that for granted. Except to play with Legos, Mai had hardly let go of them since Thursday. She wanted him and Lisa to go everywhere with her.

"It's going to take some time," the regional psychiatrist had told them. Chris didn't mention that he couldn't let go of Mai either. How long was that going to take? He wasn't in a hurry.

Chris pointed the shirtless preteen captain toward the confluence of the Tonle Sap and Mekong Rivers on the southern edge of the city. The rivers ran high, still full of an entire half-year's rain, and the sandy islands that appeared later in the dry season were nowhere in sight. On the opposite shore, naked children dove from their waterborne homes into the roiling waters. Fishermen paused only briefly to take a look at the group, adjusting their conical hats before casting their nets again. Chris looked at Lisa. She looked beautiful today.

With no one talking much, they reached the point where the two great rivers met. The captain killed the engine and let the boat float freely, and the mourners shuffled to the bow with the wind mangling their hair and tossing their shirt collars about. Lane Connelly took the lid off a ceramic jar, and a puff of ash floated away. Everyone stood in silence for a moment, staring at Connelly and the jar.

"Does anyone want to…"

Chris cleared his throat. "I guess I'll say something." He began to cry and had to take some deep breaths to continue. It had occurred to him over the last two days that, since leaving college and getting married, he hadn't had anyone—except for Lisa and Mai, of course—he could call a best friend. His heart ached with grief. "Um, I only knew George for about a year. But I could see that he affected the lives of many people. And the way he died was kind of a metaphor for his entire life here in Cambodia: selfless sacrifice for others.

"George saved many lives, and he saved my life and my daughter's life. He knew what he was doing." Chris's voice wouldn't cooperate and slipped an octave and back. "He made a conscious decision and…um…it's…um…well, it's been a long time since I picked up a Bible, but I thought it would make George proud and…um…I found this."

Chris tried to unfold a scrap of paper, but the wind carried it away. He stared after it and laughed a very sad laugh. "Damn it. I needed that paper."

"It's okay, Daddy," Mai shouted above the wind. "Just make it up."

It seemed as if everyone breathed again. Chris gave Mai a kiss on the head to thank her for the strength to continue.

"Well, what it said was something like this. It said, 'Greater love has no man than this, that he lay down his life for his friends,' and, well, that was what George was all about."

Chris couldn't look at the other tearful faces. "Anybody else want to say something?" He turned to the river.

Silence.

"I think you said it all, Chris," Lane Connelly whispered after a time.

Chris turned to face the group again. "Well, now, I know George would like it, so I'm going to say a prayer."

Chris closed his eyes and sucked in the warm air. "God, here is one of your good children. Please take him home."

Connelly reached over the side of the boat and let the ashes fall from the urn.

Epilogue

Tuesday, May 2, 2017

"Hey, you're not going to believe this. Page twelve."

Lisa Kelly folded the newspaper and threw it to Chris across the living room of their Arlington, Virginia, apartment, almost hitting him in the head.

"Hey, watch it!" He opened the paper to page twelve and read.

The Washington Post
Tuesday, May 2, 2017

Cambodia: Leader of Popular Rebellion Forms Government

In a solemn ceremony in Cambodia's Royal Palace, Sochua Nika, leader of December's popular uprising that ousted longtime Prime Minister Thul Chorn, was sworn in as Cambodia's first female prime minister. In polling widely regarded as free and fair, Sochua's United Democratic Alliance took an overwhelming majority of seats in...

Sochua has received accolades both at home and abroad for making public a long list of promised reforms, including abolition of the military, but she recently stunned supporters—and overcame stiff opposition within her own party—when she selected Chea Phyrom to be deputy prime minister. Chea, a nephew of the

*former prime minister and rumored to have ties to organized crime, was convicted
of manslaughter in 2002. Although this conviction was later overturned…*

Chris stopped reading, lost in thought. He didn't think of Chea Phyrom,
the man who'd kidnapped Mai, or Sochua Nika and whatever in world had
compelled her to bring that scumbag into her government. Frankly, he didn't
care. He thought about George, the gentle giant who'd been his best friend.
He thought about Mai and Lisa and how lucky he was to be in their lives. He
thought of the little Cambodian girl he'd rescued—and then lost. Just one of
thousands he couldn't help. He wondered what she was doing now. What was
her name? She was about the same age as Mai.

⟁

Two foreign men sat at a sidewalk table eating foreign food. Quynh rubbed
her belly and extended a hand.

"Nyam, nyam?"

The men pretended to ignore her, but she saw one of them watching her
from the corner of his eye. She touched him.

"No," he told her.

She moved closer and touched him again.

"No." This time he spoke angrily.

"Nyam. Eat. Very hungry. Please."

A waitress brandished the back of her hand. "Get! Get out of here!"

On the street Quynh saw a group of boys. They were bigger than she was,
and one of them threw a rock at her.

"I told you this is our territory! Don't come here again, you stupid *yuon!*"

She walked south until she met her friend Raksmei. She grabbed her
hand. "Come on!"

They wandered side streets until they found an unattended moto. Quynh
twisted off a black hose and gasoline spilled out.

"Hey! Hey!"

A man ran toward them. Fast. The girls didn't stop until they reached
the Royal Palace Esplanade. They sat facing the river and took turns sniffing

their gasoline-soaked rag. A fat foreign couple approached, snapping pictures of the palace.

"Nyam, nyam?" Quynh giggled in spite of herself. She thrust out her hand.

The End

From the Author

I moved with my wife and three young children to Phnom Penh, Cambodia, in 2004. Cambodia was a beautiful and impoverished nation experiencing rapid economic development and an unprecedented influx of foreign tourists come to see the UNESCO World Heritage Centre of Angkor, which had been off-limits for decades due to armed insurgency and general lawlessness in the area. Upon our arrival, I was immediately struck by Cambodia's thriving sex industry, in general, and the prominence of sex tourism, in particular. Most disturbing of all was the evident trafficking and prostitution of children.

I reached out to a foreign nongovernmental organization involved in the rescue of children from prostitution to see how I could help. This organization asked if I would volunteer to venture into Cambodian villages known to traffic in children, posing as a foreign pedophile, in order to support their efforts.

There were many reasons to say no. For one, my personal safety would be at risk; the sex industry was operated by violent organized crime gangs with reported high-level connections in the Cambodian government. Second, as the primary caregiver of three small children—including an adopted child who could pass for Cambodian—and the kind of parent who always checks for the fire exits, the safety of my family was no passing concern. This book, in essence, is a product of my worst nightmare.

In the end, the decision was made for me. On December 7, 2004, police under the direction of General Un Sokunthea, head of Cambodia's Anti-Trafficking and Juvenile Protection Department, raided a Phnom Penh hotel and found dozens of women and children working there as prostitutes. These people were released by the police and given shelter by AFESIP, a French organization that served victims of sex trafficking.

On December 8, AFESIP's shelter was raided by armed men in vehicles with Cambodian military license plates. Ninety-one women and children were forcibly removed from the shelter and, for all practical purposes, vanished. AFESIP was forced to temporarily cease operations in Cambodia after receiving death threats. General Sokunthea was suspended from her post. As a result, the NGO I'd contacted ceased their rescue operations before I'd gotten started, citing a "lack of commitment and cooperation" on the part of the Cambodian government to end human trafficking and the prostitution of children.

Child sex trafficking continues in Cambodia. The US Department of State reported in 2017 that "Cambodia is a source, transit, and destination country for men, women, and children subjected to forced labor and sex trafficking" and that "Cambodia does not fully meet the minimum standards for the elimination of trafficking." Although the Cambodian government has taken some positive steps, endemic corruption, poverty, and persistent demand ensure the exploitation of children for sex in Cambodia remains stubbornly robust.

ACKNOWLEDGMENTS

I owe a debt of gratitude to a great number of people who helped with this book and encouraged me along the way. I wish to thank Miss Bryant, my first-grade teacher, who encouraged me to read; Gaurav Bansal who gave ideas and helped fill plot holes; Nathan Spande, who provided friendship, encouragement, and honest feedback; Ambassador Joseph A. "Joey Bear" Mussomeli, who gave me valuable insight; Colonel Terence Tidler, who gave me loads of information about the Cambodian military; Peter Bartu and Penny Edwards who inspired me; Aarti Kapoor, who gave me valuable information about AFESIP and the raid on their shelter in 2004; Terry West, who schooled me in the workings of an American embassy's consular section; John Davis, a nice guy; Dr. Laura Watson, who answered gruesome questions; M.S., who patiently explained Cambodian politics and provided interesting tidbits; Holly Fukuda, for encouragement and friendship; Nina Buford, for inspiration and positive thinking; C. S. Lakin, a great editor; Phnom Penh Book Group, who indulged me with a first read; and the many other friends and family who have encouraged me in my writing. I also wish to thank my father, Ron, and my mother, Doris, who taught me everything. Finally, I would not have been able to complete this book without the understanding and encouragement of my wife, Dana R. Williams.

About the Author

Greg Buford has lived in Japan, India, France, Cambodia, and Switzerland. He's settled down (for the moment) in Austin, Texas, with his wife, Dana, and their children. This is his first novel. Learn more and see images that inspired the novel at http://gregorybuford.com/.